WINDRUNNER'S DAUGHTER

WINDRUNNER'S DAUGHTER

BRYONY PEARCE

First published in January 2016 by Xist Publishing.

This edition is by Telos Publishing, 139 Whitstable Road, Canterbury, Kent CT2 8EQ, United Kingdom

www.telos.co.uk

Telos Publishing values feedback if you have any comments about this book please email feedback@telos.co.uk

This book is dedicated to my beautiful daughter, Maisie,
my superhero of a niece, Blythe,
and to all the girls who know there is nothing they cannot do
if they try

Prologue

'We've lost them.'

White-faced, Captain Kiernan stared at the viewing station, where his view of the tiny blue planet remained unchanged. Perhaps in a few minutes they would see flashes of light or the spreading fungal splotches of mushroom clouds; or maybe, from this distance, it would remain at peace.

'Who started it?' There was no point to such a question.

The Captain shrugged. 'The Caliphate, the Pan-Asian Alliance, the Russians, the Western Blockade?' His lean body curved as though a sudden gravitational increase had dragged at his spine. His hands hung loosely at his sides. Impulsively he flicked his fingers, changing the view to the 100 km orbiting mirrors, wiping out the Earth altogether.

'Captain?'

'We'd better annou –'

The control room rocked sideways and a cloud of oxygen-propelled debris puffed silently in front of the viewers and filled the window with mist.

'Sector three – report!'

'No answer, Captain.'

'What the hell?' The Captain's fingers danced as he called up displays. The mirrors that had been filling the screen slowly began to realign, turning their reflective surfaces away from the planet below.

'Get a security team suited up and over to three. Send Phelps to engineering and find out who's altering the mirrors,' the Captain shouted. 'Where are the redundancies?'

More silent explosions of atmosphere and bodies: dandelion fluff blown towards the turning mirrors.

The Captain's face hardened. 'Sabotage.'

'They were waiting for the earth event?'

'Had to be. Now they know there's no chance of resupply. Hail the *Intrepid*.' The Captain's foot started to beat on the tile, a hard sound in the thickening atmosphere.

'Nothing, Captain. I – I think –'

'They're in the Molniya orbit, it might take them a minute.'

Seconds ticked by.

'Still no answer, Captain.'

'Keep hailing, if the *Intrepid* is down, then there's no way to get the colonists up to the emergency habitat.'

'Captain, word from Mariner Canyon, the CFC factories have been targeted.'

'Co-ordinated attacks.' Trembling with rage the Captain spun to his communications officer. 'Find the messages. They'll be buried in code but find them. I want to know who's doing this.'

'Everyone's Deep Vetted.' The reply was almost a wail. 'How could this happen?'

The Captain's eyes filled with tears as the wreckage of the *Intrepid* swung past the viewing screen, moving in a majestic ballet towards Phobos, the largest and closest of the Martian moons.

Alarms blared and he started. His screen blinked at him, emergency warning lights strobing furious red lines across his face. 'Get the scientists and their families into the shuttle.' His voice cracked. 'Hail the ten colonies. Let them know …' He closed his eyes. 'Let them know that now the CFC factories are gone, they'll have to rely on the positive feedback loop.' He shook his head. 'That last orbital asteroid transfer would have had us a decade away from a breathable atmosphere, Lieutenant – a decade.'

'And now?'

'In a few years they won't need their pressure suits to go outside, but they'll need oxygen canisters for generations.'

'*They*, Captain?'

'We have to try and give them a chance – those mirrors need to be put back in alignment. It's a manual job now they've blown the Stack. The last thing they need is sunlight being reflected *away* from the surface.'

But instead of rising from his chair the Captain switched the view once more. Swirling below them was the red planet. The Martian Delta was gouged with patches of brown-green and half obscured by the clouds that thickened and rolled in its new atmosphere. The sun glittered from the shallow water that covered Lake Lyot, turning it into a mirror that reflected back the racing clouds.

'They'll have to remain in their separate habitats, won't be able to spread out as planned.' The Captain was dictating furiously as the communications officer transmitted in a low voice. 'The dust storms are worsening, so no leaving the safety of the biospheres in the afternoons.' He wiped his forehead. 'God help them when the next big one comes around. There's a mega-storm due in six months and no way to get them off surface.'

'And what about –?'

The viewfinder switched to the bio-labs. They were burning.

'The indigenous organisms we modified appear to be restricted to the sand, at least at the moment. They'll have to find a way to survive alongside them.'

'We were *so close to* full terraforming.'

A shuttle burst onto the main view screen and started to fall towards Mars; a tiny burning seed, carrying the last of the colonists.

'They could be on the shuttle – the saboteurs.'

The Captain sighed. 'Lieutenant, they're already on the ground. Keep working on the messages, send what you find down to Harris and the other nine colonies, maybe they can pinpoint the terrorists. The important thing is that the families have dropped to safety.'

'Safety?' The word was a sneer.

'Earth's irradiated.' The Captain sagged in his chair. 'If the biospheres can hold, Mars is the safest place in the solar system for humanity now.' He turned off the view-screen. He'd had family back on Earth, been coming up to the end of his posting; had been looking forward to sunlight and true-blue skies, not the florescent glow of the space station or the half-light on the Martian surface. He stood, just as the low oxygen warning began to flash. 'If they all left on the shuttle, at least we'll able to realign the mirrors.'

'And if some of the saboteurs have stayed behind?'

The Captain smiled dangerously, and lifted his weapon. 'Lieutenant, a part of me hopes that they have.'

Runner's Elegy – Fragment: Unknown author

When I fly, I fly alone
If I'm lost it'll be far from home
When I die don't search for my bones
For I'll lie as I lived – under wings, under sky
Don't bury me deep in the dust when I die

1

Elysium Mons was littered with the bones of Runners. Most, but not all, were bleached white. There was always *something* for the Creatures on the flats below the cliffs.

Amongst the corpses lay the Runner's wings. Half buried they shone like fallen stars; heartbreakingly beautiful, even broken and twisted. There were so many shattered wing-sets down there that after a mega-storm the dust shone silver for days, until the sand blew back over them.

Wren squinted over the desert, her O_2 canister light on her back, barely aware of the mask that rubbed against her cheek as she turned her head. Ignoring the bone-yard beneath her, she was seeking the tell-tale glimmer that would warn her a Runner was flying in.

Despite the warmth of Perihelion she shivered. The Runners had never gone this long without contact. The Patriarchs were meeting at Convocation, but that left plenty of Juniors still flying; someone should have arrived from one of other colonies by now or, if there was a problem, sent a message over the central communicator in Elysium.

When the sky remained empty, Wren's heart sank. She glanced back at the Runner-sphere on the cliff edge. Avalon, as the Runners called it, looked like a low mollusc, clinging to the rock, as close to the Running platform as practically possible. But she wasn't heading home. If the Runner's weren't coming in, she would have to send a message out. She needed someone to fly for her.

Turning her back on the sphere she started to run. She had to talk the Councillors of Elysium into letting her use their communicator.

The path curved along the cliff edge, so close that each step sent red-brown stones flying past the marker-posts and into the desert, kilometres below. The few who walked the path from Elysium to the Runner-sphere did so with care, looking over their shoulders to see how close to death they stepped.

Wren *sprinted* down the trail as though Creatures were on her heels. The rattle of kicked gravel followed her footsteps and her long blue-black hair flew from her scarf.

As the green-belt came into view with its low-slung gingko trees and clinging ferns, she put on another burst of speed. A rock slid under her foot. Her ankle twisted but the sharp pain vanished in a gasp that was half scream as she realised what was about to happen. Frantically she wind-milled her arms, but there was nothing to stop her from falling; her whole world tilted towards the sky.

Wren spat curses as her right hand slammed into a marker post. Instinctively she grabbed hold and her whole body swung; her fall arrested.

Closing both hands around the creaking pole, Wren looked down. Below her feet the branches of a spindly bush clawed the sky. Beneath its browning leaves a sheer drop plummeted towards tendrils of cloud then finally, the bone yard, kilometres below.

A hysterical giggle bubbled through her mask.

There was no point calling for help. Even in normal times visitors from Elysium were few and with no incoming Runners for the Council to interrogate there would be no-one taking the path. Even if there were ... Wren closed her eyes. There were those in the biosphere who would happily watch a Runner fall. Sweat began to prickle on Wren's hands; she was running out of time.

With a swift exhalation she pulled herself higher and wrapped her elbow around the post to secure her grip.

Wren was lucky to be on Mars; on dead-Earth such a move would have been impossible. Baring her teeth in a humourless grin, Wren swung again and, moving her legs from side to side, made a pendulum of herself.

At last her right leg reached high enough that she was able to hook her ankle over the cliff top, halting her swing.

Dragging her body back onto the path, Wren lay for a moment with her arms clamped around the post that had saved her. Then she pried her fingers free, sprung to her feet and limped into a run once more.

She had to get back to Avalon before her mother woke up.

Inside the line of gingko trees, the path began to meander. Wren narrowed her eyes and glanced at the sun. 'No time for the scenic route.'

She plunged into thick ferns, her boots scraping carefully cultivated lichens and algae from the rocks. The Green-Men would be furious, but what choice did she have? At least she wasn't in the GM soya fields.

Deeper in the green belt the ferns were at shoulder height. Dense, damp tendrils clutched at her clothes and hair and a thin mist blurred her vision: O_2 being synthesised moment by moment. Wren had a strange, suicidal desire to rip off her mask and inhale the fresh made oxygen.

All around her, ferns absorbed the sounds of Mars: the howling of faraway dust storms, the hissing of the air filters in the biospheres, the eerie distant shrieking of the Creatures. Here the rustling of ferns and creaking of branches filled her ears; even the buzzing of the pollinators was muted, their tiny wings brushing against her cheeks, surprising her and making her jump. She ran her fingers through the hair-like greenery, then shook her head and pushed on, directly towards Elysium's dome.

Hexagonal, dust-pocked solar panels covered the top two-thirds of the biosphere and thick plastic storm-proofing ran around the bottom. Wren staggered to a halt in front of the airlock. Vast farms of cyanobacteria kept the air inside breathable and, once through, she would be able to remove her mask. She never did, so used was she to wearing hers at all times that Wren felt naked without it. The feel of air on her lips was terrifying, like falling.

She clapped her palm on the lock and waited, stamping impatiently, for it to cycle green. Then she stepped inside, allowing it to hiss closed behind her.

For a moment she hesitated, getting her bearings: she had come in at the South entrance. Ahead, low buildings ran in long diagonal terraces; workshops on one side, dwellings on the other. Generations-old gingko trees clustered where gusts of wind would have collected on the lee side of each structure.

The houses had been built to be battered by winds but had never been exposed to them. Now bunting dangled between each building and colourful flags hung, breathless. Snatches of music twisted through the eaves and gathered in the Dome's apex while shouts of laughter burst like seed pods. Wren stared, had she really forgotten what day it was?

A small boy ran from the nearest house squealing and waving a tiny space shuttle. 'Happy Kiernan's Day,' he shrieked when he saw her.

His mother loped after him, her face flushed, her arms spread wide; when she saw Wren she stopped as if she'd run into the dome. Then she grabbed her son, all humour erased from her face. 'Leave my boy alone!'

Wren sighed. 'Happy Kiernan's Day,' she offered.

'Not for the likes of you,' she snapped. 'Damned Runners.'

'Captain Kiernan sacrificed himself to save *everyone* on Mars,' Wren reminded her coldly. 'Runners and Grounders alike.'

The woman snorted and pushed her son towards the house. 'The Originals might have fought and died for all. But if they could see you now ...' Her voice faded into disgust and her husband appeared in the doorway.

His eyes widened when he saw her. 'Clear off, you.' He gripped the doorframe.

Wren didn't stay to watch mother and son hasten back inside the house.

'Kiernan's Day,' she whispered, rolling the words around her mouth, as if she'd never spoken them before. If the others had been at Avalon, they would have been celebrating but, left to herself, she had completely forgotten.

Soon the dust storms would start to roll in. She had less time than she had thought.

'I can still get a Runner to fly, if I can use the Communicator,' she muttered.

There was only one man in the colony who might take her request seriously and even on Kiernan's Day, he and the other Councillors would be in the Council building.

Unlike the Runners, who had a central Convocation presided over by a President and centred around the votes of the Patriarchs, the Grounder colonies were each run by annually rotating Councils of six. It was easy to tell who was Councillor because each wore two weighty pendants: one white and one black.

Wren drew close to the squatting Council building and pulled her shoulders back. The entrance gaped before her; she merely had to walk in, but she froze. Now, in this moment, there was hope. Her heart fluttered. They had only to say yes: just one little word. She wasn't asking for Phobos, just for five minutes on the Communicator.

Yet ringing words popped like bubbles in her gut: *clear off, you.*

With stiff legs Wren marched through the open door and into a short corridor made of slowly rusting shuttle panels. The waiting area was empty, but still a mechanised voice asked her to 'take a number and a seat'. There were no seats. A tab with the number '001' dropped into a waiting basket. She picked it up and rubbed the indented plastic with her thumb. Ahead of her a second door slid greasily open. She dropped the tab back into the basket, hid her shaking hands behind her back and stepped forward.

The Council building was low ceilinged. There was room enough inside for eighty or ninety colonists to gather, more if everyone stood, but the tallest would have to duck their heads. Wren had been inside only twice in her life. The room featured in her nightmares.

In the centre a raised dais, around it a table and six chairs. Five were occupied. The sixth sat askew, achingly empty, a missing tooth in an adult mouth.

'Where is he?' Wren blurted, unable to stop herself.

A thin man, his features like twists of twine raised his eyes. Beside him his flat chinned companion gawped. 'It's one o' them Runners,' he sputtered. 'What's he doin' out of Avalon?' He lurched from his seat, slab feet slapping on the panelled floor. 'It's Kiernan's Day,' he snapped. 'Have some respect!'

'Are you blind Hawkins? That's no *he*.' One of the Councillors was a woman. Wren staggered back, as if shoved. 'It's one o' their Sphere mistresses.'

'No – too young,' Twine-face suggested. 'A *nothing* then. Too female to be a Runner, too young to be a Sphere-Mistress.'

'What're you here for?' The woman leaned forward and raised her voice to speak slow and loud as though Wren were deaf, or stupid. Her pendulous breasts squashed against the table top. 'Want to petition to get into the Women's Sector?' Her chuckle shook the chair beneath her.

The men around her sniggered. 'Would you let her in, Tee?'

'No–one would have her to wife, but we always need fertile wombs for the exchange programme.' The woman smiled. 'Is that right, Runner-girl, are you sick of running errands for fly-boys, do you want to come and join Tee's noble girls?'

'Shut up!' The words, flung into the air, seemed to float between them, shocking red. Wren's eyes widened. 'I mean, please, I do have a petition, but not that.'

'And why should we listen?' A third man spoke, his voice rasping, like tearing skin. 'Send your Patriarch, or your Sphere-mistress.' He turned his back on her, as if she'd already left.

'I need to use the communicator,' Wren called. 'It's –'

Laughter rolled through the hall; loud as a cannon, it ricocheted from the low ceiling and surrounded Wren, mocking her trembling fingers and reddening ears.

'The nothing wants to use the communicator!' Hawkins thumped the table, making the water jug in the middle jump.

'What's wrong? Got a boyfriend you want to talk to? Won't

the other fly-boys carry yer love notes?' Tee nudged the frowning man on her left and he barked in acknowledgement of her joke.

'Use the *communicator!*' The final man, whose beard covered half of his face shook his head as the laughter petered out. 'Even if it wasn't a fragile piece of equipment with irreplaceable components that are breaking down, even if we didn't have to save it for essential use only, why on Mars, would we allow someone like *you* to use it? You're just a girl. What possible reason could you have?'

Wren opened her mouth.

'That wasn't an invitation to speak.' Tee sat straight. 'You Godless Runners believe you're more important than us. You think the rules of the colony don't apply to you. If we let you play with the communicator and it breaks down, what happens when an adult actually needs to send an important message? What then?'

'This *is* important.' Wren lurched forwards, her fists clenched.

'I'm sure you think so.' The bearded man, who Wren now realised was the colony Smith, nodded indulgently. 'Let a Runner take your message, girl. They might not charge you more than a kiss.'

'You have to vote.' Wren was horrified to find that tears made her voice almost unrecognisable. 'That's the rule, you have to vote in response to a petition.'

Hawkins sighed. 'Let's vote.'

'You can't do it without Win. Where is he?'

They ignored her. First Tee, then Hawkins, then all five, closed their fists around their pendants and lifted them into the air.

Black, black, black, black ...

The blacksmith looked at her with something approaching sympathy and, for a moment, Wren's heart rose. His hand closed around one of his pendants, the other remained in his shirt; she couldn't see which he had chosen. He lifted the bulb slowly, his big hand obscuring the colour. Wren leaned forward, her breath solid in her lungs. Then his fingers opened. He held black.

'Five of six, a clear majority, we don't need Win to tie-break.' Tee dropped her chain back onto her breast. 'Vote's against you Runner girl. Now get out.'

'But –'

'The decision's been made and recorded.' Hawkins was tapping on a sticky keyboard.

Wren clenched her fists. 'At least tell me where he is.'

'Meeting with people a lot more important than you.'

Wren backed out, her blood roaring like thunder in her ears. She wouldn't turn her back on them. She flayed the Councillors with her eyes until the door slid closed on the chamber; then her shoulders sagged. What had she expected – that they'd just allow her to use the communicator?

Maybe this *was* better: she should have asked Win himself to make the request in the first place. She would wait at his door for as long as it took him to come home.

Wren ran past the trees and under the bunting, weaving through stinking shafts of recycled air. She saw hardly anyone. After first worship, Kiernan's Day was a family occasion. Warily, she approached the gaping gateway of the large property at the far West edge of the Dome. There she made an effort to slow to a walk, but her knees shook and threatened to tip her forward. She grabbed the gatepost, which was almost as tall as she was, and caught sight of Win. The old man was standing in the garden, speaking earnestly with two Senior Technicians and a uniformed Green-man. The three were gesticulating widely, their voices angry.

'We haven't had a Runner in for three weeks and Tir Na Nog haven't yet replied to our hails –'

'Yet you can see that we are managing perfectly well. The seedlings have taken, we have samples of the last set of drugs being reproduced, so why do we need them? I say we cut ties –'

'Cut ties! What about the baby exchange? Genetic diversity is –'

'We can manage four more generations before inbreeding

becomes any sort of problem.'

'And what then?'

'By then the Runners will be under our control.'

'It's true that they have too much power over trade and distribution … great hells Win, what's that supposed to be?' The youngest of the Technicians had spotted her.

Wren's ears were ringing; she staggered into the garden where chunks of rocks and coloured dirt formed mesmerising patterns around the pathway. 'You can't be serious?'

'How much did you hear?' Win flew forwards, his jacket billowing. Stick thin, like a wing-stand, he loomed over her, and bony fingers on spidery hands grabbed at her wrists.

'You can't be considering cutting ties with the other nine colonies!'

'This doesn't concern you.'

'I'm a Runner!'

Win's long face drew into a sneer. 'Whatever you are, you're not a Councillor, you've heard a tiny piece of a long discussion and drawn your own conclusions. More importantly, you're derelict in your duty. Why are you here, instead of at the Runner-sphere waiting to serve incoming Runners? No landings have been reported.' He cocked his head, silently demanding an explanation.

'I –' Wren drew herself up, but Win refused to release her wrists, twisting them painfully, so that she had to hunch again to keep them straight. She stared as his scornful face, a weathered parody of her mother's, curved into disdainful lines.

Then, as if bored, he shoved her to one side. 'Go back to Avalon, Wren, and tell no-one what you heard.' He began to stride towards the house.

Wren chased after him. 'Grandfather, I need to talk to you.'

When he turned and she saw his face, she faltered.

'Don't call me that. I'm no Runner relation.' The old man's eyes flickered. 'How could your mother let you come to the 'sphere looking like that?' He marched towards her and pinched her elbow. 'Wild. Uneducated. Useless to the colony. You're an embarrassment.'

'I'm not uneducated. I can run the whole of Avalon if need be –'

'Useless.' Win spat again. 'Get out of here.' He drove her through the gateway and started to pull her towards the nearest airlock.

'Wait.' Wren tried to pull free as his grip tightened to leave marks on her skin. 'I need you to get permission for me to use the communicator. I have to contact Father. He's in Convocation at Lake Lyot.'

Win snorted. 'Ridiculous. The whole point of having Runners is that we don't need to overuse the communicators.'

'It's essential that I get hold of him.'

He strode on, dragging her behind him. 'I do nothing for any of your brood. Mia knows that.'

Wren heaved a breath. 'She's ill.'

Win hesitated for only one step. 'So what?'

Wren closed her eyes and spoke the words she could barely make herself say out loud. 'I think she's dying.'

Win yanked Wren in front of him and her eyes flew open. 'Are you lying to me?' His nose, with its network of tiny veins, almost brushed hers as he bent to look into her face.

'No,' Wren whispered. 'She's had a fever for three days.'

The old man straightened up. 'Let your father deal with it.' He renewed his hold and marched on toward the edge of the settlement.

'Lyot's the longest Run we do. He might not be back for a month. He'll be too late,' Wren gasped. 'I have to get word out. I need help.'

'Help yourself,' he spat. 'I told Mia to get pregnant before the Choosing.' His eyes swum with nostalgia and Wren could almost see a picture of her young mother in the dark of them. Then he shook his head. 'She could have been married to an honourable Grounder. She could have joined the exchange programme and increased the genetic diversity of the colony, but she disobeyed me. She accepted your father's offer to become Sphere-Mistress when his sister died and now she's paying the price.'

Wren blinked at him. 'You'd rather she was in the Exchange programme, than married to Father?' She tried to pull away, but her grandfather's grip was pitiless.

'She allowed herself to be chosen by that Runner, so let him take care of her. Living in that Runner-sphere, exposed to the storms, our every conversation monitored in case "the ex-Grounder" reveals the secrets of flight. She might as well be dead.'

Wren gasped. 'But she might really die. She's your daughter.'

'She disobeyed me; she's no daughter of mine.'

And now their raised voices attracted attention. Loping around the corner like Creatures scenting blood, the boys. They took position around the airlock, lounging, bodies relaxed but eyes sharp, predatory. Seeking entertainment.

Wren's vision blurred. 'She never asked you for anything,' she shouted.

Win made no reply, only dragged her past the line of watching eyes. One pair in particular snatched at her attention. Green eyes that burned with more than scorn; they glittered with pure hatred.

Wren's eyes skittered away and snagged on the face below the eyes. The whole left side was scarred; a twisted landscape of grey, islanded with patches of pink skin. When he curled his lip, the flesh pulled tight. Painful. Caro's disease, left untreated for too long.

Wren stumbled as her grandfather pinned her against the airlock and slapped his palm onto the pad.

'Looks like you're cleaning house, Councillor,' Raw murmured and Wren clenched her fists. She and Raw were the same age: fifteen. The other boys were younger. Despite, or perhaps because of, his scarring, Raw inspired worship. There was something about him. His cruelty was fascinating.

Her grandfather ignored him, simply waited for the airlock to cycle green as though Wren wasn't struggling beneath his arm. As soon as it opened, he tossed her through.

'Don't come back again without a chaperone,' he growled.

Then he turned his back and walked away.

Clutching her arms to her chest, Wren heard Raw's laughter through the opaque walls that shut her out of Elysium's Dome.

2

With the 'sphere at her back Wren climbed up the cliff path. The afternoon had become close, a minor dust storm was coming. Sweat dripped down her neck but she dragged her feet, her mind racing. What should she do now?

Behind her a hiss told her the airlock had opened. It could be a Green-Man checking on the belt. Still she turned, her heart rising in the hope that Win had changed his mind and was following her out.

Instead she saw Raw striding up the path after her, his oxygen mask covering half of his scarring.

Wren considered running from him, but her heart wasn't in it. Her mother was dying, what more could he do?

She turned her back to him and kept walking. Raw's legs were longer than hers, he caught her in moments. Then he simply walked beside her. Wren shivered as the shriek of a Creature whispered up from the flats. As they drew level with the belt, she lifted her eyes to Raw's narrowed gaze. 'What do you want?'

Raw moved to block her, stop her walking. Wren blinked. He was big; more muscled than her brothers, despite their wing-training, and he had a wiry leanness that made her step backwards out of his reach. Her heart thudded.

'Is your mother really dying?' Raw asked his green eyes gleaming.

Wren caught her breath. 'You heard …'

'So she *is*.' Raw rubbed the scar on his face, massaging the tight skin above his mask. 'Good.'

Wren flinched as if he'd struck her after all. 'You can't mean that.'

Raw met her eyes once more. 'I really do.' He smiled then stepped to one side, out of her way. 'Oh, and happy Kiernan's

Day!'

Wren opened her mouth then slammed it shut. She'd never wish death on anyone. And wouldn't he have died from Caro's disease if the Runners hadn't brought medicine for him? He'd pay for his words. One day.

With a sob clinging to the back of her throat, Wren set her feet back on the path. With half of her mind she noticed that dust was beginning to rise into swirling eddies around her feet.

By the time Wren had reached the cliff top, tears were making mud of the dust on her face. If only her brothers would only come home. They could fetch a cure from the scientists in Aaru and do something about Raw. Where were they?

It was possible that one or both had found their future Sphere-mistress. They could be courting. Wren knew that one day, probably soon, Colm would leave and Runners would begin to come for her, hoping one day to take over the Patriarchy of Elysium from her Father.

It seemed too early for either of her brothers to leave and the idea of being married off to some hoary Runner who her father liked, made her own skin crawl, but the possibility that Colm was moving on his own ambitions was better than the other … she dashed away fresh tears and tried not to look over the cliff towards the bone-yards. She would wait for news before she believed them gone. Her mind had room for only one problem now: Their mother was dying and Wren had failed to get a message out.

As Wren sloped towards Avalon, the dust rose to her ankles like a flood back on dead-Earth. Still she faltered. She had to get home but she paused again, driven to search the sky above the Martian delta.

Surely this time she'd see a Runner coming in?

The wind shoved her dangerously towards the marker posts, so Wren lay flat, rested on her elbows and shaded her eyes with her hands.

Russet mists churned over the flats. In a few weeks, when the wind was at full strength the desert would disappear completely, but today the sand flirted with the ground. She looked higher into a vast purple sky, hazed with gauzy streaks of grey cloud. The sun glowed to her right, a half-light, she had been told, compared to that of dead-Earth. She could barely imagine brighter. She peered directly into its corona, desperate to see figures racing the storm.

'Colm, Jay, where are you?'

There was nothing. They weren't coming.

Wren waited one more minute as the spark of hope was doused. Then she jerked as horns blared from the roof of Elysium.

Her eyes widened. 'What? No! It's too early!' She tried to stand but the wind snarled and knocked her off her feet. 'It's *Kiernan's Day*!' She shrieked, as if there was anyone to listen. It was only just Perihelion, the big dust storms were days away, weeks even.

But the alarm wailed.

The dust wasn't going to remain low on the ground. Elysium had detected a big front; it was going to rise and rise and …

'Oh, *Kiernan*!' She shrieked as she crashed back onto her elbow. Dust clogged the filters of her mask and she gasped as stinging crimson particles whipped into her eyes. Panic began to cloud her thoughts. If her mask failed she would suffocate. The atmosphere was years off breathable, even this close to the green belt.

The alarm was one continuous shriek now and the dust had risen already. She was almost out of time. Squeezing her eyes tightly shut, Wren dragged herself forward on her elbows. She used her instincts to remain on the invisible path and felt out to the left in case she encountered a marker post, or worse, dead air.

Suddenly the wind crept under her shoulder and inflated her shirt. Wren was boosted a hand's width from the ground and tumbled sideways.

'No!' With fingers curled into claws she stabbed at the path and rolled, deflating her shirt. She thumped onto her back, her O_2 canister digging painfully into her shoulders. Wriggling frantically, she tucked her shirt into her pants, flipped onto her belly and continued to crawl, panting sharp little breaths that now tasted frighteningly of sand. Her lips dried and she tasted grit on her tongue. How much longer would her mask operate? With a full tank on her back, she could die from a lack of O_2. A giggle forced its way through her lips and Wren bore down on bubbling hysteria.

Her lungs tightened and she gasped into the darkness, bright lights flashing in front of her eyelids. She daren't stop, if she wanted to live, she had to keep moving.

Gritting her teeth, Wren reached ahead, gripped what felt like a marker post and pulled herself towards it. She could use the posts like this as long as she kept far enough to the right.

After an eternity, Wren's fumbling fingers bumped into what had to be the porch of the Runner-sphere, where she knew safety lines were coiled in a box on the first step. They hadn't been used in years, but Colm maintained them. He liked backups, safety nets; he planned for every possible eventuality. Thank the skies.

The clips were slotted into a grooved post for easy access. She reached for the lowest and her fingers brushed silver fibres that glimmered even through the whirling dust. Growling, she pushed once more until she was right underneath the box and stretched. The line was too high for Wren to unclip without raising herself higher.

With a yell, she drove upwards, but as she lifted her chest the wind howled its triumph and took her. Wren's fingers brushed the line and a scream dragged from her mouth as she was tugged back towards the cliff edge. Then the gale changed direction with a fickle huff and hurled her as hard towards the box as she had been torn away from it.

As she hurtled past, almost completely blind, Wren grasped a safety line in both hands and fumbled for her belt. She snapped the cable on just as it pulled tight and whipped her sideways by the waist. Wind roared around her and she was pummelled on the end of her line like a kite. The leather stretched, but held. Turning inside the maelstrom, Wren caught the rope with both hands, closed her eyes once more, and began to pull hand-over-hand towards the house.

It seemed to take hours. Wren was already light headed and nauseous, and now O_2 deprivation needled at her vision. She was going to suffocate before she reached the 'sphere.

Still, Wren focused on the movement of her hands and body. She reached with her left fist, fought the wind as it tried to drag her arm behind her, gripped the rope and took a step; then she did the same with her right. Gradually she drew nearer to safety.

Eventually Wren's feet knocked against the porch. Two more sluggish paces and the wind lessened enough for her to leap for the airlock. Wren wrapped a fist around the handle and held on until her knuckles whitened. She crouched, making the most of the shelter, and then unclipped the line and, in one movement, slammed her palm on the pad. As the door hissed open she rolled in, ripped her useless mask from her face and lay on her side, gasping.

Now that she was back she didn't want to move from the airlock. On the other side her mother lay dying. In here she could pretend everything was all right. However, she felt naked without her mask, exposed to air that she was sure could fail at any moment. Her hands began to shake. She had to refit her mask and quickly.

Her mother stirred. 'Wren?'

Wren exhaled guiltily, shocked to see a puff of air from her own lungs dissipating in front of her. Swiftly she cycled the lock around. 'I'm here.'

'… so thirsty.'

The room came into view and Wren looked for the jug of water. It had been on the floor by her parent's bed. A little remained. Before she helped her mother though, she *had* to replace her mask.

Once a near inaudible hiss of O_2 shivered through the new filters, Wren's heart began to slow. As soon as her hands stopped shaking, she tossed the old mask into the recycling, poured water into a clay mug and made her way over to the recess that hid her mother.

She hesitated in front of the curtain. Clutching the mug tightly, she closed her eyes and pictured her mother smiling and reaching for the water, as if the thought could make it so.

'Come in here, Wren, it's a cold morning and I'm not ready to get up.'

The curtain was flung back. For a moment all Wren could see was a tangle of bedding and limbs.

'I'm hungry,' she mumbled, but her bare legs were cold and Jay was already snuggled up next to their mother, which left a Wren sized gap. 'Where's Colm?'

'He went to check the skies.'

'The airlock's what woke you. Now get in here!' Her father lifted the covers. It must have let in a chill, because her mother shrieked and slapped his arm.

Chayton raised his eyebrows and Wren decided that her belly could wait. She sprinted for the bed and leapt into the space, wriggling into the warm gap. Jay pinched her leg to make her move over and she huffed and slid across slightly, making her father growl as the blanket pulled off his chest.

'You're all getting too big,' Chayton grumbled, before pulling her close and sniffing her curls. 'Mmmm soft.'

'Or we need a bigger bed,' Mia used the ends of her blonde hair to tickle Wren's cheek and she squealed just as the airlock cycled open.

'Incoming.' Colm announced, slapping dust from his hands.

'Already?' Mia was dismayed. 'They must have set off at first light.'

'Just a bit longer?' Wren wrapped her arm around Chayton's elbow, holding him in place. 'They'll be ages yet.'

'I need to make sure the platform's dust free,' Mia said unconvincingly. 'And set up the massage table and oils, warm some stones, heat water for a brew and get some soup and bread on. Jay, you'll need to wrap up warm if you have to run down to Elysium with his message. Colm, you know what to do. Wren, you can help me.'

'Can't I help Colm check the netting and look after his wings?'

Mia frowned, her brown eyes suddenly hardening. 'No. Wing checks is men's work. If they need a repair you can help with the glue, but it's more important that you learn to do Sphere-Mistress tasks. After all, you'll have to take over from me one day.'

'Not for years and years.' Wren scowled back. 'Alright then, can I at least record the arrival and his message in the big book?'

'How's your handwriting?' Chayton frowned down at her.

'As good as Jay's. I've been practising.'

Mia thawed. 'Fine. You can write in the book, if you get dressed and start the water.'

Wren sat up straight and Chayton rolled out of bed.

'I hope it's news from Arcadia.' He rubbed the stubble on his head. 'I'm getting worried.'

Mia smiled at him, her cheeks still flushed from sleep and warmth. 'Don't be worried yet, it's too early in the day.' She stroked his back with gentle fingers and Wren wrapped her arms around his neck.

He flipped her over his back and onto his legs. 'Does anyone want a bite?' He offered her shoulder to Jay who grinned and growled.

'I do.'

Wren screamed as her brother pretended to snack on her arm. 'Let go, let go.'

Colm rolled his eyes.

Wren stared at the curtain. How old was the memory? It had been a long time since care had worn away her father's humour. When had he last played with them like that? She glanced at the thick record books. Easy to find out, she simply had to look back to find the first time her handwriting appeared on the tightly pressed lines.

'Wren?' Her mother's voice again. She couldn't put off the moment any longer.

Kneeling, Wren drew back the curtain. She swallowed against the smell of sickness that wafted towards her, bit her cheek to keep her terror from showing and finally, looked.

The flesh had melted away from her mother's face, leaving hollows in her cheeks and wrinkles on her throat. Her skin looked like dead leaves: crispy and transparent, and the blonde hair that had once tickled Wren's cheek lay in greasy tangles.

When Mia opened her eyes to look at her daughter, they were bloodshot and the colour so faded they were almost grey.

Yesterday she had moaned and thrashed in her sleep but now she seemed too weak even for that.

'Water?'

Steeling herself for the feel of her, Wren lifted her mother's shoulders. 'Here.' She held the mug steady as Mia sipped and when the liquid made her cough, Wren rubbed her back, wincing as she felt her mother's bones through the sweat-stained shirt.

After a while Mia stopped coughing and fell back onto the bed. 'Is your father home?'

'Not yet.'

'Didn't I hear the airlock?'

Wren bit her lip.

'Are your brothers home?'

'Nobody's home.'

'How long?' Mia had lost track of time.

'Jay and Colm have been gone for a week.'

'A week.' Her mother fell silent. They both knew what that could mean. Then Mia tried a smile. 'Colm's found a little-Mistress maybe ...' her voice faded. He would have told them if he had.

Wren squeezed her fingers. 'They're still partner-Running, they'll be looking out for each other.'

'I suppose. *Did* I hear the airlock?'

Wren cleared her throat. 'That was me.'

'You?' Her mother struggled to sit upright.

'I went to Elysium.'

For the first time, Mia looked at Wren properly and her face changed as she took in her daughter's expression. 'Oh, Wren.'

Wren took her hands. 'I'm fine.' Her gaze swept the empty sphere, over the long table, empty of the usual tumble of brothers, visiting Runners and her father's glowering presence.

Books lined the back wall: treatises on flight, maps of Martian air currents, details of every trade and exchange ever made by their colony. *Useless. Uneducated.* Win's words clanged in her skull. 'I went to see Grandfather.'

31

For a terrible moment Mia's face lit up, then her eyes reflected the misery on Wren's face. 'He wouldn't help, would he?' She turned her face to the wall.

'He said Father had to look after us,' Wren replied as she buried her face in her mother's lap. Exhausted, Mia closed her eyes and, stroking the snarls in her daughter's waist length curls, was dragged almost immediately back into sleep.

After a while Wren disentangled herself. She rose carefully from the sick bed and quietly drew the curtain. Then she strode to the viewing window, a single hexagonal panel that was transparent, though pocked from the seemingly endless storms, and squinted in a vain attempt to see the landing platform. But the storm still raged and she couldn't make it out through the red-brown sand. She stared for a while and then turned away.

In the corner Jay's training wings leaned against the wall. He had outgrown them, but there was a rent in the graphene that needed repairing before they went away to be used by the next son of their line. *Her* son.

And if she failed to bear a son, to Colm's or Jay's.

Wren snorted. No Runner had yet come calling just for her, but she had seen them begin to look, peeling the humanity from her, considering her as wares.

It helped that she was smaller and thinner than the colonist girls, she looked young, not Mistress material. But when Colm really did go courting, her father would look at her and remember how old she was. Then the bidding would begin.

She shuddered.

'Father refused to marry the girl the Council wanted him to after Uncle Hawk went to the bone-yards and Aunt Blue got Caro's.' She spoke to her own fingers as she removed the mending kit from Mia's dresser. 'So why do I have to make the union *he* wants?'

She didn't need to hear the answer. Colm had explained it to her so many times that he had stopped arguing about it.

'The men in the Sphere have to live and work together. So the Sphere-Mistress takes the man approved by the Patriarch.'

'But I'm the one who'll have to bear the children of some pig-faced –'

'It's your job to get on with whoever Father picks. Imagine living here with someone who caused friction.' Colm looked deep into her eyes. 'Father loves you, he won't choose badly for you. He'll consider your feelings.'

'What if he doesn't? Why can't I fly to find a husband? Why do I have to wait here for one of Father's friends to come to me?'

'You know the reasons! We lose enough wings as it is without letting girls take them. Girls don't Run. You're not strong enough or fast enough. It isn't safe.'

'If a girl could Run, just once, to make her union, then you could stay here instead of having to go live in some strange Runner-sphere.' Wren's voice broke. 'I can't think of you leaving.'

Colm sighed. 'And when the girl I choose gets blown into the desert on her way across the wastes? Give it up, Wren, the rules are there to protect us.'

'I might welcome any union.' Wren whispered. 'If I could fly there.'

Colm was quiet. He wrapped an arm around her shoulder. 'It'll never happen Ren-Ren. And would you really want to leave Mother?'

Wren sighed as she picked up Jay's precious wings by their struts and carried them to the table. Even folded they were bigger than she was. The ancient material shone as she spread the wings and located the rip that made them dangerous to use.

'How did he *do* that?' She touched the tear. Graphene was resistant to heat and *strong* – it could be stretched by twenty percent without damage. 'If they were mine, they'd *never* need repairing.'

Still, the wings were more than a century old. Wear was to be expected, even in graphene.

With nimble fingers Wren glued the tear and held it closed until it bonded with barely a crease. The area would be weaker than the rest but there was none of the original material left on Mars with which to properly restore the wing. All that they had the colonists had brought with them from dead-Earth. Although the original landing parties had searched, Mars had no graphite with which to process the wonder material. There was a limited supply.

One day the problem would become acute enough for the Runners to try and retrieve the wings in the bone-yards, braving the Creatures in the sand to bring them back up the Mons. But they were not that desperate. Not yet.

Instead of folding the wings and putting them away, Wren carried on stroking them. The Sphere had never been so empty before; only Wren and her sleeping mother. No brothers, no fathers, no visitors. Her fingers walked up the straps. What would it feel like to wear them, just once?

Her mother coughed in her sleep and Wren froze. She should be thinking of ways to get access to the Communicator. Her mind raced, fruitlessly. There was no way to break into the Comms Room, no-one who might help her, no-one who would ask for permission on her behalf.

She considered the Doctor again. He was an agoraphobe: never left the safety of Elysium's Dome, had refused to journey to Avalon even when Jay broke his ankle. But he knew Mia. Maybe if Wren pleaded, or took enough payment.

But not on Kiernan's Day. Wren glanced out of the window. Not while a storm raged and the alarms on the Dome screamed warning.

Tomorrow then.

She stood the wings back in the corner and stood them up. More sounds from behind the curtain. Her mother was restless; in pain.

What if her illness was the result of another hybrid microbe, like Caro's?

Even if the Doctor agreed to come to Avalon, if her mother had something new they would have to send to the scientists in Aaru for a cure. And for that they would need a Runner. Wren laughed bitterly.

Where were all the Runners?

Wren was sprinting again, almost to the Dome now, trailing

clinging vines and pieces of fern. It had been a bad night and she had set off the moment the fingers of dawn made shadows of the old CFC factories on the delta.

Her pockets sagged with the weight of the valuables she had filled them with. Anything shiny, anything she thought the Grounder Doctor might value. Grounders weren't like Runners, unimpressed as they were with graphite glue, or massage oils, fresh goggles or clean paper. They liked … pretties. She closed her hands over the bulkiest pocket. Her mother had come to the Runner-sphere with jewellery. Wren didn't think she'd mind using it. There was little else she could offer. The message-slips were tightly locked away: no giving away free Runs.

And what if the Runners never came back?

No, she had her mother's jewellery, her father's good penknife, Colm's screwdrivers, Jay's small kite, her own collection of hair pins and an almost full ration card. They had nothing else portable that a Grounder might value. And she wasn't that sure about the kite.

Suddenly the rustling of something out of place pierced the thumping of blood in her ears and Wren skidded to a stop.

Was it possible that a Creature had finally, inevitably, left the dust bowl? Holding her breath, she squinted into a stand of gingko. A rock fractured the leaves and smacked into her elbow. She cried out and, as though her voice was the signal, a hail of stones rattled around her. Wren threw her arms over her face and three boys in light sphere clothes, their storm jackets gaping open, strode from the trees.

'Raw.' Wren stared as he hefted a branch. 'What are you doing with *that*?' Even Wren, who had blithely ripped her way through the ferns, was horrified at such wanton destruction of a big photo-synthesiser. She jerked forward, but as Raw's smile reached his eyes, she realised what she was doing and backed away. She lowered her gaze. 'I just need to get past, all right.'

Raw dangled the branch in big hands. 'I don't think so. Call us 'protectors of the biosphere'. We're keeping the unsavoury elements out.'

Wren pursed her lips. 'I need to see the Doctor. You know

why.'

Raw laughed. 'Yeah, I do and you're not going anywhere.'

A snort from behind told Wren that Raw's friends had her hemmed.

'You can't be serious.' Wren tilted her head. 'I need a Doctor. She's *really* bad today.'

'Really bad?' Raw smiled. 'Really, *really* bad?'

Wren ground her teeth as he mocked her. 'Yes.' She bit off an insult. She had to persuade him to let her pass. 'Please.' She swiped inky curls from her eyes.

Raw picked thoughtfully at a burr on his club, then he caught Wren's eye. 'Go back to Avalon. No-one wants you here.'

'No-one? Really?' Wren leaned forward, almost spitting. 'You know what happens if Mia dies? We'll have no Sphere-Mistress. Do you know what'll happen then? Either Chayton will have to choose another Mistress from your precious Grounder colony, or *I'll* be put in charge of the Sphere when the Runners are out. *Me*. I'm old enough now. *I'll* choose which of your trades are worth making, *I'll* choose which of your messages the Runners take. *I'll* decide when or *if* your babies are taken to exchange. You don't want to upset the Runners, Raw. You don't want to upset *me*.'

'You refuse our messages and we refuse to feed you, *Runner*. You think you're so special. You'd be nothing without the workers in the 'sphere.'

Wren lifted her chin. 'We do the most important job. You think we should use crusky equipment to carry babies between 'spheres, or bring back trade goods? You think we should go hungry? Without us you'd have had no way to replace the seedlings destroyed by the last mega-storm.'

'Liar.' Raw lurched forward and gripped her shoulders. '*You* should be in the women's house with the other girls, not out there, breaking Designer Law, thinking you're too good for Grounder men. It's unnatural.' Raw's smile was hard edged as he shook her.

Colm's screwdrivers fell from her pocket and thudded to the

ground.

'What's this?' Raw brightened as he picked them up.

'They're for the Doctor, give them back.' Wren reached for them, but he kept one hand around the meat of her arm and held her tightly. She twisted and he laughed.

'Nice. Do you want them, Bone?' He tossed them over her head. One of the other boys caught them and cheered.

'What else has she got?'

'Nothing.' Wren wrenched sideways but Raw pulled her close. His cold green eyes trapped hers, hypnotic. There was gold in the irises. He pinioned her with one arm and used the other to pat her down.

'Look at this.' He yanked out Jay's kite and her hair pins scattered over tree roots. Her father's penknife followed, then the ration card that she had tucked into her belt. The boys shared the things out. Raw took nothing.

Last was her mother's jewellery.

'Not that.' Wren whispered.

Raw hesitated, a bracelet dangling from his closed fist. 'You were going to give it to the Doctor, it's meaningless to you. Why shouldn't we take it? There are a few Grounder girls who'd give even *me* a kiss for this.' He leaned so close that his mask pressed against hers.

Tears gathered. 'If I've nothing to pay the Doctor he won't come.'

For a moment Raw looked almost sympathetic. 'Stupid Runner.' He shook his head. 'That man won't leave the Dome for anyone. Not for you, not for your pretty jewellery. He's terrified of open sky.' He looked up scornfully. 'There are more and more like him now. Generations who've never left the Dome. It's only the Green-men who go out now and even they don't leave the tree canopy.'

'And us,' one of the younger boys shouted.

'Yeah, Bone, and us.' Raw tossed over his shoulder. 'He won't help you,' he murmured.

'I can describe the symptoms. He can give me medicine.' Wren bit the words out.

'Perhaps.' Raw nodded. 'But the colony is running low. Do you think he's likely to give our last analgesics or antivirals away on the word of a Runner girl? *I* wouldn't.'

'*You're* not a Doctor.' Wren gave a massive heave and ripped free of Raw's grip. She stumbled backwards and looked at the airlock. He let her go.

'You're wasting your time, Runner.'

A cloud of pollinators whirred overhead and automatically Wren tracked the sound, her eyes going upwards past the pale green, fan-shaped leaves of the gingko. The sun was climbing towards mid-morning. There would be another wind-storm later. She had to get moving.

'It's my time to waste.' Frustration burned Wren's eyes, but she wouldn't let a tear fall, not in front of the boys.

Raw spat between the tree roots. Then he tossed her the bracelet back. 'Here you are then, much good it'll do you.'

The fragile chain tangled around Wren's fingers. She closed her hand around it and backed along the path towards the Dome. When she was far enough from the laughing boys, she turned and ran once more.

Compared to the day before, it was as if the colony had repopulated. Men were up ladders removing bunting, or racing in and out of buildings, industrious, like insects in a mound. Elysium created the lungs of Mars. Its botanists, or Green-Men, worked endlessly on the production of seedlings hardy enough to withstand mega storms. The Green-Men could be clearly identified by their intense focus and specialised masks.

The women were less easily seen, but Wren knew they were there by the pools of judgemental silence that followed her progress. They gathered at the corners of buildings, or in front of tech houses, children at their ankles. They collected around the schoolhouse and grouped by the laundry. Their twittering laughter petered off at her approach and their chirping gossip developed hard edges. Their eyes were granite.

Thankfully, the youngest women and in Wren's experience,

the cruellest, lived in the Women's Sector on the other side of the Dome. Controlled, in case they used their wombs irresponsibly. Wren suppressed a shiver. To be locked in a dormitory until your approved Choosing, not even allowed to see the top of the Dome, let alone the vast delta or the rosy sky: hell.

The Surgery was near the food store. Long and low it had more original shuttle parts incorporated than any other building. It shone even in the low Dome light. She edged nearer. After yesterday's quiet, today there would likely be a queue.

She was right. Three Grounders stood outside the door: a pregnant woman, swaying on her feet, a man with an obviously dislocated shoulder, his round face pale and a teenaged boy, his skin rash red.

Wren spoke without thinking. 'I can help with that.' She gestured to the man's arm. 'We have bad landings sometimes. That's basic first aid.'

The woman shrank back. 'A Runner!' She gasped.

With an effort the man turned. 'I'll … wait … for the Doctor.'

'That must hurt.' Wren frowned. 'Why wait longer than you have to? I can fix it here and now.'

'He doesn't want you touching him, *Runner*.' The pregnant woman spat the word like it was an insult.

Wren narrowed her lips and the boy stared at her. 'You can fix that? You're a girl.'

'Like the woman said, I'm a *Runner*.' Wren folded her arms.

'What're you doing here?' Curiosity provoked him. 'You don't look sick.'

Wren swallowed. 'I'm here for my mother.'

'For Mia?' The woman's eyes flickered. 'What's wrong with her?'

'I don't know.' Wren felt suddenly very tired. 'That's why I need the Doctor.'

The woman licked her lips. 'He won't go up there, you know. Nobody would.'

'Some do. With messages.'

The woman shrugged.

'I can pay.'

'That's not ...' She caressed her belly. 'He won't give you medicine without seeing the patient. He just won't.'

The man shook his head. 'She's right. It would be a waste of what we have. You said you do first aid – you fix her.'

'She needs *medicine*.' Wren ground out. 'Whatever he gives me we'll replace it next time Chayton Runs to Aaru.'

The woman shook her head. 'He won't help you; you should go.'

'I'll stay.' Wren folded her arms.

The woman grunted and the Grounders turned from her. The boy kept stealing glances back but Wren ignored him, and the hour wore on. The man went in and came out again, relief in his eyes. The woman took her turn and queue grew behind her: a technician with a burned hand, a Green-man with a hacking cough that sounded frighteningly like her mother's.

Then the door slid open and the boy went in. It was Wren's turn next.

After an eternity the door slid open again. She tried to step forward and the technician barged past as if she wasn't there.

'Hey!' Wren leaped for the door. It closed in her face and the red 'locked' light flashed at eye level. 'He can't do that.' She appealed to the man behind. 'Did you see?'

The Green-man ignored her.

'He can't do that!' She was shrieking now.

'You're a Runner.' The Green-man muttered. 'Grounders go first.' He pushed her to one side and took her place.

'But –' Wren tried to push back in, but he turned his shoulder, a wall of muscle, against her.

Over the next hour more Grounders turned up to see the Doctor and each of them pushed in front of Wren. She tried running for the door whenever it slid open, she tried pleading. They kept pushing her to one side. '*Grounders first.*'

Raw stood two buildings away, watching, his green eyes frigid. Beside him the boys showed off their stolen belongings.

'Why won't they help me?' She sobbed. She wasn't speaking

to anyone in particular, and the two families queuing with her ignored her completely. But Raw sauntered over.

'I told you –'

'Don't say it.' She tore at her shirt with frustrated fingers.

'Do you know how many trades and messages get turned down by the Runners?' he asked. 'How many of these people had things they thought were important, that your family decided weren't?'

'I –'

Raw sneered. 'They're only doing to you what you do to us.'

'We can't take *every* damned message!' Wren yelled. She turned towards the door, towards the Doctor behind it. 'Runners risk their lives on every journey – you think we should risk our lives to get you something you don't really need?' The door remained impassive.

'Who are you to judge what we need and what we don't?' Raw said quietly.

'Someone has to.'

'Well, *they've* decided that *you* don't need the Doctor.'

'But I *do* need him.' Wren's voice was a wail. 'She might die.' She bent over double, a sudden pain cramping her gut. 'I can pay,' she sobbed.

Raw shook his head. 'This isn't about what you can pay.'

Suddenly the door opened and a mother with a crying infant made to move into the gap.

Raw stepped into her path, blocking her, almost as if by accident. Wren's eyes widened but she took the opportunity and leaped between their bodies and into the open door. She didn't know why, but Raw had given her a chance.

The Doctor was sat at a desk. Greying brown hair, an elongated body, long arms, legs crossed at the ankle; he seemed a broken limbed doll, splayed uncomfortably at a tea party. She could see the balding patch on the top of his head.

Behind him was an array of tools: air syringes, small hammers, sterile knives. The shelves behind him displayed a few bottles of tablets or thick liquids, but most were bare. Wren swallowed, Raw hadn't been lying, the colony was almost out of medications. They would need a Runner to go to Aaru soon. But there were none.

She cleared her throat. The Doctor looked up. 'A Runner?' His lips and tongue moved constantly, nervously as if he was chewing on the air. 'Take off your mask.'

Wren shook her head. 'I'm here about my mother. You need to come.'

'To Avalon?' He shifted in his chair. 'I'm far too busy, she'll have to come to me.'

'She can't.' Wren leaned her fists on his desk. 'I think she's dying.'

'You're a Doctor now, are you?' He smiled tightly.

'She's had a fever for three days.'

'Then it'll break soon,' he said dismissively.

'We need medicine.' She pressed forward. 'She has this cough –'

The Doctor sighed. 'I can give you analgesics.' He reached behind him and chose the smallest bottle. 'This is all I can spare.'

'We'll get more, as soon as Colm gets back in, I'll send him out …'

'Well, when he gets back, return for another bottle – if you still need it – until then, there are Grounders who need these more: people who do *real* jobs, women who contribute to society.'

'My mother contributes –'

'How many babes has she sent for exchange?' he snapped. 'It's all I can spare. Take it or leave it.'

Wren closed a hand around the bottle. It fit inside her palm. 'These won't be enough.' She pulled out the bracelet and thrust it at him. 'I can pay.'

The Doctor snorted. 'What do you think I am? I've given you all the help I can, now get out so I can see someone who's actually sick.'

Wren staggered backwards. 'What if she …?'

'Get your father to bring her here and I'll examine her.'

Wren's back hit the door. 'He's not here.' It slid open

automatically, tipping her onto hard packed dirt. The Grounder mother stepped over her, kicking dust into her mouth and the door shut in her face.

Wren scrambled to her feet. Raw was nowhere to be seen, but the boys remained by the tech house. She looked at the bottle clutched in one hand. Analgesics! She had tried them already, used the family's whole supply in the first two days. Wren was tempted to throw the bottle, but she held herself back; some pain relief was better than nothing.

Raw had been right, the Grounders weren't willing to help her. She was on her own.

Avalon was quiet when she returned. The skies were clear, the platform empty. She hadn't expected anything else. She cycled through the airlock and stood, trembling, in the centre of the room, listening for her mother's breathing. One day, soon, she'd open the curtain to find her dead. Would it be today? Wren couldn't bring herself to step closer to the alcove and find out. It was too quiet.

But the sphere didn't have a feeling of abandonment, not yet, and her mother coughed in her sleep.

Wren placed the bottle of capsules on the kitchen counter ready to administer them when she woke.

Jay's wings remained in the corner where she had left them and Wren drifted nearer. Dreamlike, she touched the straps. She was about the same size that Jay had been when he first started running. So, if she tightened the straps like *this* and swung them behind her like *that* ...

Wren slid the wings over her own shoulders, tightened the straps over her chest and clipped her wrists onto the struts.

Her breath caught. Sheer terror twisted her gut. This was blasphemy. She glanced at the doorway -if someone should come in now ... but they wouldn't. She was completely alone. Outside, Elysium's alarms began to sound. It was mid-day in dust storm season. No-one could come to Avalon now, even if they wanted.

She did a half turn, like a Grounder with a new dress, and the wings swished around her ankles. They were lighter than she had expected them to be. She lifted her arms; they moved with her, as if they were part of her body.

She giggled and immediately clapped her hands over her mouth. If she was caught like this she'd be killed: dropped screaming from the Runner platform. Convocation's rules were unambiguous. Girls were forbidden from wearing wings. No room for argument, no loop hole. No Running for Runner women. She swished the wings again. Graphite glimmered in the soft light.

She had to remove the wings, but she couldn't make herself undo the straps. Her fingers were frozen.

Wren pressed her teeth together so hard they ached. There had to something more she could do for her mother. Was she really supposed to just watch her die?

She had seen her father and brothers Run a thousand times.

She touched the straps again; she had to take off the wings.

With shaking fingers, she unclipped the straps and shrugged them carefully from her back. But she didn't hang them up. Moving with a new sense of urgency, Wren folded the struts, pulled the quilt off her bed, wrapped them with it and laid them down.

Now she couldn't see them. She turned her back to the wings and started to prepare lunch; perhaps her mother would eat something today.

As she worked, the dust storm raged outside the window and the back of her neck itched. She fought not to turn around.

Convocation could only kill her if they *found out* she had Run. She'd seen no other Runner for so long. She had only to find her brothers, send them to Aaru and return home. No-one else need ever know. Colm would be livid, but would he turn her in? She thought not.

Silently, the wings called to her. The dust settled back to the ground, clearing the windows.

She gripped the knife tighter in her hand.

Walking as if in a trance, Wren left the kitchen and entered the airlock. If she was even going to consider doing this, there was something she would need to do first.

'Give me a sign,' she whispered and she looked one final time at the storm-cleared indigo skies above the delta. 'Send a Runner in. Anything.'

Nothing.

She nodded. Then she caught her long hair in one hand. Ignoring the tears that gathered in her eyes, she reached above her with the knife, placed it beneath her fist and started to saw.

The blade sliced easily through her thick mane and Wren was soon left with a handful of hair. Steeling herself, she held her fist in front of her and opened it. Gleefully the wind scattered the gathered coils. With the strange sense of lightness on her head, Wren watched, unmoving, as her hair blew into the wind like charcoal smears.

'No-one need ever know.'

Glowing with new purpose she returned to the sphere, found her warmest outdoor clothing and pulled on the padded jacket. She put a spare mask in her pocket and checked the levels of cyanobacteria in her O_2 canister. There were enough in there to keep cycling her air for another couple of weeks. Plenty of time before they would need flushing and replacing.

Lastly, she scooped up the water jug. The family's drinking water came from filters deep underground. Surface water, apart from that in Lake Lyot was still limited, although more was appearing every year as the air temperature continued to increase, unfreezing the Martian water and, with it, more and more dormant indigenous life. That was where the Creatures had originated, and Caro's disease.

As the jug slowly filled Wren looked at the closed curtain and listened to her mother's shallow breathing. What if her illness was the result of another hybrid microbe, like Caro's? If it was, would any of the colonies even have a cure? Aaru housed the scientists, who might be creating new drugs, but Vaikuntha had the biologists, experts in the local species, they too might have an answer. Eden might even have some herb that would offer a solution, a genetic modification perhaps.

She shook her head, unwilling to acknowledge, even to herself, that she was already planning a Running route: Vaikuntha to Aaru via Arcadia, then to Eden … and back. She would look for her brothers at each stop.

She looked at the jug and frowned. How long would she be away? If her mother drank the jug dry, she would never be able to reach the tap herself. Quickly, Wren filled every mug, cup and pan in the house. When that was done, she surrounded the alcove with the containers.

Her mother hadn't eaten since she became ill, but Wren cut a loaf into chunks and left that by the bed with some of the hard soy-chiz she knew she liked.

There was only one more thing for her to do. Back in the cabin Wren tipped the bottle of analgesics onto a plate, then she opened the curtain.

She bent to give her a kiss and Mia groaned as she woke. 'Wren?'

'No-one's home. I'm going to find help.'

'What kind of help?' Her mother struggled to sit.

Wren pushed her gently back. 'There's medicine here.' Wren put the plate on the floor. 'Have some when you need to, I'll bring more back with me.'

'You're scaring me. What have you done to yourself?'

Wren pushed one hand through her shorn hair. 'All these cups have water in and here is food. Do you understand?' She held her mother's hand until she nodded.

'Where are you going?'

'I'm going to find Colm and Jay.'

'Y-you're going on a Run?' Her mother sagged.

'I can do it.'

Long fingers tightened in Wren's, so dry the skin crackled. 'It's forbidden.'

'I know.' Wren hid a shiver. 'I'll be fine.'

'It's dangerous.' Shadows filled her mother's eyes. 'I know you've listened to your brother's lessons, but you can't do your first flight alone. And you don't know the route your brothers took.'

'Then I'll find a cure myself.'

Tears teetered on her mother's cheekbones. 'What if something happens to you?'

'I won't let you die.' Wren set her jaw.

Her mother huddled over a coughing fit that brought tears to Wren's eyes. 'You'll be leaving me alone,' she gasped. 'Like your father and your brothers.'

'I'll be back in two days. Three at the outside. I promise.'

'Three days.' Her mother touched Wren's face with hands that still shook from coughing. 'You look so much like your father.'

They sat like that for a moment, neither wanting to let go, then Mia's arm dropped, too exhausted to hold on. 'But you have my eyes,' she sighed and closed her eyes. 'When you see your brothers, tell them I love them.'

Wren nodded and her throat felt like wood. 'I love you.'

The reply was so quiet she could hardly hear it. 'Love you too.'

Wren left her mother's curtain open so she could see the airlock from the bed, then she hung Jay's spare goggles over her wrist, scooped up the wings and walked away.

With a breath that tasted of hope, Wren pressed her palm on the pad and, when the airlock cycled round, she stepped outside. She did not look back.

3

It was a short walk to the Runner Station perched on the landing strip. No-one had been in since Wren had cleaned up after her brothers a week before and the smell of stale sweat lingered; she could taste it even through the filters of her mask. Wren left the airlock open in an attempt to freshen the room and a tiny sand snake slithered inside.

All but one of the wing stands stood empty. Wren stiffened as she tried to remember the last time there had not been at a full complement of wing-sets in here. Where were all the Runners? Maybe she would find out.

Reverently, Wren unwrapped Jay's old wings. When she hung them from the stand the silvery material dropped in folds to hang a hand-span above the floor, only slightly shorter than the larger pair on the stand behind them.

The thin metal struts of 'her' wings looked fragile as snake bones and when Wren breathed out through her mouth, the material rippled.

Her hands shook as she stroked one rubbery airfoil; then she turned and slipped her arms inside the straps that hung from the front. She buckled the belt tightly across her throbbing chest and found that her wrists fit comfortably into the bracelets.

Wren studied her hands; unexpectedly steady. She took a deep breath. She was going to find her brothers and help her mother.

'What are you doing?'

Wren spun as the airlock filled and, instinctively, she stepped back, trying to hide her wings in the gloom.

'I knew it – I knew you'd do this.' It was Raw. Triumph glowed as emerald fire in his eyes.

'What are you doing here?' Wren hissed. Her hands came up and Raw laughed.

'You think you can fight me?' He stepped forward and the lock cycled shut behind him. 'Do you know what the Council will do when they find out what you're planning?'

'And you'll enjoy telling them. Go on, run.' Wren glanced towards the closed exit and her heart thudded.

'You think I'm stupid as well as ugly.' Raw glowered. 'I leave you alone and you'll be gone when I get back.'

Wren glared.

'Give me the wings.' Raw held out his hands, as if she would just take them off and hand them over.

Wren shook her head. 'I can't give wings to a *Grounder!* I'm going to find my brothers. You can't stop me.'

'Watch me.' Raw stepped closer, his bulk filling the hut. 'Women don't Run. You said so yourself. It's sacrilege.'

As he reached for her, Wren retreated behind an empty stand. Swiftly she grabbed the heavy tripod and hefted it in front of her. Raw paused long enough for Wren to give the wood a swing. The stand whistled past his face and it was his turn to take a step backwards.

'I hate you,' he hissed. 'I hate your family.'

The wooden stand felt as heavy as a tree under the weight of his hatred. 'But you helped me before, why?'

Raw sneered. 'I wasn't thinking straight. Give me the damned wings.'

'No!' Wren gripped the stand tighter. 'Why do you hate me so much?'

He made no answer, but his eyes gleamed.

Wren blinked. 'I've done nothing to you.'

Raw's sudden laugh made her scuttle backwards. She stumbled against a low shelf and almost fell. At the last second, she remembered to raise the stand and caught Raw in the ribs as he lunged. The impact shuddered along her arm.

He stopped his advance. 'You've done nothing to me?' He turned his face so that his scarred cheeks caught the light.

Wren flinched. '*I* didn't do that.'

'*Runners* did it,' Raw spat.

'Did not.' Wren's denial was immediate, but Raw simply

looked at her until her defiance faded.

'Five years ago, my mother was ill, remember Caro's disease?' He didn't wait for her to answer. 'Your father was having a dispute with the Council. He wouldn't Run for the cure until they agreed payment terms. We thought she was going to die. So, I came up here ...'

Wren gasped. 'You tried to steal some wings. That's ... that's ...'

'I had *no choice*.' Spittle spattered her wings like beads.

'But if we lose wings they can't be replaced. Every time a Runner goes down, another wing-set gets lost and there can be fewer trades, fewer messages.' Wren shuddered.

Raw gestured at the straps over her chest. '*You're* doing it.'

Wren opened her mouth then closed it. She'd heard her brother's lessons, she was better prepared than Raw, but really, was what she was planning any different?

Raw saw her face and snorted. 'Your father beat me and kicked me out, then he Ran for the medicine. Gave us enough for my mother ... but nothing for me. That was my punishment.'

'You *got* the cure.' Web frowned. 'You wouldn't be here otherwise.'

'He relented ... eventually. But not before *this*.' Raw ignored the wavering stand and leaned so he could hold his scarred face close to Wren's. She winced as he pointed, unable to take her gaze from the pocked landscape that was his left-hand side. Her hand with the stand in it began to sag.

'You want to know the worst thing?' Raw's fists clenched. 'It isn't that my mother nearly died because of *your* family. It isn't that I'll never be able to take my turn on the Council, because no-one will deal with me. It isn't that I've been forced into apprenticeship engineering and maintaining the solar panels, so no-one will see me in the Dome. It's that I'm now so *ugly* and so *useless*, that the Women's Sector won't even consider my application for the choosing. I'll *never* have a family.'

Wren's eyes widened as the truth of his words crushed her heart like a fist.

'That's right.' Finally, he reached for her. 'Why should you get to save your mother when I had to wait for your father to save mine?'

Wren used the stand to knock him sideways. 'Get away from me.'

His hands clawed at her shoulders, but she twisted and ran for the door. She felt her wings catch on something and knew he had her. But the material was slippery as oil and Raw's curses followed a crash as he lost his grip and fell into one of the other wing-stands.

Wren tossed her weapon aside and slapped at the airlock, racing out before it had completely cycled open. Then she sprinted like never before, heading unerringly towards the edge of the cliff. She had thought to take some time to prepare herself, to replay her brother's lessons in her mind, but now she would just have to Run.

Raw's shouts spurred her on, but she couldn't lift off without Jay's goggles. Barely missing a step, she pulled them from her wrist and slipped them over her eyes. She was pulling up her hood as her feet hit the platform; it bounced slightly under her soles, boosting her to run even faster.

Wren returned her focus to her sprint. She knew Raw was behind her, but she didn't turn. She had to be running as fast as she could when she leaped, and she couldn't go any faster than she already was.

Her arms pumped by her sides and her wings flapped noisily, muffling Raw's shouts with their music.

A blue line blurred past her feet. This was her last chance to stop. Once she passed the red line, a few strides further on, her momentum would take her over the edge, even if she changed her mind.

For his sake, she hoped Raw stopped chasing her in time.

Wren did not even consider stopping. She pounded past the red line and the ground fell away. She was no longer on Elysium Mons. Now she was running on a platform built over air.

Twenty feet below her feet a net waited, but a falling Runner could miss it if caught by the wind, and kilometres below there was only the bone-yard, where every Runner who had ever made a mistake lifting off or landing at Avalon inevitably ended. She put the idea from her head. She had to think only about her own launch.

The end of the platform was a blur. Wren's heart pounded in time with her feet. She had seen her brothers do this a hundred times. She had heard their lessons. She could do it too.

Two steps before the platform ended there was a green line. As her right foot thudded onto it, Wren threw out her arms. With a flick of her wrists she locked the wings. She allowed a wave of relief to wash over her then she squeezed her eyes closed and leaped from the spring-board. Her body arched.

At the end of her jump she lurched downwards, but Wren kept her elbows locked as she had seen her brothers do it and the wind caught her. It swept her up, filled her wings with a rattle and whisked her away from Raw's angry cries, the safety net and Elysium.

At first, Wren let the air simply carry her. Fighting an impulse to return to Avalon, she focused completely on the tension in her arms and legs and the anticipation of another nauseating drop.

Gradually she became used to the idea that she hadn't plunged to her death and her breathing began to slow. She kept her legs stretched behind her and her arms straight, but, tentatively, she relaxed her muscles, allowing the wind to hold her limbs in position.

She still hadn't opened her eyes.

She was picturing her brothers reciting their lessons at the table. The boys often struggled to recall the instructions that her father gave them while Wren stabbed her sewing with vicious frustration and offered the answers in the confines of her head. A thrill of fear shivered through her as she thought of how her father would react to her flight.

Had Raw been telling the truth? Her shoulders shook and she wobbled and scrubbed the thought away. She had to picture her father's flying lessons, not imagine him refusing medicine to a dying boy.

His voice rippled through her memories. 'Relax your tongue first and your other muscles will follow. You don't believe me? Try it now.'

She tried it. Only when she focused on her tongue, making it flop loosely in her mouth did she realise how much tension she held there. Pleased that the trick had worked she thought about his next instruction.

'Open and close your fists to make sure the blood continues to flow.'

She clenched her fists and realised how numb they had become. Opening her hands, she repeated the exercise until her arms started to tingle.

'If you want to go right, dip your right shoulder by one thumb joint.'

In her memory her father held up his right thumb and shook it to make his point, but one joint didn't sound like much. Wren ducked her right shoulder as far as she could and tipped into the wind. Her body turned towards the dipped shoulder but, with rising alarm, she realised that she could not straighten herself out: she was in danger of rolling.

She teetered like a balancing toy as she fought the wind, unable to bring her right arm up. Then it struck her: instead of bringing up her right arm, she should dip to her left. She would need to be very careful, if she tipped too far her wings would flap shut and she would fall.

Moving her attention from her right arm to her left, Wren shifted her shoulder muscles. Gradually she felt a slight relaxing of the pressure on her right. Again, she shifted her left shoulder and felt herself straighten out a little more. One more dip and she was level.

Unclenching her fists, Wren tried shifting her left shoulder no more than the length of one thumb joint and rolled gently left, changing course again, but maintaining her smooth flight.

'Sorry, Father,' she whispered.

The only noise in Wren's ears was the rustling of her wings.

Soothed, Wren finally allowed herself to open her eyes.

She had been imagining that the wind cradled her in gossamer arms, so when she saw nothing between her and the desert but wisps of cloud, the shock made her squeeze her eyes closed again with a whimper.

Several shaky breaths later, Wren cracked her eyes open once more. Unable to look down, she peeped straight ahead.

For a moment, confusion clutched at her thoughts. She was staring towards a cliff with a tiny 'sphere gripping its edge.

Where was she?

She circled, mystified. Beyond the 'sphere a belt of green surrounded a much larger biosphere, the sun glinted from the panels that ringed its roof. Trees stole out from it, merging into ferns, then into wide flats of green, which looked almost like lakes themselves, and only then finally into the red wasteland of the mountain top, like a patchwork quilt creeping from a bed.

Her eyes went back to the stubby Runner platform which ended by a 'sphere that looked tiny as a shell on a riverbank.

Wren had turned herself completely around. She was looking at her own home.

Suddenly her breath caught in her throat. Out by the Runner hut someone was moving: a figure wearing wings. While she had been flying with her eyes closed, one of her brothers had finally come home.

She had her sign. Wren smiled on a long exhale as she circled low towards the Runner-sphere. Tension lifted from her shoulders. She wouldn't have to commit any further transgression. Whichever of her brothers was back, she didn't care. She would land, send him to set out again to save Mother and hope he didn't tell Father what she had done.

But the Runner was heading *away* from the house. He was running towards the platform and he wasn't removing his wings.

Wren frowned as she swept closer. The Runner's build was unfamiliar; too wide to be Colm, too tall for Jay. It certainly wasn't Father.

The figure started to sprint along the platform. The metal

juddered with the thudding of his feet. Suddenly the straps over her chest felt too tight. It couldn't be … but there had been one more set of wings in the hut.

'Raw!' Wren's voice sank like a rock into the wind. 'What're you doing?'

With tension winding her shoulders together, she willed herself faster. What was Raw thinking? Did he imagine he could catch her? Punish her? He'd heard none of her brother's lessons. He would fall from the platform, plunge through the clouds and be lost in the bone-yards – with the last set of wings on his back.

'*Stop!*' she cried as she hurtled towards him. But it was too late – he was passing the red line.

Wren howled and Raw looked up, his eyes narrowed in bright determination. He wasn't even wearing goggles. '*Jump* you idiot.' She swept past and wheeled as hard as she could. '*Jump!*'

4

Raw leaped from the end of the platform and his arms whipped out in a fair imitation of Wren's own launch. The breath whooshed out of her as the wings locked into place and lifted his weight.

Then he panicked.

'*Turn back.*' Wren yelled so hard she thought her throat would tear, but Raw was beyond hearing. Instead of trying to circle back to Elysium, he lurched into a current and headed beyond the safety net and over the delta.

His flight was no smooth meeting of wings and air; he rocked like Jay's lost kite launched into a gale, yawing and wobbling alarmingly.

Wren could barely swallow; her throat was blocked with fear as hard as gristle. Any moment those wings would snap shut, he'd be gone and she knew who would be blamed.

She drove herself into the same current that had taken him and felt the wind flow around her, drawing her past the cliff. Refusing to look down she kept her gaze focused on the fluttering wings ahead of her.

Wren's flight was much smoother than Raw's and her wings held a better angle. It wasn't long before she caught up. From above, Wren saw Raw fighting his pinions. 'Can you hear me?'

Raw's flight didn't alter in the slightest.

Wren dipped her right wing and circled, hoping he would see her. He gave no sign. She would have to dive to draw level with him.

Taking a deep breath, Wren brought her father's instructions to mind. 'To drop, you must lift your legs from the hip. Lift them higher to descend more sharply.'

Wren recalled watching her brothers lying face down on the floor, lifting their legs stiffly from the ground. With a deep breath, she tensed her thighs and lifted. The air rushed beneath her and she started to tip.

Straight away Wren's heart thudded and she levelled out as fast as she could, but the wind still embraced her and when her chest stopped aching she saw that she had dropped closer to the guttering wing-set below.

'Okay.' With another breath Wren lifted her legs again and the wind tipped her like a favourite child. As soon as she could see Raw's wings glowing silver at the tip of her fingers, she pulled up. 'Raw!'

He still couldn't hear her. Even over the flutter of wind in wings, Wren caught the frenetic pants that heaved from his mask. She tried to catch his eye but without goggles, his eyes were watering madly. He couldn't see her.

As she considered circling round and trying again, Raw yawed more violently and overcorrected.

Their screams harmonised as the inevitable happened: his wings unlocked, lost their shape and were abandoned by the wind.

Raw's cry mingled with hers' as he dropped towards the formless clouds.

Instinctively Wren threw herself into a dive to match his crazy tumble.

Raw's arms and legs flailed as he tried to catch the insubstantial air and he hit the cloud cover like it was water.

Wren followed a moment later. Automatically she braced, but although she went face first into the mist, there was no impact, just moisture that clung to her goggles and blinded her.

'Raw!' She could no longer hear or see him but Wren had to hope they would break through the clouds together and that she would have enough time to save his life – and the wings – on the other side.

She counted as she dived. Her cheeks and fingers went numb and drops of water poured into her hair like tears.

'One, two, three, four …' Wren had reached ten when the light on her goggles grew abruptly brighter and warmth tickled her back and fingers. She was through.

Putting her face into the wind, she forced the air to whip the spray from her goggles. In moments she could see.

The red desert was still far below, spotted with flashes of silver as sand moved lazily over the bone-yard. But where was Raw?

Frantically she turned her head one way, then another. There was no sign of plummeting silver.

A deadening blow smashed her right arm downwards and she spun in the air. Wren sobbed as Raw plunged past and fought to keep her arms locked as the wind tried to close her wings against her body.

She had overtaken him inside the clouds.

Three times she turned; so fast the ground and sky blurred together. Then a gust of warm air slid beneath her and she yawed level.

Her right arm ached as if it had been struck with a hammer, but she had to hold it steady. With a shake of her head Wren took a single deep breath; then she pitched downwards once more. At least Raw now knew she was there.

As she dived, she saw that he was finally trying to straighten out. But each time he attempted to thrust out his limbs, the wind shoved his arms and legs back in. Still plunging, he tried to spread his arms. The wings fluttered above them, useless and lank. Suddenly though, they netted the wind and billowed.

Wren gasped and her heart leapt.

But Raw's wings hadn't locked. For a short moment the spreading material arrested his fall, but then his arms were pulled behind him with a crack that even Wren could hear.

The wind carried his cry and trapped it under her hood. It pealed in Wren's ears until she quivered at the sound. She hissed, moved her arms to a slight backward cant and pushed herself to dive faster.

Raw was rolling again, wings tucked round him like the shell of a louse. Wren's eyes flicked to the ground, then away. She could already make out individual boulders at the base of the Mons. Among them she could make out clusters of bones, where unlucky Runners had made their last landings. Jumbles of curving ribs and grinning skulls showed where the majority had met their end. In the distance she spotted skeletons that appeared whole, spread-eagled for the sky. But soon she saw that even these were missing limbs; taken by the Creatures.

Her stomach lurched, there was very little time before both Raw and the precious wings were smashed to pieces.

Then she reached him.

'*Raw,*' she screamed.

His eyes rolled, terrified and staring. He'd never understand instructions; there was only one thing to do. Wren's heart beat a terrified rhythm: *please don't, please don't, please don't* ...

She had never watched her brothers practise this move, she'd been too scared, but she knew the theory and now, if she wanted to save the wings Raw had stolen, she had no choice.

Before she could change her mind, Wren flicked her wrist just so, unlocked her wings and pulled her arms into her body.

Now she was falling too.

Wren pulled her legs in to imitate Raw and her dive immediately became a chaotic tumble. Panic clawed into her throat and her heart pounded faster: *don't die, don't die, don't die* ...

The ground rushed towards her, but she only saw it in pieces; patch-worked into a dizzying jumble with the sky, the cliff and the fool plummeting with her.

Somehow on a roll, she caught his eye. He had to understand what she was doing and watch her do it.

Wren inhaled, glad that her mask kept pumping O_2, because the air, even if it had been breathable, now whipped past her too thin and fast to do any good. The ground rose like dough, a blur of bronze that started at the corner of her eye and then filled her whole vision.

Furiously Wren thrust her legs out behind her and forced herself back into a dive. Every instinct fought against the streamlining of her shape; demanded that she make herself less aerodynamic; called for a few extra precious seconds of life.

Over-riding her terror, Wren drove her arms back so her hands touched her thighs. She shot past Raw and saw him roll as he tried to follow her descent.

Then Wren thrust her arms out from her sides, making a T.

The wind battled her, trying to pin her limbs back to her body, but she was fighting for her life. Her shoulders threatened to give way. Suddenly she passed the halfway point and the wind allowed her to flick her wrists and lock her wings into place.

She was still heading at insane speed towards the rocks below – oh and a small patch of greenery, it seemed the ferns had spread to the delta. But she had her wings once more. Hysterical laughter hissed out of her as she began to bend her torso upwards.

Just as with her arms, it was a matter of reaching that point where the wind stopped fighting her and got beneath her straining body. But Wren wasn't strong. She grunted with effort, unable to tear her eyes from the ferns. In moments she'd drive through them so hard no-one would even know a Runner had crashed there.

Would she feel her bones breaking, or would it be over too fast?

Abruptly the wind pushed her upwards. With a crazy whoop Wren straightened out, blood pounding in her ears so loudly she could hear nothing else. Then she wheeled back to Raw. *'Now you!'*

There was no sign that Raw had taken her display on board.

'Do it,' she cried.

He won't, he won't, he won't. Her pulse goaded her until, with relief, she saw Raw thrust his legs behind him.

Raw was stronger than Wren and it seemed easier for him to create a disciplined dive. She wheeled over his head, heart banging in her throat, as he accelerated towards the ferns.

His right arm was slower to move than his left, but it looked straight enough. Maybe the wind hadn't broken it after all.

Still it took Raw a couple of tries to lock his wings into place and Wren held her breath until he had his wings extended, seconds away from control. Too many seconds away.

'Pull up,' Wren murmured. Her eyes were glued to his body as he struggled to bend his torso as she had done.

When she knew it was too late, she closed her eyes.

5

There was no sound.

Surely Wren should have heard the rustle of ferns being crushed, the snap of wing and bone as Raw drove into the desert?

She risked cracking open her eyes and peeped towards the ground. There was no sign of a crash landing; no broken body or twisted wings poking from clusters of greenery. Holding her breath, Wren turned her head. Was it possible that Raw had flown?

She was too low; all she could see were long scarlet rock formations. Smoothed by millennia of abrasive storms and with no water to add grooves, each was so organic that Web could imagine the breath that would make them rise and fall. Looking away from the bubbles of rock she wheeled into a warm gust but, even circling slowly, she could see no sign of Raw.

Then, as she searched upwards, a spot appeared in the centre of the lowering sun. It darkened and grew until she could see Raw, finally flying upwards, whirling just as she was, in the centre of a thermal.

For a single inhale Wren allowed herself to feel a wave of relief that almost washed away the strength in her limbs. Raw had lived, but more importantly, her father's spare wings had survived his crazy impulse. If she could just get him to land, no-one need ever know what had nearly happened.

'*Raw!*' She flew up behind him as fast as she could force the wind to lift her. Automatically he turned his head and yawed alarmingly. Immediately he turned back. He was holding his body stiff as thin ice, ready to shatter at the slightest pressure. He had to relax. 'You're all right,' Wren called. 'You won't fall.'

Either he didn't answer, or the wind snatched his reply away.

Wren circled until she flew on his right flank and then looked at him. His eyes were watering badly. His jacket was dark with crescent shaped stains and there was blood smeared on his lip and chin.

'Can you hear me?' she called.

Raw nodded tightly.

'I'm going to help you land.' Wren tried to catch his eye. He'd crunch on the runway if he didn't loosen up.

She could hardly hear his croaked response. 'Are *you* going back?'

Wren snorted. 'No, but I'll guide you in – tell you what to do.'

Raw stared ahead and the muscles on his jaw stuck out like struts. Then he shook his head. 'Then I'm not landing.'

It took a moment for Wren to absorb his reply. She almost choked. 'What do you mean?'

'If you're not landing,' he yelled, 'I'm not. I'm coming with you.'

Tears of frustration pricked Wren's eyes, threatening to mist up her goggles. 'Why do you want to follow me – to get me in trouble? I won't help you if you come after me. Go back.'

Raw risked a slight twitch of his head and wobbled as his body jolted into the wind.

'You have to,' Wren raged. 'You don't know how to fly.'

Raw said nothing; he simply set his face into the wind.

Furious, Wren narrowed her eyes and pointed her toes. She'd gained enough height, so she could leave the thermal. She should leave Raw right here, circling endlessly upwards into the cooling air until she returned. Or until exhaustion overtook him and he fell.

'Burn you.' She glared viciously through her goggles, wishing she could force Raw to obey her. 'I'm not going back to Avalon. I have to find a cure.'

He continued to ignore her, but Wren noticed that the longer they circled the less terrified he looked.

If he followed her, she would have no choice but to help him. The wings were precious, she couldn't risk their loss. 'If you're coming, you'll have to keep up,' Wren growled. 'I'm not waiting for you.' Then she dipped left and the thermal released her into the cooler air.

For a while Wren burned with a fury so hot and deep that she could hardly see anything through her goggles. She paid no attention to the landscape below, simply headed in the direction of the Mons, kilometres lower than Elysium, but still visible against the horizon, which she knew would steer her to Vaikuntha.

Her mind raced with the problem of her hanger-on. When he crashed, the Runners in Vaikuntha would instantly see that he was not one of them. Even if he watched her and managed to pull off a landing, he knew nothing of etiquette and then, if he still escaped notice, he would give Wren herself away. Why else was he following, if not to ruin her mission? She clenched her fists. 'Just because his mother almost died …' she muttered.

Her wings rustled louder as she shuddered. But as the afternoon wore on, and her arms began to ache, rage burned itself out and Wren was filled instead with quiet awe.

Below her, the Martian delta stretched out, seemingly endlessly. A vast orange desert pocketed with patches of green, seeded from Elysium. Rock formations like giant sculptures dotted the emptiness, smooth as sanded wood, shadows growing black as the sun sought its nadir.

Then she saw an arrow moving in the sand, following her own shadow as it wove over rocks and dipped in and out of crevices. It persisted with her, keeping pace as she sped through the sky.

Wren shivered as one trail became two, then three. She saw nothing of the Creatures themselves. As far as she knew, no-one ever had. Generations ago early colonists had tried to modify the Creature's antecedents, which had been woken from dormancy by humanities' terra-forming efforts; they thought they could use the burrowers to loosen soil and release more greenhouse gases. But they had grown at an alarming rate even as rivers began slowly to form in empty beds and the dampening sand filled with Martian bugs. As far as the Originals had been concerned the Creature was a relative of the sand snake; some kind of serpent. But who really knew what they had turned into since man's modifications?

The Creature's persistence as they waited for Wren to make a mistake reminded her to check on Raw. He too was on her tail, waiting for her to fail, a scavenger no less than the Creatures below. She glanced back. Her enemy remained in sight, silver wings glinting in the reddening sunlight, but she was drawing further ahead of him. Soon he would be nothing but a mote. Wren sighed and tilted into the setting sun, looping in lazy circles as she waited.

The joy of feeling the wind against her cheeks sent from her mind the Creatures, Raw and their hunger for her demise. At some point her hood had blown back and her shorn hair streamed in the currents. The sheer speed of flight amazed her. In mere hours, she had travelled so far that Elysium's massive peak was barely more than a bump in the landscape. She imagined that if she had no O_2 mask, the wind would have long ago whisked the air from her lungs, but instead she had tamed it and forced it to carry her in its currents.

When Raw began to catch up, Wren swung towards Vaikuntha. He could stay at her back; she did not want him at her side.

As she flew, Wren started to think of the wind as a solid, living thing and gradually became adept at choosing the gusts that were strongest and longest lasting.

As she did so, she began to see that the shape of the ground affected the character of the wind. Where the desert was smooth and flat the wind rushed in a straighter path; where the ground gullied and rolled, it swirled and bounded in flurries that took her up and around more often than forward. So, Wren started looking at the ground ahead to anticipate where the wind would be kindest. It meant that she veered from a straight path more than once, but she flew even faster.

Behind her Raw grew tiny and, with a strange lurch in her belly, she found herself wishing she could share her discovery with someone, even if it had to be him.

Despite her resolution to leave Raw to himself it was as if Wren's head was on a string and although her loathing of her partner burned as brightly as ever, she was drawn to keep checking on him.

The wind's whisper in her ears was comforting, but somehow desolate. The silence which filled the air above the wind pressed in on her like a weight.

Wren was coming to know the Runner's truth. Flying was freedom, but freedom was lonely. And so, each time Wren saw Raw dip into the wind, she had to fight the upturning of her lips. She did not know what would happen once they landed, but at least she wasn't alone.

Hours of flying meant that Wren's wrists felt burdened as if by ballast and the sharp arrow of her flight was beginning to sag. To the East the bright star that was Deimos began to burn, brightening the heavens. She looked to the West as Phobos faded into view, pallid against the bronze sky. For a while the battered asteroid hung in balance with the setting sun and Wren poised between them on a thread of air.

All too soon, the desert quenched the sun. The sky smouldered and gold-edged wisps of clouds changed to grey as twilight descended in a cloak decorated with mirrors and stars. Now both moons were in the sky together, the orbital array between them, reflecting the last of the sun's heat back to the surface. Moisture from her breath started to freeze in Wren's mask and cold ate through her clothes as the air cooled. She flexed her stiffening fingers and exhaled shakily. They had to be close to Vaikuntha now, simply because night-Running was not an option; particularly for a beginner. Already she could feel the thermals wilting; flaccid and unable to bear her weight.

Although Wren pitched her torso desperately into the wind, trying to turn upwards, her flight tilted into a gradient and she began to descend.

The V-shaped wake of the Creatures seemed to surge closer.

Was it possible they knew she was in trouble?

'*Wren*!' It was Raw. He was only a few wingspans above her and his voice was filled with fear. Wren looked up; his wings glowed red and purple as they reflected the dying sun. 'I'm sinking. What do we do?'

She offered no answer; she would just have to search the deepening darkness for a rock on which to land. It was their only chance. If their feet hit the sand, the Creatures would have them. Raising her head, Wren searched desperately for tell-tale shadows.

Rocks littered the delta, but boulders large enough to land on were too low to the dust, Wren could imagine Creatures lunging for them out of the darkness. To her right was a high tower of stone, which seemed promising, but when she circled towards it, Wren realised that it was too narrow: they would fall off if they tried to set down. Her breath was coming in sobs now, as though her O_2 canister wasn't operating properly. Wren ground her teeth. She would not die like this, eaten by Creatures, not even one colony investigated for a cure. There would be somewhere safe to land; there had to be.

She shook her head to flick away the useless tears that were starting to mist her vision and regular shapes: rectangles on the delta, caught her attention.

Quickly she leaned towards them. Her descent had already taken her into dust. Now the wind carried particles that stung her exposed skin and gathered in the rims of her goggles: she was too low.

The sand trails that told Wren where the Creatures lurked, seemed larger now, as though they were closer to the surface. Dust surged, showing the Creatures lunging towards the shrinking shadow of her wings, but they had not yet broken cover. Wren could no longer count their wakes as they wound back and forth, wriggling like greenbelt-worms, and she pictured them fighting over her when her feet hit the desert.

She shivered and pushed towards the rectangles: their last hope.

A shout told her that Raw was right behind her, but she

ignored him. The wind brought her lower still, the rectangles developed ragged edges, and suddenly Wren knew where she was. They were flying above the CFC factories. Already Wren could see that sand had swallowed at least one of the buildings; only a rectangular shadow showed where it had once stood. Others were half absorbed, protruding from the dust like broken teeth, rotting into fragments.

Only one still jutted unbroken above the delta, its rooftop a wide grey expanse in the titian desert. Tentacles of sand curled up its sides and boulders were rolled against its walls, hurled there by mega storms and never pushed off. But, as far as Wren could see, the sand clung only about half way so the roof was safe. Explosions had not marred its flatness, it would provide a fair Runway, possibly a little shorter than she'd like, but she had no choice.

As the light faded even further, Wren aimed herself at the rooftop and reminded herself of her father's instructions to her brothers. 'When landing, dive until level with the platform. As soon as you are overhead, drop your legs below your body. After two body lengths bring your arms together. When you feel your feet touch the platform, start to run.' His voice in her mind was calm and her chest loosened as she started to follow his directions.

She glanced back to see Raw copying. He was following as close to her as he dared.

Rather than dive, Wren sought to angle herself so that the wind would drop her as close to the edge of the roof as she dared.

Terror had shortened her breathing into little shallow gasps. Light headed, Wren struggled to slow her inhalations down, dragging in lungs full of oxygen, until her head spun. The rooftop seemed to move below her, shifting sideways as she dropped her legs to prepare her landing. The Creatures now surrounded the building like a besieging army, as though they knew what she planned.

A gust of wind caught under Wren's wings and, just as she was convinced she would miss the roof altogether, it propelled her forward and slammed her toes into an uneven lip of concrete. Then it dragged her upwards again and she cycled her legs vainly in mid-air as she was carried towards the centre of the parapet.

Wren had to close her wings, or risk being pulled all the way off the other side. She bit down a cry and started to pull her arms shut, but the wind was stronger and kept them stretched out behind her, pulling them backwards and making her wings billow. She had no control.

Now she understood why her brothers had been crunching weights since they were old enough to hold them above their heads. Their shoulders were strong, Wren's were not.

But Wren herself had been climbing up and down the side of the Mons since she was old enough to use a net repair kit. Her trapezius muscles might not be powerful, but her biceps were. You couldn't climb from the net without doing pull ups.

Instead of trying to force her wings down against the strength of the cooling wind, Wren focused on bringing her hands towards her chin, using her biceps to tuck them in.

She heard the click as her wings unlocked. Agonisingly slowly her elbows bent and her wings fluttered more loosely. Yet all the time she was being dragged towards the sand.

An impact crushed Wren's toes and shook up her ankles; she had met the concrete once more. Remembering her father's wisdom, she started to run. To go with the wind, at least a little way, was the only way to gain control without hurting herself. She risked a glance towards the end of the roof; she had maybe the length of a wing span in which to stop. Ten steps.

She tried to count, while she hauled her wings in closer. One, two, three …

Abruptly her wings sagged as the wind fled from beneath them. Then a sharp gust got behind her and caught in the baggy material, trying to lift it the other way. Wren had to flatten her arms against her sides.

It was easier now that the wind was no longer pulling, but pushing. She staggered sideways with the power of it. Five, six, seven … then she slapped her hands onto her thighs. Her pennons slid closed, billowing only slightly, but her momentum kept carrying her forward.

'Wren, stop!'

She ignored Raw's shout, staggering eight and then nine steps. At ten she found herself teetering on the roof edge, staring down at sand that boiled beneath her as if alive.

Then she was still.

She backed away from the ledge on trembling legs. Her knees collapsed, and she crunched to the floor, the wings settling round her like a cloak. She dug her fingers into crumbling concrete and a nail snapped with a sharp pain as she pressed down hard enough to persuade her thudding heart that she had made it to safety.

Then she looked up. Raw had wheeled into a circle and was swinging in behind her like a scythe. 'Drop your legs,' she shouted and she rolled as he swooped over her head and crashed into the rooftop. His long legs pounded as he battled to stop. Raw yanked his own right arm closed with barely a hint of struggle, but his left wasn't moving so easily.

The crack of the limb snapping backwards during their first flight reverberated through Wren's memory and she caught her breath. If his shoulder was as badly damaged as she feared, that wing wasn't going to close.

Raw snarled as he wrestled with the wind, but his feet jerked sideways as his wing billowed and hauled him against his will.

Ignoring her own aches, Wren leaped to her feet and sprinted across the rooftop after him. Her own wings started to flutter again; if they caught a gust, they were both dead.

Raw yelled his fury as he stumbled closer to the edge and he tried to turn his sideways propulsion into a spin. He rotated on his toes, but still tottered, a fingernail from doom.

Wren launched herself at him, arms spread. She punched into his chest and closed her arms around his wings as her weight slammed him down. Raw grunted as he crashed on his back into the rooftop.

Wren's own wings finally caught and swelled like sails. '*Raw!*'

Immediately his own right arm wrapped around her, crushing the foils against her back. They rustled as the wind squeezed out of them and Wren exhaled shakily.

For a long moment they lay still together, as twilight darkened around them.

Raw's arm was a tight band hot against her back, and his heart beat against her cheek. He smelled sour and his sweat dampened her face where she lay on his shirt. She lifted her head and saw him looking down at her; his eyes deep in shadow, unreadable. She struggled out of his embrace, pushed onto her knees and wrapped her arms around her chest, remembering how furious she was with him.

'You bloody fool!'

Raw flicked his hair so that it covered his scarred face. 'It's getting cold,' he replied. 'Let's do this inside.'

6

'Do you think there's a way into the building?' Wren examined the flat rooftop. To her left the remains of a communications array twisted like arthritic fingers towards the stars.

'There's a ladder.' Raw pointed. He was right; beside the broken satellite an aluminium ladder clung to the lip of the roof. 'It must go somewhere.'

Wren nodded and they made their way across the concrete. 'It doesn't look very secure.' She knelt and gave it a shake. The bolts holding it down rattled in corroded joints.

'Hold my legs.' Raw made to lean over the roof, but Wren shook her head, lay flat and inched her way out until she could see where the ladder ended. 'There's a window.'

Raw pulled her back and Wren hissed as her stomach scraped on the ragged edge. She slapped his hands away as she sat up and shivered. The temperature was already plummeting and her drying sweat felt like frost as it lined her forehead and shirt.

'How cold do you think it's going to get?'

'At night on the delta? We'll be lucky if it stays above freezing.'

'No choice then,' Wren's breath was misting up the inside of her mask, the filters hissing as they cleared the condensation. 'We'll have to risk the ladder.'

'It won't be much warmer inside,' Raw warned. An icy gust rattled through their wings and he shivered. 'But at least it'll be out of the wind.'

Wren stamped as her feet began to grow numb. 'You first. Or me?'

Raw tilted his head, the scarred side of his face merging with the dark. 'If you go first, I can hold the ladder at this end in case the joints snap. But I won't be able to help you if a rung breaks, and I don't know what you'll find inside. There could be sand up to the ceiling … Creatures.' His face hardened as he made his decision. 'I'll go first.'

Wren shivered again. 'What if the ladder's not strong enough for you?'

Raw shrugged. 'Then the Creatures get me; probably quicker than freezing to death up here.'

Wren opened her mouth and then closed it again. He was right. They both faced a choice between a quick death or a slow one; at least the quick version came with a chance. Wren clenched her fists. For tonight, at least, she would have to trust him.

As Raw knelt in front of the ladder, Wren's skin felt too tight for her bones. Tension thrummed through her as though the rooftop itself vibrated. 'Wait.' She lay down, anchoring herself as best she could and gripped the arches where they were driven into the roof. 'All right. Now.'

Raw flexed his fingers and his eyes met hers. Then he took a breath, swung his legs over the edge of the roof and gripped the rail with both hands. Although it was almost full dark, Phobos' light revealed the movement of the sand beneath him. Slow at first, but then, as he started to climb and the ladder creaked with his weight, faster.

'They're below you,' she whispered.

'You think I don't know?' Raw took another step and the ladder groaned. Wren tightened her grip.

'I don't think I'll be able to hold this if it –'

Raw's eye twitched. 'I know.'

He went down to the next rung and darkness absorbed his legs to the knee. Wren heard his gasp and a clatter. He jerked and slid suddenly downwards. She held her breath until he halted his fall.

'One of the rungs was corroded through,' he managed to gasp. 'Watch it when you follow me.'

Wren nodded without answering.

'I'm nearly there,' he said conversationally. 'Three more rungs and I can swing inside … it's been left open all this time.'

'It'll be full of sand,' Wren called.

Raw hesitated. 'If the Creatures could climb,' he said eventually. 'They'd already have me.' And he swung out of sight.

There was silence. Wren kept her hands wrapped around the railing and counted her heartbeats, straining into the darkness for sight or sound. If a Creature had him, wouldn't he scream? What if he couldn't – what if it had happened too quickly? The chill was seeping through the concrete, through Wren's clothes and into her gut.

'Wren!' She'd never been so happy to hear her name spoken.

'Is it safe?'

'I think so. Come down, I'll hold the ladder at this end and catch you if you fall.'

'I won't fall.' Wren slid her legs around and over the railing, feeling for the rungs with her toes. Her wings trailed after her, fluttering as she climbed.

'Take your time.'

'Shut up,' Wren muttered. Who was he to tell her what to do? Her toes found a gap and she realised that this was the rung that Raw had knocked into the desert. She looked down and her heart pounded. The sand below boiled; there must be dozens of the Creatures beneath her.

She gave a scream as something wrapped around her ankle. Wails bubbled through the sand.

'It's me.' Raw gave her ankle a shake. 'You can swing in.'

Wren looked down to see his hand move to her shin. Would he keep hold of her, or would he let her go? He'd said he hated her.

'Let go,' she snapped. Carefully she swung around the ladder rail and found herself in front of an entrance barely large enough for a man's shoulders.

'You're sure there're no Creatures in there?'

'I'm still here aren't I?' Raw held his arm out. 'I'll catch you.'

The wind snatched her hair and tried to yank her back into its embrace. Her fingers were so numb the tips were almost burning. Would he catch her?

She leaned forward and took a step away from the ladder,

reaching with one hand for Raw. Her palm slapped into his and he pulled her towards him. She half fell in through the window and thudded to the floor below the aperture, sand padded her landing.

Immediately the wind let her go and without its spikes drilling into her clothing, Wren felt instantly warmer. 'You didn't let me fall!'

Raw's face hardened. 'You thought I would?'

'You said you hated me. What was I supposed to think?'

Raw turned from her and his fists curled at his sides. 'What kind of person would let you fall ...' His voice faded.

'Why are you even here?' Wren cried. 'Why didn't you land at Avalon when you had the chance? You're trying to ruin my mission.'

'Mission, hah.' Raw hunched his shoulders, his back still to her.

'I mean it, Raw, if you ruin things for me ...'

'You'll what?' Raw asked, his voice quiet.

'Just remember,' Wren warned. 'You'll be in just as much trouble as me. When we get to Vaikuntha, you remember that.'

Raw nodded but did not look at her; instead he went to a panel in the wall by the door. He pulled it out and examined it intently.

'What are you doing?'

Raw didn't answer. He reached into his pockets and pulled out a tiny pair of pliers; then he began stripping and twisting wires. 'It's corroded, but if I reroute ...'

'What are you –?'

She looked up as a single glow tube in the centre of the room began to brighten. Surrounded by the shattered components of its companions, it was the only light, and it cast a bluish aura that blackened the shadows and made them crowd into the corners and crawl over the floor towards her feet.

'You got a light on.' She stared.

'I figured it was worth a try. There must be a solar panel still working somewhere.'

Raw retreated into the shadows as Wren stood up. Her legs

felt like noodles and as she straightened, she almost fell. She groped behind her for the window sill and used it to hold herself up. She winced as the movement stretched her shoulders, they were already seizing.

She looked at Raw more closely and saw that he too was half curled. He slid his pliers back into his pocket gingerly, wincing at the movement.

'Your shoulder?'

'I'm fine.'

'I can look at it. It's one of the responsibilities of a Sphere-Mistress – helping Runners with minor injuries.'

'Leave it.' Raw pointed towards the window. 'That's going to be a problem. We should find another room, one that'll be warmer.'

Wren bit her lip. 'We know it's safe in here.'

Raw shrugged. 'Up to you then. I'm moving.'

'Wait.' Wren wrestled with herself. She could huddle in the lee of the window, out of the worst of the wind, but gusts still blew in, bringing an insidious chill that was already seeping into her bones. She could wrap her wings around her head and survive the night, but it would not be comfortable. If they explored, they might find the scientist's beds, maybe even some retort pouches of thermo-stablized food, the stuff from dead-Earth that the colonists were eating before Eden got the soy crops established.

Her stomach rumbled, and she avoided Raw's gaze.

Worry gnawed at her. Creatures might have broken in from the ground level and for all they knew, this could be the only secure place in the building. Wren had a responsibility to her mother to remain safe. If something happened to her, there would be no-one to seek a cure.

'We should stay here,' she repeated, but Raw heard the doubt in her voice. He cocked his head in challenge.

'Neither of us has ever left Elysium, do you really want to huddle in the first room you find? No-one's been here in over a hundred years, don't you want to investigate?'

'It's dark. Even if there was something to look at, we

wouldn't be able to.' Wren glowered at the flickering light above her head.

Raw said nothing, simply stared at her with his arms folded. Eventually, he sighed. 'I thought you were more interesting than this.'

'Who cares what you think?' Wren snarled. But a part of her rose up in challenge. The door beckoned to her, a portal to mystery. She rubbed her elbows, wings trailing on the floor behind her. For the first time she understood the meaning of the term 'bone tired'. Her arms and legs, even her stomach muscles ached where she had been holding tension for hours; she wanted to collapse. But she knew she wouldn't sleep, not with the door right there, beckoning.

'Fine.' She dragged fingers like spikes through her tangled curls. 'A quick look.'

She strode over the sand carpet. dust clung to her boots and stuck to her ankles like static. Raw stepped aside, allowing Wren to be first to touch the door. She pressed her palm against the reader and it hissed, jerked and slid open half an inch. Then it stopped.

Stale air puffed through the gap and made Wren cough. The door shuddered as it tried to open. 'It's stuck.'

Raw shook his head. 'I don't think there's enough power.' He grabbed the door with both hands and winced as he strained his shoulders.

'You don't have to –' Wren began.

Ignoring her, Raw gave a massive heave. The door groaned as it squeaked sideways. Tendons stood out on Raw's neck and he threw his head back, his mask tightening across the lower half of his face. As soon as the opening was wide enough to allow them to pass sideways, he dropped his arms. Wren peered past him into the darkness, her ears pricking for the sound of slithering, or the chilling wail of a hunting Creature.

She jumped as electricity hissed and crackled through glow tubes. Suddenly a corridor was illuminated in front of her.

Wren looked down. The sand stopped at the doorway, a line drawn in the encroaching desert. She glanced at Raw, the glow brightening her eyes, then she turned and side-stepped through the door.

Her boot heels clicked on the floor, stifled by layers of dust and a silence so intense that it seemed to absorb all sound. Even the hissing of the single operational glow-tube seemed stifled. A muffled curse told her that Raw was squeezing through behind her. She turned to see his wings caught in the mechanism.

'Stop.' Alarmed she sped back to him and gently pulled them free, stroking the material as it settled back around his legs. 'If you rip these you'll be trapped here.'

Raw nodded and wrapped them tighter around his legs. 'Can you see anything – any other rooms?'

'I think there're stairs.' Wren pointed to a hollow blackness ahead. 'Do you want to go down?'

Raw raised his eyebrow. 'You want to go back?'

'Well ... we're out of the wind.' Wren fidgeted, but her eyes kept flicking to the staircase.

'Come on.' Raw pushed past her. Wren watched as he reached the corridor's end. He vanished into the dark as if it had swallowed him whole. Another crackle as power followed him and the stairwell appeared.

Wren was moving towards it before she had time to consider her actions. Despite her aching legs, she was going down.

When they had descended a single full flight, glow tubes started to come on below them, illuminating floor after floor. 'The building wasn't that tall.' She stared.

'They must have built down into the delta, to protect it from dust-storms. Look.' Raw pointed to a number painted on the wall, in faded crimson: 21.

'There are over twenty floors,' Wren gasped. 'Which do you want to look at?'

Raw shrugged. 'Pick a number.'

'Fifteen.'

'Your age.'

'Yours too,' Wren whispered.

Raw shook his head. 'I turned sixteen a week ago.' He too had lowered his voice. The sheer size of the building suppressed sound.

'Sixteen then.' Wren shoved past him and started to descend. The stairs were a kind of gridded metal that bounced slightly as she walked, but had barely corroded with time. Each floor was marked with a closed and numbered door. By the time they had reached the number sixteen, Wren's thighs were trembling.

'We're here.' Raw sounded out of breath.

Wren pressed her palm to the reader and this time the door slid open with barely a creak, the mechanism almost as smooth as the last day it had been used.

Wren stepped through with Raw at her heels. Then she stopped. He caught her elbows as her knees folded. 'By the skies,' she gasped.

'By the Designer,' he echoed and trembled against her.

She shook him off and staggered to the guard rail that ran along the platform they had emerged onto.

Ahead of them glow tubes were sputtering into life, dominos of light that had been set off when the door opened. The glow was spreading across a cavernous space, sixteen floors deep, illuminating massive machinery with a faint bluish glow.

'I've never seen anything like it.' Raw gripped the railing beside her.

Wren stared downwards, her eyes still following the trail of lights as they broke into the darkness, dropping like a Runner from a platform.

The machine looked like a cylinder, with struts protruding from it, floor by floor, like the legs of a Martian bug. It sat silent, but Wren could imagine the vast wall of sound that it would make as it plunged into the rock, breaking it up to create the fluorine-based gases that would then be pumped into the atmosphere through giant chimneys that had long ago collapsed.

'How many of these were there?' she muttered. 'How did they build them?'

Raw looked surprised. 'You don't know?'

Wren glared at him. 'A Runner's education is different.'

Raw shook his head. 'Still, you *should* know.'

'Why? What use is the information? Did you know how to stop falling when your wings unlocked?'

'I –' Raw fell silent and shook his head.

'Right then.' Wren turned her back on him. The silence drew out.

'There were twenty machines,' Raw said. 'They built them in orbit then dropped them onto the delta and built the factories around them.'

Wren was quiet for a while, thoughtful. 'Did the saboteurs destroy all twenty? This one looks okay.'

'How would you know?' Raw laughed. 'Trust me, it's dead, they all are.'

'What if it isn't? What if we could restart it?' Wren leaned forward bending almost double over the railing. The light had reached the ground now, the whole machine illuminated with the faint glow.

Raw laughed. 'If it could have been fixed and restarted, they would have done it. We don't have the technology any more, things keep breaking and without resupply from dead-Earth we can't train engineers to operate the machinery. God, Wren in a few generations even the bioengineers in Elysium will be reduced to ancient farming and breeding methods. We can only hope that the biospheres last long enough for the atmosphere to become breathable and that if they don't, we have enough equipment to keep making masks.'

'We're going backwards.' Wren nodded. 'That's why the wings are so precious. When we lose the last of them, we'll be grounded, just like ...'

'Just like *you*, that's what you were going to say.'

Wren nodded.

Raw offered a twisted smile that she could just about see inside his mask. 'I'm a Runner now.'

'No, you're not,' Wren sneered. 'You're a wing thief.'

Raw stepped back from her as though she'd hit him. 'So are *you*.' Wren hadn't noticed that the cruel edge to his voice had vanished from his speech until it reappeared. 'You're a *girl*. You aren't a Runner any more than I am. Thief. Blasphemer.'

He stamped back towards the stairs.

Wren lifted a hand as if to call him back, then dropped her arm. He was right. She was only a Runner's daughter; no more a Runner than he.

She stared down at the glowing behemoth, blackened twists of metal glimmered. Then she heard it: the eerie wail of a Creature. It wound around the machinery, warped by the echoes. She shivered.

They were not alone inside the factory after all.

7

Wren sprinted back towards the stairs, her stiffening muscles forgotten. She burst into the stairwell. 'They're here.'

'I heard.' Raw didn't turn around. He was powering up the stairs, his wings wafting behind him.

Wren's back prickled and she jerked and looked behind her, convinced that she was about to be pulled back. There was nothing there. 'They're hunting us.'

'Yes.'

'What are you doing?'

Raw had stopped at the eighteenth floor.

'The machine cavern only went a couple of floors above sixteen. I figure these are the living quarters.'

'Don't,' Wren called, but Raw was already pressing his palm on the reader, cycling the door open. Wren tensed, half expecting Creatures to boil out like spaghetti from a pan. Nothing but darkness emerged.

This time the light flickered on and off, the power refusing to catch as Raw stepped through. Wren bit her lip as she looked behind her and then back to Raw's vanishing wings. The keening of the Creatures swirled up the stairwell, reverberated from the walls and shivered inside her head. She looked down, trying to see all the way to the bottom. How had they got inside?

Then she remembered the sand snakes, they could burrow into the smallest gaps. Was there a hole down there under the sand?

Could they climb?

Did she see movement in the shadowy depths, or was it simply just that her eyes were over-strained?

Wren spun around and chased after Raw.

He was waiting for her just beyond the door. As soon as she

was through, he cycled it closed, muting the terrifying sounds. Darkness embraced her; then light flashed on again, pushing it away.

Wren stared at him, panting. 'What's the matter with you?'

'I've almost died once today already.' Raw shrugged. 'Invisible monsters don't seem so scary right now.'

Wren glared at him, then looked past along the corridor as the light burned, then died. Above her the tubes hissed like snakes. The light came back on, dimmed, brightened. 'Lots of rooms.'

Raw nodded. 'If the layout is what I expect, there'll be a kitchen at the end.'

'A kitchen?' Hope like a spreading fern rose in Wren's chest. 'Food?'

'Food a century old.' Raw warned her.

'Space food,' she reminded him. 'Lasts.'

Just the thought of something to eat made Wren's gut shrink to the size of a stone and before she knew it, she was running through the cycling light and dark.

Doors flashed past until they stood side by side in front of dusty glass. Wren wiped it clean and squinted through. 'It *is* a kitchen, there's a table and stools.'

'There'll be one on each residential floor.'

This time the door pulled towards Wren instead of sliding sideways. She exhaled shakily as she stepped forward, desperate to search for pouches, but afraid that her hopes would be crushed.

She held her breath as Raw opened cupboard after empty cupboard. Then he froze.

'What is it?' Wren stood on tip-toe and he stepped aside. There, at eye level, was a box half full of unopened retort pouches.

Wren blinked, but then held her eyes closed, as though the box would disappear if she looked again. 'Are they real?' she murmured.

In answer Raw took her hand and closed it around something cold and pliable. She opened her eyes. In her palm was a pouch the same colour as her wings.

'Do you think it'll be all right to eat?' Raw tore open the top of his pouch. 'It's more than a century old.' He looked at it doubtfully.

'In theory.' Wren pulled the tab on her own.

Raw lifted his mask then stopped with the pouch halfway to his lips, guilt painted on his face. 'I almost forgot.' He dropped his mask back into place and gestured towards the ceiling. 'Thanks to those who brought us here, who gave their lives so we might live, thanks to He who keeps us safe who had this planet made to give.'

'You observe the rites?' Wren stared, surprised.

Raw paused with the pouch raised. 'Everyone observes. Don't *you*?'

Wren stepped backwards. 'Runners do things differently.'

'I know you have a whole different set of rules. I didn't know you don't thank the Designer and Originals,' Raw sneered. 'You're so arrogant.'

'It's not that we're not grateful.' Wren squeezed her pouch so hard that the ancient seam burst, wet slime coated her hands. 'We have more important –'

'That sounds about right.' Raw turned his back on her.

'We know we'd be dead if we'd stayed on dead-Earth. It's just we haven't deified Captain Kiernan like you …'

'What were you going to call me just then?' Raw spun around. 'A Land-crawler, a Grounder, I know your terms for us.'

'And you don't call Runners names, treat us like –'

'No more than you deserve,' Raw growled and he loomed over her. 'You keep flying in families, you cling to your power like a dead-Earth monarchy – no-one *else* gets a chance to escape Elysium. At least in the biosphere you get the job you're best suited for.'

'Unless you're a *girl*,' Wren yelled.

'The bioengineers tried other methods, only a womb works. It's plain wrong that Runner girls don't do their womb-duty to the colony. Women are valued and protected.'

'As long as they do as they're told and produce the proscribed number of children for exchange.'

'We have *families*.'

'You have brothers and sisters you've never met and never will.'

'So, you're against genetic diversity too!'

'Of course not! I just don't want the life they say. Can't you understand that?' Wren sank down onto a metal stool and stared at the slime drying on her fist as the light blinked on and off, making her eyes water. 'When it's time, some Runner friend of my father's is going to just come and claim me.' She hung her head. 'No matter what I think of him, I'll have to produce sons with life expectancies of sand snakes and daughters to do the same.'

'And you've no choice?' Wren jumped as Raw touched her shoulder.

'No more than your *Grounder* women.'

'They have some choice.' Raw frowned. 'They don't have to accept the choosing offered them. It's frowned on, but it does happen.'

'Then what?'

'Baby exchange – they can be impregnated with seed from the stores. Or back into the choosing pool for the year after.'

He moved inside the darkness so it seemed he had simply appeared beside her. 'Maybe, it isn't exactly fair.' He pulled his hand away as the glow tubes shone once more. 'But it's the Original's decree.'

Wren shivered. 'The originals messed up. It's *their* fault we're stuck inside mouldering biospheres when we should already be spread over the surface of the planet.'

'The saboteurs –'

'Were originals too, weren't they?'

'Devils disguised as angels.' Raw said seriously. 'The wheel turns and what has happened before will happen again.'

'It's human nature, not some stupid wheel.' Tears pricked Wren's eyes. Raw moved away from her and leaned against a cabinet. She looked at him with her hand on her mask. 'We should eat.'

Wren pulled her mask up, licked sticky gel from her fingers and dropped her mask back down. She glared at him as she swallowed. 'It's sweet!' Her taste buds sparkled like sun from quartz. 'If you're waiting for me to throw up or something, you'll be waiting a while.'

Raw lifted his own mask and took a pull from his pouch. His eyes widened. 'What's it made of?'

Wren shrugged. 'Dead-Earth stuff. Let me see your packet.'

Raw handed it over.

'It's a kind of fruit.' She pointed at a small picture on the front. 'See? A plant.'

'*Edible* fruit?' Raw frowned. 'Gingko seeds are poisonous.'

'Chayton said they were developing some in Eden, I wondered what it would be like.' She licked her hands again.

'Give mine back.' Raw finished his packet and started to pick through the others in the cupboard. 'We should have some protein too. Here.' He tossed another pack over. It had a different picture on it.

'That looks like a GM bun-bun pet.' Wren peered closer. 'Why would it have a bun-bun pet on it?'

'We didn't always live on soy and supplements.' Raw shrugged. 'Don't you Runners know *anything*?'

'Of course we do. I know a lot. I know how to repair a net, mend wings, read semaphore and the whole theory of flying. I can fix the solar panels at Avalon when they break down, sort out the water pumps when they break, massage an incoming Runner for over an hour, feed my family with soy beans that anyone else would have thrown out. I can –'

'You've made your point.'

'But *you* think I should go to the Grounder Women's Sector and make babies. You think what I'm doing is blasphemy.'

'I'm … starting to rethink.' His eyes slid away from hers.

'Why?'

'Like you said, I'm doing just as much wrong.' Raw took another swallow from his pouch. 'If I'm caught, I'll be punished.'

'Killed probably.' Wren nodded. 'Both of us.'

'That's what I figured.'

'Then why?' Wren leaned forward. 'Why did you follow me? Why risk your life?'

Raw said nothing.

When she realised that she wouldn't get another word from him, Wren sighed. 'We have to talk about what happens when we get to Vaikuntha. You need to pass as a Runner.'

'I'll just do what you do.'

'You can't say your Rites before meals, or at bedtime.'

She saw Raw flush. 'Fine.'

'You have to be respectful to the Sphere-Mistress. No talking about the Women's Sector or anything like that. She'll be responsible for treating your injuries, massaging you, making sure you're okay to fly again when we set off.'

'Do you think I'm an idiot?'

'You don't know our ways.' Wren gnawed at her lips. 'You should go back to Avalon.'

Raw set his jaw and Wren dragged her hands through her hair. 'Just … do what I do. Don't speak unless you really have to. I'll have to think about who we say we are and why we haven't Run to Vaikuntha before.' She opened her second pouch and put it her lips. 'Yuck.' She threw it down. 'Tastes like garbage.'

'Stick to the sweet ones then.' Raw picked her discarded packet up. 'Who knows when you'll get to eat again?'

'Tomorrow,' Wren said firmly. 'As soon as the sun gets high enough to warm the thermals we'll take off. We'll be in Vaikuntha before noon.' She looked at the corridor outside the kitchen, at the lines of closed doors. 'If this is residential, do you think there'll be a bed?'

A distant hunting cry came through the floor. Raw ignored it.

'There's only one way to find out.'

Raw had to force the door, the power was barely enough for

him to get his fingers through. Wren stood peering into the gloom. Then the corridor lights cycled on again. Sure enough, she could see a low cot made up with a mouldy foam mattress and a foil blanket. On the wall was pinned an ancient picture; a smiling trio standing in front of a forest of greenery.

'Dead-Earth.' Wren pointed. She held her wings close and wedged her way through the opening. Raw followed.

'What're you doing?' She glowered at him.

'There's not enough power to open another door. And do you really want to be alone?'

Wren was about to say she was perfectly happy by herself when yet another eerie wail reverberated through the factory. 'You'd better stay.'

Raw nodded. 'I thought you'd say that.'

'But there's only one bed.' Wren fidgeted anxiously.

Raw pulled his hair down over his scarred cheek. 'I'll take the floor. It's not a problem.'

'Not the floor.' Wren pulled the disintegrating mattress from the cot and dumped it by the door. 'This'll be less cold to sleep on.' She looked at the cot. Beneath the mattress thick plastic was pulled taut over struts. 'That'll be fine for me.'

She tested it carefully, bouncing her fists on top to make sure it would take her weight; then she climbed on, wrapped her wings around her shoulders and pulled the foil blanket to her chin.

Raw watched her from behind his dangling wave of hair; then he sat on the mattress and leaned against the wall. He sighed. 'I've got observances to make.'

'So, make them.' Wren rolled over, turning her back on him. Her breath fogged her mask and she was soothed to sleep by the soft murmur of Raw's prayers to dead-Earth, the originals and the deified Designers who had at least started to terraform the planet.

8

Wren woke to the flickering of lights. She was curled up in the exact same position in which she had fallen asleep and her legs and arms were numb. She tried to stretch and roll over. Pain spiked through her; electricity that curled fire around her muscles and cramped her fingers until they went into spasm. She cried out.

From the floor Raw groaned as her cry woke him.

Wren rolled from the cot to land on the floor in a tangle of wing and blanket. Beside her Raw moaned again, his own limbs shaking as he tried to sit.

'It hurts,' he gasped.

'That's why we offer massage when a Runner comes in.' Wren forced her cramping fingers into her thigh. 'To prevent *this* from happening.' She winced as feeling started to come back to her legs.

'What time is it?'

'I don't know. Morning?'

Raw staggered as he tried to get to his feet. 'No way to know unless we go and have a look. It feels warmer.'

'The room's small. Could just be our body heat.' Wren managed to get to her knees, then her calf seized and she rolled again, clutching it.

Raw had dropped to the floor and was leaning on his hands. His wings flowed around him like sand. All she could see was his hair as it hung over his face.

'How are we going to take off like this?'

'It'll pass.' She spoke through gritted teeth. 'Give it time.'

'How much time?' Raw groaned again.

'Get moving.' Wren trembled as she tried to stand again. 'It'll help.'

'Hah,' Raw spat and he finally looked at her. 'Guess it's not *all* fun being a Runner, after all.' Then he clutched at his shoulder. Even Wren saw the muscles twitching beneath the silver material that lined them. He wouldn't want her watching him.

She used the wall to climb to her feet. 'I'm going to eat something. Follow when you can.'

Wren squeezed through the opening and into the flickering light-dark of the corridor. She lurched to the kitchen and, after some swearing, managed to stretch high enough to pull down a fruit pouch. She swallowed it down, the pain of her cramped and aching muscles almost over-riding her sense of taste.

Then she leaned against a cabinet as she silently pleaded for her legs to come back to life. Raw was right, if they couldn't Run, they wouldn't be able to take off. They could stay here another day, until they both felt stronger, but Wren had promised her mother that she'd be back in three. If they remained in the factory her mother would be a day closer to death and Wren would have achieved nothing.

She tossed her pouch on the table and clenched her fists, wishing there was something to strike. The opening door made her look up. Raw stood in the entrance, still shaking. His jaw was set and his scar deformed his face in the half light. Automatically Wren leaned away from him and he jerked so that his hair flopped over his face. He stepped close, reached past her without looking her way and snagged a pouch.

'After this we should go to the roof,' Wren mumbled.

He nodded, still without looking at her.

'We should at least see what time it is,' Wren pressed. 'We don't have to take off straight away, we could rest up there for a couple of hours even, until we've loosened up.'

Raw muttered his obligation and turned from her to remove his mask. His back moved as he drank and then he threw his empty pouch onto the floor. He replaced his mask. 'Let's go then,' he muttered.

Wren followed him to the end of the corridor, where dust motes floated in the stale air, lit by the faint blue light of the glow tubes. She stumbled through them like a drunk, making whorls in the atmosphere. Raw had stopped at the door. He pressed his ear to the metal.

'I can't hear anything,' he said eventually and before Wren could speak, he put his palm on the reader and the door cycled open.

Wren tensed her abused muscles, but nothing sprung towards them. Raw stepped into the stairwell, his footsteps echoing in the silence. Once more the opening door triggered the lights and they clicked on.

Wren shivered as Raw leaned over the rail and looked down. Then he carefully leaned back. Beneath his scarring, Raw's face was white. 'There's something in the stairwell.' He spoke so quietly that at first Wren couldn't make out his words. Then her eyes widened and she clutched her fists to her chin.

'Creatures?' she barely mouthed the word.

'Must be.'

'You can *see* them!'

'Only movement. They're right down at the bottom.'

'They can't climb the stairs, or they'd have been waiting for us to come out.' Wren spoke too loudly, the Creatures stirred and their cry echoed around her. She clapped her hands over her ears.

Raw grabbed her arm and shoved her towards the stairs. 'Run.'

'They can't climb,' she gasped again, as Raw pushed her ahead of him. Her legs could barely take her weight, and she collapsed as she tried to take two steps at a time. Wren grabbed the rail and sagged. 'You're not thinking.' She wrapped her arm around the rail. 'Slow down.'

Raw tried to pull her free. 'Listen.'

Wren tried to quiet her breath, but all she could hear was the slithering and wailing of the creatures below them. 'They're no closer.'

Raw grabbed her face and, as she tried to fight free, he pushed her cheek and ear into the cold wall. 'No,' he hissed. '*Listen.*'

Furious, Wren tried to kick him, but he held her against the concrete until she calmed, and then she heard it: the rattle of debris, the dragging of great bodies through stone.

Her eyes widened. 'They're in the walls?'

Raw nodded. '*Now*, will you run?'

'How are they in the *walls*?' Wren half screamed at him, as though it were Raw's fault. 'I *said* we should have stayed in the upstairs room.'

'They're burrowers,' Raw closed his hand around her elbow, drew ahead and began to pull her after him. 'They can't climb the stairs, but they can …'

'Burrow through concrete? They can't get through rock. None of the colonies would be safe if they could.'

'The walls won't be solid inside, they'll be filled with some kind of insulation. Easy as sand.'

'But then they can't get through the wall to reach us.' Wren's legs were quivering jelly now.

'You're right.' Raw halted suddenly as the lights flickered above them. Wren bumped into his back and stood panting on the step below. 'They shouldn't be able to get to us. So, what are they doing?'

Wren watched him silently. Now he had drawn her attention to the slithering in the walls, it was all she could hear. She clenched her fists, staring from side to side as though the concrete would burst open at any second, and sprout teeth.

'They're driving us,' Raw said eventually.

'Driving us where?' The warmth Wren had rediscovered overnight, fled, leaving her chilled from top to toe. Then she answered her own question. 'The saboteurs – the explosions. We didn't see any sign downstairs, perhaps the bombs here went off –'

'In the living quarters.' Raw finished. 'Somewhere up here there are holes in the walls.'

Wren froze, as though another step would take her in reach of one. 'We didn't see any on our way down' she whispered finally. 'Did we?' She remembered entering the building, exhausted, in the dark. They hadn't been looking for gaps in the walls. Shadow still clung to every corner, even in the stairwell.

'Did we?'

Raw groaned. 'We could have missed something – we didn't know to look.'

'Then they could be waiting in the top room.'

'Or somewhere else. I don't know.' The sounds around them intensified and Raw shivered. 'They want us to go up.' He looked up at the stairwell curving around and out of sight. 'So, wherever the hole is, it has to be above us.'

Wren closed her eyes. 'What are our choices?' Her heartbeat slowed and her breathing grew more deliberate as she thought. 'We can go back to the corridor we came from – that was safe – but we can't stay there forever, there were only about ten food pouches: we'd starve. We can't go down, that takes us towards the ones in the stairwell. And if we go up …'

'We end up in their trap.'

'We might,' Wren conceded. 'Or we could move fast enough to get past them. It's our best chance.'

Without another word, Raw started up the stairs once more.

The glow tubes burned with their low blue light, on and off, light and dark, almost in time with Wren's steps. Just above her she could see Raw's wings flapping around his legs, billowing slightly with each step, as if the air could take them even in here. As she climbed, she kept one hand on the rail and wrapped the other around the growing knot in her stomach.

The sounds in the walls grew louder, almost anticipatory. Wren could imagine them speaking to one another.

'How intelligent are they do you think?' she whispered.

Raw did not answer.

Then, two floors up, the sounds abruptly stopped. Wren climbed higher and a wail curled down the stairwell. She froze and backed downwards. The cry halted.

'Raw?'

He was standing with one hand over the palm reader. 'It's quiet in there,' he murmured. 'No Creatures and there could be more food in the kitchen, enough to last us until they give up and leave.'

'Don't open the door.' Wren caught his elbow. His hand

halted bare millimetres from the reader.

'Why?' Raw glowered at her.

'You said we were being driven. If it's quiet in there, it's because that's where they want us to go.'

'Or it's because they aren't in there.' But Raw didn't move. 'You think they're *that* clever?'

'I don't know.' Tension thrummed through Wren's body, like the flickering lights overhead. 'You're betting your life that they're not.'

'And if we keep going?' Raw looked up. 'You're betting our lives that they *are.*'

'They're hunters,' Wren bit her lip. 'The safest place has to be where they don't want us to go.'

'That would make sense if they were people.' Raw exhaled. 'But they're not.'

'No, they're not.' Wren withdrew her hand from his. 'You decide.'

Raw looked at the door again, then up the stairs. A susurrus hummed from the ceiling as if the Creatures could sense Raw's hesitation and were hurrying him.

Raw stepped back from the door. 'Up,' he said.

He turned and pounded up the stairs as the Creatures wailed. Wren raced after him, her legs shaking with each step.

Thuds against the concrete made the walls shudder and there was a scraping sound like that of teeth against rock.

'They can't get through,' Raw shouted. 'Keep going.'

Wren realised that she had faltered to a stop. She shook herself and pushed on. It felt as if she was running through a near solid barrier made up of noise and terror and she found her arms swinging widely in front of her as though to push it aside.

Then they were at the top of the stairs.

'This is where we came in.' Raw was standing in front of the reader, his palm spread. 'Are you sure about this?'

'Do it,' Wren just wanted to be out of the stairwell. Her fear was suffocating, she wanted it over, one way or the other.

Raw slapped the reader and from the ground floor,

Creatures *screamed.*

Jerkily the door cycled open and Raw slid through sideways, pulling Wren after him. She slapped it closed and they stood in the room, panting. Shadows swirled around them as the glow tubes softly burned into life. Was the darkness deeper in the far corner? Was that a hole in the wall?

Wren sprinted for open window, kicking puffs of dust as she gripped the ladder and swung outwards in one smooth movement. She looked down and her eyes widened. The sand, which seemed strangely close to her feet given the length of the stairs they had climbed, was moving as far as the eye could see. Creatures must have converged from across the whole desert.

Her fists turned to ice and refused to open.

'Move it, Wren. I can't get on the ladder till you're off it.'

Wren looked up and her heart sank like a rock fall. 'Oh skies.'

'What is it?' Raw grabbed and shook her leg. 'What's the problem?'

'It's not morning,' Wren spoke with a shuddering voice.

'But its light out.' Raw strained past her.

'It's not morning,' Wren repeated. 'It's *midday,* or near enough.'

'Midday?' Beneath his scar, Raw paled. 'But that means –'

'There's a dust storm coming,' Wren swallowed as sand began to swirl upwards from the boiling mass. Wind caught her hair and wings and snatched them outwards.

'But we can't stay *here.'* Raw yelled. 'I can hear them – they've found a hole. They're widening it. They're *coming.'*

Almost without thinking, Wren started to climb the ladder. It groaned with her weight and the sudden rage of the wind that pulled her as she tried to hold onto it.

She dragged herself onto the roof top and lay flat. Raw was swinging out onto the rungs even before she could call for him.

He stared at the ground, just as she had done, then climbed.

She caught his hand and helped him onto the roof. He flattened himself next to her and his eyes swept the desert. 'Now what?'

'If we stay here the storm will blow us from the roof.' Wren was pale as ice. 'But we can't take off, that would be suicide.'

Raw groaned. 'Which way will the storm come?'

Wren's wings lifted from her back, almost pulling her into the air. Raw flattened them with a strong arm as Wren pointed. 'The storm should sweep across this way, from Deimos, towards the South.'

'And which way do we want to go – which way is Vaikuntha?' Raw shouted to be heard over the rising gale.

Wren pointed towards a curving hillside. 'That way.'

'It's not that far, is it? We were nearly there yesterday.'

'Yes, but –'

'Then you know what we have to do.' Raw caught her chin and turned her to face him. As her eyes met his, he automatically tried to tug his hair over his face, but the wind pulled it back, exposing him to her gaze. He looked like a winged demon, his mask hiding his grinning lips. 'We have to outfly the storm.'

9

'Are you *insane*?' Wren wrenched her face away.

'It's the Creatures or the storm,' Raw growled. 'If you don't want to fly, you might as well jump off the roof now and be done with it.' He grabbed her again and pointed to the churning sand. 'Go on. They might be distracted enough fighting over your body that I can get away.'

'Stop it.' Wren kicked him hard and he flinched and released her. She stared; the dust had already risen to knee height. Soon it would form a wall. She blinked particles from her lashes and pulled her goggles over her eyes.

She wasn't going to throw herself to the Creatures and she wasn't climbing back into their trap. Grinding her teeth, she rose into a Runner's starting position and flexed her arms. She was in agony. She wasn't even certain that she was going to be able to fling out her arms, let alone fight the wind.

'Stay with me,' she ordered Raw. Then she started to run.

Wren had barely taken three steps when the screaming wind swept into her wings and lifted her from the rooftop. She hadn't even opened them. With a moan, she forced her arms wide and gave the flick of her wrist that would lock the struts. Instantly she was lifted so fast that the factory was gone, vanished in a blur of ground and dust and sky.

Was Raw behind her? There was no way to know. She was tossed and buffeted in the leading edge of the storm, debris clattering against her legs and torso. She twisted, trying to see Vaikuntha, but the dust blurred everything and she had no idea which way she should be fighting to go.

Suddenly it was no longer about getting to Vaikuntha, but about survival. She faced forward, where the sand was curling into waves to meet the wind. She had to get further ahead. Forcing herself to streamline, she pushed faster, racing the dust, a tiny figure in the vast desert.

Her eyes and ears strained as she listened for Raw, but all she could hear was the gale that raged at her foolishness like an un-caged beast.

She pitched and yawed almost uncontrollably until she gave up the struggle to remain level and, with a feeling of terrifying elation, let the wind take her.

There was no longer anything to see but churning orange mist. Wren's goggles clogged until she was blind, her senses shut down. She focused instead on the feel of the wind, tossing her like a rudderless kite, wondering at what moment she would crash into a cliff, or the ground.

Inside her mask, she laughed. With all the Creatures converged at the CFC factory, she would likely be buried in sand before they could get to her. She had chosen her death and it was a Runner's death; glorious and in full flight.

Buffeted up and down, Wren's stomach rolled with every sudden jolt. Then the real storm caught her and she was tossed into a somersault. Her feet went over her head, her wings collapsed and refilled and she had no idea whether she had come back level. She was as helpless as a leaf in the storm, and just as fragile.

Wren fought against nausea; if she threw up, the hose to her canister would block and there would be no air. Already her breath was shortening as dust clogged the filters. She wished she had some sense of time; she might have been in the sky for moments, or hours. The storms usually lasted between thirty and sixty minutes, she could only pray to the skies that this was a short one.

Where was Raw – was he with her? Behind? Ahead? Already dead?

It seemed impossible that they could both survive: ridiculous odds. And yet she hoped. It made it seem less terrible if Raw was somewhere near, being hurled across the desert with her.

Time stretched and ballooned and the wind's screech grew louder. The skin on her fingers and face had long gone numb, not with cold, but with the pain of constant abrasion.

And then, with a strange abruptness, the wind, as though out of breath, began to drop. A lessening of the darkness that covered her vision told Wren that the sand had fallen away from her, but she had no way to clean her goggles to find out for sure.

Still she pitched side-to-side, wobbling, not even certain which way up she was flying. Her head was spinning, her gut clinging to her throat. There was no way to regain any kind of control, not only was she blind, but she had gone beyond exhaustion, she didn't think she *could* make her body move; her shoulders were pure agony, wrenched, as they had been, by the gale. Gusts warmed around her, gentler now, and she could feel the wind, exhausted as she, losing all its strength.

Some instinct, some sound, or change in the atmosphere around Wren, made her brace. She tensed just as she slammed into the desert.

The breath was, knocked out of her, and her mask ripped from her face. She rolled, spitting sand, and her wings unlocked as she scrabbled for the O2 canister, blindly seeking the hose that should end in her mask.

Gasping, feeling her throat already burning from the chemical atmosphere, Wren fumbled until her fingers closed around her mask. She shook it to empty the sand, then shoved it against her lips, inhaling with grateful desperation as the oxygen hissed from the bacteria in her tank.

She was on her knees. With trembling fingers, Wren pulled her goggles off, blinked and swallowed. Dust settled around her as a gentle breeze caressed her hair, almost apologetically. She turned to see a long furrow where she had ploughed into the ground and rolled. Martian bugs were already fighting inside, a miniature world at war, their armoured backs and sharp pincers ripping into those exposed by her landing. She shaded her eyes, staring around with growing desperation. She had landed in the middle of the desert, so the Creatures would be coming. It was stupid to think that the whole population of the delta had congregated at the CFC factories.

Wren tried to stand so that she could see further and immediately fell back to her hands and knees. She pulled her mask from her mouth just in time. She vomited a heavy, warm stream of purple fruit gel onto the desert floor and watched through sticky eyes as green grey bugs swarmed around her knees, seeking the sustenance.

Then, still shuddering as if she was in flight, she managed to refit her mask, and rise up again. Removing herself from the pain of her limbs she stared out across the desert. A short distance to her right there was a rock formation. If she could make it there, she could at least climb off the sand and there was a chance she might be able to work out the way to the nearest settlement. She wrapped her arms around her chest, her wings dragging and airless. She doubted she was anywhere near Vaikuntha. Wren hung her head. She was likely hundreds of kilometres off course; she could be anywhere … anywhere at all.

Barely able to keep her feet, Wren staggered, with her head hanging and her feet dragging through the sand; great weights on the ends of legs that felt like twigs. Her wings slid along behind her, wiping out her footsteps as she walked. Every so often she looked up to check that the rock remained ahead, then she looked back down again, her ears straining all the time for the wail of a hunting Creature, the skin of her spine already tingling in anticipation of an attack.

When she looked up again the rock was right in front of her. If she lifted her arm she would be able to touch it. She blinked and swayed; then she stroked its smooth surface. It was real, it was smooth and it was too high for her to climb. A giggle forced its way through her lips, then another.

She trudged along the rock looking, with increasing hopelessness, for some kind of hand or foothold in a formation that millennia of storms had sanded to polished smoothness. The rock itself, striated with black obsidian, sloped slowly until it entered the delta at the height of her waist. She flung her arms over the end of it and kicked her legs, trying to gain any friction, seeking to lift her body from the sand. She dangled uselessly;

then dropped. As if the thud of her feet wakened something she felt, rather than saw, a Creature stir and its attention rise towards her.

Terror gave her speed. She ran backwards, out into the desert; then she turned, flicked out her aching arms until her wings locked and raced back towards the rock.

Her heart pounded and the dust dragged at her feet, making her slip and slide, but at the very last moment she leaped. Her jump forced wind into her wings and made it lift her, not far, but far enough. This time Wren managed to get her whole chest onto the rock; her stomach, her thighs. She wriggled forward like a sand snake, until she lay flat on the sun-warm stone, her breath coming in small rasps.

She lay with her face pressed against a seam of quartz, arms splayed out, hugging the rock. She lay still and quiet for what felt like an age until she felt the pressure of the presence vanish once more into depths. Then she lay longer, allowing the stone's heat to soothe her quivering muscles and throbbing bruises. By the way the warmth moved across her back, Wren could feel the sun tracing its way across the sky and knew that she had hours to find some kind of shelter before the desert grew cold once more.

Her thoughts turned to Raw. By forcing her to fly he had saved her life, but for how long and to what end? She thought again of her mother, dying alone in Avalon, and of her missing brothers. She had no right to be lying here on a rock, wasting all of their time.

With a moan she dragged herself to her hands and knees. Careful on the slippery stone she crawled to its highest point. Only then did she raise her head.

To her right and left there was nothing; only desert stretching out as far as the eye could see. A bump in the distance could be Elysium Mons, or not.

She turned to look behind her. She rubbed her eyes and then she rubbed them again, just to be certain.

Right before her the sun glittered from the distinctive shape of a solar panelled biosphere. It was difficult to judge distance in the delta, but it looked like half an hour's hike through the dustbowl. Wren giggled at the ridiculousness of her situation.

Again, her choices were limited. She could sit on the rock until she froze to death in the desert night and in sight of shelter, or she could set off across the sand, hoping that she could outrace the Creatures, most of which would have to come from the CFC factories to reach her.

She locked down the sob that threatened to constrict her chest and held her head up high. She'd come this far, hadn't she?

Wren stood up. She flung out her arms with a wince, heard the click as her wings locked; then she started to run.

The rock *was* smooth, she had gone barely three paces before her left foot slipped. Instead of allowing herself to slide, she pushed off as hard as she could with her right, turning the fall into a leap. The wind caught under her wings and lifted her.

It was a light wind. Wren had been hoping for a thermal, thinking that one might have developed above the warm rock, but she was carried almost straight forward and gained no height.

The desert raced below her. The longer she could remain in the sky, the better. She angled her body upwards, rolling slightly into the wind, trying for more elevation. The faster she moved, the higher she flew. She looked ahead: the sphere was getting closer.

With a whoop, Wren twisted towards another rock, once more hoping for a thermal, but again the wind remained low and steady and she was already dropping.

From this height she could see the different colours in the sand; reds, oranges, yellows, browns and small patches of burned looking green that were still iced with dust from the storm. It was strangely beautiful and far less colourless and uniform than she had imagined when looking down from Elysium.

Bug colonies swarmed in and out of cone-shaped nests, fighting endless wars. Carapaces glimmered in the sun like the dust-polished stones that were piled in odd little cairns.

But now she was dropping again, her wings fluttering as the wind died inside them, curling up and away from her, ignoring her desperate lurches to catch it.

She looked ahead: the biosphere was closer, perhaps a ten-minute walk. Not so frightening.

She dropped her legs. This time she would alight gently, less likely to waken a Creature from its sleep. As soon as Wren's toes touched the sand, she began to run, the wind still giving her a little lift, sufficient to make her light. So instead of landing properly she continued to bound along, half-running, half-carried. It was almost fun. Each footstep took her twice the normal distance. She would be at the sphere in no time.

Then she saw the wake in the sand: at least one Creature had found her. And it would only take one.

Now it was a simple race, could she make it to the biosphere before the Creature reached her?

10

Wren put down her head and bounded, pumping her legs to make each jump count. She dared not look to her left, where the Creature arrowed towards her.

There was a thud so loud that even she felt it through her boots. Wren looked up, towards the biosphere. A figure stood at the edge of the 'sphere, just outside an airlock. He had just hurled what looked like a stove into the sand.

'Move it, Wren,' he yelled and he pointed towards another airlock that was cycled green and standing open for her.

When the Creature started to turn back her way, Raw threw something else.

The wake turned again, heading towards the noise Raw was making and Wren sprinted as fast as she could.

She skidded into the airlock without closing her wings. They scraped against the wall with a hissing sound, like claws. Wren gasped, suddenly terrified that she had broken or bent the struts. She pulled in her arms, hearing the click as the wings unlocked and turned to slam her hand on the palm reader, closing the door behind her.

Then she sank into a crouch, shuddering as some *thing* slammed against the 'sphere just outside, making it shake.

A slithering sound, a wail that spoke of hunger, frustration, perhaps even fury, and the Creature was gone.

Wren didn't know how long she sat inside the airlock as her heart slowed to a steady beat. Eventually though, the door was opened from the other side and she fell backwards into the biosphere.

She stared up at Raw, his scarred face upside down to her. His eyes were red and swollen, the skin around them bleeding. He had gone through the storm with no goggles. And he was no longer wearing the wings.

'Where are they?' She rolled and leaped up, fright bearing her in its updraft.

'They're safe.' Raw rolled his shoulders. 'I just wanted them off for a bit.'

'*Off for a bit*!' Wren shrieked. 'You don't even know where we are, anyone could take them. Runners never remove their wings unless they're in a Runner station.' She hesitated then and looked around, realising what was missing. No-one had come to see who had entered the 'sphere: no curious child, no Councilman seeking news. No-one. 'Where is everybody?'

Raw didn't answer.

'And how did you get here?' she hissed, and placed her hands on her hips, forgetting for a moment the absence of the colonists.

Raw pointed upwards. Wren followed his gaze. At the apex of the sphere there was a jagged line through one of the solar panels. Her eyes widened.

Raw nodded at her understanding. 'That's where I landed.'

'Skies, you've cracked the sphere.'

'It'll hold.' Raw did not meet her eyes.

'They'll throw us to the Creatures.' Wren wrung her hands. She frowned. 'If everyone's in a meeting, we can look for the Runner station, wherever it is. We'll hide out there until we can fly again. What did you do with your wings?'

Raw shuffled his feet. 'The wings are fine and we don't need to hide.'

'What do you *mean* we don't need to hide? Do they already know – what did they say? Where are we?'

She strode towards the nearest buildings. They were arranged like those of Elysium, low to the ground, built in diagonals. But the colours were different. These colonists had favoured stone that shone and glowed and preferred decals of dazzling minerals. Each home was built from an array of gem laden rocks that gleamed in the afternoon light, like a treasure box recently opened. When the sphere was removed the colony would glow.

Abruptly Wren stopped. 'I know where we are.' She turned,

grinning. 'I always wanted to see it – the twinkling colony – Tir Na Nog.' She turned and walked faster. 'We should find the council building, my brothers said it's *amazing*.' She sped ahead, her fear of punishment all but abandoned. Then she halted. 'My mask is all clogged up, but ...' she inhaled, her nose wrinkling. 'I shouldn't be smelling ...' gingerly she lifted her mask from her nose. She was inside the biosphere and would be able to breathe, but she struggled to convince herself.

'*Don't.*' Raw reached for her but she shook him off. Carefully she took a tiny breath, her eyes watered and she pressed her mask back against her face. She stared at Raw. He too was still wearing his mask.

'What is it? What's the smell?'

Raw had tears in his eyes. 'You don't want to know.'

Wren stepped up to him. 'Tell me.'

Raw shook his head.

'Where are all the *people*?'

'Listen, this place is pretty, isn't it? It's safe from storms and Creatures. There's plenty of food and water, we can rest here as long as we need to, then we'll fly on. Just keep your mask on and don't ask me that question again.' Wren's toes were touching Raw's, she curled her fists at her sides. The expression on his face was pleading. 'Let me make you something to eat. I can rub your aches.' He reached for her and she jumped out of his grasp.

'Why won't you tell me? I'm not a child.'

Raw's green eyes flicked towards the far side of the 'sphere. It was enough for Wren. She began to run.

'No!' Raw strode after her, his long legs eating up the distance between them. He grabbed her arm. 'Why can't you trust me? You don't want to know.'

'I *have* to know.' A horrible premonition had wrapped Wren's heart with icy fingers. Cold was spreading to her fingertips and down her spine.

She no longer saw the jewel-crusted houses and almost missed the giant council building that sloped into the earth, gold plated, engraved with pictures of earth fruits and flowers, fantasies of a long-dead home. She ran past it with barely a second look.

Raw followed a step behind, no longer trying to stop her. Whenever she looked back, his face screwed up to reveal his concern.

Then they were there.

Wren stopped, her heart shrinking in her chest as if it was hiding from the scene in front of her. Although she had nothing in her stomach, Wren bent double and vomited. She heaved until nothing came out but bile. Raw's hand was warm on her back where he was making small circular movements beneath her wings.

'I tried to tell you,' he said.

She closed her eyes, but she could still see it. Most of the bodies had been burned, but not all. Not the last ones.

'They can't all be ...'

'I haven't found anyone else,' Raw whispered. His hand stilled. 'I tried to stop you.'

'I know.'

They had started with the proper rites; there were line after line of urns. Then they had given up. A giant pile of ash and bones told Wren where they had piled the bodies and burned them all at once, with no regard for the obligations. Then the last of them had – what? Dragged themselves to the fire pits to lie with the remains of their families?

The bone shards were grey with ash. Wren clutched her hands to her face. White pearls shone among the remains 'Are they ... teeth?'

Raw nodded.

Skulls grinned at her, filthy rags of half burned material lay among the bones, clinging like fingers to scraps of flesh.

She gagged again and turned, only to come face to face with a bloated corpse, his yellow face dark with veins and rot.

She staggered and Raw caught her in both arms.

'What happened?' she murmured.

'I don't know.' Raw sounded as though he had been wounded. 'Come away.'

Wren let him guide her back towards the council building but a memory made her squirm.

'I overheard the Councillors when I went to Elysium.' She muttered. 'They said Tir Na Nog wasn't answering hails. This must be why.' She whimpered then. 'I don't understand. Why didn't they let anyone know? And where are the Runners?'

'Whatever it was it might have happened quickly.'

'The Creatures?' Wren froze.

Raw shook his head. 'There wouldn't be bodies.'

'The scientists here were looking at new ways of producing vast quantities of CFCs,' Wren tilted her head. 'Could they have poisoned their own air somehow?'

'Perhaps.' Raw bowed his head. 'It makes sense.'

They had passed the Council building and were heading back towards the airlocks.

'We should leave.' Wren looked up at the sky. 'Right now.'

'Not yet.' Raw's voice was strained and Wren looked at him properly for the first time. Apart from his abraded eyes, which she now realised were reddened with tears as well as dust, his shoulder was so badly swollen it looked as if he had a hunch and he walked with a limp. He must have been really hurt when he crashed into the sphere.

Wren bit her lip. 'I know where we are and which way to go. We could be at Vaikuntha in a couple of hours.'

'A short rest then?' Raw swayed on his feet and Wren saw how tired he was, how tired they both were. 'We can at least eat something.'

Immediately Wren curled her lip. 'Not here.'

'Perhaps not,' Raw sighed. 'But I'm hungry, I'm tired and … I'm hurt. I don't know how you're still on your feet.' He stared at her.

Wren fidgeted awkwardly. 'We're both still alive. It seems impossible. I – I'm glad you made it.'

A small smile flashed beneath Raw's mask and then vanished like a Creature into sand. 'There's an open house near the airlock. That's where I stored my wings. We can rest there.'

Inside, the house was much like Avalon; the colonists had built to the same plans. Raw's wings were lying on the bed, carefully arranged. Wren glanced at him and away before he could see her surprise. Then he slumped into a chair.

'That's it.' Wren marched up to him and grabbed his left arm. He tried to pull back, but she held on. His eyes were pools of surprise and pain.

'What're you –'

Wren put her foot on his chest. His eyes widened.

'No, Wren!'

She twisted and yanked, ignoring his scream of pain, feeling for the click that would tell her that his shoulder had returned to its socket.

The pink patches of skin on his face lost all colour and the grey darkened. His eyes rolled back in his head.

Click. She rotated his arm a couple of times and then placed it carefully in his lap. He groaned.

'Better?'

He nodded, unable to meet her gaze.

Then she sat on the chair opposite him.

This far from the cemetery fires the smell was barely noticeable. Still, neither of them removed their masks.

Raw's shoulders curled and he leaned his head on the table. His hair, long for an Elysium colonist and longer now than her own, slipped with its own weight over his neck and onto the table. Sweat soaked curls, darkened to black, stuck to his nape and with a long sigh he let his fists dangle between his legs.

She could see only a little of his scarring, running down his left cheek and into the collar of his shirt. Was it true that her father had withheld medicine to punish him?

Wren's fingers twitched as if to touch the grey scales on his skin and she had to admit, if only to herself, that it was likely. If there was no punishment for trying to take wings, Runners would lose them to stupid Land-crawling adventurers all the time.

She caught herself thinking the insult and blushed. Land-crawlers, Grounders, the Land-locked. These were the terms that kept Runners apart.

Raw had never received a lesson, yet he was flying. He had Run ahead of a sand storm – no other Runner she knew of had ever done that. He was no longer Land-locked. And how many other so-called Land-crawlers would be excellent Runners given the chance? She clenched her fists, her mind racing.

How many girls?

Yet what they had done was blasphemy and if they were caught … she was unable to complete the thought. Still in the back of her mind she could picture how they would scream when they were thrown from the cliff.

If nothing else though, she had news of Tir Na Nog. Wren's hand lifted to touch Raw on the arm. He had saved her life, drawing the Creature away from her. He was a good Running-partner. She still didn't understand why he was helping her; perhaps it was simply that he had not encountered any other Runners yet. She would have to be cautious when they reached Vaikuntha.

Had she thanked him at all? She couldn't remember. She opened her mouth.
Raw shivered once, snorted and a deep snore rattled from his chest. Wren stared, then, as he snored deeper and louder, she laughed.

Wren tried to sleep alongside Raw, but she could not. Her mind was racing too fast to allow her exhausted body to slip into unconsciousness and she was uncomfortable on the chair. She didn't want to move Raw's wings from the bed and so she walked around the room, trying to keep her muscles from stiffening any further. She stared out of the window port, watching the sun creep across the sky. They dare not leave it too late to Run to Vaikuntha, they could not be caught in the dark again. But Wren wanted to let Raw sleep for as long as possible.

She slipped from the house; she could at least find the Runner platform so that she would be ready when they decided to go.

Wren knew that it would be high up and likely on the edge of the 'sphere, if not outside it, so she started at the airlock and began to walk, following the line of the wall. The colony was eerie in its silence, Wren could hear a faint buzzing and when she looked up to follow the noise she realised that it was the sound of electricity being collected in the solar panels, a sound that was normally too quiet, buried under the sounds of humanity, for anyone to hear. No air moved inside the sphere, there was no wind to move curtains, or blow leaves from the clusters of gingko. Dead brown foliage lay beneath the plants, half burying the roots, turning to mulch exactly where they had fallen.

She reached the science block, the door swinging open on its own weight. She had no intention of entering. There would be no cure for her mother here, not with the work these scientists specialised in. *Had* specialised in.

Behind the science block a stairs climbed towards the top of the sphere. There was an airlock placed at roof height and above that more stairs curved around the outside. At the top, a Runner platform. Wren wondered which building was the station: Raw needed goggles.

She hesitated outside the most likely looking; it nestled at the base of the stairs. What if they hadn't all made it to the cemetery? What if there was a dead body inside?

Wren thought of Raw's eyes. He couldn't do another flight without goggles. She opened the door and ducked inside.

Everything in the station was covered in dust. There were no wings on the stands; it was as though it had been abandoned for months. Wren found the goggles in a drawer of spare parts. Feeling as if ghosts dogged her every step, she clutched them to her chest and ran, her own wings billowing behind her as she went.

Wren wanted fresh air. The stench here was muted by her mask but still she could feel it, winding into her nose and lining her throat, the phantom smell of burning bodies, ash in the air.

Wren raced as fast as she could back to the house and her

sleeping partner. It was time to wake him.

She paused with one hand raised over his shoulder. How should she do it? She could shake him, but that seemed cruel. Instead she pulled gentle fingers through the dusty tangles of his hair. He made no movement at all. Wren frowned and patted his head. He twitched, turned so that his cheek rather than his forehead was lying on the tabletop, and continued to snore.

It was the first time that Wren had the opportunity to really study Raw's face, covered as it usually was with his long hair, the disguise he had grown to make the lives of others easier. Barely breathing, she pushed the remaining tendrils from his eyes and chin. The shape of his face was strong, his jaw wide. The hair on his chin was starting to roughen and thicken, like Colm's, but only on the right-hand side. The scarring would suppress the hair on his left. Unless he shaved, he would have half a beard. His skin though, the unblemished skin, was clear and smooth. Apart from the abrasions he had earned while flying, he had no spots or craters marring his face. It made the thick grey scarring even more of a shock. When she looked closely at it, Wren realised that it actually did look like scales; patches of skin like the leather of a sand-snake. The unbroken pale patches between the scales looked strange, almost as if they were the wounds, something inflicted rather than the parts of him that had not been touched.

Without thinking she touched a fingertip to one of the pink patches, almost the exact shape of Phobos, that sat just above his mask, and instantly Raw came awake as though she had electrocuted him. As if that skin was both sensitive and painful.

Wren leaped back. 'Sorry to wake you, but we've got to go.'

Raw rose groggily to his feet, already pulling his hair down over his face, hiding his scales from her gaze.

'I got you these.' Awkwardly, Wren held out the goggles and Raw swiped them from her, still half asleep.

He blinked at them, confused, and then his eyes cleared. 'Goggles.'

She nodded. 'You need them.'

'Yes, I do.' He pulled them roughly over his head, arranging his hair so that enough was trapped beneath the strap to keep his face covered. 'You went looking for these by yourself. Was it okay?'

Wren half smiled. 'There's no-one here to stop me.'

'That's not what I meant.'

'I know.' She examined him as he finished settling the new eye-wear. 'You don't have to do that. Not for me.'

'Do what?' He saw that she was looking at his face and jerked, spinning around so that she couldn't see. His fingers pulled restlessly at his fringe, pulling even more to his chin, thickening the curtain.

'Sorry,' Wren gasped. 'I didn't mean –'

'It doesn't matter,' Raw muttered. 'Knowing it's there and having to look at it – that's two different things. People say it's okay, but then I see them flinching, trying not to gag. They tell me I can no longer work inside the Dome, that I have to learn how to repair airlocks, but I know that what they mean is, they want me where people don't have to look at me.'

'Even your friends and family.'

Raw shrugged. 'Forget it.'

'They don't –'

'I said *forget it*.' His words were a snarl. He stalked to the bed and grabbed the wings, swinging them over his shoulders. They settled down around him like a silver cloak, only just touching the floor. 'Let's go.'

Wren led the way to the Runner platform and pointed to the stairs. 'Up there.'

'Makes sense.' Raw began to climb. Halfway up Wren turned to look back over the colony. It really was beautiful, but now there was no-one to maintain the already cracked 'sphere, no-one to work in the science block, or fill the houses. The sphere would eventually collapse, probably in the next mega storm and the desert would start to absorb it, as it had done the CFC factories.

'We might be the last to see this,' she said, tears standing in her eyes.

The council building reflected the sun and the houses around it looked like lines of scattered ornaments, gem stones on a cloth. A blackened patch on the far side reminded Wren why everything was so quiet and she started to climb once more.

Raw wasn't moving.

'What's the matter?' She followed the line of his pointing arm and her eyes widened. 'That can't be right.'

In the far distance a thick grey line marred the horizon, bringing it higher and closer.

'We've got maybe a week, do you reckon?' His voice was rough.

Around the sphere, the dust was whirling and eddying, no longer still. It would keep moving like that until the mega-storm reached them.

'But it isn't due for another four months,' Wren whispered. 'No-one will be ready.'

11

'Nothing we can do about it.' Raw stamped up the stairs.

'But why is it happening? A mega-storm has never been early. Not in fifty years of Runner records at least.' Wren stumbled to catch him and they paused at the airlock.

'Will it affect our flight?' Raw said, holding his hand over the palm reader. 'Will we make it to Vaikuntha?'

'We tend not to fly this close to a mega-storm, because there's likely to be more turbulence, but it's only just rising. We should be all right.' Wren placed her hand on top of Raw's, feeling the warmth of skin against hers and the chill of his surprise. She pushed his hand onto the reader. 'We'll be in Vaikuntha before sundown.'

The airlock cycled open and they stepped out together, into the Martian atmosphere.

'What will you do when we get there?' Wren said suddenly as the wind caught in her hair. 'What are you planning?'

Raw went still, only his wings moved. 'What do you mean?'

'You know what I mean,' Wren insisted. 'You followed me for a reason …

'Things have changed,' he said roughly. 'I won't betray you.'

Wren pressed her lips together. Her mask rubbed her cheeks. 'That's the thing though, isn't it? If you *were* planning to, you wouldn't tell me.'

Raw made a sound that was half laugh, half snarl. 'You either trust me, or you don't, Wren. You could have left without me while I was asleep. I'd have been forced to wait for another Runner to come in, or risk flying myself without a guide. But you didn't.' He cocked his head at her. 'That must mean that a part of you does trust me.'

'Or that I don't want to fly alone.' Wren pulled on her goggles. 'Well, come on then, follow me.'

She climbed the last few stairs and stood on the edge of a Runner platform, a long metal walkway balanced on thick struts. She peered down. There was a net hanging beneath it, taut, yet bouncing slightly in the growing wind. The colony itself was mostly hidden by the curve of the solar panels on top of the biosphere.

Wren straightened and shook out her arms. The aching was so all pervasive that her limbs felt almost numb. She would be able to fly.

She bent into a starting position, wincing as she took her weight on bended knee. Then she lurched into a shambling run. She hurtled straight ahead, keeping her eyes on the lines. The blue line first. She ran towards it, her arm pumping. The wind got behind her, lifting her wings to play with the fabric. She hit the blue line with her leading foot and hammered out two more steps. Then she had reached the red line: if she tried to stop, she'd go right over the edge and into the net. Finally, the green: she flung out her arms and her heart thudded relief as her wings clicked into place as she leaped.

This time the wind took her straight into its arms and she kept her eyes open as she raced towards the scudding clouds.

She circled down to see Raw leap from the platform.

He had opened his wings before hitting the lines and his launch was wobbling and unsteady as a result, the wind fighting with itself, the currents confused beneath the foils. Then he straightened out by sheer force of will, it seemed, and flew to meet her.

They circled one more time, wordlessly saying goodbye to the tomb beneath the 'sphere. The further away they flew, the lighter Wren felt, until she was smiling again. She tilted her wings, thinking of the maps on the walls of Avalon. She knew where Vaikuntha was in relation to Tir Na Nog, she just had to remember.

The land speeding below her reflected the image drawn on her wall. A straight formation of stone that led to the deep wriggling lines of a long-dried riverbed: those were the landmarks that needed to be on her right-hand side. She flew until she was sure that she had found the configuration. Then she turned from it and headed into the lowering sun.

It had grown later than she had thought. The rising mega-storm was straight in front of her now, a thick grey line moving terminally, across the surface of the planet, destroying everything in its wake.

Only during the mega-storms were Runners made welcome inside the 'sphere. They joined the colonists inside underground bunkers, where they would remain for two whole days, united briefly, in their fragility.

Wren had only ever seen the devastation a storm had left after it had gone by, never the build-up.

The wind around her had a different tone to it, almost as if it knew what was coming and longed to be embraced into its power. It sang a higher note and tossed her more joyfully.

Wren turned her face to the ground, seeing the desert spread out beneath her. The wakes of Creatures followed like old friends and patches of green reminded her of Elysium. Endlessly her colony turned out the tiny oxygen factories that were gradually, permanently changing the Martian atmosphere. What would happen to the Creatures then? Would they be able to breathe in the new air? She hoped not.

A gust of wind whipped Wren upwards and she whooped as Raw slid into view, his great silver wings catching the light and turning it back on her.

He leaned into the wind, his hair streaming and the foils of his pinions fluttering so loudly that she could hear them even over her own.

She found herself racing him, streamlining her body and arcing her wings so that the wind took her away from him. Then she grew lonely and turned, but he was right there, overtaking her above her left-hand side and she grinned.

Almost leisurely, Wren rose towards him. She angled herself so that she would flatten out ahead of him and twisted into a thermal that pushed her higher, faster. She whipped past him with a whoop, hearing the rustle of his wings and his cry of surprise, before she levelled out.

Then, with a lurch, the wind fled. It vanished as though it had never been, as if her flight had been nothing more than a dream.

Wren's scream was cut off by her own jolt, as she dropped instantly, like a stone.

Over her silent screaming, her mind threw up one word, louder than all the others: *turbulence.*

Her wings rattled again, whipping out behind her as she fell. Raw's own shout: her name, loud and horrified, faded above her. At least he had missed the patch of dead air.

Wren wanted to roll into a ball, close her eyes and pretend this wasn't happening, but her father's voice spoke in her mind. Years of listening to her brother's lessons meant that she knew what to do. She locked her elbows in a slightly bent position, bullying her wings to remain locked, yet allowing a bit of give so the pressure of her fall did not break the struts. Ignoring her instincts, she remained flat and slowed her descent as best she could. Her only hope was that the wind would pick her up again before she hit the ground.

She risked a glance down. She was speeding towards the dust bowl unimaginably quickly. A sob burned her throat and her goggles filled with tears, which at least meant she couldn't see the ground filling her vision, getting closer with every heartbeat.

Frantically she shook her head. How would she know when her time had run out? It suddenly seemed very important that her very end did not come as a surprise. Angrily Wren shook the tears to the edges of her goggles and forced the rest back. She would look death in the eye and spit in it at the last.

Now she could make out individual rocks, bug cairns. Her stomach lurched: she was going to crash into one of their cone nests. Tears filled her eyes once more and her heart pounded so hard it was ripping her chest open. Maybe she'd have an old woman's death after all: a heart attack.

Giggling hysterically, she realised that it was time to spit or close her eyes. Viciously Wren curled her lips and braced. This was going to hurt, but not for long.

She body-slammed into something so strong it stole her breath. Before she could blink at the strangeness of her continued existence, she was being lifted back up towards the sun. The wind had – returned and caught her with the finesse of a ball-player on a holiday. With her heart fluttering like a bug's wing Wren trembled in its embrace, unable to control her ascent or direction.

Soon she was high enough to hear Raw's cries. 'What was that? What happened?'

Wren shuddered silently until he drew closer, then she turned to look at him. 'Turbulence. It could happen to you.' She swallowed, her throat dry. 'Did you see what I did? How I kept my wings out.'

Raw nodded and his face was grim. 'There was no warning.'

'No.' Wren said and she set her face for Vaikuntha. 'There wasn't.'

It was not the end of the turbulent air. With the mega storm so close, only days away, the wind was unpredictable and cold. When it deserted Raw's wings, Wren could only watch and pray. But he did not fall as far as she had done and he did not panic.

They flew beside one another, no longer racing, long shadows growing as the sun dropped and the Creatures returned, tracing their progress with anticipatory cries that the wind carried to their ears.

The jerk and jolt of the turbulence began to feel horribly familiar. One moment Wren's wings were plump and full, the next they were hanging in empty tatters. As the afternoon wore into evening they juddered up and down, getting closer to the ground and the waiting Creatures, their onward progress slowed.

'Night's falling,' Raw yelled and Wren clenched her fists, glaring at the moons which were materializing on opposite ends of the sky, Deimos already two days into its slow orbit. He was right. Wren had left it too long. She had not expected their progress to be so slow.

She laughed as she saw the CFC factories clustered in their rectangular lumps, illuminated by Phobos' weak glow and the twilight of the dying sun. They were back where they had started that morning.

'We're not landing there again.' Raw shouted following the direction of her gaze.

'We won't need to.' The wind still carried them; they could reach Vaikuntha.

Wren's eyes strained, desperately looking for the colony. Her stomach began to knot. Had she forgotten the maps and badly misjudged? They were descending now, the cooling air too weak to hold them. A curve in the line of the delta ahead told her a hill might take them down even earlier than she anticipated. Wren blinked. They had turned from the sunset, putting it to their side, but the hill seemed to be outlined with its own glow, almost as if it had its own sinking orb to consume.

'*Over there!*' She wheeled, trying to see around the curve of the landscape. Then, suddenly, stars were reflecting at her from the desert floor.

'A biosphere.' Raw's cry of relief drew an answering cheer from her lips. They were mere kilometres from Vaikuntha now.

Wren tried not to look at the sand. Still, a part of her brain was frantically calculating: which would they hit first, the desert, or the 'sphere?

Distracting herself from the horrible question, Wren focused on the 'sphere ahead. It was much, much bigger than Elysium. Laid out, as it was, on the flat at the foot of a Mons, these colonists had been able to spread out wider.

The dimensions of her home colony, Elysium, were restricted by the slopes of the Mons shelf, the rise of the summit. It was well placed for the distribution of seedlings into the wind, but Wren had not realised how small the 'sphere was until she saw the vastness of Vaikuntha.

The diameter of the 'sphere was so wide, and Wren now so low that she could not see from one end to the other. Like Elysium, Vaikuntha was not perfectly round; instead walls, black in the evening gloom, but with a subtle obsidian sheen, rose towards the moons.

Panels topped the walls, fitting together like a lid on a pan. The originals had used Martian rock to create an airtight barrier and their panels to top it. The shape was, Wren mused, more like a stadium than a sphere.

She blinked. As stars emerged in the sky around her, something glittered to one side of Vaikuntha's walls. 'There's water,' she gasped.

Raw flew at her side now, his pinions fluttering in the edge of her vision, his fingertips almost touching hers. 'Look at it, above ground. Why doesn't it fill with sand?'

Wren shook her head. They were approaching obliquely now, but she could barely take her eyes from the enticing shimmer.

Closer they drew, lower and lower. The wall loomed before them like a cliff that had been flattened by a giant hand. But where was the Runner-sphere? Hard as she looked, Wren could see no structure outside the wall. Then, as they drew close, a fragile looking Runner platform emerged from the highest point on the blockade, as if a painter had touched up the sky with a splash of jet-black ink.

'Do you see the platform?' she shouted and angled her body towards it.

Raw nodded and Wren's heart thudded: it was going to be close. She fought desperately for height, while below her the Creatures that had been tracing their progress stopped racing and began circling in front of the wall. The sand pushed into tapers that mirrored the waves that rose and fell in the river.

'Could we land in the water?' Raw's hopeful shout turned her head.

'How would you get out again?' Wren indicated the Creatures, invisible but for their wakes. They would be waiting in the sand. There would be no climbing from the water. 'Follow me. Do what I do.' At least the dim light should provide some cover for their amateurish landings.

The wall was racing towards them at a breathless pace. The

ground too was rising faster than thought. Wren could only hope they reached the platform before they dropped too low. At the last possible moment, she stopped fighting her descent and allowed the plunge that would put her level with the runway.

She started to lower her legs.

A masked figure sprinted along the boards, shouting wildly and waving a red flag. Did he want to get knocked off? No-one was allowed on the platform when a Runner was coming in.

Trembling with tiredness, Wren instinctively whipped into a twist that took her away from the platform. Then she realised that she would never be able to regain the height. She had just doomed herself.

A curse revealed that Raw was copying her move. She had killed them both.

With a sob she cast her eyes back to the platform that was now level with her shoulders. The man started to point his flag, gesticulating furiously.

Was there somewhere else to land? Somewhere below them?

She tried to call to him. 'Where should we go?'

The words were torn from her mask and scattered by the turbulent wind.

Raw's wings were just above her. She glanced up just as they flared orange like a blooming sun. She blinked. He was reflecting lights that had blossomed on a rock just to the left of the wall.

She yawed sideways, there was no choice: alternative landing area or not, Wren and Raw would land on that rock or hit the sand.

Wren had just enough height left to circle the rocky outcrop; it was shorter than a traditional Runner platform, but someone had painted the correct colours on it and lit flares at the end to guide them in.

She dived and levelled, knowing Raw was right behind her. Fighting for balance, she reached the first painted line and dropped her legs. She slapped her arms together and her toes grazed rock as the last of the air was forced out from under her wings. Beside the stone, wakes in the sand followed her progress.

As soon as she felt solid ground beneath her feet, Wren broke into a run, her knees stiff and unyielding. At first the wind pushed her from behind then a gust of air caught her folded wings. For a single thud of her heart she stood still; then she was stumbling backwards towards the sand.

A Creature slithered against stone and Wren gasped, but before she could cry out, hands grabbed her and expertly unbuckled the wings from her chest and wrists.

The Creature wailed and Wren's knees collapsed. Strong arms caught her and a man's low voice spoke over her head.

'It's a boy, barely muscled. He can't have been Running long.'

Another answered him. 'Get him into the hut; I'll wait for his partner.'

'No, wait.' Although her limbs felt like wet laundry, Wren struggled free of the arms that were guiding her from the runway. 'Let me see him in.'

It was good to know a real Runner was going to catch Raw when he landed, but the Creatures still circled. The wail, like that of a hungry baby still shivered across her skin. Wren wanted to make sure that Raw landed well – and that when he did, he kept his promise and did not betray her.

12

As he came into land, Raw's arms shook so hard that Wren could see the effect on his wings. They juddered as if they were coming free of his back, the pinions flapping violently. Eventually he dropped his legs, only a little late, and thumped onto the rock with the sound of washing hitting stone.

He grunted and his knees buckled, but he staggered forwards, just as she had done, trying to run as the wind fought to pull him back into its embrace. His jaw was set and his eyes glittered madly in the firelight. Wren saw him wince as his shoulder was strained. Then he forced his wings together, choking the wind from their vanes.

She blinked as figures barged past her and caught Raw before his wings were fully empty. She strained to hear his voice, but she could hear only the strangers.

'You all right, Runner? You timed that Run close. Set out late did you?'

'That was a hard landing. Better get something cold on those ankles.'

As Raw was led past her he met her eyes.

Wren's knees trembled and the man who held her shoulders leaned down to look into her face. 'You ready to go in now, boy? Your partner's safe landed.'

Her cheeks were so numb she could barely speak. With fingers that felt like lumps of ice, Wren pulled her goggles off. After a glance at the flares that were now burning themselves out on the far end of the rock, she allowed herself to be led after Raw.

As they walked, Wren heard the Creatures slithering alongside them, wakes shrinking as they burrowed deeper into the sand.

'Pay them no mind.' There was a smile in the man's voice.

'We're used to 'em. They've never left the sand yet, so if you stay on't rock you'll be fine. In a way they're company for us.'

'They'd eat you if you slipped!'

'They would at that.' The man gave her a quick hug. 'Probably we'd eat them too, if we could catch 'em. Works both ways see. Just don't step off the rock and you'll be fine.'

Wren nodded but her eyes kept sliding to the side, where the whisper of shifting sand followed her all the way down the smooth slab and she could not help remembering how clever the hunters had been in the factories.

Long and wide, the rock sloped down to a plateau, metres above the sand, where a low clam-shaped building clung like a limpet; the reinforced polyethylene walls shining with the glow of the dying fire.

Wren stared. 'Where's your biosphere?'

The man who held her upright gave a bitter laugh. 'This is temporary-like, Runner. We only use it when the main platform's out of commission. No 'sphere out here – just the building. Won't last past the next mega-storm, but it'll do for now.'

'So, don't tek yer mask off.' A second voice snapped.

Wren had been about to draw their attention to the approaching storm, which she realised was hidden by the curve of the mons, but she jumped as a man pushed past her, wiping his hands, and her words fled. He opened the exterior door simply by turning a handle, as if the house was one of those inside Elysium. Here there was no sphere to protect the occupants.

Wren put her hand to the mask that nestled on her face, she knew it was secure, had trusted it all this way, but suddenly it seemed flimsy and insufficient.

'I don't often take it off anyway,' she muttered. 'Except to eat.'

'We've some like that here too.' The man nudged her. 'We call 'em argonophobes.'

'How do *you* eat?' Wren's curiosity stopped her in her tracks.

'You ain't seen our masks yet have you?' Get inside and take a closer look. The man reached for the door handle. 'It'll be crowded in here. Ready?'

Wren took a breath. Was she? The worry that the day's events had banished from her mind suddenly reared again. So many strangers – what would they do if they realised that she wasn't a boy? 'Ready,' she whispered.

He opened the door.

Wren stared, unmoving until the man pushed her into the press of people.

'Shut the door, Adler, you're lettin' all the heat out.'

Behind her the door slammed shut and Wren jumped, already wistful for the emptiness of the sky. The small building was so crowded Wren could barely make out individual bodies.

The air was fetid with the stench of sweat and a poorly operating latrine. The scent of over-spiced soy-stew wound around the other odours, unappetising, but enough to make her stomach growl. She clutched her mask, holding it onto her face, as her breath shortened. Never had she seen so many people in one place. Men crammed like trees around her, so close it took her a moment to see the Sphere-Mistress who had spoken, standing near the cook-pot.

Adler raised his voice. 'These Runner's need something warm in their bellies, Genna. And one of 'em needs cold wrap on his ankles.'

The woman nodded, wiped her nose and picked up a ladle. She started serving stew into bowls and immediately men sat on benches set into the walls, clearing a space around Wren so that she could breathe once more. Now she saw Raw, heading purposefully towards her.

Automatically she stepped backwards, almost tripping over outstretched legs, and Raw grabbed her as she swayed. One hand closed around the top of her arm. This was it: he was going to tell them what she was.

'What my partner needs, is to sit down.' His voice was rough, and Wren blinked, slow to catch up with what she had heard, still certain he must be outing her. But he couldn't, she reminded herself. If he revealed the truth about her, she'd do the same to him. They were at a stalemate.

Adler gestured and several of the men shifted to reveal a plastic table pushed up against a wall with two metal stools nestled beneath. Wren and Raw hobbled to the seats.

'Thank you, Sphere-Mistress, for your hospitality,' Wren said, quickly before she could forget. She nudged Raw and he echoed her.

Then her eyes widened. 'Where are our wings?' she whispered.

Raw looked around. 'I – I don't know.'

Wren pulled away from him. She knew better than to let their wings out of her sight. As she had already warned Raw, Runners were occasionally downed in settlements where lost wings put them at a premium. Convocation disapproved and most Runners would be appalled at the idea of wearing someone else's wings, but if you had none of your own and a Runner was stupid enough to lose track of his …

'Where are our wings?' Panic raised her voice.

One of the men grunted. 'We ain't nabbers Runner. There ain't room for them in here, they're outside, under tarps.' She blinked again. The man's voice was offended, but his face was long and mournful.

'Sorry.' She sank onto one of the chairs and it wobbled under her, one leg shorter than the others. She grabbed the table with a small inhalation. That too lurched under her hand and she balanced herself gingerly then glowered at Raw until he sat with her, his knees almost touching hers.

Bowls were thumped onto the table in front of them.

'Here, Runners, you need to eat, but you won't be able to till you change those masks.' Wren frowned and looked up. Adler grinned down at her. His teeth gleamed beneath a black moustache that bristled along his upper lip.

Then she realised what she had been seeing all around her: the men's full faces.

She surged to her feet. '*Your mask!*'

Adler crouched and pointed to his nose. Then she saw it – instead of a full mask, Adler wore a tube that clipped into his nostrils and hooked over his ear, unobtrusive and, as far as Wren was concerned, inadequate.

She shook her head. 'I'm not wearing one of those.'

But Adler was already gripping her O_2 canister. 'Hold your breath.'

Before Wren could protest, he had unhooked her mask from her canister, attached another tube, pulled the visor from her face and, as she choked, in one smooth movement clipped the other end of the new tube over her nose. Wren lurched backwards, but it was too late, her mask was gone. She pawed at her face but Adler held her hands down.

'Just breathe, I know you don't like it, but you'll soon see this is better. You can eat. Full masks are good for flying, they keep your face clear of the wind, but here, we use these halfies for everything else.'

Stars were bursting in front of her eyes; Wren couldn't hold on any longer. With her heart pounding, she tried a small inhalation. Automatically her lungs fought for air. It flowed into her chest without the plastic smell that usually came through her mask.

Adler held her eyes as her breathing slowed. 'There now, that wasn't so bad.'

Wren grabbed her full mask from him and clutched it tightly.

Then she looked at Raw and Wren forgot her fear of the halfie as she recognised his expression: he was about to start his obligations. She cleared her throat, trying to get his attention and he looked up. She gave a sharp shake of her head and he paled. The prayers would have given him away as a Grounder. With a shaky exhalation, he leaned to pick up his spoon, ignoring his own 'halfie' as though he'd been born to it.

Then, as he raised his left arm, he blanched and changed hands. A wave of sympathy made Wren study his shoulder more carefully; although it was no longer dislocated, the bruising and swelling made it mountainous.

Wren winced at the sight and Raw looked up, his attention

caught by the tiny movement. His face tightened and he ducked his head. When he made sure his hair flopped over his cheek to hide his scarring, Wren realised that he thought she'd been flinching at the way he looked with his mask removed.

She opened her mouth then stopped and snapped it closed. What could she say?

Pretending she hadn't seen his reaction she turned her eyes to her own bowl.

Despite its spicy scent, the soy stew was a dirty grey colour, unappetising, but Wren couldn't remember the last proper meal she had eaten. Still breathing through her nose with great care, she gulped the food down, glad suddenly of the halfie that allowed her to do so.

When she slid her empty bowl across the table, Wren felt the eyes of the men on her. Nervously she glanced up, finally able to properly take in the Runners who surrounded her.

Adler remained nearest, his big hands resting on his knees as he watched her become acclimatised to her halfie. Behind him others viewed her, and Raw, with looks that seemed just a little too hungry.

Wren gripped her chair, and edged towards Raw, seeking the comfort of his familiarity.

The men were mainly olive skinned, with dark hair and close-set eyes. Several of them sported facial hair, like Adler's. There was the mournful one who had spoken to her earlier and beside him a stocky fellow whose frown lines cut deep as knife wounds. By the cook pot was a Runner so large he was a wall of sheer muscle. Nearest to Raw was a shorter figure, whose smile was sudden and bright.

The flash of his teeth teased a twitch of her own lips and she fidgeted in her chair. Immediately the smiling man went down on one knee. 'Well, Runner, if you're done eating, can we hear your messages?'

'Messages?'

The Sphere-Mistress, Genna, pushed her way through the men, carrying her record book close to her chest with one arm. 'We've been waiting for a Runner to land here for a while.' She glanced in the direction of the main settlement as if she could see it through the walls and Wren's eyes were drawn to the fingers of her free hand, where they twisted inside her skirt, making small tears in the weave.

Raw dumped his spoon in his bowl. Quickly Wren offered her own answer before he could speak. 'We don't have any messages.'

Shock palpably thickened the hut's dank air and Genna returned the book to its place on the shelf. She frowned. 'No messages. Then why come here?'

Wren straightened. She almost had to think to bring her real mission to mind, it seemed so long since she had set off. 'I'm looking for my brothers. They were due back a few days ago and they had planned to come this way.'

'Your brothers,' Genna murmured. 'Still partner-running?'

Wren nodded tightly, trying to squash that familiar rush of hope that still burned each time it flared. 'Have you seen them?'

'Like I said, no Runners at this station for a while. But they may've landed at the main settlement.'

'Where we weren't able to?' Raw interrupted and Wren bit her lip. Had he forgotten that he wasn't supposed to speak unless he absolutely had to?

Adler spread his hands. 'The flaggers are meant to be out for all the Runners, but we've seen some go in anyway.'

Wren groaned. Colm's grasp of the flag code was spotty at best. Even if he had seen the red, he might have led Jay onto the wall. 'How do I find out if they're there?'

For a moment silence draped the room then Adler nodded. 'Go, Saqr.'

The mournful looking man sighed deeply. Then he put his bowl down, opened the door and set out into the darkness.

Genna gestured. 'You're best getting out of those clothes while you wait, or you'll be too stiff to fly by morning. I'll give you both a rub.'

Wren spun to look at Raw, panic tasted like acid on her tongue.

Steadily Raw's eyes met Wren's, and understanding cleared in their green depths. Slowly he stood and gave a stretch that cracked his tendons. 'As you can hear, Sphere-Mistress, I definitely need that massage you're offering. Do me, then *I'll* do my partner.' Genna opened her mouth to protest and Raw shrugged. 'He's a bit shy, is Wren. He'd rather eat more stew and wait for me.'

The second portion of soya sat in Wren's stomach like clay. She watched Genna rub Raw and paled each time the woman's hands teased a crack from his muscles and ligaments.

He lay on the bench by the cook pot, having displaced the big man, and his head was turned from Wren. Half of his body was lit by the low light that flickered over the long lines of his muscles. The other half of him was in darkness. His hair tangled in the deep shadows that pooled beneath his head.

Wren turned towards the door and grimaced as her neck cricked. Genna was right, she desperately needed a rub, but although she felt warmer towards Raw, there was no way she was letting him get his hands on her.

Perhaps Saqr would return soon with her brothers and her own massage would be forgotten. Colm would surely forgive her for using his spare wings if it meant they returned to their mother with the medicine she needed to save her life.

Yet the door remained stubbornly closed and she drummed her feet on the floor as she glared at it.

With agonizing inevitability, Genna worked her way down Raw's body until she lifted his feet from the bench and rubbed the arches. Now Raw looked relaxed and Genna exhausted. The Sphere-Mistress dropped his feet and flexed her fingers.

'All done.' She touched his shoulder with gentle hands. 'I'm not sure what you did to that shoulder, but you need to rest it as long as you can.'

Raw rolled over and Wren quickly closed her eyes.

'Thanks.'

Wren heard rustling as Raw redressed.

'Your turn.'

She opened her eyes to see Raw looking at her, his expression unreadable.

She shook her head. 'I'm fine, Sphere-Mistress.'

'Don't be stupid, Runner.' Adler glowered at her from the place he had taken across the table. 'What if your brothers ain't 'ere? You'll want to fly again tomorrow. It's not like you can trek across the desert.'

As if thinking of the Creatures drew their attention, their eerie cries split the night. Wren shuddered. 'Well …' She tried to rub her own shoulders, but could barely lift her arms.

'You're hurting, Wren, and it's best if *I* give you the rub.' Raw moved so that he was standing right next to her, almost knee-to-knee. Wren could hardly bear to look at him, certain he'd be smirking. But when she raised her head, he looked serious. He took a step backwards 'If you'd rather the Sphere-Mistress do it …'

'No.' Wren jumped to her feet and moaned as her muscles protested the sudden movement. These were her choices: let Raw rub her, or let one of the strange Runners do it. One way would give her away for sure, the other was a nightmare.

'Fine,' she snapped. 'Just …' she inhaled suddenly and looked around. The other Runners were watching her curiously. What Runner would refuse a massage then berate his partner? It was so much easier when they had been alone.

Wren bit her tongue and mercilessly thrust back the tears that fought to reach her eyes. 'Fine.' She squeezed past her audience to reach the bench.

'Lie down.' Raw cracked his knuckles.

Genna frowned. 'You'd better take them clothes off first, Runner.'

'Of course.' Wren looked at Raw with frantic eyes. If she took her clothes off everyone would see her breast bands. Raw hadn't given her away yet, so maybe he wasn't planning to. He had to get her out of this.

Raw's mouth twisted in what Wren could have sworn was a wry smile; then he pulled his own shirt over his head and handed it to her. 'Here, put that on. You can wear it as I rub you, keep warm.' He looked at Genna with an easy grin. 'He feels the cold.'

Genna nodded, she hardly seemed to notice Raw's scarring, her eyes instead focused on the crags of his chest.

For some reason Wren was compelled to turn away from Genna's flirtatious expression and her eyes fell on the shirt in her hands, still warm from Raw's body. She crumpled it between her fingers and shivered; it would almost be like wearing a piece of him. Resignedly, she pulled it over her head. It settled around her like a tent. Underneath its folds she started to undo her buttons.

Although she had warmed up since coming inside, her fingers tingled. After a moment of fruitless fumbling Raw's large hand covered hers'. 'Let me do it.'

'I don't think so.' She continued to scrabble stubbornly beneath the shirt.

'For the Designers sake,' he hissed under his breath. 'I'm going to rub you anyway, let me undo your damned buttons.'

Wren flushed angrily. Her eyes were level with Raw's naked chest, and she glared at the hairs frosting his skin, refusing to meet his eyes as he deftly unbuttoned the toggles beneath his shirt as though she were a three-year-old.

'What about your trousers?' He looked at her legs.

'I'll manage,' Wren snapped. She pulled at her laces, swearing under her breath, until they came apart; then peeled the trews away from her clammy skin. The material stuck on her boots and she kicked at it crossly.

Raw caught her under the arms and, before she could shout at him, dumped her on the bench. Then he knelt down and dragged her boots off, pulling her trousers after them with one fast yank.

Wren went still.

The heater burned her back. In comparison her front felt cold, yet her cheeks still burned. She clenched her fists impotently. She had to let Raw rub her or the others would get suspicious. If they found out she was a girl ... she took a deep breath. For her mother, she could take the humiliation.

Narrowing her eyes in silent warning, she swung her legs over the bench and awkwardly lay down. Every muscle protested and her skin tightened as her chest met cool aluminium.

For an age nothing happened. Having closed her eyes in miserable anticipation, Wren cracked them open. Raw was standing above her, holding his hands an inch over her shoulders, as if he was touching some part of her that she couldn't feel, almost as if she were still wearing her wings. The light reflected from his eyes and brightened them; underneath his scars were dark. Wren turned away once more, not wanting to see the evidence that her partner really did have every reason to hate her family.

As his fingers dropped onto her shoulders she tensed. Every muscle shrieked at her to get away. She forced herself to lie still and submit to his hands on her back. At least she was wearing a shirt.

But his palms burned through the material as if it was melting ice. She could feel every callus on his fingertips, every tiny change of pressure as he moved.

First, he rubbed her shoulders, working on the wing-made knots as if he actually knew what he was doing. For ages it felt as though he was pressing on bruises and she groaned as lumps of tension moved under her skin. Her own muscles popped and stretched but finally her shoulders stopped hurting.

As she let herself sag on the bench, she heard Raw's weary exhalation and knew it was tiring him out to be working so hard, and probably hurting his own shoulder.

He lifted his hands and she felt the loss of them for a moment before they returned and started stroking the knots in her spine.

When he had forced her back to loosen, Raw moved to her arms.

It was quiet in the hut. The other Runners had retreated to

the edges and corners and she knew some were working. One hummed under his breath.

Raw laid Wren's arm back on the bench and pressed her wrist between his palms, lengthening the tense ligaments and kneading as he worked his way up her fingers.

Wren snapped her eyes shut.

His hands moved again. This time he lifted her foot from the bench and started to work his way up her leg. There was no way she was going to relax now, not with his hands so intimate.

He kneaded her calf, then, hesitant as if he was reluctant himself, he moved up to her thigh. As her heart pounded, Wren turned her face towards the heater and inhaled hot air until her head started to spin.

Suddenly a gust of rain blew into the hut as the door slammed open.

Wren lurched onto her elbows; had Saqr brought her brothers?

13

A stranger walked in. Younger than the other men in the hut and darker skinned, his curls gleamed in the lamplight and his skin looked smooth as silk under a scattering of stubble. He was flawlessly beautiful.

Wren's mouth went slack as he shook back his hood. Then he shrugged off his tunic to reveal wide Runner-muscled shoulders and hung the garment on a peg behind the door.

Genna embraced him tightly. 'Orel. What did you find out?'

Orel's eyes went to the tableau by the fire. 'Later, Sphere-Mistress.' Shaking Genna off, he strode forward with his eyes on Wren.

Raw still had one hand on her leg. As Wren writhed, trying to feel less exposed, Raw half raised his other hand to greet the newcomer.

Orel's eyes never left Wren's. They were dark as sin and glinted with un-nameable mischief. A frown flickered over them as he gauged the weight of Raw's hand on Wren's skin, as if he somehow shared her fury at such intimacy.

Then he slid his gaze from Wren to Raw. 'Who are you?' he demanded.

Raw subtly shifted so his muscles caught the light and his scars slid into shadow. 'I'm a Runner. Who're you?'

Orel ignored him and looked back at Wren with the same question in his eyes.

She fidgeted under his gaze. 'I'm a Runner too.' Snappish under his scrutiny she sat, pulling her legs up under Raw's shirt.

Orel raised his eyebrows. 'If you weren't Runners you wouldn't be here. I asked *who* you were.' He narrowed his eyes in the direction of Wren's legs and she tightened her hands over her calves.

'I'm Wren,' she stuttered.

Raw placed a hand on her shoulder. 'I'm Raw. We're partner-Running.'

Wren shook him off and glared at Orel. 'Happy?'

Orel's chin dipped. 'In from where?'

Raw growled and Wren just knew that behind her back he was flexing his fists. 'We're from Elysium.' He spoke through clenched teeth.

'I thought I knew all the Elysuim Runners: Chayton's family.' A frown creased Orel's forehead.

Wren nodded quickly. 'I'm the youngest.' Her head spun as she tried to remember the story she had planned. 'Chayton's my father. Raw's from Cockaigne, he came to see about courting our sister. It's our first partner-flight in this direction.'

Cockaigne and Paradise were the colonies furthest from Vaikuntha. Cockaignians were known for their reclusiveness, its Runners least likely to be known to those here. Wren couldn't remember the last time a Cockaigian had landed in Elysium. Still there was a huge risk: a one in ten chance that the local Patriarch had Run from there to partner the Sphere-Mistress.

Orel said nothing, his chest rose and fell as he watched her with those intense brown eyes. Under his scrutiny, Wren had to force herself to remain still. But she jumped when the door burst open once more.

A gust filled the room with dust and Wren began to cough as Saqr stomped in, leaving smears of red sand on the blackened floorboards.

He wasn't alone. A figure lurked in the darkness behind the door, but Wren's tearing eyes and the smoke from the fire meant she couldn't see who it was. She rocketed off the bench. Her newly loosened muscles obeyed her much more easily, but still she lurched across the room. After such a long time lying down, she was unsteady on her feet and she stumbled.

Orel caught her with one hand. His fingers closed around

her arm like a bracelet and he raised his eyebrows as his fingers almost closed around her bicep.

Her skin tingled and she met his brown eyes. For a long moment neither of them moved; then Orel released her arm. Wren licked suddenly dry lips and resumed her run forward. But quickly she saw that the figure Saqr had brought was taller than Colm. This was not her brother. Her feet stuttered to a stop.

'Lister.' Genna blocked Wren's view of the man who was now sweeping off his long coat.

'I'm not staying.' His voice was smooth as soy-cream.

Wren turned to Saqr. 'Did you find news of my brothers? Who's this?'

Saqr nodded slowly. 'This is the Lister.'

'The Lister?' Wren felt like a puppet with no strings, unsure where to go. Her eyes automatically looked for the familiar and Raw slid from behind the massage table to stand by her side.

'What does that mean?' he asked.

Ignoring the question, the Lister stepped into the light and Wren's eyes widened; she had never seen anyone so completely bald. The light burned on the dark skin of his pate and shadows clung to the contours of his forehead and deepened his eyes.

At first, she thought he must be old, but then she realised that his eyebrows were black as beetles and she saw that as he stalked towards the table he moved purposefully, like her father.

Her eyes fixed on a bag that dangled around his neck.

When he reached the table, the Lister lifted the bag over his neck. When it thudded onto the wooden surface, he rubbed his shoulders and relief lightened his expression, as though the bag weighed on more than his muscles.

Then as the Lister opened the flap Wren leaned forward to see what was inside.

The bag contained a simple flat screen; solar powered, useful for doing straightforward calculations and containing information, notes and the like, that would be uploaded to central data banks later on. There weren't many operational ones left; Wren had only seen a couple of them in the hands of the Green-men at Elysium. They had run out of the components to repair them fifty years ago. To have one, this Lister had to be more important than he appeared.

The Lister pressed a button on the side and the screen brightened. He flicked to an application and opened it out, pulling the device to his chest to hide it. He sniffed at Wren and Raw. 'You're looking for your family?'

Raw's hand folded around Wren's wrist and she let it stay. She nodded her reply, barely breathing.

The Lister grunted. 'You think they arrived a week ago?'

Wren nodded again, her voice caught.

'Give me their names.'

Wren forced her words free. 'Colm and Jay. M-my father's Chayton.' She leaned closer, leaving Raw's hold. The fearful catch in her voice sounded strange to her ears.

The device uplit the Lister's face as the screen glimmered with a brightness that reminded her of the glow tubes in the CFC factories. He scrolled down pages, searching.

Wren edged closer and he turned and glowered, forcing her back into Raw's aura.

The Lister stopped reading, pursed his lips and sucked air through his teeth as if he was considering withholding what he knew. Then he spoke. 'Two of those Runners are here: Jay and Colm. Arrived seven days ago. Being held in block 7b.'

He switched off the flat screen and closed it back in his bag. Wren flinched as if her brothers themselves were being shut inside.

Part of her wanted to spin around the room; after all, her brothers were alive and she knew where they were. But her feet froze to the ground as a nameless dread slowly deadened her body. 'What do you mean *being held*?' she whispered. 'When can they come home?'

Above her Raw's breath warmed her newly shorn neck which now seemed sensitive to every disturbance in the air.

The Lister sniffed again. 'What's *your* name?'

Wren curled her tongue around the information. Suddenly she didn't want to give her name to this man; she didn't want it trapped in his bag.

But Genna answered for her. 'His name's Wren, in from Elysium.'

Wren cut her eyes to the Runner woman, then straight back to the Lister.

He nodded, as if committing her name to memory. 'Well, Wren, your father never landed here. Presumably his route took him towards a different colony, perhaps Tir Na Nog.' Another curl of his lip showed Wren what the Lister thought of that.

She opened her mouth to tell him exactly why she knew that was impossible, but for some reason Raw closed his hand tighter on her arm. Instinctively she obeyed his wordless warning and remained silent about the twinkling colony.

'Your brothers are being held with the other Runners who landed on the main wall – in quarantine.'

Raw's sharp breath seemed to suck the air from Wren's canister. Her chest tightened. 'In quarantine?' She spun to face Genna. 'What's going on?'

The woman twisted her hands in her rumpled skirt. 'We were going to tell you after you'd rested.' She gestured helplessly. 'There's an illness in the biosphere. It spread through the streets like a dust storm.' She gave a little moan. 'It starts with a fever and ends with death.'

'For everyone?' Raw asked, weak voiced.

'So far.' The Lister sighed.

The illness started with a fever? Wren thought of her mother. Then she thought of Tir Na Nog. *Had* they poisoned their own air, or had something *else* killed them?

A whimper tickled her throat and impulsively she clawed backwards until she felt Raw's arm under her own. His hand closed around hers' and she dug her nails into his flesh.

'That was why you couldn't land on the main platform.' Adler was saying. 'No-one, but the Lister, is allowed in or out of the town till this thing burns itself out. The Lister's got a free pass because well, we need someone who knows what's going on everywhere. You don't think there're usually this many of us in this hut, do you? Most of us are Runners who were out when quarantine started. Your friend over there ...' He indicated the smiling man, whose face was dropping. 'He's a Waller, his job is to make sure the wall remains air – and Creature – tight. A Grounder, not a Runner, but he was stuck outside, same as us and can't go back in.'

The Waller shrugged at Wren's hard look and Adler carried on.

'We don't know how the illness started and we can't risk it spreading until we find a cure. If your brothers landed on the main platform, they were taken into custody to prevent them from spreading the plague.' He rubbed his mouth. 'If this thing *does* spread it could wipe us out. Every colony: every last human on the planet. We might as well walk into the sand. We have to keep it trapped *here*.'

'*If* it spreads.' Raw's voice was a pale echo and Wren pictured her dying mother.

Wren swallowed. 'But ... are my brothers ill?'

The Lister consulted his tablet. Shook his head. 'Not yet.'

'Then you have to let them out. Send them home before they catch it.' Panic pounded through her veins and set her heart racing.

The Lister stroked his bag as if it were a restless baby. 'You Runners live in a different world, don't you? None of us can escape it, so why should you? Just because your brothers aren't ill now, doesn't mean they aren't carrying. They could fall ill tonight, or tomorrow. They're going nowhere.' His mouth flattened and he glared around the room. 'We don't know for sure where the plague came from but we've got ideas. It came from you Runners, from your travels.'

The Runner men grunted as if he'd struck them and the Lister narrowed his eyes. 'Maybe they made it in Aaru – all their work with crazy drugs – or in Paradise, or Arcadia where they mess around genetically modifying Martian species.

Maybe it's a local thing brought to life by the stage of the terra-forming, like Caro's. We don't know, but we're checking our records right now for surges in illness after landings. Once we can prove this is your fault ...' He fell silent, as if only then realising that he was surrounded by the very people he was insulting.

Adler started forward and The Lister shouldered his way past Saqr and out of the door. His bald head floated briefly in the darkness then the night wrapped itself around him and he was gone.

Wren stared at the men glowering murderously after the Lister.

'What does the Lister do that's so important?' she whispered.

Saqr turned to her with tragedy on his face. 'He's our record keeper. Right now, he's mostly keeping lists of the dead.'

'It's bad in there.' The Sphere-Mistress nodded in the direction of the walled Vaikuntha. 'Really bad.'

'Is it true?' This time Wren turned to Orel, her eyes pleading. 'Is it possible that *we* spread this? Runners I mean.'

Orel stepped towards her, his face dark. 'They can't know for sure. If it's like Caro's it could be carried in infected seed – that's how it started in Olympus. But it could be airborne, carried by Martian bugs, anything. They don't even know if the plague *is* anywhere else, so how can they blame us for bringing it here?'

'For *spreading* it,' Raw spat. 'He's right. Runners could be carrying it around the colonies – to *Elysium* Wren.' He shook her bruised elbow until she pulled away with a hiss.

'I *know*.' Tears sprung to her eyes. She didn't dare believe her mother's illness was caused by the Runners. If Mia had this plague the whole colony was in danger. She thought of the man coughing at the Doctor's surgery, had it already moved from Avalon to Elysium? But how was *that* possible? No, sometimes a cough was only a cough.

Another thought struck her like a rock to the chest: she had to hide the truth of her mother's illness from these people. If they thought Wren was already a carrier she'd be quarantined and left with no chance of finding a cure.

The weight of her secrets was suddenly too much and she sank onto one of the chairs. 'What do we do?' She looked at Raw. 'Fly on? If the plague is elsewhere, someone else will have a cure, won't they? What about Aaru?'

For a moment there was silence. Raw turned towards the door as if he was considering the wings leaning on the wall outside and wondering how much further he could go.

Then Orel sighed. 'We *have* a cure.'

'Orel!' Genna lurched forward.

Orel shrugged. 'Why shouldn't they know?' He held Wren's eyes with his own. 'Our biologists have been working day and night. The first patient's fever broke during the dust-storm.' He held up his hand to subdue her elation. 'We have something that works, but not *enough* of it. Not even close. We don't have enough ingredients and we lost the auto synthesiser years ago. Everything's slow time now. The Council's favourites will be all right perhaps, but the rest of the colony … I don't know what will happen to them.'

'*That's* what you found out?' Genna looked stricken and her skirt suffered another series of brutal twists. 'How?'

Orel squinted across the room at her. 'People don't look up. You'd be amazed what you can hear from a rooftop.' His eyes were bleak. 'The Council needs scapegoats. When the rest of the settlement realise the cure isn't reaching them, the Council plan to aim their anger somewhere else – at the quarantined Runners.'

'Their anger …' This time Wren's voice created the echo. 'It doesn't matter how the disease is spread; they're going to blame us anyway.'

'I think so.'

'How much time do we have?' Adler's fists were clenched in front of him, as if he planned to personally rip through the walls of the biosphere.

Orel shrugged. 'They're looking for proof, anything they can use. If a Runner comes in with news of plague elsewhere, or if they *can* find evidence ...' He exhaled. 'Not long.'

His words rung in Wren's mind – *news of plague elsewhere* – shaking, she dropped her head into her hands. They could not tell them about Tir Na Nog, not if it was possible that the plague had destroyed the colony. Her mother was dying of what sounded like the same illness. Her brothers were about to be thrown to an angry mob, and she was pretending to be a Runner, leaving herself open to the most horrifying of punishments. 'What am I doing?' she murmured.

'What?' Orel frowned at her.

'I – I –'

Raw grabbed her hands, pulled them from her face and shook her. 'Get a grip, Wren.'

Suddenly Adler leaned over her, throwing a twisted shadow on the wall. 'You're not a real Runner, are you?'

'What?' Raw spun to face him. 'Don't be ridiculous, man.'

'Not you.' Adler growled at him. 'That one.' He indicated Wren with a tilt of his head. 'He's far too young to be Running. No muscles where a real Runner would have 'em.' Abruptly he crouched so he and Wren were eye-to-eye. She flinched. 'You took those wings without permission, didn't you, boy?'

Wren's breath caught, but ... Adler had called her 'boy'. He thought she was too young to Run; he did not suspect the truth. Still holding her breath, she gave a tiny nod. Raw edged closer to her side and Wren's eyes widened. It almost looked as if he was ready to protect her. Perhaps she could trust him not to give her up.

She swallowed. 'What are you going to do to me?' Involuntarily she glanced at Raw.

Adler straightened. His eyes slid past the Sphere-Mistress and the Waller, to the other Runner men.

Genna shook her head. 'We can't have wings going without permission.'

Wren pressed herself into her seat.

Orel nodded towards Raw. 'At least they were partner-Running. And they are looking for other Runners.'

Adler sighed. 'There's protocol. If the last Runner in a settlement is lost, the Council have to wait for the next arrival, then they can send a message to Convocation for a replacement.'

Genna wrung her hands. 'So many Runners are in quarantine here.'

'We haven't had a Runner in for weeks,' Wren whispered.

Raw raised his chin defiantly. 'How long should we have waited? No harm has been done. We did a partner-Run and we did it fine.'

Wren looked at Adler with pleading in her eyes. 'I know I did wrong,' she murmured.

Genna caught Adler's arm. 'He's only a boy – a Runner boy – one of our own. These times aren't normal.'

'Do you think we should ignore the law?' Adler narrowed his eyes.

Saqr took his arm. 'We can't make a decision like this without the Patriarch, brother, and there're more important things to talk about than disobedient children. What do we do about the quarantined Runners? If we don't get them out of the settlement –'

'They'll be killed.' Raw stated the fact unemotionally, but his eyes slid to Wren and he flinched.

'More than that.' Saqr looked miserable. 'When Convocation finds out what they've done here, it'll be war between the Runners and Grounders.'

Wren's eyes widened. The Runners would refuse to fly and trade would end. The baby exchange would vanish and inbreeding would decimate the Colonies within generations. In return the Runners would lose their support and they would starve. It could be the end of everything.

'We have to get them out,' she whispered.

'Yes, we do.' Orel nodded. 'But feelings against Runners are running high. They'll have blocked off my usual route in and out by now. I barely made it out this time.' Genna gasped but Orel shook her off. 'I'm fine, and I have another way in, remember. I'll have to start using it.'

Adler nodded. 'So, we use your 'other way' to go for the others.'

Orel shook his head. 'No offence, big man, but *you* can't get in my way and the other Runners can't get out.' He looked at Wren and Raw. 'There're only two here who could go with me.'

Raw closed his hand over Wren's shoulder. 'No chance. It's too dangerous.'

Wren whirled around. 'Since when do you tell me what to do?' She stepped to Orel's side. 'I'm going after my brothers.'

Raw hesitated. 'At least rest for tonight.' He appealed to Genna. 'We've been flying non-stop. '

Genna looked at her son. 'What do you think?'

Orel shrugged. 'A day to plan – it might be a good idea. I can't break the others out on my own – we need them.'

Wren nodded. 'All right then, one night to rest.' She sighed as the idea of sleep brought a flood of weariness. Head in her hands she wondered how her mother was and if she'd managed to eat anything. She would be expecting her home around now.

Fingertips pressed against her neckline. 'Are you sure about this?' Raw's voice was low and deep.

Wren spoke into her palms. 'My brothers are in there and –' She stopped herself before she mentioned the cure. 'I'm going in,' she snapped.

Raw sighed. 'Fine.' He turned to Raw. 'We'll go with you tomorrow.'

14

'It's a reasonable request, Chayton. The children are old enough not to need their mother so much. The girl could even come with her. She could enter the Women's Sector like a respectable female instead of training for this … unnatural life.'

Wren was beneath the Runner-sphere, balancing a pile of rocks, when the voice floated up the path.

Her father's footsteps crunched on the gravel but the sound of his tread was offset by a quicker, heavier step she didn't quite recognise. These must belong to the owner of the voice. Strange; it sounded like her grandfather, but he never left Elysium.

The men didn't know she was there. A thrill shivered to her toes; she was hearing something she shouldn't. Kicking over her rock tower she wriggled further into the shadows; maybe she could hear more.

'I'm not talking about this any longer. You asked me to meet with you, I heard your 'reasonable request' and I denied it.'

Wren clenched her fists: her father's tone held a clear warning to the speaker; he had to back off.

'Chayton, you aren't thinking. She's given you children: two boys to be Runners and, if you insist on keeping the child at Avalon, a girl to bear more. She's met your needs your line will continue. Now let her go.'

Let who go? Were they talking about Mother? Did she want to leave?

Anxiously Wren wormed her way to the front of the house. There she saw her father and Grandfather. She clenched her fists to her chest, fighting not to cry out: 'she doesn't want to go, you nasty old man, she doesn't want to leave us.'

'There's a good partnership waiting for Mia in the settlement if you let her go. The man has waited a number of years for you to grow tired of her.'

Wren shoved her knuckles into her mouth to stifle a gasp and saw her father's shoulders shoot back.

Then her eyes widened as her grandfather's face crumpled. His shoulders slumped as though someone had cut an invisible set of strings and his voice was almost a whisper. 'I'm only going to beg once, Chayton. We miss her. Please, let her come back to the Dome.'

Her father shook his head and she saw him spread his hands. When he spoke, his voice was astonishingly gentle. 'Win, she wouldn't go.'

'Have you asked her? Have you?'

Her father shook his head and made no reply.

What did that mean? Wren held her breath. Had he asked her, or not? Did her mother yearn to leave Avalon and live in the Dome again? She leaned forward until the sunlight teased her fingertips.

'Well then.' Her Grandfather glanced down at his tunic and slowly flattened the material against his thighs. When he looked back up, his face was once more set in hard lines. 'Aside from Council business you'll not hear from me again. Mia's no longer my daughter, she's a Runner. Make no mistake I'll have nothing more to do with her, or any of your brood.' He raised his voice until it carried into the house. 'You hear, "Sphere-mistress"? Don't ever come crying to me, because you'll get nothing.'

Wren woke with a gasp. She was curled up under the table with Raw's shirt gripped in her fists like a blanket. Despite the eerie calls of the Creatures, the snores of the other Runners and the pressure of Raw's O_2 canister against her side, Wren had fallen asleep almost immediately, exhaustion dragging her under. Perhaps it wasn't strange that this particular memory would resurface now. She should have remembered it earlier; recalled Grandfather's warning against asking him for help.

At least now she had another way to help her mother. There was a plague, but there was also a cure.

Slowly she unfurled, muscles protesting as she adjusted her O_2. The others were snoring in bags around her and she carefully stepped over bodies. She needed to pee. Web hesitated at the latrine curtain. She was used to going with her brothers around, but not these strangers. And what if one of them opened the curtain and saw her sitting? There were many things she could do just the same as any boy; going to the toilet wasn't one of them.

She glanced at the door then made up her mind. She would go on the rock. It was probably where the latrine was emptied anyway.

Tiptoeing to the exit, she pushed her halfie further into her nose. She licked her lips as she touched the door handle. Without a biosphere there was no difference in atmosphere between the hut and the night sky. The air might even smell better outside. She *would* be able to breathe. Still her heart raced, and she held her breath, as she opened the door and slid beneath the stars.

At first, she clung to the wall and made no attempt to inhale. The sky above her seemed vast and the stars further away than they did from Avalon. Phobos was already starting to set in the West, the bright star of Deimos almost directly overhead. Her chest tightened. If she wanted to pee, she would have to inhale.

Breath shivered from Wren's lips, tinting the cold air with mist. Grimacing, she forced herself to trust the tube and sucked air in through her nose.

Her O_2 canister held, oxygen filling her lungs as it ever had. She just had to remember to breathe through her nose and not her mouth. Wren released her hold on the hut and slipped her toes along the rock. The Creatures were quiet now, perhaps seeking other prey.

She glanced towards Vaikuntha. The walls rose overhead, so vast that she could see nothing past them. The shimmering biosphere even blocked out the stars. She edged around the hut and saw that the rock the Runner-hut was built on formed a kind of bridge that ran all the way up to an airlock set into the black wall.

She undid her trousers and crouched on the rock, out of sight of the door. Urine streamed between her feet, steaming as it hit the cold.

She continued to stare at the black walls. How was Orel planning on getting them inside? Surely the airlock would be guarded. If she was caught or shot, her mother would die alone.

Wren shivered as she gathered her clothes back together.

She turned automatically, searching through the dark for Elysium Mons. Maybe she *should* just go home. She was only a girl. What could she do against a colony bent on murder?

If she went home, she could at least be with her mother when the end came.

Wren closed her eyes. Perhaps her father would return in time to take word to Convocation about Vaikuntha's plan. *He* could save her brothers.

She clenched her fists. Somewhere behind those walls there was a cure. Maybe her brothers had a little time, but her mother did not. If there was any chance that she could get to the cure along with her brothers, she had to take it. Wasn't it better to try and save her mother, than to be there to comfort her while she died?

She pressed her lips together and opened her eyes. Then she blinked. A figure was slipping into the Runner house.

She frowned. Had the Council of Vaikuntha decided to bring their remaining Runners into quarantine? She had to warn them.

Heart pounding, she ran on padded feet back to the door, but it was firmly closed against her. She put her ear to the panelling. There was no sound from inside.

Her imagination ran wild and she threw the door open, a shout already building in her throat.

There was no sign of an intruder. The Runners slumbered on, mouths slightly open, eyes tight shut.

Her eyes sought out Raw. He was stirring next to her spot, trying to get comfortable. As she watched, his eye opened. 'What're you doing?' he mouthed.

She shook her head. 'Nothing.'

Confused, she stepped back over bodies and crawled under the table once more. Maybe she'd seen only shadows after all.

As she settled into place her gaze fell on Orel, wrapped in a blanket near the doorway. He was studying her with serious eyes. After she had curled up, he kept his eyes locked on her for a moment more; then he rolled over.

Wren clenched her fists under her chin. There were a few

more hours till dawn and she'd need her sleep. She squeezed her eyes closed.

'Can you feel it now?' Jay pushed her hand further into the hole.

'What?'

'The nest is in there, just reach a little further.'

Wren stretched and her knuckles scraped against the stones that enclosed the side of the hole. Grit dug into her armpit. Then, suddenly, her fingertips brushed something smooth, hot, and oddly soft. She gave a little cry.

Jay grinned smugly. 'There you go. Those are her eggs. I've been watching her for weeks.'

Wren withdrew her arm. 'Where is she? Isn't she going to be angry?'

Jay shrugged. 'I'm going to catch one when they hatch – I'm going to have my own sand-snake.'

The sound of shouting from the Runner house stopped Wren's reply and she jumped to her feet. 'Another visitor?' she asked.

Jay shook his head and the sun shot highlights through his dark blonde hair. 'Mother would have called if there was a landing.'

Wren tucked escaping curls into her headscarf and caught her brother's elbow. 'Let's find out what's going on.'

Together they ran the short distance to the cliff path. There they were halted by a terrible cry: fury, frustration and grief wound together and punched the air, Wren had never heard such a sound. She gasped and Jay shoved her behind him. 'What was that?'

Jay shook his head. She gave him a shove and they pelted towards the house.

Just as they reached the safety lines the door slammed open and their father stomped onto the curved porch. His face was pale and his blue eyes almost black with rage. It was an expression that had become increasingly familiar over the past months. She shivered and dropped her eyes. Only then did she see the Grounder lying on the floor behind him, a pair of wings draped on a chair between them. The boy was trying to get up, but blood dripped from his mouth and he collapsed again, to face away from her.

'Jay, take your sister somewhere else.'

Wren's eyes flicked towards her brother.

'Who is that?'

'Do it, Jay,' their father snapped. A sun-shaft illuminated crimson spots on his shirt and knuckles. He looked down at himself and then he took a shuddering breath. 'Go somewhere else, both of you.'

Clearly it was not a good time to appear disobedient.

Jay had frozen. Gently Wren gave his hand a squeeze. 'Let's go find your snake,' she said.

'Wake up, Wren.' Raw's face floated above her, his scars glowing in the dawn light.

After her dream she couldn't stop herself from recoiling and for a moment she thought she saw a flash of hurt before his face assumed its usual hardness. It must have been Raw's voice that had screamed in her memory.

'Get up. We're eating and they're starting to plan.'

He stalked to the fireplace where Genna was serving bowls of soy.

Wren scrambled out from beneath the table and stretched. She rubbed her eyes and found Orel watching her again. He was leaning against the far wall with his breakfast on his knees. When he saw her looking, he saluted her with his spoon.

Her stomach rumbled and Raw shoved a bowl and spoon into her hands. 'Eat,' he snapped.

Although she hated appearing to obey him, Wren's hunger forced the spoon into her mouth.

Raw looked at Adler who was pulling his goggles over his eyes. 'Where are *you* going?'

Genna spun around. 'Adler! You can't Run – the only reason we're not quarantined with the others is so we can deal with incoming. If you leave, the rest of us will be on lock-down.'

Adler raised a hand. 'I know, but someone needs to let the Patriarchs at Convocation know what's happening.'

Genna tugged at her skirt and there was a long silence. 'All right then,' she said. 'It's a risk we need to take. But if the guards see you leave –'

Wren jumped up, grabbed Raw and pulled him towards the door. 'We're going to check on our wings,'

She dragged him into the open air and closed the door behind them.

'What's the matter?' Raw frowned.

'We can't let Adler go.' Wren dragged her fingers through her short hair.

'I don't understand – your father's at Convocation isn't he? I thought you wanted to get a message to him. You can ask Adler to speak to him when he gets there.'

'I did. I do. Chayton needs to know about Mother. But things have changed ...' Wren dropped her voice and stared at the walled colony. 'This is hard to explain.'

'I know it's torturous for you, but *look at me*.' Raw snatched her attention back to him and Wren swallowed a flash of anger. 'What's the problem?'

'What do you know about Convocation?' Wren asked.

'Just that you Runners have your own separate Government. Why wouldn't you want them here?'

Wren swallowed. Then she reached out a hand as if to touch Raw's face. Her fingertips stopped a feather's width from his scar and for some reason her skin tingled with the almost touch. She pressed her lips together before she spoke. 'You think my father was harsh when he refused to give you medicine when you got Caro's. When he beat you?'

Raw jerked back, as if propelled by the idea that she really would touch him. 'Harsh?' he spluttered.

Wren dropped her arm. 'Yes. You think he was wrong, that he went too far, hurt you too much?'

Raw grit his teeth. 'You could say that.'

'If he had told Convocation, you would have been tortured to death. That's what happens to Grounders who take wings. No mercy. If they find out about me, I'll be thrown off the platform at Avalon. The High Patrions never bend the law. They don't have families, so they can't be influenced.' She shivered.

'High Patrions.'

'A bit like your Council, but there's no rotation. At Convocation the Patriarchs debate an issue and the High Patrions decide.'

'Don't you want these people punished?' Raw gestured towards the colony. 'They've got your brothers.'

Wren shoved her hands under her armpits. 'Chayton tried to keep relations good between us Runners and you Elysium Grounders.'

'Rubbish.' Raw curled his lip.

Wren shook her head. 'Now you know what *should* have happened to you, but it didn't. Do you know what he should have been demanding as payment for his Runs? Do you have any idea how hard he works to keep Convocation from interfering in your deals? There's a faction that thinks we'd get more respect if we lived like Councillors. Father won't join them, but I think that's why he's at Convocation now, the High Patrions are making some sort of decision.'

'No way would we pay you more,' Raw snarled. 'He knows it.'

Wren's eyebrows raised. 'Even if Elysium was sanctioned – if you were unable to trade seeds for food, medicine or tech, even if Elysium was taken off the baby exchange register? Even then?'

'You –' Raw clenched his fists and stopped.

Wren hung her head. 'Chayton thinks we're heading for a breaking point, that it won't be long before people like you try to take our wings.'

Raw turned on her. 'That *should* happen.'

Wren rounded on him, her own fists curling. 'Really? You did so well without me that first flight.'

'I –'

'You don't understand how hard Running is. Runners have years of lessons before flying. And whoever took our wings wouldn't find out till it was too late. Not until the Runners were gone and they had broken the wings trying to fly for themselves. Then what? One day the last of the communications arrays will be broken by the mega-storms and the last of the spare components will have rusted. What if, on that day, there are no Runners, or no Runners willing to carry messages between the colonies? You need us. But we need you too. We need each other.'

Wren stopped. Raw's face was pale and drawn. She turned back to the biosphere looming above them. 'Things could be better.' The sun was rising above the walls, a blazing ball that pitched the stone into black shadow. 'But they could be so much worse. If the High Patrions find out what the Vaikunthian Grounders are planning it'll mean war. And if the Patriarchs come here and find us – you know what'll happen then.'

Raw's jaw tightened. 'We can't let Adler Run.'

Wren nodded. 'I know.'

The hut door opened behind them and Adler ducked beneath the low frame. He nodded at Wren and Raw. 'I'm heading out.'

Raw blocked Adler from reaching the waiting wings in their clips. Only when he squared up, did Wren see how broad Raw really was, how huge he would become in a few years.

Adler noticed too. 'What're you doing?' The big man frowned.

Wren stepped close to him. 'Don't Run yet. Give us a day.' She touched his arm. 'If the Runners haven't been freed by tomorrow night, *then* Run to Convocation.'

Adler shook her off as Genna joined him on the rock. 'What's going on?' she looked at Raw.

'Our visitors don't think I should make the Run to Lake Lyot.'

Genna frowned. 'We've made our decision. He has to go *now* – every hour could count.'

Raw folded his arms and his biceps became subtly more defined in a way that, for some reason, dried out Wren's mouth. 'Orel said he needed us to get the Runners out. If Adler Runs to Convocation now, *we* won't go into Vaikuntha.'

Genna faced Wren full-on. 'That so, Wren? I thought you wanted to get your brothers.'

Wren swallowed. 'If Convocation comes here, you won't be able to control what happens. It'll lead to war.'

Genna looked at Adler. 'The boy's right. The first thing the Patrions'll do is place sanctions.'

'And the rest of the colonies will lose the expertise of the macro-biologists.' Raw spread his hands.

Genna twisted her hands in her blouse and looked at the wall. 'It'll mean more mutated babies.'

'And when your current batch of soy crops run out the colony won't get fresh seeds from Eden or Elysium. There'll be no tech plans from Olympus, no drugs from Aaru. Everyone will go hungry.' Wren touched Adler's arm again. 'Do you understand why we're asking you to wait?'

Adler glared. 'And if we wait too long and the Runners get killed? Convocation will punish *us*, the Grounders will have who knows how many wingsets in their possession *and* there'll be war.'

'*One* day.' Genna straightened. 'Give Orel one day to get the Runners out. He says he can do it. Once the Runners're free we can tell Convocation what happened here. There'll be a cost, but not so far reaching.'

Adler glared; then he wheeled back into the hut. 'We're giving them a day to get the Runners out,' he snapped at those inside. 'I'll go to Lake Lyot tomorrow.' He looked sourly at Wren who was hovering in the doorway. 'We have news by twilight tomorrow, or I Run.'

Orel rose to his feet. 'Big man, you'll have *good* news by then.' His smile seemed to be for Wren alone. 'Now, we have some planning to do.'

15

Wren sat on the sun-warmed rock. Only the blinking of her eyes betrayed her alertness; she was watching the sun go down.

The rock beneath her legs had been steadily cooling as the afternoon wore on but it continued to radiate a gentle heat that soothed her still-tight muscles and made her unwilling to move.

They had talked until a dust storm had made speech impossible, and planned for every contingency. Wren's throat was hoarse, she was done with talking. Now she was just waiting for the sun to go down.

The door closed behind her and Raw stretched out next to her. She did not take her eyes from the sun. It had reached the top of the wall. The black stone cut a slice from the orb and swallowed it. No longer a perfect round, the sun continued to sink, sending a glowing line along the top of the biosphere, as if it was setting it on fire.

'Looking for the way in?' Raw squinted at the settlement.

Wren shrugged. Now the sun was nothing but a bright sliver and the wall's shadow slithered over her rock. She pulled her feet up to her chin, needing to stay in the light for as long as possible.

'We don't have to do this.' Raw's words made her turn her head. When she looked back the sun was gone.

She allowed her legs to slide back onto the blackened rock. 'Yes, we do.' She looked at his frowning face. 'At least *I* do. You don't. Why don't you go home, Raw?' His mouth opened and she pushed on. 'You don't know my mother, you fight with my brothers, you don't like me. Why not just leave me here?'

Raw's fists clenched on his thighs. After a moment he spoke. 'I already told you, you saved my life. What kind of person would I be if I left you alone?'

Wren swallowed. 'Think of it as payment for what Chayton

did to you. We're even. If you want to, you can go.' She hesitated. 'Orel will look after me.'

Raw snorted. 'I bet.'

Wren narrowed her eyes. 'What's that supposed to mean?'

'Nothing.' He turned his face away.

'Raw?' Wren frowned and he snapped a reply without looking at her.

'I've seen the way he looks at you.'

Wren snorted loudly. 'He thinks I'm a boy.'

'Then I've seen the way you look at him.'

'I –' Wren fell into silence. Orel was beautiful, there was no denying it. How it must hurt Raw, who had once been handsome himself. Suddenly her chest bands felt tight and uncomfortable and she fidgeted, snappish. 'What do you care who I look at?'

Raw shook his head still without looking at her. 'I just don't trust him.' His eye met hers' again. 'I'm not leaving you alone.'

'He's a Runner, Raw. Runners don't betray other Runners. And he's going to rescue my brothers.'

Raw's eye twitched. 'You're trying to get rid of me because you want to be alone with him.'

'Yes, so he can figure out that I'm a girl and have me tossed from the top of the wall for blasphemy. You're being ridiculous.' Wren ground her teeth. If anything, she wanted Raw to stay. He was a breath of the familiar, a part of her home, and the way that he was trying to protect her made him seem much less hateful. But how could she tell him that.

'Understand this then.' Raw leaned against the hut. 'The more of us go in, the better chance we have of some making it out. If I go in, your brothers have a better chance. So why are you trying to talk me out of it?'

Wren closed her mouth just as the door opened behind them.

'Sun's down.' Orel nodded at the biosphere. 'Time to wing up.'

As Wren lifted the tarp, the breeze caught her wings and they fluttered with welcome, pearlescent in the twilight gloom. Wren stroked hers gently almost as if calming them; then she unhooked them from the clips that held them secure.

For a moment they billowed and pulled, as if desperate to be away, but Wren held them to her chest. With a sound like a sigh they relinquished all but the fluttering edges of the wind and bent to her will.

'May I?' Orel took her wings and held them out, waiting for her to slip her arms into the straps.

Raw grunted and lifted his own wing-set. As he did so one of the pinions flopped and dragged on the rock. Wren gasped, her own half-worn wings forgotten. 'They're damaged!'

Saqr pushed his way from the hut. 'Let me see.'

Wordlessly Raw handed his wings over and Saqr ran his hands over the weakened pennon. 'How did this happen?'

Wren winced as she remembered their first flight, Raw's arm being almost ripped from their sockets as he failed to get his wings to lock. Then she thought of all the punishment the wings had taken since: crashing into Tir Na Nog and fighting turbulence.

Next to her Raw rubbed his shoulder. 'We had some problems on the way.'

'But he landed fine.' Wren pushed towards Raw's wings; her brother's spare set. 'He was wearing them then.'

'They've weakened. This strut –' Saqr flexed the light metal with one hand. 'And here, see this connection? It won't hold for a long flight.'

Wren's eyes burned. As a future Sphere-Mistress she should be able to repair the wings. But if she tried, she'd give herself away: men didn't repair their own graphene.

'Can Genna fix it?' Wren refused to look at Raw. He didn't yet realise he could be stuck in Vaikuntha for the rest of his life.

Saqr rubbed a palm across his chin with the sound of a snake on sand. Wren watched him as though she could force his words to come out the way she wanted. 'Not fast.' He shook his head 'And not permanently. Right, Genna?'

The Sphere-Mistress stroked the wings. 'I could do a patch job on the connection, but it'll take me all day.'

Orel stepped into Wren's line of vision. 'We just need to get to the watercourse. Will they last that long?'

Genna nodded slowly. 'Probably.'

'*Probably*?' Wren felt as if a hand was around her throat and her voice was high-pitched. 'What if they fail?'

'Then I fall.' Raw swung the wings around his shoulders. He shoved his arms through the straps and tightened them in one smooth movement, as if he'd been doing it for years. 'They've got me this far.'

'Raw,' Wren's voice tailed off as if the hand around her throat had closed. She grabbed his arm. 'If the wings fail you could die.'

'If we get caught on the other side of the wall I could die.' His green eyes glittered and Wren knew the words left unsaid. *'and if anyone finds out what we've done.'*

Then he gave a tight smile. 'Anyway, you're my partner. You think I'm going to let you go in there alone and unprotected while the Sphere-Mistress works on my wings?'

'I'll be there.' Orel loomed on Wren's left.

'Yeah.' Raw's eye narrowed. 'Like I said …'

Orel's wings caught the breeze. The silver material swelled and glowed gold in the light from the hut. He looked heroic even with the offended frown that marred the smoothness of his forehead.

Raw casually curled his hands into fists.

Wren gripped Raw's arm. 'If your wings break you won't be able to get home.'

He hesitated and his scar darkened as he flushed. Then he looked at Genna. 'If I let them break into Vaikuntha without me, you could fix my wings up enough to get me home?'

She nodded. 'My patchwork would get you back to Elysium.'

'But if I stick with the plan and fly now and *then* they fail?'

She grimaced. 'If this shears,' she indicated a point on the dragging wing. 'I won't be able to do a thing.'

Raw looked at his feet, motionless as a rock in the wind. Then he raised his head. 'I'm going with you. The wings might hold.'

Wren's eyes widened. 'They might *not*.'

Raw gave a lop-sided grin and she blinked with surprise at the unfamiliar expression. 'Hey.' His eyebrows twitched. 'I've been lucky so far.'

He started to buckle Wren's straps for her. 'Remember, the more of us go in –'

'The better chance we have of some making it out.' She shivered.

'Right.' He patted the strap over her chest and glanced at Orel. 'Are we doing this or not?'

'We're doing this.' Orel gazed at the biosphere and Wren's heart gave a little skip as the wind lifted his hair from his forehead. She really had never seen anyone so handsome. Quickly she looked away, allowing herself to wish for one short breath that she didn't have to be disguised as a boy.

'See any guards?' Adler squinted in the same direction.

'I think we're all right. They're not looking down here.' Orel nodded towards the empty Runner platform on top of the black walls. Then he sidled closer to Wren. 'Stick close.' He raised his voice so Raw could hear. 'Follow me and do exactly what I do.'

'How are we getting into the settlement? You wouldn't say inside.' Raw sounded angry.

Orel tilted his head slightly towards the hut. 'We aren't all Runners in there, remember? I need to be able to use this entrance again and there're some secrets I don't want to just hand over. Even if Mahad seems a decent bloke, he's still only a Waller and Land-locked.'

Raw inhaled at the insulting term, and Wren quickly gripped his forearm. 'Fair enough,' she said to Orel. 'So, we just follow you.'

'It'll be obvious what you have to do.' Orel rolled his shoulders and moved towards the painted lines at the end of the rock. Then he looked back at them. 'Just make sure you do it.' He pulled his goggles over his head and started to run.

Wren's eyes were drawn to him as his toes thudded on the stone. His thighs bunched beneath his tunic and her heart pounded in time with his heels as Orel spread his arms, flicked his wrists and locked the struts. His muscles tensed again as he leaped from the end of the rock, toes pointed like a dancer, wings flowing like dreams in Deimos's starlight.

He swooped without hesitation into a funnel of air and ghosted into the darkness behind the hut.

Wren turned to catch Raw glaring poisonously. He pulled his borrowed goggles over his face. 'Your turn,' he grunted.

She glanced at the audience hovering in the hut doorway and lowered her voice. 'We launch in order of seniority – you're older than me, so you have to go first.' His shoulders tensed and Wren almost stroked his arm. 'You'll be fine. Just do it like Orel.'

This time Raw's grunt was wordless, but he straightened his back and turned to the launch lines.

Wren tensed as a shriek like a baby crying burrowed into her ears. The Creatures were back. She could hear them slither along the rock, a teasing of skin to stone, on and off, up and down. She grabbed Raw's arm. His skin was warm, almost hot despite the rapidly cooling air. He swallowed.

'They're waiting for a mistake.'

'Yes.' Wren nodded. 'Are you sure –'

'Shut up.' Raw shook her off and without looking at her he began to run. His feet hammered the rock like flat-irons and his wings fluttered erratically as the damaged strut kept them from evenly scooping the wind. His head was bowed, and the tendons in his neck stood out even in the near-darkness.

Wren held her breath. If he slipped off the rock, if the wind didn't take him, or the damaged wing failed, Raw would hit the sand. With the Creatures so close they'd never be able to rescue him. He'd be dead; bones at the end of another platform.

Heart in her throat, Wren saw Raw hit the red line; it was too late to turn back now, even if he tried to stop, he'd go over the edge. There was a hissing sound from the sand.

She gasped as Raw hurled himself from the end of the rock.

His legs flailed over the drop and he tried to lock his wings. His yell of frustration carried cleanly through the desert air.

Wren's fists clenched beneath her chin; she couldn't tear her eyes from him. She heard the watching Runners surge forwards as one, almost as though they could catch him and bring him back. She did not turn.

Raw kicked his legs, thrashing at the wind as if it would help. A gust caught his good wing and pulled it outwards, swinging him up and away from the sand. He flicked his left wrist again and again, trying to force the wing to lock the way it should, but it remained only half extended, slack where it should be stiff.

'We should never have let him try with those wings,' Saqr cried.

Wren's breath had stopped in her throat. Raw started to spin back towards the desert and Wren's eyes widened as the hiss she had heard sounded again, louder.

And then the wing locked.

Skimming the sand, Raw finally released his own relieved cry as the gust pulled him upwards. Throwing himself this way and that, he fought to find the thermal that had carried Orel.

Eventually he stopped fighting the currents and found his way, gaining height as he spun past the hut.

Shakily Wren released her breath and glanced at the door. Genna had pushed to the front of the group and was watching her warily. Wren pulled her own goggles over her eyes, trying to banish the sound of hissing from her ears. She gave Genna a little wave, shook her arms and touched her toes, overcome with gratitude for the massage and the rest that had loosened her muscles. Then, with a little hop, she started to run towards the slashes of colour.

Wren's wings filled and lifted behind her. Their noise encouraged her onwards like whispers in her ears *'time to fly.'*

She looked at her toes, which were barely brushing against the rock as she raced along.

First, she saw the blue line; grey in the shifting darkness. Then just one step later a stripe that seemed black: the red. If her take-off failed now, she would fall, a long drop with a short ending.

The hissing intensified as she came to green stripe, threw her arms out to her sides, felt both wings click into place and leaped.

There was a flash beneath her and Wren's eyes widened. Had she really seen a gaping saw-toothed maw surrounding a throat bigger than she was? She stared at the sand which was innocently sinking into a new depression. Whatever she had seen had vanished as swiftly as it had come.

Unearthly shrieks filled her ears, seeming to echo from the very walls of Vaikuntha. Briefly her arms vibrated as she withheld a turn. Her body wanted her to head home, away from the Creatures who lived so close here, the Runners who had been forced into a tiny hut, the dying Grounders and the situation that felt like the start of a war. But she overrode her impulse and veered.

Immediately the air around her warmed slightly. She was inside the thermal that had carried Raw and Orel away. She allowed herself to relax and turn her head, searching for them.

The darkness had grown and all she could see were flashes of Phobos' light from silver as the two Runners circled a little way above, waiting for her to join them.

Her eyes flicked to Vaikuntha. Along the length of the wall searchlights blossomed, but as the edifice curved towards the uninhabited desert, the light spots scattered and it went almost black. Assuming Orel headed in that direction, how would she and Raw be able to see him? And how long would the cooling air hold them up?

A flash of colour to her left told her someone had dropped and was pacing her. She glanced across to check the smoothness of his flight and her lips pulled into a grin: it was Orel. She dropped her head, presenting as small a target for the wind as possible. Then she pointed her toes and bent her arms into a slight vee. The wind rushed faster over her face and whistled like an accolade. Orel started to fall behind and she chuckled.

Then something made her look up. Orel had caught a

higher, faster current and was above her. She raised her torso, seeking the same height and Orel rolled. Starlight shimmered from the tops of his wings, the light of Phobos burned in his goggles. He looked almost inhuman.

Wren tipped her shoulder and rolled her wings back at him. The rushing wind tried to tumble her but she merely rolled back.

Then she caught sight of the wobbling figure dropping behind. They had almost lost Raw. Immediately she stopped racing until he had caught up.

When she turned again Orel had been swallowed by the darkness.

'Orel?' she panicked.

'I'm here.' His voice floated from her right.

'How do we know where to go if we can't see you?'

There was silence for a moment and she glided directionless, hoping he was still on her wing. 'Orel?'

'Runners fly in the sky.'

Wren frowned.

'Come on, both of you. Runners fly in the sky.'

Suddenly Raw's voice dropped from above. 'Creatures hunt …'

Words flowed across Wren's tongue, burning with memories. 'Boys lie,' she choked.

'Runners fly
    In the sky
    Creatures hunt
    Boys lie'
    Thunk, thunk. The rope swung along its arc, whipping the ground with each downward blow and then scything up, as if into the clouds. The two girls on each end sang as they turned their arms in huge circles.

    'Nitrogen, oxygen, argon rise
    Carbon dioxide fill the skies'
    Three other girls jumped in and out of the cable, kicking up puffs of dust as they ran from one side to the other, clapping one another's hands as they passed.

'Soy will grow when it gets warm
Hide us from the sand-filled storm.
Creatures hunt,
Boys lie.'
Wren watched from behind a rock, her fists clenched. It looked fun.
'Runners fly free
In the sky.'
She'd never be allowed to join them.

'Nitrogen, oxygen, argon rise.' Orel's voice was lower and further left, Wren dipped her shoulder. If they stuck close to the sound, they'd be able to stay on his tail.

'Carbon dioxide fill the skies.' Raw's voice blended with Orel's, deeper and more melodious than she ever imagined it could be.

'Soy will grow when it gets warm,' she called.

'Hide us from the sand-filled storm.' Orel's voice was still moving away and curving to the left.

'Creatures hunt.' Raw's voice was almost on top of her.

'Boy's lie,' she choked.

'Runners fly free in the sky.' Orel's voice grew fainter. Suddenly light glimmered round the curve of the wall and an alien sound interrupted the whisper of the wind.

Nothing like the shrieks of the creatures, or their strange hissing, this was more like the whispering of the leaves when Wren had run among the Gingko trees. Yet it was louder, somehow more purposeful, a determined rushing from one place to another. She stared downwards. Something below her moved and glittered and a gust of wind brought a splash of cold onto her face.

'Water!' Wren's heart jumped. They were over the course, close enough to hear it, touch it even. She inhaled. Her nostrils, even filled with the plastic tang of her halfie, still picked up a fresh perfume, clean, something that reminded her of Elysium's ferns. She wanted to taste it.

She wished she could see better in the growing dark.

Raw flew beside her, his own fingers spread as if to catch the flying droplets on his palms.

'We're here,' Orel called.

Wren squinted downwards. 'I don't understand. Where are we meant to land?'

16

'Just follow me.' Wren's heart jumped as Orel's voice plummeted. He was heading downwards, but she couldn't see much of anything, let alone a swathe of rock large enough to make a safe landing away from the Creatures.

She followed closely, the cold air even colder above the river and knew that if she got this landing wrong, she was in deep trouble. There was no way she could fly back to the rock before morning. In Phobos' light, she watched Orel drop his legs. Wren frowned. All she could see was the dark ribbon of water that widened with each passing moment.

'What's he doing?' Raw echoed her thoughts. 'Is he landing?'

'Where?' Wren's frustration made her loud.

Orel's legs started to kick; he was well into his landing sequence. He must know about a rock or platform hidden beneath the wall but did he realise she and Raw could not see it?

She started to call out, but before her lips could open, there was a splash and Orel's wings blinked out as if snuffed. Wren gaped. He had landed in the river.

She tore into a circle in an attempt to arrest her own descent and scanned the rushing water frantically.

'Did you see that?' Raw's voice stabbed into her ears.

Wren ignored him. There was no sign of Orel. Was it possible that he had landed in the river *on purpose*?

'Burn it.' Wren stared at the river, straining for a sign of the other Runner, but he had utterly disappeared. Curses stained her lips but she bit them off, who knew who might hear her.

The wind was growing colder and the air thinner. Wren risked a glance behind her. The night-weakened air threatened to drop her, but she wobbled in place and maintained her height, seeking a sign. Behind them the lightless wasteland stretched back around Vaikuntha. They had to follow Orel; he had known they would.

She recalled him telling them to follow him *exactly*.

'What're you doing?'

She ignored Raw's shout and started into her own landing sequence.

Wren tensed as she dropped. Foam rushed her legs, soaking her boots and trousers. She gasped; it was freezing, a cold so bone deep that her heart stuttered. But she was coming in too fast to change her mind. Hoping to see Raw, she flicked her gaze behind her. He remained overhead, blotting out the stars. Not following, but not trying to leave either.

Wren started to kick; swimming in the air as a prelude to the real thing.

She began to inhale but before she'd planned it, her legs plunged into the river. Shock stole the breath that was meant to sustain her.

Her trousers stuck to her thighs as the wind tugged at her one last time; then she was submerged up to her armpits.

The water dragged her, heavy. How could it be heavy? And it was so bitterly cold that it burned.

Frantically Wren lifted her face, forgetting for a moment that her O_2 canister would keep her breathing even as the water dashed into her nose and over her goggles. She tried to haul in a deep breath but the cold constricted her lungs and she couldn't.

Her wings pulled her arms back; then the water took over. The silver material caressed the air one last time then fluttered to the surface, bulging and swelling as it was swamped.

Wren was buffeted along, gasping and spluttering. Her wings only just kept her afloat and she had no sense of the river's bottom.

Panicking, she swallowed a lungful of icy water and flailed, sobbing for breath. In the depths something touched her ankle. A Creature? Could they swim?

Graphene tangled round her like a cocoon as she threw her arms about. Suddenly she was rolling and kicking against her own wings.

Pain crackled through Wren's shoulder as she bounced from a rock and spun back towards the centre of the watercourse. The shrinking rational part of her knew she had to calm down.

A wave washed over her head and plunged her underwater. She closed her eyes and tried to shut her ears to the river's roar. Struggling madly, she felt the brush of air on her cheeks and opened her eyes again.

It was pitch dark.

Kicking and thrashing she tried to roll, her mind blank with dread. Why couldn't she see anything? Had the blow to her head blinded her?

The water still carried her forward, but the noise had changed, it was deeper, denser and more echoing. She was travelling under the wall.

Wren fought to free one of her arms and managed to tear her right one loose. Floundering madly, she tried to keep her head out of the water, but she was tiring.

In a terrible counterpoint to the cold that seeped into her bones, Wren's throat burned. Cramps gripped her muscles and tremors made her waving hand spasm.

Suddenly she caught a flash of light, but she was so disoriented and moving so fast that she couldn't tell where it was.

'This way.' Her ears carried Orel's voice and she tried to reply, but couldn't open her mouth. *I can't get to you.* She thought. *I can't swim.*

Abruptly her boot caught on something and she kicked feebly.

'It's me. I've hooked you.' As Orel pulled, she tilted and water rushed over her face.

She was being drawn against the current but it fought to keep her. Her ankle hurt where Orel held it, but it was a dim secondary pain compared to the cold.

Suddenly she swung round, thumping full length against a solid surface. Hands shoved into her wings and round her shoulders and she was wrestled out of the river, over a stinging boundary and onto a hard floor.

The world spun once more as her wings were untangled and pulled to her sides. She coughed, rolled and pushed herself up with flattened palms. Slowly her heart stopped hammering. She still panted, but now it was cold rather than terror that shortened her breath.

Sitting in front of the small heater at home, her feet in her mother's lap and her head on Colm's shoulder, she had not believed such a chill could exist. She tried to move her feet and found her legs completely numb. Her lips quivered in a weak sob.

She leaned her head against her frozen right arm and groaned. The violence of her clattering teeth made her jaw ache.

'You all right?'

Wren wiped her tangled hair out of her face with unfeeling fingers. She could barely control her hands.

'Speak to me.' Panic rose in Orel's voice.

She glared at him. 'S-so, c-c-cold.'

Orel nodded. He was shivering almost as violently as she; his clothes clung to his skin and his wings hung limp at his sides. His goggles were tucked into his belt and his grey eyes were bloodshot. 'Here, take this.' He held out the solar light, and Wren realised that the bulb was giving off a little warmth. She pulled off her goggles and wrapped her hands around it, willing the heat over her exposed skin.

'Your partner's coming.'

Raw! Wren spun around. A furious shout echoed around them and immediately following the noise, a silver figure bundled from the tunnel mouth and into the slower water by her feet.

Now Raw stroked strongly against the current, jaw held high, solid as a rock and determined as ever. How did he know how to do that?

Orel held out his hand, but Raw ignored it, powered to the riverside and stopped with one hand on the edge. He ripped off his goggles and threw them to the floor; then he looked for Wren. Only when his eyes had settled on her did he haul himself free of the river.

Wren watched him emerge, wings dragging behind him, shedding water as if it was oil. One of them hung at an awkward angle and she bit her lip hard enough to draw blood. The water had finished the job the wind had started. Raw wasn't flying from Vaikuntha after this.

His face was white even in the gentle solar light and his lips were compressed with barely suppressed rage. His scars had darkened in the water; they were blacker than she had ever seen.

'You could have warned us.' He poked Orel viciously in the chest. 'We went in there completely unprepared.' His teeth were chattering as badly as hers and his lips were blue.

Orel knocked his hand away. 'I told you why I didn't tell you. We made it didn't we?'

Only then did Wren look round. They seemed to be inside a cave, but it was like no cave she had ever seen. She touched the wall with tingling fingertips. It was smooth but the light showed tiny cracks where blocks had been mortared together. 'What is this place?' she stuttered.

Orel dropped to his haunches. 'We're inside the wall, within the watercourse. The colonists invented a way through the wall for the river that wouldn't affect the seal on the biosphere. This cave was built for the workers.' He gestured with hands that still shook with cold.

Wren rubbed her hand over the stone. 'We're *inside* the wall.'

Orel nodded. 'To get to the other side, there's a small, one-man, airlock further down. It was built for the original engineers but it won't be guarded. Since the water level submerged it, they've forgotten it even exists.'

Raw's shadow suddenly fell over the torch. 'Fascinating as this is, how do we get to that airlock?'

Orel's eye twitched angrily and Wren stared around her. There was no other way out of the cave. 'We have to go back in the water, don't we?' Her dismay brought Raw to her side.

Orel nodded. 'And now you'll see why the other Runners couldn't come with us.'

17

At some point the cavern they were in had been blocked off by a huge grid. When Orel pointed, Wren held the solar light higher to see that there was a gap, about the length of a man's body, between the grating and the brick wall. Debris nudged up against the lattice: bones that bobbed and banged, floating ferns and pumice-like stones unable to move further in.

Raw frowned at the barrier then folded his arms. 'We're trapped.'

Mischief glimmered in Orel's eyes. 'Looks like it, doesn't it?' Orel knelt down and reached his arm into a gap between the wall and the grid. He tugged and the grid peeled upwards.

Raw nodded understanding as Orel tugged until there was a gap big enough for the three of them to slip through.

'The wall doesn't go down to the bottom of the river. Water has to get into the settlement. And as I said, there's a small airlock down there, beneath the wall, drowned and forgotten.' Orel glanced at Wren. 'Be careful, the edges here are sharp.'

Wren bit her lip and Orel leaned down to squeeze her shoulders. 'I'll go first. I'll open the airlock and keep it cycled green for you, so you won't need to do anything but float through. You'll need to be quiet though, so no-one hears you on the other side. Leave the light.'

Reluctantly, Wren moved out from beneath his arm and propped the light against the wall nearest the hole. Then she looked at Raw. He was glowering at the black water as if it had offended him. 'You all right?' she murmured.

Raw turned the force of his glare on her. 'Fine,' he snapped.

There was a gentle splash as Orel slid beneath the grid and into the river. Wren watched his muscles flex as he fought for control against the sucking current.

He glanced at Raw and pushed his water-darkened hair

back from his forehead. The flame caught on his chiselled cheeks and turned them from dark olive to pale copper. Wren's breath caught and she had to struggle to focus on his words.

'We won't be coming back this way, so last one down needs to pull *that* back into place.' He gestured at the grid, registered Raw's curt nod, then turned with the current and dived. His feet kicked once on the surface; then he was gone.

Wren's breath shortened.

'I don't want to go back in either.' Hesitantly Raw patted her shoulder. 'You'd better go next if I have to pull this thing shut behind us.'

She pressed her lips together, skin already crawling at the memory of the cold. Then she thought of her mother and brothers. Somewhere past that wall her brothers needed rescuing and she had to get hold of the cure Orel had mentioned.

'Suck it up, Runner,' she muttered to herself. She sat on the rock, careful not to trap her wings beneath her. Gingerly she slid one foot into the sucking water. Immediately her leg was pulled away from her. She tugged it back out and took a deep breath. The cold didn't seem as bad as she'd remembered: her skin was still numb. Before she could change her mind, she threw her whole body into the current.

Unable to stop a gasp, Wren at least managed to keep her head above water by holding onto the grid with fingers turned to claws. Her wings floated out behind her, then slithered underneath, tugging her down, in league with the current.

'Go.' Raw was sliding his legs into the river, just as she had. 'I'll see you on the other side.'

Wren released the wire. She barely had time to turn her face in the right direction before she was pulled down. Pretending that she was flying, she shaped herself into an arrow and let the river tug her towards the wall. She forced her eyes open, saw the gap as a darker hole and reached towards it. Her fingers jarred against stone with a thud that made her whole arm shudder. Her hands were too deadened for her to tell if she'd broken bones and she had no time to try bending them.

She groped for the gap and pulled herself through, easily clearing the breach.

As soon as she thought she was past, she started to kick. Her heel smacked against brick, but she kept going, aiming herself upward and breathing through the halfie in her nose.

And then there was the light of an airlock, flashing green, cycled open as Orel had promised. Struggling towards, it, Wren managed to grab the edges and haul herself inside. She floated in the lock, her wings streaming around her. Orel was on the other side of the aperture, his palm pressed against the reader, holding it open.

He gestured to her to come forward, his arm laggard in the dragging water. Wren nodded and kicked, bubbles streaming out behind her as she reached him.

He gripped her shoulder with one hand and steadied her against him.

Wren looked behind her. The water was black and there was no sign of Raw. She squinted into a darkness that was alleviated only by the glow of the airlock, seeking the brightness of his silver wings. Where was he?

She shook Orel's arm and pointed, trying to get him to understand. He shrugged, eloquently uncertain.

The airlock began to beep. Wren's eyes widened: the automatic cut off was kicking in and it was going to cycle closed with or without Raw.

Raw couldn't swim any better than Wren; if he was left behind, would he manage to operate the reader and turn the handle underwater as Orel had done?

Wren wanted to shout for him, the words bubbled in her chest, but water pressed against her from every direction, filling her mouth. Was it possible to get lost in the tunnel; what if he was turned around?

She watched in horror as Orel pulled his hand from the now useless palm reader and the airlock cycled shut, leaving nothing but murky water on the other side.

She kicked to the door and, as the water drained out, she pressed her face against it. As soon as air touched her face, she shouted his name: 'Raw!'

Orel pulled her back and pressed his hand over her mouth. 'Quiet, someone might hear you.'

His fingers dug into her cheek until Wren nodded acknowledgement. He released her and she stepped back, her wings pooling around her like a cape, the water already at her knees.

'We can't just leave him.' Tears burned on Wren's icy cheeks as she whispered.

'Once he reaches the airlock, he can open it himself.'

'And what if he can't?' Wren thought of Raw thrashing in the water, fighting it as thoroughly as he fought the air with his wings. 'What if he's hurt?'

'He's got his canister on.' Orel tried a smile. 'He won't run out of air. Worst case he'll go back to the cave and wait for us.'

'But there's no other way out of there.' Water sucked at Wren's ankles, foaming in the blinking airlock light, as it was pulled through grids to either side of her. She looked back up to see Orel watching her with a strange intensity to his gaze.

Then Wren remembered the stone gap. She had cleared the brickwork easily enough, but Raw's shoulders were almost as broad as Adler's. Orel had refused to bring the big man, telling them he couldn't use the route he planned.

'You knew this would happen,' she gasped. 'You knew he wouldn't get through that gap.'

Orel leaned over her, his breath warm on her face. 'Do you want to save your brothers, or not?'

'Of course –' Wren stepped backwards, her feet splashing gently on the drying floor.

'He wouldn't have let you do this without him. He wouldn't even stay behind for a damaged wing. It's easier this way. He'll wait in the cave and we'll come back for him when we're out. He's safe.'

'No.' Wren hissed. She flung herself back at the airlock and pounded on the palm reader.

'It won't open until the floor is completely drained,' Orel sighed.

Desperate, Wren peered through the scratched window and out into the endlessly moving darkness beyond. Was that a flash of silver? She pressed her nose to the glass.

The silver was gone, if she'd ever seen it.

Slowly she turned back to Orel. 'You tricked us.'

Orel had the grace to hang his head. 'I had to. I'm sorry, but I have friends in here too. I need you to help me get them out. This isn't a one-man job.' He looked up at her, his brown eyes damp with pleading. 'Forgive me.'

'He'd better be all right,' Wren snapped, but her heart was melting as fast as her skin was drying in the cycled air.

Orel nodded. 'He'll be fine.' He kept his voice low. 'We'll get the rest of the Runners out and then go back for him. I can take a rope through and Adler can pull him out along the river.'

Wren leaned her forehead on her arm. 'I can't believe we have to leave him. What if something happens to us? No-one will know he's trapped there.'

Orel didn't move.

Wren looked at him again. He wrapped an arm around her shoulders and she shivered with more than the cold.

'If I don't make it out, promise me you'll go back for him.'

Orel squeezed her hand. 'I promise. He might even find another way out.'

Hope warmed Wren's frozen chest. 'You think so?'

'Sure.' Orel turned around and pressed his palm against the opposite wall. The door cycled open with a sigh and he stepped through, pulling her with him. On the other side there was a tunnel; in it the water came up to Wren's knees. She splashed towards lights that glimmered at the other end.

The tunnel ended and Wren moved out of the shadow of the wall with Orel at her side. He gestured at the city beyond as if her were offering her a gift. 'Well, we're in.'

Wren followed his gaze, her heart pounding. She had never thought to see a colony other than Elysium and now, with Tir

Na Nog, she was seeing two. Part of her shrank back: Tir Na Nog, despite its exotic beauty, had been horrifying. What if Vaikuntha was the same, or worse? But excitement made her pulse race. She was going to see inside the great walled colony, perhaps even the giant pyramid, her brothers had told her about.

Ahead the water channelled in different directions; creeping in squelching boots, Orel led her along the widest course. The river's complaint formed a backdrop to the more familiar sounds of human habitation.

True night had fallen now and the settlement was lit wholly by solar lamps and the flickering glow of gas hobs that burned through windows like blue eyes.

'It's so quiet,' Wren muttered. Her wings moved over her sopping jacket. 'Is it always like this?'

Orel shook his head. 'There's a curfew – it's part of the quarantine.'

They slunk between the first clusters of houses huddled in the gloom and Wren was hit, almost physically, by how different they were from those she knew. Like Elysium and Tir Na Nog, Vaikuntha had been built by colonists who assumed their biosphere would be coming down and it had been built to withstand Martian storms.

The wall was the first of their defences, a vast barrier against the Creatures and the wind. Its presence allowed the houses to grow taller: two-storied, rather than one. The ground floors were each broader than the next floor up and they reminded Wren of a child's brick tower.

The streets themselves were protected from the winds that would one day come, by canopies made from a thick material. Wren could imagine them snapping with a night breeze, but they had remained unstirred for more than a hundred years.

As they scuttled along on numb feet Wren hunched her shoulders, feeling trapped by the boards over her head.

She looked up between the warp of two mismatched sheets

and saw the biosphere far above her, so high that it felt like part of the sky. Near transparent from this side, she could see Phobos almost at apex. The amorphous silicon made the moon seem stained and decayed.

Wren swallowed back a moan, unable to banish an image of Raw trapped under the wall. She should have made him stay behind. She clenched her fists. One rescue at a time: first her brothers, then her Running-partner.

A loud cry cracked her determination. Orel's hand closed around Wren's wrist and they froze. The wail sounded again, close by and he pulled her into him and leaned them both against a wall, trying to melt into the shadow of an overhang. Her wings trailed in the dust, so Orel caught them up and wrapped his own wings around them both.

'Creatures?' Wren whispered.

'They can't burrow beneath the wall. Just to make sure, the Council let off concussions directed into the earth every few months. The Creatures come no closer than the Runner Station. They don't dare.'

'That was human?'

Orel nodded and, as Wren wondered what kind of throat could have made the sound, it came again and Wren jumped as a door across the street flung open and something was shoved over the threshold by a stooped man, who was choking on his own coughs. The high-pitched wail continued inside, but was muffled when the door slammed closed.

'What is it?' Wren frowned.

Orel looked furtively left then right and then he wrapped Wren's hand in his still damp palm. Their wings billowed behind them as they scuttled over to the bundle. Orel lifted the corner of the tattered blanket with the toe of his boot and Wren shoved her bruised fingers into her mouth to stifle a shriek: he had uncovered a small hand.

Orel propelled her from the house and they ran into a lightless alley the length of a terrace.

Across their path a fallen joist had snapped like a broken limb. They scooted underneath. The awning above their heads flapped unsupported and there was a long tear in the fabric. They ran with the narrowing of the alleyway as if driven.

Wren's hand remained in her mouth and as air whistled from her halfie into her nostrils, she noticed the smell, a scent her own full-sized mask would have protected her from: pungent, slightly sweet and overwhelmingly rancid. It was the smell of a poorly ventilated sick room and it tainted the air all around them. Now that she was aware of it, the odour clung like a shroud she couldn't shake.

Then her foot slipped in something soft. Bones splintered under her boot and she gagged, instantly horror-struck. Orel caught her by the elbow as she squinted to see a dead bun-bun pet rotting against the wall.

'The sooner we get out of here the better,' Orel muttered.

They helped one another navigate the rubbish that was strewn across the end of the alley. Then they peered past the final corner into a narrow street. Here the houses formed taller stacks of blocks with gently sloping roofs. Solar lights were secured to posts outside each door, but most of them were unlit. Only two glowed, like the last beacons on a battleground.

Windows gaped like gashes in each wall and most of the doors had splashes of crimson paint daubed on the metalwork. Grey dust clung to the doorsills.

Five more rolled bundles lay in the street and Wren swallowed as Orel's bicep moved against her neck.

'Let's go,' he whispered.

She nodded but just as she was about to step into the open an oscillating squeal jerked her to a stop and her eyes narrowed as a heavyset man plodded from the gap between two houses, pushing a huge barrow with a squeaking wheel.

Behind him, bald head shining in the lamplight, followed the Lister.

Orel's arms tightened around her again and they watched, barely breathing, as the Lister paused by the nearest wrapped bundle. As he leaned over, the bag containing his flat-screen dangled over the body.

'Stop,' he snapped and his companion dropped the barrow

with a thud. A whisper of cloth carried like an echo as something inside shifted and settled.

The Lister pulled the screen from his satchel. He glanced at the door of the house and his hand moved as he added text. Eventually he nodded and the attendant bent down. He twitched the blanket aside, and the Lister seemed to hesitate. Then his hand moved once more as he added to the note.

'Done,' he muttered and the big man scooped up the bundle then tossed it into the barrow, blanket and all.

Wren dug her nails into Orel's arm. They clung to each other like children hearing nightmares rattling their shutters.

At each bundle the Lister repeated his actions. Wren burrowed her face into Orel's clammy shoulder, terrified of the small glimpses of the dead that the collector was inadvertently offering them: a wilting hand, a tangle of hair, a still foot.

Then from the corner of her eye Wren saw the Lister bend over. Curious, she had to see what had detained him. A shaft of light revealed a small doll dangling from his hand. It had fallen from one of the bundles. He held it for a moment then his shoulder jerked as though he were going to toss it into the barrow. Eventually though he shook his head and gently tucked the beloved thing back inside its blanket.

Wren's eyes watered and her throat closed. Then the Lister and his companion started to move away, the squeak of the heavier laden wheelbarrow accompanying their otherwise silent journey.

18

Wren stood silently in the circle of Orel's arms until he gave her a gentle shake.

'This ... this ...' she had no words.

'I know.' He squeezed her shoulders. 'But when it burns itself out, then we'll rebuild.'

'You think it'll burn out?'

'It has to.'

Wren thought about Tir Na Nog. Everyone there had died. But it must have happened quickly; too fast for word to get out. Why had it hit them so fast while the Vaikunathans had time to find a cure? Were the Vaikunthans stronger? Or had the disease originated in Tir Na Nog, and weakened somehow since? Perhaps Orel was right and it would burn itself out before it hit all ten colonies.

Her hope felt naïve, but if the disease had been generated by the microbiologists of Tir Na Nog, then it couldn't have been the fault of the Runners.

She met Orel's eyes with a frown. 'You sound like you hardly care.'

'Of course I *care*,' he growled. 'You want me to curl up on the ground and cry like a baby. I'll do that.' He paused. 'It won't help get your brothers back.' He held her shoulders tightly. 'Wren, this isn't as much of a shock to me as it is to you.'

'I know but –'

'Do you want to stand here and talk about how awful this thing is, or do you want to rescue the Runners? What if they have a more effective cure somewhere else? What if they've developed a replicable drug in Aaru? If we let the Council execute the Runners, who'll fetch it?'

'No-one.' Ruthlessly Wren pressed both horror and hope back into her stomach. Orel was right. If the Runners died, the colony would die, one way or another, if the illness didn't destroy it, the inevitable war would.

As she drove herself to a semblance of calm, something rattled in the alley behind them. 'What was that?' She jumped.

Orel turned. 'What?'

'That noise?' Wren stepped backwards.

'I'm sure it's nothing.' Orel blocked her body with his own. 'But if some Grounder is breaking curfew we'd better move. We can't be seen.'

Wren frowned into his broad chest then nodded. 'Which way?'

Orel looked into the street. 'They're holding the Runners in the centre of the colony, in a part of the council building. We've got some way to go.'

'Then we'd better move.' Wren turned and started to march. Orel squinted doubtfully down the alley then followed.

It wasn't long before Orel had to take the lead. The layout of the settlement was too confusing for Wren to aim herself in any one direction and the floor was so covered in litter that she had to watch her feet all the time.

When she tripped noisily on a discarded cook pot, Orel gripped her arm. 'We're going to get caught,' he growled.

'I can't help it.' Wren snapped. 'How are you missing this stuff?'

Orel seemed to float through the alleyways like a ghost.

A noise inside the nearest building made Orel drag her into a tiny lane. 'You're right, this isn't working.' He looked up. 'We can do it here.'

'Do what?' Wren tried to follow his gaze, but there was nothing above them but another canopy.

More noise behind them filled Orel with urgency. 'Up you go.' He grabbed Wren around the waist and she gasped as he boosted her upwards. 'Grab the roof – got it?'

Wren stretched, but her fingers touched only smooth wall. 'No,' she gasped.

Orel got his shoulders beneath her knees and shoved her higher. 'Now?' he asked.

Wren's fingertips curled round the lip of the first floor and Orel managed to balance her toes on his shoulders. Wren got an elbow onto the roof and, with Orel pushing from below, managed to pull herself up.

She held a hand down for Orel but he waved her away, took a few steps back and jumped. With one foot against the wall, he pushed himself up and caught the roof just as she had, with one hand. Wren grabbed the neck of his tunic and when he was beside her, she looked up. They were sitting on the top of the first floor of the house. The canopy was attached to the brick just above her head. If she rose, it would brush her hair.

'Now what?' she whispered.

Orel ripped the canopy away from the brick. It flapped onto the ground like a broken wing and Wren blinked at the destruction.

'A few months ago, that would have been repaired by morning,' he sighed. Then he held his fingers to his lips. 'Sleeping quarters are usually on this floor. There'll be someone right there.' He pointed to the wall by her shoulder then he helped her to her feet. 'Up again.' He boosted her once more upwards.

She reached towards the sky and caught the roof of the next level.

Sitting on the highest point, Wren stared out over the settlement. Although it was mostly dark, solar lanterns glowed intermittently like sickened stars. Sporadically illuminated by their guttering glow she saw a sea of canopies. The river's prattle was distant and Wren almost relaxed, allowing herself to imagine that the scene below the material was tranquil and safe.

She could see a pattern to the rooftops now. The lights cobwebbed into the centre of the settlement and in the middle … her mouth fell open … there was the pyramid her brothers had told her about. It rose through the darkness, one, two, three, four … eight stories high. And that building was still lower than the walls, which hemmed them like the edge of the world.

She shivered, still damp from the river and hugged her arms to her chest. At least the colonists in Elysium could see the desert and sky through their biosphere. These people saw nothing but ceilings and walls.

Orel crouched behind her and smiled. 'What do you think?'

Wren exhaled. 'Is that the council chamber?' She pointed to the pyramid.

'Yes, and the labs where the scientists work on the GM. That's where the bun-bun pets were developed from dead-earth rabbits. Even if the Runners have been moved, they'll be nearby.'

'It's huge.'

'Bigger than the council chamber at Elysium.' His eyebrows twitched. 'But then we have a much larger population. Are you ready to run?'

'Run?' Wren judged the rooftop with a frown. 'This isn't big enough for a take-off.'

'Not a real Run, we'll jump between houses and use our wings to make the extra distance.'

Wren squinted at the space before the next roof. 'There's no wind under the Dome.'

'We'll be making our own.' Orel walked to the far edge of the roof. 'Try and be light on your feet and *don't* shout – if a guard sees us, we'll be in trouble.'

Wren's heart thudded. 'You're sure they're *all* looking outwards?'

'They're watching for incoming Runners, aren't they?' Orel bent into a starting position. 'Don't lock, just let your wings lift you.'

Wren inhaled nervously. The nauseating smell was less strong up here, but the air was still tainted and she shivered in her sodden clothes.

'Here we go.'

She hopped out of the way as Orel hurtled towards her. He hit the edge with one foot, leaped towards the next roof and opened his arms. Wren noticed however, that he kept his elbows slightly bent, allowing his wings a flavour of the blighted air, but not letting them fully engage. As he'd said, they lifted him just enough to bring him the last couple of lengths to the next house. A thud told Wren he had landed and his wings glittered as he shook the air from them.

He gestured at her to follow but, instead, Wren tip-toed to the edge of the building and stood over the wet footprint he had left behind. The gap she had to cross was around four of her own body lengths. If she didn't make it, she'd crash through a criss-cross boarded canopy before hitting the ground below.

She took a deep breath. Orel had done it, and although she was smaller than him, she was lighter. Her wings could carry her.

She turned her back on the drop and walked, as Orel had, to the far end of the building. Then she dropped into a crouch, took a deep breath, rose to her toes and ran.

The jump was easy; it was harder to remember to keep her arms bent. Her muscles wanted to listen to the wings; both demanded that she fling her arms outwards to catch a full lock, but Wren resisted.

Even when her jump started to turn into a fall, she held steady until her wings billowed and powered her over the brickwork.

Orel caught her as she crashed into him. 'Okay?' he whispered.

Despite herself Wren grinned. 'Race you to the middle.' She broke away from him, stepped backwards and sprinted for the next roof, arms held crookedly outwards. This time she was lifting almost before she jumped and she glided higher with no jerkiness. On the next roof she barely landed – just let her toes touch the brickwork with the barest of brushes, before jumping for the next.

In the corner of her eye she could see Orel one rooftop over. If she leaped diagonally, she'd cut him off. With a silent whoop, Wren sprinted to the corner of the building and leaped across, almost swiping him with her wingtips as she overtook him.

He was bigger than she and his legs were longer, but Wren was lighter and ultimately faster. Each jump took her slightly ahead of him until she looked back and found herself three buildings ahead.

Then she gasped and her feet tangled together, dropping her full length onto the roof. Was that a figure behind them? Wren rose onto her hands and squinted into the darkness. But as soon as she tried to see more clearly, the figure, if it that was what it was, vanished into the shadows.

Orel landed next to her with a gentle thud. 'What happened?' He offered her a hand up.

'I thought I saw someone.' Wren leaned around Orel still trying to see.

He looked over the twitching canopies. 'I can't see anything,' he whispered.

'Not any-more.' Wren continued to glare into the shadows. 'Could someone be following us?'

Orel's frown matched hers'. 'Maybe on the ground, but not up here, how could they be?'

Wren shook her head. 'I don't know.' Then she straightened. 'Look. There. Something moved.'

Orel stepped towards the roof edge. 'I still can't see anything.' He clenched his fists and leaned into the darkness. Then he turned back to her. 'The Runners are what's important. If there is someone following us, wouldn't he have shouted for the guards by now?'

'I guess.'

'You're in a strange place. This must all seem very odd.' He gestured at the rustling settlement. 'It's probably just your imagination. But just in case, let's run faster.' He smirked down at her. 'Or maybe you can't go any faster.' He suddenly sprinted away from her.

'Oh, no you don't!' After a last quick glance behind them, Wren bounded after Orel. She'd beat him to the centre and they'd get her brothers out, strange pursuer or no.

They stopped at the rooftop just before the giant pyramid. Now it appeared even bigger, rising above Wren's head and taking up the whole world.

'This is where we get off.' Orel slid off the roof edge, used his feet to create a gap in the canopy below and dropped silently through the hole. Wren followed him. As she dropped, Orel caught her by the waist then gently lowered her to the top of the ground floor. His hands pressed her wings to her sides and almost touched at her belly.

When he released her, he remained where he was, so close that Wren's breath fogged on his wings. He tucked a tangle of hair behind her ear and then turned away.

'Nearly there.' He dropped the final storey to the ground and held his arms out for her.

Wren dangled from the roof and let go, trusting that he would catch her. Again, Orel paused before releasing her. Then he faced the pyramid. Only the bottom level of the building had windows and when Wren peered to her right, she saw that faint light illuminated the street with stripes. Her heart started to pound. Those windows were barred.

'There! That's where they are.' She started forward and Orel seized her, enclosing her so that her back was pressed against his chest.

'Wait and watch a minute. They won't be alone.'

'All right.' Wren subsided into his arms then she craned her neck backwards. He was hunched over her and their position put her lips were a breath away from his.

'Wren,' he croaked. 'You *are* a girl aren't you?'

'I –' Wren was caught between the need to run and the desire to stay. The possibilities made her gut tighten.

'It's all right.' Orel's breath warmed her neck. 'I knew from the moment I saw you.' His mouth twitched into a smile. 'I know a girl when I see one.'

Wren twisted to face him. 'Why didn't you say anything?'

He shrugged. 'I guess if you had already got here, you had already proven you could Run, right?' His thumb touched her cheek and she froze. 'Anyway, you are partner-Running, it isn't like you're alone.' He stroked his thumb down to her jaw. 'And you're better than *he* is.' He trapped her chin in both of his hands. 'I've seen you Run, you're better than a lot of grown Runners out there.'

Finally, his lips closed the tiny distance between them and his insistent hands pulled Wren to her toes. She gasped into his mouth. Her eyes closed and her whole body tingled with a new awareness.

Then rough hands grabbed her from behind and she was dragged into the open.

19

Orel's yells faded behind her and Wren struggled, frantically kicking but still keeping silent as if her quiet would prevent more joining the mêlée.

Hard hands closed around her shoulders, more around her hips and legs and she was carried, squirming, trying to see what was happening to Orel as he disappeared into a wall of bodies. Everything was happening so fast. How had they been caught so easily?

Finally, Wren found her voice. When she started to scream the guard holding onto her legs pinched her calves and tears came to her eyes. Still she kept shouting for Orel. Her wings were dragging in the dirt, tangling in the feet of the men who carried her, as if they were trying to save her. What if they got damaged? She struggled more frenziedly. Who would rescue her brothers now?

A heavy door slammed opened and the men manoeuvred to get her inside. Wren looked up, desperate for a last glimpse of the sky. Phobos winked at her through the Dome, then the ceiling closed overhead, the door slammed and the sky was gone.

The men dumped her in the centre of the room and stepped back. Wren leaped to her feet, already looking for a way out, but she was surrounded. She turned to the doorway, looking for Orel, but the door remained stubbornly shut. Had he escaped, or were they taking him somewhere else?

She didn't want to be alone. Her knees shook, almost unable to hold her weight, but something told her she had to remain standing.

She wrapped her arms and wings around her chest and her

eyes darted around the room. There were five men with her: two by the main entrance, one by the barred window, two by another door in the rear of the room. The room itself was empty, apart from a desk and chair against one wall.

The Vaikunthans had the look of brothers, dark eyed and thick necked, but Wren noticed their flaking skin and red-rimmed eyes. Two had weeping sores around their mouths. She didn't want to feel anything for them, but it was obvious that they were sick, exhausted and scared. Her heart shrivelled and she turned, trying anxiously to keep each of them in sight.

The one by the window stooped like a gingko in a storm. Then he coughed into his hand.

The plague! Automatically Wren covered her mouth with one sleeve.

Fury in his eyes, the coughing man lurched across and, half choking, pulled her hand from her mouth. Wren flinched back from him as he raised a hand to strike her and the door in the back of the room opened.

Wren's eyes flicked to the swinging door and stayed as a man emerged from the darkness. A satchel hung from his neck and his eyes drew the shadows until his face looked like a skull beneath his bald crown.

'Lister!' Wren cried and the guard dropped her arm and scuttled from her side.

The Lister ignored her. Instead he stumbled wearily to the desk, lifted the satchel over his head and dropped it on the table-top. It landed with a thud and settled with a puff of air, as if it were sighing.

Freed of his burden, the Lister stood a little straighter. Then he turned and looked at one of the guards. 'You did as ordered?'

The guard gestured towards the middle of the room, where Wren stood, still trembling with damp-infused cold.

With a whisper of flesh-on-flesh, the Lister rubbed his palm over his bald head; then he crossed to her. 'You shouldn't have come here.' He took her chin in one hand. 'Yes, I see it now.' He nodded. 'The Councillor can use this.'

He turned his back, dismissing Wren. 'Usual procedure. Take the wings. Put the Runner in 7b.' He remained standing with his back to her. 'There's a space in Cell Three.'

The coughing guard returned to her side, spat and gripped her elbow painfully. 'Three's occupied, Sir.'

The Lister's hand hovered over his satchel. 'After dawn it won't matter. For now, let the little beast have company.'

Instinctively Wren had started to pull free of the guard's sweaty fist, but the Lister's words stopped her. 'What do you mean, *it won't matter after dawn?*'

The Lister's hand rested on the satchel now, as if it was too heavy to raise. 'At dawn the whole settlement will hear who caused the plague.'

'You found proof?' Wren whispered. '*Runner's* did this?' All she could see was her mother's face.

The Lister ignored her question and Wren was pushed into a short corridor. At the end was a gaping storeroom piled high with wings.

Time seemed to slow as Wren took in the sad condition of the discarded beauties, dumped any which way. She inhaled and her fists sprung closed: the room had been used as a toilet.

Incandescent with rage, Wren struggled wildly. The guards fought to restrain her as she battled to reach the wings that she had spent her life maintaining.

'Stop it, beast.'

'Well, this proves it, don't it?'

'Let me go.' Wren flinched as one of the guards laid greasy fingers on her chest array. 'Don't touch my wings,' she shrieked, but he mercilessly unbuckled the straps and pulled them free, adroitly avoiding her thrashing limbs.

As the man lifted her wings from her back Wren felt suddenly exposed. The air cooled the wet patches of her shirt and she felt unnaturally light.

In the guard's arms, her wings were lifeless. He wasn't holding them properly and his fingers left greasy smears on the glimmering graphene.

'You'll break them,' Wren sobbed. But the guard ignored her

and tossed her wings over-arm into the storeroom, where they cart-wheeled over the pile and clattered towards the back where they stopped with a sickening crunch.

Wren gasped and slumped in the men's hold. Bereft of her wings she barely protested as they dragged her along a second corridor.

Soon they stopped outside a repurposed airlock with a number three daubed on it. Dried crimson paint had dripped down the metal like blood. The guard palmed the reader and it slid open. Wren had no time to peer inside. A hand shoved her in the back and she flew forwards. As she fell against the far wall the door slid shut and she heard the locks click into place.

In every way possible, she had failed.

Although Wren wanted to curl up and die, she forced herself to remain upright. The Lister had said something about 'company'. Was there another Runner in here?

Slowly she took in the cell. The musk of body odour irritated her suffering nostrils and the stench of a full toilet burned the back of her throat. The smell was shatteringly bad, but it finally chased away the taint of sickness that had lined her tonsils since she had landed.

And there was something familiar about the scent, Wren took a hesitant step towards the window where light from a distant alcove ignited the bars and created a striped pattern on the floor.

There were two figures in the cell with her. Neither seemed particularly large; young Runners, she was certain.

Then one of them stepped across the light.

As if hurled from her feet, Wren threw herself at the Runner and wrapped her arms around his neck. Sobbing she buried her nose into his collar. He smelled as if he hadn't washed in a week, but it was her brother – it was Jay.

'What the …?' Jay tried to push her off, but she clung on.

'I'm *so* happy to see you.'

'Who are you? Colm get him off me.'

'Colm!' Immediately Wren released Jay and looked for her older brother. At first, she could see nothing but his eyes glittering through the darkness.

Colm was watching with his usual serious expression, but in response to Jay's outrage, he stepped into the light. Wren clutched her throat. His cream jerkin had turned to grey and a yellowing bruise flowered on his cheekbone. He still wore his full mask, and it covered his face so that she couldn't tell what he was thinking.

Unable to control her feet, she ran towards him but he raised one hand. The gesture was so like their father's that she almost skidded as she halted her charge. 'Colm, it's me.'

Silently he rubbed his thumbs over his curled knuckles and made no move towards her, but Jay's gasp echoed through the cell. 'Wren?'

'It can't be.' Colm lifted her to her toes. His eyes widened. 'It *is* you.' He shook her, hard and her head snapped back and forth, a sharp headache crackling at the base of her skull. 'How did you get here?'

When Wren didn't answer, his eyes blazed with fury. 'You took the spare wings! How *could you*?'

'Colm …' Jay tailed off.

Colm dragged her so close that his words left spit on her cheeks. 'You've no respect for your family or Runner-law. For Skies sake, Wren, was it worth it? You'll die for this.' His jaw tensed. 'Then what happens to Avalon? There'll be no next gen Sphere Mistress. You selfish *brat!*' Wren tried to wriggle free, but he gave her another hard shake. "Father's no due back from Convocation for ages. Is that why you did this? Did you think no-one would find out?'

'I had no choice.' Wren twisted under his grip to find Jay. 'Do either of you have the plague?'

Jay blinked and answered her in a strange high voice. 'No. We're fine.'

Colm's eyes were, in shape and colour, just like their mother's, but the beetling brows curving over them were their father's, as was the expression burning in their depths. 'What do you know about the plague?'

Wren swallowed. 'Mother has it.'

Colm released her and rocked as if she had swung at him with a joist. 'And you just *left*?'

'You don't understand,' she cried. 'Father's still away, you never came home. I needed *help*.'

Jay wrapped his arms around his chest. 'What about Grandfather Win?'

With a shudder, Wren thought back to her humiliation at their grandfather's hands. 'You think I didn't try? He sent me away. The Grounder Doctor just gave me a few analgesics and they wouldn't let me call Lake Lyot on the communications array. What would you have done?'

Colm bumped onto the bunk by the far wall and his shoulders hunched.

'Colm?'

'This is my fault.' He spoke through his long fingers. 'We should never have landed here.'

Jay backed against the airlock door. 'You *know* it isn't your fault.' His eyes were hunted. 'Colm wanted to wait because he wasn't sure of the flags, but I was so damn tired. I went to land and Colm *had* to follow me, he's my partner.' He gulped. 'How is Mother?'

Wren closed her eyes. 'She's dying.'

Colm sighed. 'And you didn't know how to read the flags.'

Wren shook her head. 'I didn't *land* here. We broke into the colony to rescue you.'

'We?' Colm frowned.

Wren opened her mouth; then closed it again. He couldn't know about Raw. 'Me and one of the local Runners, Orel.'

Colm nodded. 'I know him. Why would *he* want to rescue us?'

Wren swallowed. 'We didn't just come for the two of you. The Council here are going to blame the Runners for spreading the plague. We think they're going to execute you … us.' Colm hissed through his teeth and Wren nodded miserably. 'We've got until dawn.'

Her brothers leaped up and scanned the cell as if a way out would present itself. Restlessly Jay's hands searched the airlock door as if the metal would melt under his touch.

Colm's cheeks were so pale they looked transparent. 'Father was right. They think they don't need us anymore.'

'What are you doing, Wren? Come to the greenbelt.'

'Shush.' Wren waved. 'Listen to this.'

Jay crouched next to his sister and they pressed their heads against the curve of the wall. After a moment he groaned and stood. 'It's only Father and that Runner. What do you want to listen to them for? Anyway, we were told to make ourselves scarce until he left.'

'Why do you think I'm listening?' Wren grinned.

Jay tugged at her arm. 'You'll get in trouble if Father sees you. He told us to go away as soon as he saw him over the Runway; he even made Mother leave Avalon.'

Wren tossed her hair over her shoulders and pushed him off. 'Don't you want to know why?'

Jay shook his head. 'Not really, it'll be boring business.'

'Go to the belt then. I'll join you in a little bit.'

Jay huffed out his cheeks and turned away. His footsteps receded along the cliff path and Wren tuned him out as her father's voice grew louder.

'I'm not asking for greater payment, Ira. I don't want to discuss this with you again.'

'We should get more for what we do.' The man's voice was whiney and rasping. Wren curled her lip and wondered what he looked like.

'We have enough. We have food and clothing and we can maintain our equipment, what more do we need?'

'We should live better than the Councillors, Chayton. We have the power but we give it to them for free. Runners living like this, it's criminal.'

'We have a duty to our colony, Ira.'

'Bah.'

Wren heard the man's heavy footsteps on the floorboards. He was pacing. Her father's voice was muffled; he must have turned away from the wall, or perhaps covered his face. She pressed her ear harder to the sphere.

'I know things have got more difficult recently, Ira and that's why

we're having these talks. But asking for more isn't a solution.' She heard a thud. When her father got impassioned, he often thumped the furniture. 'It used to be that the Councils and Runners worked together, agreeing which Runs would be best for the colonies.'

'But they no longer ask, Chayton. They demand. It's been a long time since any of us were treated as equals by the Councils.'

Wren's father groaned. 'I know. They risk our lives as if they were nothing, sending us on pointless Runs. Did you hear about the Arcadian, Hawk?'

There was a pause and Wren held her breath.

Ira's voice filled in the blank space. 'I heard. He was sent out too close to the dust storm and crashed carrying a bolt of Cockaigne cloth for the head of their Women's Sector.' There was a pause and the footfalls stopped. 'See, Chayton, that's what I'm talking about.'

'It's wrong, but I don't know what we can do. Being as greedy as they are won't help.'

'We can do Runs for ourselves, not for them.'

'Why, because it's better to die carrying a pointless luxury if it's for other Runners? You'd better leave, Ira, because I won't do it.'

'You've no choice, Chayton, the other Patriarchs are in agreement, and Convocation will debate it soon. We have to demand more from the colonies, it's the best way to regain the respect of the Councils. If they see us living like beggars, they'll continue to treat us like servants. When they see us living like them, they'll treat us as equals. Maybe more – why shouldn't we be in charge? When the communication arrays finally go, we could be kings.' He paused. 'And why shouldn't the communications arrays break sooner rather than later?'

Her father's gasp was loud enough for even Wren to hear through the wall. 'You're talking about Sabotage? Don't mention that in front of me again!'

Sabotage – the dirtiest word in the Martian lexicon. Wren covered her mouth.

'All right, I was only thinking out loud.' Ira's voice faded, but Wren knew he hadn't just been 'thinking out loud'. He had been feeling Chayton out. Other Runners must have agreed with him.

She tried to think objectively about his proposal. What would it be like if Runners were kings of Mars? What would it mean for them?

She looked round. Would she really want to spend time telling Grounders what to do – she had enough on her plate already. Avalon couldn't be built any bigger; their biosphere was the size it was and there was no enlarging it. They couldn't have more things; where would they put them? More food? There was a good reason there were no fat Runners. Maybe a few new clothes would be nice, but she'd only ruin them when she climbed down the Mons-side to mend the nets. She shook her head and heard the airlock start to cycle open. Quickly she scrabbled round the side of the 'sphere and threw herself under the porch.

After a while she saw the figure of a Runner soaring into the currents, shrinking to nothing as he flew away. She toyed with her hair, teasing it between her fingers, playing a solitary game of cat's cradle. She waited until she was sure her father had gone; then shimmied out of the crawl space and climbed thoughtfully down the path to look for her brothers.

River water had created a damp patch on the bunk where Wren was sitting with her brothers. She didn't try to move somewhere drier; Jay's fingers twined in what was left of her hair as he tried to untangle the knots. He made little sounds of grief as he encountered each ragged curl and tried to pull the short length over his fingers.

Wren caught her breath as footsteps thudded beyond the barred window of their cell. She looked out. The light was changing from black to grey. Dawn wasn't far off; they'd been talking most of the night.

Colm looked at her, his eyes almost black in the burgeoning light. 'You say they have a cure?'

Wren dug her nails into the struts of the rickety bunk. 'Yes, but no way to synthesize enough.'

'Why aren't they sending samples to Aaru or Paradise to ask for help making extra?' Jay whispered.

Wren sighed. 'Quarantine. They're worried anyone they send might spread the plague further. It's almost ... noble.' She sighed. 'And ... I guess they aren't thinking clearly. They believe we brought the plague. They hate us – and they need us here if they want to carry out a punishment.' She rubbed her aching eyes. 'If any of us escapes we have to find the cure, or head straight to Aaru, to see if they have anything.' Her exhaustion caught up with her and she slumped. 'But we've had no Runners to Avalon from Aaru either. If they've not been quarantined here, the situation there could be just as bad.'

'We aren't going to escape, are we?' Jay stroked the last of the tangles from her hair. Now he could get his fingers through the curls without Wren flinching and she knew the small task had soothed him a little.

Colm's fists were on his knees. He sat, staring out of the window, as if carved in stone.

Wren's eyes wanted to close, but every time her eyelids drooped, terrible images chased their way across the darkness and they sprung open again: Mother breathing her last as she waited fruitlessly for Wren to return, Father returning from Convocation and flying into Vaikuntha to find the wingless corpses of his three children hanging from the walls.

Her fists flexed under her chin and she wished she could sleep. Beyond their window a sliver of sky peeked through one of the unused windbreaks. Wren could see tongues of pink licking at the grey. Phobos was still overhead, but the sun was rising.

20

Sounds from the corridor outside propelled them to their feet.

'They're coming,' Wren whispered.

Colm pulled Jay up beside him. Her younger brother had his fists closed so tightly that his knuckles looked like pebbles straining against his skin. Wren tried to stand by them, her own hands raised, but Colm shoved her behind him.

'You're my little sister,' he murmured and the look in his eyes made her stand back.

They heard a hiss. Then the airlock cycled open.

Silhouettes became a pair of guards. There were smudges beneath their eyes and, as Wren took in the sweat stains and smears of dirt on their uniforms, she felt another twinge. But when the men saw the three Runners up and waiting for them, their cruel smirks killed Wren's sympathy.

Boots thudded as the bigger of two aimed himself towards Colm.

Jay's throat bobbed as he faced the shorter, rounder man who smiled as he advanced.

Wren flew round Jay, slipped between the guards, who turned too slowly to catch her, and hurtled into the corridor.

There she stumbled to a halt. Along the line of cells bleary-eyed Runners, more than she had ever seen in one place, were being shackled together. How long had Vaikuntha been collecting Runners who were foolish enough to land? No wonder none had reached Elysium for weeks.

Before she could break into a run again a rough hand caught the back of her neck.

She tried to see who had her, but a thumb dug into the pressure point under her ear and she cried out. Unable to wriggle free she had to stand, cringing and gasping as her left arm was yanked behind her back. Metal circled her wrist then the weight of a chain pulled her hand down as it was released.

'This one's small.' The man holding her squeezed a little tighter. 'I've had to wrap the chain twice.'

Another voice rasped from her left, but she couldn't turn her head to see who spoke. 'He'll just have to walk closer to the one behind. It won't be for long.'

The hand released her and, simultaneously, someone shoved the small of her back. She stumbled, but the chain round her left wrist jerked her to a stop. She whipped her head round to look for her brothers.

They were behind her, flanked by the guards who had entered their cell. Their arms were already manacled and Colm was holding his forearm, his face pained and drawn. She hadn't even heard him cry out.

A thickset guard waggled the other end of Wren's chain; then looped it through Jay's. She focused on her brother; it was a mistake; the panic in his blue eyes made her own rise like dust in a storm.

'Move.'

The column jerked into motion, guided by kicks and prods. The Runner in front of Wren jolted into a shambling walk and Wren's left arm jerked forward, pulling at Jay's. Immediately her brother bumped into her back; the shortened length of chain between them allowed no leeway. Quickly she shuffled her feet and fell into step, with Jay's toes catching at her heels. She shivered as the Runners were forced, cursing and stumbling, down the corridor, around a corner and through a huge portal.

Awe consumed Wren as they entered the chamber beyond the archway. She'd known the building was big, but hadn't expected anything like this. The ceiling was so high she could barely make it out; only gatherings of shadows clinging to dark recesses told her that the chamber ended at all.

Windows pocked the walls around them. Through them, Wren could see the sun's corona glimmer through the biosphere; setting wisps of cloud on fire as it rose.

Between the windows, solar lights bled orange onto a row of iron posts that protruded from the floor in front of a raised platform. The posts cast shadows that pointed finger-like towards a single empty cage in the very centre of the room. Swiftly put together from what looked like canopy joists, it hung ever so slightly above the floor, high enough for it to swing with an ominous creak.

The door banged shut on the last of the Runners and Wren anxiously peered along the line.

'What're you doing?' Jay hissed. 'Stop drawing attention to yourself.'

'Where's Orel?' Wren craned her neck, seeking his face among all the gaunt and bruised Runners. 'He has to be here.'

'Colm?' Jay breathed over his shoulder. 'You're taller, can you see him?'

Wren heard the murmur of Colm's denial.

'Where is he?' She bit her lip.

'Maybe he got away.' Jay squeezed her elbow, meaning to be comforting and she flinched. The pressure on her bruise reminded her of Raw and tears sprung to her eyes. If Orel had been killed, there was no-one to rescue Raw from the chamber beneath the wall. He would die down there.

A loud crash and a torrent of swearing and yelling made the line of Runners jump. Chains rattled as all eyes turned towards the sound. A second set of figures were hustled through the main entrance and hauled towards the posts.

'Adler.' Wren gasped as the huge man roared and tried to pull free. A guard ran from Wren's line to club him and he went to his knees as another wrapped the chain holding his wrists to the stake in front of him.

Behind him stood all the Runners from the station outside the wall, including The Sphere-Mistress, Genna, who stared, wide-eyed and stupid, her feet twitching beneath her skirt.

Wren stumbled and Jay caught her. 'This is my fault,' she murmured, horrified. 'Adler wanted to Run to Convocation and I wouldn't let him. Orel said we'd be able to get you all out. He said there wouldn't be a problem.' Her voice broke. 'Now look.'

Her eyes went to Genna again. The woman was staring around her, shocked into stillness.

'Why are you all just standing there?' Colm's voice rang around the walls. 'Fight for your lives.'

Runners raised their heads in sudden realisation.

The redheaded Runner chained in front of Wren turned and looked directly at her, as if he thought she had the answers.

'He's right,' she whispered. 'They're going to kill us.'

Although dulled and weakened by weeks or perhaps even months in his cell, the Runner lurched into motion, lunging for the nearest guard. But the Runner ahead of him had twisted the other way.

Wren was yanked off her feet as the panicked Runners tried to fight and simply brought themselves down in a heap. Guards laughed as they grabbed chains and shackled the Runners to the line of posts. When the jowly guard reached Wren, however, a shout from the platform stopped him.

'Not that one.'

The guard's sweaty forehead creased into rolls like soysages on a griddle.

'That one's to go in the cage.'

Colm and Jay brawled like madmen, but they were chained and Wren was unhooked with barely a moment's interruption.

She went limp and dragged her feet, but the guards simply picked her up and tossed her inside. Wren's shoulders crashed into the bars.

There she swung, disoriented, as she watched her brothers hooked to the post directly ahead of her.

Why had *she* been singled out?

Once the Runners were secured, the guards abandoned them.

Finally, as the sky lightened, footsteps sounded behind Wren's jail. She whirled, making the cage rock, and watched as the Council assembled around her. Just as in Elysium there were six: five men and a woman Wren assumed was the head of the Women's Sector. None met her eyes. They all had black and white pendants around their necks.

She shrank into herself as her mind fired the question at her over and over: why was *she* in the cage?

The fattest of the Councilmen stepped forward. His long sleeves fell back and revealed fleshy elbows, which wobbled as he spoke.

'We have called you here to administer justice.'

The head of the Women's Sector bent and started to cough. The Councilman's eyes flickered. 'Are you all right Leanne?'

Time dragged as the thin woman choked into her palm. Her back heaved and her hair hung over her face. Then, slowly the coughing abated and she straightened. Her voice was a rasp as she replied. 'Keep going, Erb.'

The Councillor, Erb, smiled at Wren, as if she was some sort of co-conspirator. It was a bright, hungry smile that showed too many teeth.

'Where's the Lister?'

The bald man stepped from the shadows. 'Here.'

'You have your proof?'

The Lister nodded. 'We have the cause of the plague.'

Wren held her breath. He was going to blame the Runners.

The Lister pointed. One single finger protruded from his sleeve; a spike of blame aimed directly at the cage.

At Wren.

21

For a moment Wren's brain felt like old soy. He had to be using her as a *symbol* for the Runners. Surely, he meant all of them, not just *her*.

The sudden shouting that rose from the chained Runners buffeted her like waves and she covered her ears, so disoriented that she almost missed the Lister's next words.

'This unnatural beast has destroyed the order of things, offended against both Runner Law and the Laws of the Designers, committed acts that have upset nature and brought the plague upon us.'

'What are you talking about?' The red-head shouted. 'He's just a boy.'

'Idiot Grounder … the plague's addled your mind …' The Runner's insults grew louder.

Wren looked at her brothers. Jay too was yelling. 'You don't know what you're talking about!'

The Councillor, Erb, smiled a predatory smile. 'Bring the witness,' he said.

Wren's eyes widened. A witness – someone who knew who she was. There could only be one person: Raw. He'd betrayed her after all.

How did they find him in the cave?

The shadows behind the Council shifted as a light was moved through them. Through the airborne dust Wren could see him, his wide shoulders framed with wings that caught the orange light and glittered as they moved in rhythm with his long stride.

His face remained in shadow as he stepped forward and his boots thudded on the sand floor loud as drums.

She strained to see his face; wanted to look him in the eye as he denounced her.

She had always known that Raw intended to give her up, but for some reason her heart felt fragile. She had been starting to trust him. He had said it himself – she had saved him. But he must still blame her family for his shattered life.

Wren recalled all the times he had hidden his scars beneath his hair, remembered his grief when he told her he'd never get to choose from the Women's Sector.

Maybe they had promised him his life and a place on choosing day.

She gripped the bars. If Raw was going to speak against her, he must have forgotten that she had the same power over him. Raw's wing theft had been just as bad as Wren's.

Then he stepped into a shaft of light from the window and Wren's spit dried to nothing.

It wasn't Raw who faced her. It was Orel. His eyes burned into hers for a moment and then he faced the Runners.

'Tell them.' Erb's expression reminded Wren of a well fed tabby. 'Tell them what she is.'

'*She* ...' The Runners raised their voices, a susurrus that sharpened the air and gave it edges.

Orel nodded. 'She's no Runner. She's a girl.'

'Tell them more,' Erb demanded.

Orel cut his eyes to her and away. Wren's fingers were almost blue, so tightly was she holding the bars.

Orel opened his mouth to speak then stopped. He was staring at Adler and Genna. 'What are they doing here?' He spun to face the Councillor. 'When I came to you, you said you'd let Vaikuntha's Runners remain free. What's going on?'

Erb curled lips like slugs. 'They're here to make sure you hold up your end of the bargain.' He spoke in a low voice that only Orel and Wren could hear. 'And if this one isn't sufficient, we'll need a few more sacrifices – for the good of the colony.'

'Wait.' Orel spun to face Wren, his eyes pleading. 'They said they'd let all the Runners go. Don't you see? There was no way the two of us could have got them out, but *this* way ... one life for ...' he gestured over the grouped Runners before them.

Wren's fingers fluttered over her lips. 'You kissed me,' she whispered.

The Lister snorted. 'And it was an excellent signal.'

Erb grabbed Orel's arm and his wings shivered. 'Bear witness and maybe we'll let the others go.'

Orel squirmed. 'You *said* this one death would be enough.'

'*Make* it enough,' Erb snarled.

Wren saw the bob of his throat as Orel gulped. He turned back to her. 'You're dead anyway when Convocation gets hold of you. This way you can save all the Runners – not just your brothers. Tell me you understand?'

Wren shook her head, but her instinctive denial warred with the weight of truth in his words. They dragged at her until she felt weak as a baby; hardly able to hold her head up. He was right. This was the way to save her brothers. 'Tell me you'll get Raw out of the cave.'

'I promise.'

Wren dropped her head into a nod and Orel sagged with a hint of relief. He turned back to the Runners. 'She turned up a couple of nights ago,' he shouted. 'Said it was her first Run, but it couldn't have been. I've seen her, she's better than half the adult Runners I've known. Better than her partner was.' He hesitated. 'It's unnatural.'

'What partner?' It was Jay. 'You're *crazy* Vaikunthan. Wren had no-one to Run with.'

Genna turned. 'Wren said he was your little brother, Elysian. What's the truth?'

Jay fell silent.

'Well?' She screamed. 'Tell us.'

Saqr gripped the post he was shackled to. 'Is it true?' he shouted. 'Are you a *girl*?' His voice was saturated with disgust.

Colm spoke up, but ignored the Vaikunthan Runners. 'Wren? Who's your Running partner?'

Wren shook her head desperately. She hadn't told her brothers about Raw. It was the final betrayal of everything they believed. If they ever caught him, Colm would kill him.

'Wren?' Colm tried to lunge towards her.

'Don't ask me.' She pleaded.

'I'm asking.' He roared. 'Who's your partner.'

'He said his name was Raw.' Orel called. 'Do you know him?'

'Raw?' For a heartbeat Colm was confused, but then his face cleared. 'The *Grounder?* You're not serious.' He yanked at his chains, taking out his fury on them. 'I can understand your reasons for risking a Run, and you at least know the *theory*. But to give wings to a *Grounder*. To *that* Grounder.' He bent and retched. 'How *could* you?'

'Colm I –'

'Don't. There's no excuse.' He stumbled into Jay. 'This is our fault. We let her have too much freedom, gave her your kite to play with – allowed her to dream impossible dreams.'

'So, you admit it. She is a girl.' Genna screamed. 'Damned Elysians. You've doomed us all.'

'No,' Wren whispered. 'I didn't …' She looked at Colm. He was still hauling at his chains, his face red. Tears were sweeping down Jay's cheeks. Colm was so angry with her that he might just let her die. And he should, Wren realised. She had broken the Law. She had known was might happen to her when she had made that first jump from the platform. Her thoughts turned to their mother. Her death could buy a hundred lives today – maybe it could buy one more.

'Councillor.' She had to raise her voice to be heard over the furiously shouting Runners. Erb pretended to ignore her for a moment then took the few steps needed to bring him to the cage. His pendants swung within her reach and she was briefly tempted to grab them and tighten the chains around his fat neck.

'You're going to die for this blasphemy,' he hissed.

Wren leaned her forehead on a bar. 'I've never flown before and I can prove this was my first Run.'

The Councillor snarled and made as if to turn away. Wren caught his sleeve through the bars. 'That would be no good to you though, would it?'

He snorted. 'What do you mean?'

Wren licked her lips. 'I – I know you've a cure for the

plague, but not enough for everyone. I know that once the rest of the colony finds out, there'll be riots. So, to save those who actually get the cure from those who don't, you need to provide a different target for their hatred.' Her mind raced. 'You thought to use the Runners, didn't you? But you know how much you still need us.' Wren grew stronger as she felt the truth of her words. 'So, you need to focus their resentment on one person – on me.'

'Are you *threatening* me?' Redness burned in his cheeks and he pulled free. The Lister moved to his side and tilted his head, listening.

Wren snatched at his hand, but missed. 'I can prove that I've never flown before … or I can admit to bringing the plague down on you.'

A sneer filled the Lister's brown eyes. 'To save your precious Runners?'

'Yes, and for one other thing.' Wren licked her lips again. 'Give my brother, Colm, enough treatment for one person.'

The Lister's eyes flickered as thoughts chased one another over his face. 'He's not sick – why would you want that?'

'My mother has the plague.'

The Councillor froze and he and the Lister exchanged a horror filled look. 'So, it *is* in other colonies.'

Slowly Wren nodded. 'In Elysium at least. And Tir Na Nog,' She swallowed a lump in her throat. 'Tir Na Nog is dead, completely wiped out. I don't know if it was the plague or something else.'

The Lister paled. 'Why are we only just hearing about this?'

Wren couldn't stop the curl of her lip. 'Because you've got most of the Runners trapped here – who knows when anyone last stopped there. I don't know why they didn't call for help. Maybe their communications array was down, maybe they didn't have time.' She exhaled, remembering the horrible cemetery. 'I don't know about anywhere else. So far, my mother's the only one sick in Elysium and she hasn't seen anyone from the main 'sphere for ages.' She gripped the bars. 'If she gets the cure it won't spread. You'll save our whole colony.'

She tried not to think about the man at the Doctor's Surgery and his cough, there were other illnesses.

The Councillor remained silent, his fat mouth working as if he were chewing. Wren pressed her face to the bars and splinters dug into her cheeks. 'You know you can't abandon the other colonies. You need Eden for its food, Aaru for its drugs, the technology from Olympus … without Elysium you'll lose the new photo-synthesisers.' Wren pushed on, putting pleading into her voice. 'I know you care. You quarantined your own settlement to keep the Runners from spreading this. You were too late, it *has* spread, but you *can* stop it – at least at Elysium – with enough cure for only *one*.'

'But, my dear,' the Lister whispered and Wren suddenly noticed the exhaustion in his bloodshot eyes. 'Which of *our* people has to die in order to save your mother?'

Wren's eyes filled with tears. 'I – I don't know.'

He his head. 'Neither do I.'

The Councillor measured her as if he were considering a trade deal. 'If we give you this, you'll confess to anything we say?'

Wren nodded.

The Lister's shoulders twitched. 'You realise, do you not, that if it's elsewhere then Runners *did* spread the plague?'

Wren's chin dropped again. 'My brothers know about my mother. If you let them go free, they'll make sure Convocation is told.'

A bead of sweat made its slow way over the Councillor's mountainous forehead. 'I should kill you all – that might save *more* lives from the plague.'

Wren remained silent. Erb had to know that if he did so, Convocation would do what it took to destroy Vaikuntha. What more could she say?

Finally, Erb called a security guard forward and murmured an order. Wren strained, but only meaningless syllables floated, disjointed to her ears. The guard began to jog from the platform. He had to stop at the steps for a coughing fit and then he was gone.

The Lister looked from her to the Runners, who were starting to stir as if woken from a dream. 'What's the punishment for a female taking Runner wings?' he called.

'Death,' Genna screamed.

The Councillors formed a line and slowly, each raised their white pendant. Agreement.

'Death.' the Lister echoed.

The ringing of an enormous bell shivered through the chamber, loud enough to shake dust from the walls. Wren clutched the bars. The people of the colony were being called.

The noise of the gathering crowd pressed against the building and swelled like the river. With each surge of sound, Wren's terror grew. She was going to die.

Before her, the Runners were muttering and shouting curses. Words chased one another up and down the line, unable to go anywhere but forward and back. Jay's face was pale and ghostlike and he talked in an urgent undertone to Colm, who was shaking his head.

Then she lost them as the main entrance opened.

Wren only had a moment to see an expanse of lavender sky before the crowd eclipsed the crack of light.

Suddenly she was grateful for the safety of her cage as the colony entered the auditorium. Families clustered together; the sick supporting the dying. A few healthy men and women held their sleeves over their faces as coughs blew through the gathering like the cracking of joists.

She focused on the people immediately before her, her mind skipping to the trivial and latching onto it gratefully. Fashions here were similar to those of Elysium, but women's dresses were shorter and cut lower in the front and their head-scarves were tied low across their foreheads. The men wore their tunics longer and their trousers looser. Many of the tunics were hooded, but most wore them down over their shoulders. A single man stood out to her; his hood was pulled low over his eyes, hiding his face in the folds of its shadows. He looked like death himself.

These people were here to watch her die. Wren could look at them no longer. And indeed, they soon became a faceless mass, pressing against the chained Runners; an amorphous hungry beast.

When the door closed behind the last of the crowd, there was a moment of confused hush, broken only by the coughs of the sick and dying.

Erb lifted his voice to the ceiling. 'We know how the plague started. This girl, who thought to fool us all, broke Runner *and* Designer Law by taking wings not her own.'

He looked at Wren and gestured sharply for her to stand. She rose on shaking legs, careful to balance against the swing of the cage.

'Remember our bargain,' Erb whispered. 'Make them believe and I'll let the Runners go.'

Orel leaned close to her. 'They have to *hate* you, Wren.'

Wren nodded and for some reason her eyes went to the hooded man. She would talk to him alone, persuade death to let her people be. 'I – I've been Running for ages –' she began.

'Liar!' Jay wailed, his tears showing in the growing daylight. 'Why say that? You never used wings before. You never had the chance.'

His voice drowned in the wave of disgust hurled from the crowd. The hooded man was lost for a moment in the surging crowd and Wren looked at Colm. His face was white and he was standing perfectly still.

How very like Chayton he was. Now he watched her with calculating intensity and she could almost read his mind: Wren's life or theirs? His sister, or all the Runners? A girl who'll die at the hands of Convocation anyway – a sister who had let a Grounder take wings – versus a war that could destroy their whole way of life?

There really was only one conclusion.

Tears blurred his eyes. Colm's decision had been made. He caught Wren's gaze and then, with a sudden tilt of his head, indicated Orel.

Wren understood. He'd let her die for them, but Orel would

not Run free.

But Jay was still shouting. 'Leave Wren alone,' he cried. 'She was trying to help …'

'Shut *up*, Jay! Colm, shut him up.' He read her lips. Although Colm's chains shortened his reach, he grabbed Jay around the neck and pulled him close. Jay struggled while Colm muttered urgently in his ear. Then he started to shake his head and kicked harder for freedom. Colm tightened his grip and Wren had to look away. Her eyes went to Adler, who was looking at her as if she'd eaten his children. Everywhere she turned she saw horror at what she had done. The freedom of Running had felt so right, but now it really did seem blasphemous.

As her adrenaline started to seep away, shock set in. She'd never see her mother or father again, never have a family of her own.

She was suddenly fighting for air. Hunching over, she groped beneath her shirt for the tucked end of the sheet that bound her chest and pulled it out. She wriggled to loosen the bands and as they fell at her feet and her breasts sprung free, her whole body shivered with relief.

Suddenly the cage jerked and her face was splattered with foul smelling liquid. She wiped her cheek with a shaking hand and stared at the rotted soy patty that oozed over the bars. A soiled nappy smashed against a higher joist and, as if that was a signal, rubbish rained over the heads of the Runners and struck her cage.

Most of it erupted on the bars, but some got through and her clothes were soon fouled. Mouldy soy slimed her bare arms and rancid chiz mushed against her cheek.

She cringed in the swinging cage. From the corner of her eye she saw the Council and Lister retreat. They left her cage exposed in the centre of the platform; a lone target. Even Orel went with them, abandoning her finally and completely, without even a pitying glance in her direction.

Eventually the crowd ran out of rubbish and instead used their voices to attack her.

With her eyes tightly closed, Wren started to bang her head

on a joist. Harder and harder she hit herself, because each time she knocked her head it rang and for one blessed second, she could hear nothing.

After an eternity the crowd's cries quieted. Slowly Wren opened her eyes, rubbed slime from her face and saw the guard who had been sent out by the Councillor. He stood in front of the Runners pointing a gun. She lurched for the bars, scanning desperately for her brothers.

Then she realised that the Runners were silent and that none had fallen. The gun had not been fired. The muzzle was, however, aimed squarely at Colm.

'*Oh no, oh no, oh no*'; heart thumping it's message of dread, Wren rubbed her stinging eyes and saw a second guard standing over him.

Colm tilted his hand to show Wren a small package. Then he tucked it into his belt.

The guard moved away and both stepped back to allow the Council to return to the platform. Erb stopped close to her cage. 'I am not an unreasonable man.' His eyes were yellowing as if left out in the sun too long; he turned them on her with a look that was almost regretful. 'If you don't hold up your end of the bargain, I will shoot your brother and take it back.'

Wren nodded meekly.

'Then let us continue.' The Councillor waved for Orel to come forward and her erstwhile partner strode over the boards like a conquering hero.

The sun had finally come to Vaikuntha. Climbing the wall, its rays now found their way through the windbreak and into the avenue of windows, just in time to catch his wings and turn them to pure light. He swept his hair from his forehead and, even though he was a hated Runner, Wren heard the adoring sighs of half the audience.

'As you were saying.' The Councillor gestured and Orel began to speak.

22

Orel told how Wren arrived at the secondary station, having known not to land on the main wall despite the fact that so many other *experienced*, Runners had made the mistake of landing there. How he had found her half naked at the station, yet he appeared to be the only one who could see through her disguise. How he had crept out to find the Councillors that night and told them what was going on and how they realised that such unnatural behaviour could cause a shift in the order of things, a change so great that it could cause other unnatural occurrences – such as a plague.

This was a community that had started out as scientists, who still worked to investigate the biology of awakening Martian species and who had blended Martian DNA with dead-earth organisms to help them survive on Mars. Their willingness to believe that Wren's actions could have unbalanced nature and caused a plague made her realise just how strong their superstitious worship of the Designers had grown. Wren hunched as the crowd hushed, as though her actions were so abhorrent that an outcry was not enough.

The eerie quiet was terrifying and Wren shook so hard her bones jarred against the bars.

Even Jay was silent. He stood with Colm's hand on his shoulder, eyes burning into her cage as if he could break it open with the force of his stare. The important thing was that, for now, Colm had him under control.

She realised that the Councillor was looking at her expectantly. 'I *said* the beast will now *confess*.' He glared at her; his puppet failing to perform.

Wren swallowed a mass of thorns that seemed to have lodged in her throat. Could she really do this to herself?

Her mother's face swum before her own; how could she not?

Her voice though, had left her. Devastated at Wren's betrayal of herself, or perhaps being the only part of her actually able to escape, it had fled. She tried to speak, but nothing came out; no words, only sounds: small squeaks that had her hanging her head in shame.

'Speak.' The Councillor's roar made her jump and as if in a dream she saw the guard raising his gun and pointing it towards her brothers.

Colm was stood by the curve of the house, flying Jay's red kite. His thin, serious face scrunched in concentration as he twitched his fingers and made the crimson square whirl in widening circles. Their father said it was the best way for a young Runner to get to know wind patterns. Still, when Colm saw his little sister watching, he helped her hold the string and showed her how to make the bright dot dance.

As she fought the desire of the wind and exerted her own control over the fragile mote in its grasp, Wren's chest expanded. Her feet wanted to fly off the porch and follow the kite into the air. It was at that moment she knew she wanted to be a Windrunner.

'I –' shamefully her voice returned and she looked at the bars beneath her feet.

'Louder.' The Councillor gestured towards the roof as if to tell her how far her story must reach and tears filled her eyes. She had to make the Vaikunthans hate her even more; force them to unite with the chained Runners in their horror. Her death alone had to be enough for them.

She met as many eyes as she could, challenging them from her wooden cage, then settled, once more, on the hooded figure. Eyelessly he watched her from the centre of the throng and it seemed easier to speak to a man who could not show her his disgust.

'At first I didn't realise what I was doing.'

'Go on.' Erb was like a toddler with a bedtime story he didn't want to miss.

'I – I've been flying for months. Stealing my brother's wings and going out. I don't care that it's blasphemy. I just want to fly. And why shouldn't I?' She grabbed the bars in sudden passion. 'Why shouldn't I be allowed to fly? I've heard every lesson, mended wings and repaired nets. Why shouldn't I get to fly too? I'm good enough, better than they are. But because I'm a *girl* –' She shook her head. 'Because I'm a girl the most I can hope for is to be Sphere-Mistress when my mother is gone. Is that fair?' Her eyes went directly to Genna, who was standing with her mouth open. 'Why shouldn't girls get to be Runners if they want to?'

It was Genna who broke the weighted silence. 'Blasphemy,' she hissed. 'Filth.' She patted her dress frantically as if looking for something to throw. When her hands came up empty, she clenched them into fists. 'You'll pay, you … you …' She sputtered off, unable to find words harsh enough to complete her sentence.

Wren looked away from the floundering Runner woman. 'I – I first realised that it was *me* carrying the plague a few weeks ago. The Runners had stopped coming so I went back to a colony I'd visited. They were all dead. Everywhere I returned it was the same. Places I'd never been, people were fine, but places I'd visited, people were dead or dying. It had to be *me*.' Her voice cracked at the enormity of her lie, but she kept going, forced herself to tell the tale. 'I didn't *care*,' she shouted. 'Why should I care about a bunch of … of Land-crawlers. I – I kept flying. It's what I was meant to do.'

Now the people shrieked for her blood. As if her words had smashed an invisible barrier they surged forward and Wren screamed, suddenly terrified for the Runners; certain they would be crushed.

The hooded man stood still and allowed the crowd to surge around him, like a rock in a tide. She could sense the tension in him; he seemed to be waiting for something.

A concussive blast shook the floor beneath Wren's cage and the Runners were knocked sideways; they landed in a pile of men and chains.

Shocked silence choked the air and then a second blast scattered the audience like seeds. They fell, screaming, tripping and clambering over one another. The figure Wren had been watching vanished among the panicking crowd.

'Fire!' The word started quietly, barely discernible over the panicking crowd; then grew, as if blown into a gale. 'Fire ...'

An alarm began to sound; a bright, blaring squeal that cut through Vaikuntha like wings through a thermal.

'The fuel tanks.' The Lister was yelling now. 'There are more down there. This whole level could go up. Get out!'

The Runners were abandoned by a retreating tide of people who, unsure which way to turn, started to pull towards their homes.

Wren gripped the bars. 'Let me out!' She shouted as Erb and the other Councillors ran from the stage. They ignored her. She supposed it made no difference to them. One way or another she was condemned to death.

Panic continued to rise in the audience and Wren stared as gold bloomed outside the windows; a flash of brightness that turned grey round the edges as the useless windbreaks caught and shrivelled into cinders.

Vaikunthans stampeded for the exit. Through the open door, Web saw curls of ash falling like filthy snow, turning the morning to dusk and coating the straining sun.

'What about the Runners?' She shook the bars of her cage, but there was no-one left with a key to their chains. The guards, the Lister and the Councillors had fled and the Runners were trapped, chained above the exploding fuel tanks. Only Orel remained unfettered, standing uncertainly on the platform near her cage.

Wren rattled her bars to get his attention. 'Get the Runners out, you idiot.'

He goggled for a moment, as if he couldn't believe what was happening. Then he ran towards his family and started trying to loosen their chains. As if an order had been shouted, all the Runners started to heave at their posts.

Wren watched, as though the intensity of her gaze would

make a difference. Most of the Runners were still wearing their masks, so the smoke would not suffocate them, but how long did they have before the floor beneath them collapsed.

A dull boom and another explosion made the walls shake. Dust rattled down from the rafters and made Wren cough.

There was a beat of horror, as the Runners waited to see if they were dead or not. Then their efforts became frantic. Finally, Adler roared in triumph and lifted his post high above his head. He was free. Quickly he unhooked his chain and ran to help Orel, rocking Genna's stake as hard as he could.

Another, a few down from Jay bellowed his success and Wren tightened her grip on her bars. The Runners were going to get away.

Wren's brothers were still chained, but Colm and Jay were working together with the red-head, shoving their mast between them, loosening its grip on the floor.

'Wren.'

The voice was so quiet that for a moment she thought she was imagining it.

'Wren!'

She doubled her focus on her brothers.

'Wren, turn around.'

Annoyed that her imagination was distracting her from Colm's efforts, she turned. The hooded figure from the settlement was right behind her cage. His hood still covered his face and the cage threw fire-darkened shadow-stripes over his tunic. His hands lingered in the glow, reddened as if with blood. Death had come for her. How could she have imagined that they would all forget?

He started to pat the fibres that held the cage together; he was trying to get in.

'P-please.' Wren held her hands up, as if she could stop him hurting her. And the figure hesitated. Then he pushed his hood back.

She gasped and if the bars hadn't been there would have thrown herself forward. A weight disappeared from her shoulders. Raw was alive. He was trying to save her. 'How did you –'

'Quiet.' He crouched low to the ground and held her cage to stop it swinging. 'We have to get you out of here.' His scars twisted as he glared at the cage. 'I need a knife.'

Wren shook her head. '*I* haven't got one.'

'I know,' he growled. His knuckles bunched. 'I've an idea.' He reached through the bars and grabbed her discarded breast band. 'I'll be back.'

'Raw –' Wren stammered, but he had slipped away. Her cage, released from his hold, started to swing. Quickly she checked on the Runners. More were free and helping the others. None seemed to have noticed her visitor.

Raw returned. This time he was holding a piece of metal with her flaming breast band tied around it to make a torch. 'What're you –?'

'Get back.'

Wren scuttled to the other side of the cage and held her throbbing head.

Another explosion. Genna's scream echoed to the rafters and Wren's cage swung wildly. A fissure appeared in the centre of the floor: a patch of darkness with a glowing centre, it began to radiate cracks like black fingers. They spread towards the Runners with the sound of crackling metal and splintering stone.

'They've got to get *out*!' Wren cried.

'They will.' Raw held his torch to a bunch of rope at one corner of her cage. It resisted for a moment before finally bursting into flame. He moved the torch around the side, burning as he went. When the fibres turned to tatters, thick black smoke filled the air in front of her, chemically toxic. It obscured her view of the struggling Runners, but she could hear the floor continuing to fracture.

Popping and hissing. Through the smoke, Wren saw spurts of flame, reaching through the floor. 'The fire's reached the Power Cells!' Raw shouted. He stepped back and pulled the hooded tunic from his head. Underneath he wore his ordinary clothes, still showing damp patches from the river.

He turned to toss his disguise and Wren saw his back. Her hand tightened over her halfie. His shirt was shredded and stiff with drying blood. The skin beneath was torn so badly in some places that she could see bone.

That was how he got out of the cave – he had dragged himself through the tunnel under the wall.

'Raw!' She reached through the bars, but he jerked away from her and started to pull at the rope rags. With a few tugs, they disintegrated. Then he grabbed the bars on either side of the broken seam and started to tear the cage apart.

The bars moved beneath her feet. Dazed, Wren tumbled into his arms. He pulled her close. 'It's going to be OK.' He spoke into the filthy mess coating her hair. 'Let's get out of here before they see us.'

'I – I can't go.' Wren wrestled free of his arms.

'What?' Raw's green eyes caught the flame.

'I made a promise – my life for theirs.' Wren gestured towards the Runners. 'If I escape, the Vaikunthans will kill my brothers and take back the cure.' She tried to find Colm and Jay through the clearing smoke. 'I have to stay.'

'No.' Raw tried to pull her away.

Wren resisted. 'I can't let them die.'

'And I won't let *you* die.'

They glared at each other until a glowing shred of ash landed on Raw's cheek. He cuffed it off with a wince. 'More fuel tanks could go up any second.' His eyes glittered and he looked at her. 'What if you never escaped from your cage?'

'What do you mean?'

'If this place goes up, no-one will know if you were inside or not. They'll assume you died in the explosion.'

Realisation dawned and Wren nodded. As if that first piece of ash had been a signal, a sleet of sparkling charcoal blew in through the windows. Raw slapped at her hands as they were coated. 'We have to go.'

'What about Colm and Jay? I'm not leaving them.'

Raw spun her to face him.

'What don't you understand? If the *Runners* catch you,

they'll tear you apart.' He sneered. 'They're as angry with you as the settlers. *They* need to think you're dead too.'

'But my brothers –'

Raw shook the torch. 'Colm might kill you himself. And if he doesn't – do you want them to die defending you? We *have* to go.'

Wren's eyes filled with tears. 'They're not free yet. The floor …'

Heat from the burning floor burned her cheeks and the tube to her halfie felt soft, as if it was melting.

'I'll get your brothers out.' Raw shoved at her. 'Go and get your wings. I'll follow.' He didn't stop to watch her go, but simply ran to her brothers, his back bleeding through the tattered remains of his shirt.

Despite Raw's warning, Wren lingered. If he thought the Runners would be angry with her, what would they do to him once Colm recognised him? Raw was risking his life.

Colm and Jay stared at Raw as if he had sprouted from the floor, then Jay growled his recognition and grabbed Raw's arm and Colm pulled his fist back. But before it could land, a cinder landed in his hair. Colm slapped it out, then he dragged Jay from Raw with a shake of his head. They needed Raw's strength.

With Raw's help it took only a few more bursts of effort for her brothers to haul the post that was trapping them, free from the weakening floor. Wren backed towards the far door as Raw threw the stake to one side.

Then another of the fuel tanks exploded. This concussion felt almost soft. Like a rubber hammer to her chest it slammed into her and Wren was thrown backwards off the platform, to land against a door with a thud, her head ringing.

When the smoke cleared, she gasped. There was an enormous hole where the stage had been. Fire raged inches from her feet and her cage had been completely incinerated. If Raw hadn't got her out …

She heard Jay cry out a single word. 'Wren!'

Wren leaped to her feet, but he wasn't looking at her; his

eyes were fixed on the place where her cage had been.

Wren's mouth shaped her brother's name, desperate to tell him she was all right, but this was what Raw had wanted: his best-case scenario. If everyone thought she was dead, no-one would be trying to kill her; not the religious colonists and not the rule-oriented Runners.

As the fire burned higher, Wren fell through the door and began to run deeper into the Council building. She had to find her wings.

23

The corridor was windowless and smoke free. But Wren knew the floor beneath her could vanish at any moment. She had to get moving. Her wings were in a room near the main entrance, but she was disoriented.

Picking a direction at random, she started to run. Dizzily she focused on at her feet flashing beneath her. Each time her toes hit the ground, her sore legs protested and her whole body shook with tiredness. Not knowing if she was even heading the right way, she slowed to a limping jog.

Anxious voices sounded ahead. Heart racing, Wren sought a place to hide, but the corridor stretched without blemish until it curved out of sight. She skidded to a stop, preparing to run back the other way, and the voices faded.

Carefully Wren continued along the corridor. Not far ahead she saw what had been hidden by the curve of the wall – an old shuttle door. Now she had a choice: continue down the corridor, or follow the voices. Would the doorway lead to her wings, or death?

'I don't know what to do,' she whispered. She dug her nails into her palms and stared up and down the passage as if a sign would somehow appear.

There were people behind the door, which made it a dangerous choice. But if she stuck to the corridor and someone else decided to take the same route, she would have nowhere to conceal herself.

She should at least open the door and see what was behind.

Holding her breath, she placed her hand on the mechanism as if to find a pulse, then leaned in close. No sound tickled her ears. She leaned her forehead on the still cool metal, still hoping somehow for a sign, and her body sagged. She was so very tired. She closed her eyes and when she opened them again, she was on her knees, one arm resting on the frame.

She shook her head and her ears felt full of water. Then her chest tightened and her lungs contracted. A feather light irritation grew harsher until it ripped through her throat and she had to cough.

One cough wasn't enough; she bent over her knees in a vicious fit that made her ribs ache. She must have swallowed the chemical smoke from the ropes.

Wren blinked. She had to stop coughing, or someone would hear. She fumbled her sleeve inside-out, the only way to find a clean spot, and stuffed it into her mouth, muffling her barking coughs.

When her fit had petered to nothing, she dragged herself to her feet. She needed to move on. Her mother was waiting. She listened at the door for three more long breaths then opened it.

For a moment she thought her eyesight had been affected by her coughing, because the walls of the passage before her shimmered and shifted like shadows on a screen. Then she saw the smoke rolling in through narrow windows above her head.

She pressed her forearm harder over her mouth and stepped forward. The door slid closed behind her, but she ignored the thud. The floor of the corridor felt hot even through her boots, but it looked familiar. She edged further in. To her left was the Lister's study, with its door to the street, which meant the storeroom had to be on her right.

Heart racing, she turned and relief made her stagger: she had found her wings. With renewed energy she ran through the archway. Inside, her chest tightened anew at the way the precious items had been treated. The sharp tang of urine cut through even Wren's own stink and close up she could see dangerously bent struts on the wings at the bottom of the pile.

Her fingers twitched with an impulse to just grab a pair and Run, but she knew she had to get her own. Not only were her wings trainers, and therefore unsuitable for any of the full-grown Runners who would soon be leaving the arena, but they were *her* wings. Only extreme desperation would let a Runner wear someone else's wingset.

She remembered exactly where they had fallen and her eyes followed their remembered trajectory. There, right at the back, her wings lay waiting.

She resisted the urge to scramble over the pile and edged carefully around, pushing wings to one side with her hands and knees rather than risk treading on the delicate membranes and bone-like struts.

The wings rustled at her touch and whispering silver material fluttered as if gasping for the missing air.

'They're coming back.' Wren murmured as her shoulders rubbed against the wall that hemmed the restless pile. 'They're coming for you.'

Then she was at the back of the room and could get no closer to her wings without disturbing the whole bank.

As she stood considering how best to reach them, voices rang in the corridor.

'I'm sure our wings were this way.'

Wren's eyes widened. The wall hid her from view, but for how long? The Runners were coming for their wings and she was completely exposed.

Instinct took over. Wren wasn't going to leave her wings for anyone else. She dived over the silver drift and her hand closed over the straps. Her ears strained for the sound of cracking struts, but the mound of silver slid beneath her and did not break.

Dragging her wings, she slithered to the rear of the pile just as the voice echoed in the doorway. A large storage chest was half buried beneath the wings. A quick look showed her tools and wire inside, but there seemed to be enough room for her as well.

She swiftly slid in, hugged her wings close and pulled the lid down. Sharp edges dug into her hip and back and she hoped the Runners wouldn't take long finding their wings.

'Look how they've treated them!'

As the leader raged, Wren ducked lower and squeezed her eyes closed. What if someone looked inside the chest?

Whether the Runners believed that she had brought the

plague or not, it didn't matter. She had broken their most sacred laws. These men would kill her without a second thought.

She bit the knuckles of one hand to muffle her terrified panting. With the other fist she pulled her wings closer. She curled herself as small as she could and listened.

'They're not *my* wings.' One voice whined.

'Put them on.' The leader's spoke again.

'I won't. It's disgusting.'

'Do you know where yours' are?'

An aggrieved silence filed edges on the air.

'We don't have time to each find our *own* wings. This floor could go at any second and a scrum could damage them.'

'Who put *you* in charge?'

There was a sudden report, flesh on flesh, and a sharp inhalation of breath, then the leader spoke again. 'We'll agree to meet at Convocation in seven days. We can sort out the wing-sets there. ... All right?'

His question was met with silence; then Wren heard the distinctive rustle and slither of straps which meant wings were being donned.

'You'll be giving them out?'

'I'll take that task on.'

'What if some are damaged beyond use?'

'It'll have to be first-come-first-served.'

'And you'll tell everyone to meet in a week?'

'I want my own wings as much as you do. Now, *go*.'

Footsteps rang from the room and Wren knew at least some of the Runners were escaping. She bit her lip: would they make it to the platform? Fires were raging and the colonists would likely kill any Runner they caught.

She pressed her forehead against the wall and listened as more men entered the room.

'Strap on these wings, don't look for your own. Convocation in a week to sort it out.'

This time no-one protested. Wren wished the other Runners would speak, it was the only way she'd be able to tell if her brothers had been and gone, but it seemed these Runners had nothing to say.

A distant concussion and a shower of debris on the chest lid told her that another fuel tank had blown up. Would she be buried here?

She did not dare lift the lid to see how many wings were left.

'You need to go, man. We're out of time.'

'I know.' Weariness weighed on the lead Runner's tone. Wren felt for him. 'There are still a few wing-sets left, still some Runners who haven't been through here.'

'Not everyone got out of the arena.'

Wren's heart seemed to stop. Was he talking about Colm and Jay? What about Raw?

Steps pounded from the room and Wren held her breath at the sudden silence. They had all gone. She could get out now too.

Trying to swallow her grief she began to move her stiffening limbs and lift the lid.

'That way to the wings. Convocation in a week.' She heard the shout and immediately ducked back down.

Again, the noise of booted feet intruded on the wing-room. The noise echoed more strongly, reminding Wren that the wings had almost all been taken. She held her breath and felt a familiar tickle in the back of her throat. This blasted cough would literally kill her.

Frantically she bit her own hand to take her mind from the irritation. When that didn't work, she tried to swallow, but her mouth was desert dry. The cough was coming.

She shuddered beneath her wings.

Perhaps these Runners would leave quickly. Sweat burst on her forehead and her chest heaved and quivered as she fought to suppress the traitorous cough. They had to.

'We can't just *leave* her.' The voice was muffled, but Wren's head lifted at the sound. Her brothers were *alive*.

'She's gone, you saw it yourself. We have to get home. She made sure I got a dose of the cure, so Mother has a chance. *If* we can get it to her.'

'You don't know it's real. That old bastard could've given

you anything.'

'Even so. Find some wings and *put them on*.'

'By the skies, Colm,' Jay's voice. 'They've pissed in here.'

'Convocation will hear about it. We *have* to get moving.'

Over the screaming of her lungs, Wren heard the distinctive snap of Colm donning wings. He always swung them on so hard the straps slapped together. She wished that she could jump up and let them know she was all right, but she wasn't sure what Colm would do to her and there was no guarantee that they were alone.

She was about to move the lid, just enough to check, when another voice intruded and all her muscles clenched again.

'Why haven't you left yet?'

It was Raw; Wren couldn't stop his name from trembling on her lips and a tiny bark escaped her throat, bringing a measure of relief.

'You!' Jay yelled over the sounds she was making. 'It's *your* fault she was here.'

'*I* followed *her*,' Raw hissed. 'Now I'm stuck in this cursed hell-hole, while you get to go home, so *back off*.'

'Stuck … you broke your wings!' Horror pushed through Jay's voice.

'Trying to protect your sister. She had no idea what was out here.'

'Neither did you.'

'I'm better equipped to deal with anything than she is.'

'Was.' Colm's voice was soft. 'Don't you mean 'than she was'.'

'Yes … that's what I meant.'

Wren clenched her fists. Raw was lying for her. Her eyes ached with the need to see what was happening out there and her chest heaved again as a cough lurched towards her lips.

'You two need to get out of here.' Raw again. Pushing her brothers away.

'We're leaving as soon as Jay puts some wings on.' Colm's voice receded and she sagged with relief. But then she heard his indrawn breath. Yet another Runner had appeared: someone who shocked him.

'What're *you* doing here?' Jay snapped.

'I'm just leaving.' Wren's heart stuttered and her lips tingled. Perhaps they always would at the sound of Orel's voice.

He had his wings already, why had he come to the wing room?

'You get lost smarmy boy?' That was Raw.

'A little turned about is all.'

'Grab him,' Jay yelled.

The coughing fit Wren had been fighting to hold inside, exploded with the force of an eruption.

She curled beneath her wings and coughed until she thought her lungs would burst. Then she lay limp and exhausted.

The lid of the chest lifted and light met her eyes before it was cut off by a looming figure.

She clutched her wings and her lips twitched into an apologetic half-smile. 'I was *trying* to get away,' she whispered.

Raw shook his head. 'Great job.'

As she sat up, Jay and Colm stared as though she had risen from the dead. Orel dangled loose-limbed in Colm's grasp.

He gaped. 'You're alive.' Then he straightened. 'See, everything turned out all right.' He turned to Colm with a charming smile and a toss of his dark hair. 'Now we can *all* get out of here.'

Wren looked only at Colm. 'Colm?' She left her question hanging.

Colm shook his head. 'I can't make any decision right now, Wren. You know what you've done and what should happen, but ...'

'The Runners think she's dead,' Raw hissed. 'If you can let it go, she's got a pass.'

'She's our sister,' Jay murmured.

Colm groaned. 'I know. But what she did – letting a Grounder have wings.'

'It wasn't like that,' Raw snarled.

'Raw saved your life, Colm,' Wren insisted. 'You'd be burned in the Council chamber if it wasn't for him. What are you going to do?'

'I don't know, all right,' Colm yelled. 'I'm not Patriarch. Let Chayton decide what to do.'

'So, we're all going home?' Wren's shoulders lightened.

'Yes,' Colm nodded. 'All of us who can.'

Wren stared around the near empty room. There were three wing-sets left on the floor. Colm was ready to go, but Jay and Raw remained wingless.

'Raw – you can take one of the last wings,' she pushed him towards the pile.

Raw shook his head and gestured. With horror Wren saw what he meant.

'Those have been left behind because they're too badly damaged.' He shrugged. 'Only one decent set left and that's Jay's.'

Wren's eyes narrowed. 'That's not fair.'

Raw gave his twist of a smile. 'You want me to take Jay's wings?'

'No!' Wren jerked. 'But … Orel's already home, isn't he?'

'What?' Orel jerked in Colm's hold. 'Let me go.'

Colm smiled down at him, a revelation of teeth that Wren saw her father use almost every time he dealt with the Council. 'You tried to have our sister killed.'

'To save the Runners,' Orel cried. '*She* understands.'

'First, he tried to kill *me* off.' Raw swung from Wren and sweat bloomed on Orel's forehead, caking his hair to his face.

'No, I –'

'There was no way you thought I'd make it through that gap.'

Wren glared poisonously. 'You never intended to go back for him.'

Orel grinned manically. 'I would have returned –'

'Would you really? After I was dead?'

Raw showed his teeth in a mirthless grin. 'When I realised that he meant to leave me behind, there was no *way* I was going to let him.'

'Then it was *you* following us before,' she whispered.

'You think I'd leave you?' Raw frowned at her. 'I spent all night trying to think of a way to get you out once you got arrested.'

Wren shook her head; then coughed again.

'That sounds –' Jay's expression as he looked at her changed to concern.

'Nasty. I know.' Wren wiped her head with the back of her hand. 'It's the smoke. It's getting hot in here.'

'The fuel tanks are still burning.' Colm nodded at the doorway. 'We have to get going.' He showed his predator's smile to Orel once more. 'Are you going to make this easy?'

Orel shrunk back. 'The Runners think she's dead. If you take my wings, I'll tell Convocation she's alive! It won't matter what decision Chayton makes about her then.'

Colm hesitated and his eyes flickered towards Raw.

'He isn't even a Runner,' Orel oiled. 'You said so yourself. He's a *Grounder*. As soon as they've finished with *her*, Convocation will kill *him*. They aren't worth it.'

Smoke billowed into the room and Wren coughed. Raw grabbed her wings, swung her round and tossed them onto her back. 'Do them up,' he snarled.

With fumbling fingers Wren tightened the straps around her chest. As they compressed her lungs, the cough eased. 'I'm not leaving without you,' she grabbed his arm.

Raw looked helplessly at Colm and then his shoulders drooped like windless wings. 'Get her out of here,' he said.

24

Jay's knuckles whitened around Orel's forearm. 'Colm?' His eyes were wide with panicked indecision.

'For the sake of the skies, Jay, get some wings on, I've got Orel.' Colm clamped his arms around Orel's neck, and Jay ran across the room.

Wren pressed her lips together. 'I'm *not* going without Raw.'

Colm glared at her. 'You'll do as I say,' he snapped. 'You're lucky to be alive. I don't even know if I'll be able to keep you that way when Chayton finds out ...' He tailed off then continued grimly. 'The Vaikunthan Runners know whose daughter you are. If Orel tells them you're not dead, Convocation will send someone for you ... '

Orel began to kick and Wren realised Colm was tightening his grip. 'What are you doing?' Alarm turned her voice to a squeak and suddenly Raw's arm was around her.

'He's doing what he has to,' he murmured. Jay kept his eyes averted as he did his wings up.

'*No!*' Wren shrieked.

Raw clapped his hand over her mouth. 'You want the guards here?'

Wren bit him hard and struggled free. She ran to Colm's side. 'Stop this.'

Orel's face was puce and he was clawing frantically at her brother's arms with ragged nails.

'This makes you as bad as him,' she gasped.

Colm's expression was distant as he turned his eyes to her face. 'Do you want to die?' he asked.

Stunned, Wren shook her head.

'Then *he* has to.'

'There must be another way.' Wren was frantic.

Raw stood at her back. 'There is no other way.'

Orel's brown eyes latched onto hers' and his knees buckled. Trails of smoke blew around him, dark fingers that seemed to be dragging him to his knees.

'Colm, stop it. He won't tell.' She dropped to the floor in front of Orel. 'You won't tell, will you? Tell him you won't.'

Orel's mouth gaped, fish-like.

'He can't talk, Colm. Let him talk.' Wren grabbed Colm's arm, trying to free Orel's throat.

'Get her out of here.' Colm's tone was granite and if anything, he pressed harder on Orel's windpipe.

'Don't you dare,' Wren snapped at Raw and he stopped his movement towards her. 'Let him talk – let him promise to keep quiet,' she begged her brother. Then she turned to Raw. 'How does this make you different from Father when he did *that* to you?'

Raw's eye narrowed and he raised his hand to touch his scarred face. 'He's a liar, Wren. He'll promise all you want, but as soon as you're gone, he'll tell the Runners about you.'

Orel's struggles were weakening, and one arm hung at his side, he was barely even trying to pry Colm loose now.

'Why would he tell?' Orel's eyes were closing. 'Orel did what he did because he was trying to save the Runners but now, they're free. There's no reason for him to give me up now.'

'Unless we take his wings.' Colm finally engaged with her. 'If you want wings for Raw this is the only way to get them.'

Wren gasped. 'I – I didn't mean –'

Raw shook his head. 'We know you didn't. Let him go, Colm. I already said I'd stay.'

Colm didn't move.

Orel reached up with one arm and fumbled weakly at the straps over his chest.

'Look.' Jay's wings swished through smoke as he stepped towards them. 'He's giving up his wings. Let him go, Colm.'

For another series of heartbeats Colm made no move. Then with a suddenness that made Wren jump backwards, he dropped Orel and stepped to one side.

Orel thudded to the floor, gasping. Then he rolled, pulled his wings off and threw them at Raw.

Raw didn't even try to catch them. They skidded across the floor to knock against his boots. Instead he stared down at Orel. 'You won't tell?'

Orel shook his head, hands around his own throat, as if his palms could soothe the bruising.

'If you do …' Raw crouched.

Wren coughed as Orel nodded his understanding.

Then Raw touched the discarded wings. 'If you stay quiet, I'll get these back to you. Colm can bring them.' His face hardened. 'He *will* be coming back, one way or another.' Then his expression softened again. 'I just want to get home, do you understand?'

Orel nodded again; it was all he could do.

'He won't tell.' Wren pulled at Raw's shoulders and he grimaced. 'Sorry.' She whipped her hand away. 'Can you put wings on over your injuries?'

Raw showed his teeth. 'You just lead the way.' He swung the wings up with a flourish that made swirls in the darkening air.

Wren's gaze lingered on the two wing-sets lying broken on the floor. 'Are they still alive, those last Runners?' she whispered; then she coughed again.

'I doubt it.' Colm looked at Orel. 'But if they are, will you hide them?'

Orel rolled to his knees and nodded. 'I only wanted to save the Runners. I'm glad you're alive.' He raised one hand to Wren.

Wren looked away from the offered hand. Her fingers crept to her lips as if the ghost of his traitorous kiss remained.

Jay put his arm around her. 'We're getting out of here now, right?'

Wren smiled at him with tears in her eyes. 'I want to go home.'

'We all do.' Colm hustled her towards the corridor then looked back to Raw. 'You coming?'

Anxiously, Wren twisted and caught the look of agony on

Raw's face as he tried to put his arms through the straps on Orel's wings. She almost went to him but Colm whispered in her ear. 'Leave him alone. He doesn't want you to see.'

Wren bit her lip. 'But he's hurting.'

'That's what he doesn't want you to see.'

Raw caught up, the wings tightly fastened around his chest and a forced smile on his face.

Together they headed down the passageway, leaving Orel alone with the two broken wings.

The small group hesitated in the Lister's office. 'Everyone else escaped this way,' Jay murmured.

Colm nodded and, gesturing Wren to stand behind him, he opened the door. But his sharp inhalation sent Wren darting round him. Had they walked into a trap? When her eyes were able to take in the scene outside, shock stiffened her limbs.

Fire had eaten away the protective canopies that once hung over the settlement. A few dangling threads were all that remained and those blew like trailing corpse-cloth.

Smoke had blackened stone. Triumphantly it smeared the air, blotted out the sun and brought a fake twilight to the inner walls.

Wren's chest tightened and she realised the air was thinning: the fire was eating up the O_2 as fast as it could be pumped into the biosphere.

In the distance she could see Runners leaping from rooftop to rooftop, aiming themselves at the wall.

As Wren stared, the roof of one of the nearer houses collapsed in on itself. The noise that should have been an almighty crash seemed nothing more than a sigh, and it was only then that she realised the whole scene was backed with a roar so loud it had ceased to be noise and became instead, part of the beat of her own blood tearing through her veins.

Jay's arm closed around her. 'It's ...' he fell silent.

Wren nodded and Raw's voice filled the dismayed silence. 'What have I done?'

'You?' Wren turned to him. '*You* did this?'

'I couldn't come up with anything else. I needed a distraction to get you out.' His voice trembled with horror. 'I set a fire among the fuel tanks. I didn't think it would spread like this –'

'Look.' Jay pointed and they instinctively stepped backwards. In the square before them one of the colony's O_2 pumps ruptured and the fire whipped into a vortex, fed by the burning fuel tank underneath.

The whirlwind built higher and the flames twisted. Wren couldn't tear her eyes away.

'Wren!' Raw grabbed her and she looked down to see her feet trembling on the edge of the doorway. She had been walking towards the fire.

'What do we do?' Jay was biting his lip so hard his teeth were breaking the delicate skin.

Colm shook his head. 'We can't go out there. There's no way we'll reach the platform on the wall. The rest of the Runners might, but we've waited too long.' He dragged them back inside.

Before the door shut behind them a line of houses imploded, one after another, as if sucked empty from the centre. One of the Runners vanished in a blur of debris.

'Now what?' Wren cried.

'Now what, indeed?'

Wren whirled. Behind them Erb, the Lister and another two council members had entered the room, cutting them off from the corridors. They were laden with bulging bags.

'The colony's records!' Colm whispered.

'We have to save what we can. I think the labs are safe enough *for now*.' The Lister scrubbed a hand over his bald head. 'The fuel tanks are on this side.' He thrust a bag at Wren. 'Hold that.'

She fumbled the sack as he opened his drawers, dragged out document after document and stuffed them inside.

Erb swayed. 'This is your fault.' He pointed at Wren. 'You brought this on us with your blasphemy.'

'Stow it,' Jay snapped. 'That's superstition and you know it.'

'I know nothing of the kind, the Designers –'

'Why haven't you vented the O_2?' Raw leaned over the desk. 'This fire could be out, if you just vented the Oxygen.'

'And how would we do that?' Erb spat.

'Open the damned airlocks,' Raw stabbed a hand at window.

'Can't.' The Lister grabbed the bag from Wren and slung it over his shoulder. 'Emergency protocols went into force the moment the alarm went off. We're on lock-down.'

'What kind of emergency protocols won't let you open the airlocks?' Raw tore at his hair.

'How are the Runner's going to get out?' Wren cried.

'They aren't.' One of the other Councillors, a thin tired looking streak of a man smiled with the small triumph. 'They're as trapped inside the Dome as we are for a change.'

'By the Skies.' Colm raged. 'Everything's going to burn.'

Raw caught his arm. 'Not necessarily.'

The Lister sneered. 'If you're waiting for the fuel tanks to burn empty …'

'No.' Raw shook his head. 'Think – the solar panels.'

'What do you mean?' Erb's chin wobbled as he shuffled nearer.

'You can open the solar panels on the top of the Dome. The O_2 will vent that way.'

The Lister let out a loud bark of laughter. 'On the top of the Dome! Listen to yourself. It takes days to build the scaffolding to get up there.'

'You don't *need* scaffolding.' Raw shoved Wren forward. 'I can engineer the solar panels – with Wren's help.'

'And how are you going to get up there?' Colm shook his head.

'We fly.' Raw lifted one arm so that his wings rippled. Another explosion rocked the room and Erb fell to the ground. Colm caught Wren and steadied her.

Erb looked up at him. 'You can do this?'

'Of course, he can't.' Colm snapped. 'Idiot Grounders. You

can't fly *inside* a Dome. There's no wind.'

'Wren can.' Raw pulled her from Colm's grasp. 'We've out-flown a storm, we can do this.'

'I don't know –'

Raw wheeled to the Councilmen. 'Let us try. If don't make it, you've lost nothing. You want us to die anyway.'

'And if you do make it?' Erb licked thick lips.

'You let all the Runners out as soon as the airlocks cycle open again.'

'Including the two of you I suppose.' The Lister sneered.

'Obviously.

Erb narrowed his eyes at his fellows. Then he put his hand into his tunic and lifted one of his pendants. The other two Councillors pulled out their own.

Wren was too scared to look. But Jay gasped. 'They're white, Wren.'

'I don't care what colour they are. This is a Runner decision and you're not going out there.' Colm blocked the doorway.

Gently Wren touched his arm. 'Raw's right. If we don't try, this the whole Dome burns – us too. It's our only chance.'

'You *can't* fly inside a Dome,' Colm repeated.

'I'd rather die trying than sitting here,' Wren snapped. 'If we take off from the top of the pyramid, we've got a chance.'

'Then I'll do it.' Colm decided. 'I'm the most experienced Runner.'

Wren shook her head. 'I'm lightest. I stand the best chance of getting up there. And Raw has to try too – he's the only one who can engineer the panels.'

Colm ground his teeth. 'We're going up the pyramid with you.'

Wren nodded. 'It's probably safer up there, than in here.' She cut her eyes at the Councillors.

Colm caught her hand in his. 'I don't think this is a good idea. You're not a Runner.'

Raw snorted. 'You've never seen her fly.'

Outside, the fire raged on. Raw stepped out of the door, threw his arm over his face and ran.

'Sodding *Grounders*.' Colm bit off another curse, released Wren and hurled himself after him.

'You think you can do this?' Jay's face was pale, but colour slashed over his cheekbones as if he'd been slapped. He was terrified.

Wren kissed him gently on the cheek. 'I'll get us out of here. Home by dinnertime.' She pulled him forward.

He hung back for a breath then lurched to her side. 'Home for dinner,' he smiled.

The moment Wren stepped from the protection of the lintel, the full force of the heat blasted into her.

'Come on,' Jay yelled and she whipped round to face him. His face was already scarlet from the heat.

She doubled over and began to cough. Jay grabbed her arm and started to drag her. 'I was wrong, we can't do this.' She turned to go back inside but Colm blocked her. He threw his arms around her waist and tossed her upwards. She gave a short shriek of surprise, but did not come back down. Instead, another set of hands closed around her wrists and she was pulled upwards. When she realised Raw was already on the first floor of the pyramid, she started to scramble with her legs. It had to be cooler up there.

It was – barely. Desperately she inhaled while holding Raw's shoulders to keep her upright. But when she started to let him go, he held her more closely. She frowned up at him and he glared at her in unreadable silence.

His hands tightened on her back. 'I saw him kiss you,' he snarled.

Taken aback Wren stared up at him. 'You saw that?'

'This is only fair.'

He shifted his grip so that one palm was flat on the back of her head. His fingers splayed in the sticky curls that were all that remained of her hair while his other arm circled her back. Then he tipped her, taking her balance so that she had to grip his shoulders.

Her mouth opened in a tiny shocked oh and his lips found hers.

Orel's kiss had made her tingle; Raw's ignited a furnace low in her stomach and set her on fire. The heat from the inferno below matched the flames that blazed in her chest and she dug her fingertips into his shoulders.

Raw's breath was sweet on her tongue and, instinctively, she licked into his mouth, seeking more of the taste of him. Their tongues entwined and Wren moaned and clutched him harder.

He was her anchor, solid and good and a little broken. She needed him.

Wren forgot the danger they were in as she wrapped her leg around his. He groaned into her mouth and his hand started to move, finding the bare skin on the nape of her neck.

She shivered and moved her own hands. Trusting him to hold her she found his back and the ridge of muscles beneath his wings.

He gasped into her mouth and pulled away.

'W-what?' Wren's head spun. She squinted up to see that Raw was shaking. Only then did she remember his injuries. 'I hurt you!' Concerned she jerked her hands away.

'No.' Raw grabbed for her wrists, his eyes flashed and Wren was sure he was about to kiss her again. Her lips parted in anticipation.

'A little help here.'

Wren turned to find Jay's face level with her boots. His cheeks were red and his eyes streaming. Guiltily Wren dropped to her knees and hauled him up by his wrists. A second later Raw helped Colm.

Wordlessly they stared at one another. Then Raw's great hand slid into Wren's. Her fingers convulsed on his knuckles and she inched nearer to his side then, as one, they turned to look at the colony.

From this vantage point the extent of the devastation could be seen. Half of the colony seemed to be burning and the biosphere itself shuddered as the panels began to overheat.

'Where is everyone?' Wren murmured.

Jay shook his head.

'Keep climbing,' Colm coughed. Wren nodded and he helped Raw boost her up to the second floor.

Like automatons they climbed, helping one another up floor-by-floor. Wren's eyes watered constantly, but as they got higher the air cleared slightly.

She looked back down and her hand closed around Raw's. 'I see them – the Vaikunthans.'

Raw turned his head and nodded. 'Makes sense.'

'Where?' Jay leaned back and almost overbalanced. Colm's arm slammed into him, flattening his wings against his back and pinning him to the wall.

'At the river.' Wren pointed.

Hundreds were huddled along the icy river, their O_2 canisters glittering. Wren couldn't help looking at Raw. His eyes were filled with tears.

'You couldn't have known,' she yelled.

Raw looked at her. 'I could have. I didn't think hard enough. I didn't care.'

'We're going to save them.' Wren squeezed his hand. 'Come on.'

25

'I know you've done this before Wren, but please slow down.'

Wren looked up. Her mother was a slim silhouette with the sunlight behind her. Her hair streamed around her shoulders; a golden halo.

Wren rolled her eyes. 'I'll be fine. Can you lower me a bit more? There's a tear on my right.'

Her mother braced her legs and played out a bit more line. When the slack reached Wren, she pulled herself towards the torn netting, examined the tear and ran her palm over the rock beneath it. There was a sharp outcrop and it had worn the netting away. She used her hook to mend the hole with new twine and then reached for her hammer and chisel.

Suddenly there was a tug on her belt and Wren looked behind her, Runners were coming in. She grabbed the rope and walked up the cliff. At the top she reached for her mother's hand.

Mia pulled Wren into her arms and they stood with their heads together, fine blonde hair blending with thick brown curls, as they watched the bright blurs flicker in and out of the sun.

Mia was so tense she was vibrating. Wren pulled back to look at her. Her mother's face was white and she was grinding her teeth. Her fingers flexed against Wren's shirt. Wren squeezed her hand. 'They'll be fine.'

Her mother nodded absently. 'Of course, they will.' But she did not look away from the sky, nor did she relax until Wren's father and brothers had landed safely and run into her arms.

Raw boosted Wren up onto the top of the pyramid, the flat roof was just wide enough for them to run a take-off. There she stood and looked over the colony. She had thought it would feel as if she was at the top of the world. She'd never even seen a building with eight stories before, let alone climbed one. But the wall still loomed above them, cutting the horizon short beneath the broken sphere, and the feeling of being hemmed in was as strong as ever.

The sun hung swollen and bloody behind the smoke haze and Wren was reminded to put on her goggles. Unbelievably they were still tucked into the back of her belt. She rubbed them clean and pulled them over her tangled curls. Then she looked at Raw. His hair stuck to his head in sweat-soaked clumps. His eyes were bloodshot and his face soot smeared. 'Are you sure you want to do this? You can tell me what to do. I can go alone.'

Raw shook his head. 'It's a two-man job.'

'Right.' Wren looked up. The top of the Dome still seemed far above them.

'It's almost mid-day.' Jay groped for her hand. 'The gales will be starting up soon.'

'We should get the O_2 vented before the dust storm makes it impossible to open the panels.' Raw sounded more confident than he looked but he was right. With a mega storm on its way, the dust storm would be vicious. If they opened the panels in the middle of it, the Dome would be damaged, possibly permanently.

Wren opened her wings and her pinions rippled out, undamaged. 'Are you ready?' she asked Raw.

His lips flattened and he too spread his wings. 'I'm going to copy you.'

Wren nodded. She looked again at the burning colony. The venting O_2 still blazed in the centre of the square. That was where she had to go.

'I don't like this.' Colm groaned. He was a picture of misery

'I'll be fine.' Wren insisted. 'And if I don't make it, maybe I wasn't meant to.' She cut off his reply by giving him a quick kiss on the cheek. 'Wish me luck.'

'Good luck, little sister.' Colm touched her face.

'I can't believe you're doing this.' Jay pulled her in for a hug.

Wren wriggled free. 'Look after Colm.'

Jay nodded but, as she stepped to the edge of the building, she heard him sob.

Wren tried to take a deep breath, but a cough surprised her, leaping into her chest and clenching its fist around her throat. As she straightened up she saw Colm and Jay looking at one another over her head, their foreheads creased with worry.

'It's the smoke,' she snapped.

Knowing she could say nothing more to reassure him, Wren backed up until her heels touched air on the other side of the roof. Then she dropped into a starting position and shook out her arms.

Jay paced three steps from the opposite edge of the roof. 'I'm the red line,' he said solemnly.

Unable to risk a deep breath, Wren shut her eyes to centre herself, opened her arms and started to run towards her brother.

As she reached him with no sign of slowing, he stepped back and she snapped out her wings. They locked with a satisfying *snick* and she leaped.

Wren dove past storey after storey. She forced her wings flat and prayed. Where was the hot air? Where the thermals that she hoped would boost her towards the top of the Dome?

The fountain of burning O_2 was ahead of her and on her left. The third level of the pyramid was directly below her. She was falling too fast: she was going to crash. Wren tried to force herself outwards, away from the pyramid. The air was thin, but her fall provided some wind. She angled herself and screamed as her toes brushed stone. Then she was flying towards the flames. Too low, she was going to burn.

Her arms ached as she pushed and her lungs throbbed as an endless scream trailed in her wake.

And then she was inside the flame. Her goggles filled with orange light and her tunic smouldered. Her wings glowed and her skin burned, but she was rising. The blaze jetted her upwards with the force of the venting O_2 and she screamed again as she shot in the direction of the Dome.

Frustrated flames reached for her as she was hurled upwards on their hot breath. Trembling, Wren leaned into the updraft and swooped back up the pyramid. As she crested the final storey, she saw Raw. He was clutching the edge of the roof, straining to look for her.

His scarred face twisted as he climbed to his feet. She saw him shout something at Jay and immediately her brother looked up, his face slack with relief.

'Follow me,' Wren yelled.

Swiftly Raw marched to the far end of the roof and Jay took up position again. Then Raw hunched his shoulders and started to run.

Wren circled tightly towards the apex of the Dome, not daring to take her eyes from Raw's launch. She opened her mouth to shout at him to lock his wings, but another voice over-rode her. It was Colm.

'Spread your wings, fool!'

Raw's arms snapped out and his wings flicked into position.

'Jump!' As Raw's toes hit the very end of the building, her voice blended with her brother's.

She could barely watch as Raw plummeted towards the ground. She remembered seeing him fall once before. This was different, this time she didn't care about the wings he wore, she only cared about *him* and it wasn't because he was the only one who knew how to adjust the solar panels. 'Catch the thermal,' she prayed.

Then, suddenly, Wren hit cooler air. The heat wasn't strong enough to take her any higher. She looked up. She was barely two wing lengths from the apex of the Dome and she wasn't going to make it. She started to drop.

'No!' she howled.

To her right the Dome sloped downwards, but long metal struts, like scaffold, filled her vision. They went from about two-thirds up the Dome to the very top; extra support for the weight of the solar panels. If she tilted herself correctly, she might just be able to catch one of them.

She was falling faster now. She couldn't spare a second to look for Raw. Instead she tilted her right shoulder, forcing the last of the hot air to take her circling sideways. The Dome-slope came up on her with terrifying suddenness and Wren realised that if she wanted to catch a strut, she would have to unlock her wings.

'Oh skies,' she whispered. Panic thudded in her chest and, within a finger's length of a metal joist, just as she started to fall again, Wren flicked her elbows and unlocked her wings.

Instantly her weight took her downwards. She threw her arms out and they slammed around the metal with bruising force.

Wren went from falling to dangling. She followed her arms with her legs and wrapped them around the pole, panting with terror.

Then she tilted her head and looked down. Her brothers were standing almost directly below, looking tiny. Where was Raw? She craned her neck, trying to see.

There he was, circling up the thermal, heading towards her. His voice reached her ears. He was yelling at her. Wren hugged the scaffold tighter.

Raw was heavier than she, he wasn't even going to make it as high. But he copied her, heading towards the joist to her left. He slammed into it at least two body lengths lower than she had. The whole Dome seemed to quiver with the force of his landing.

'Hang on!' she cried.

'*Holy Designers*!' Raw clung like a bug to a gingko branch. His chest heaved.

'We've got to climb the rest of the way,' Wren called.

Raw nodded and Wren looked up. Her arms already ached and the scaffold looked steep and, now she was on it, impossible to climb.

She tried to force herself to let go with one arm so that she could pull herself up, but she couldn't prise her fingers open. Her instincts said 'cling' and so she clung.

'You don't have to wait for me,' Raw shouted. 'Go on.'

'I can't.' Wren coughed.

There was a pause and then: 'I'm coming.'

Wren watched him haul himself upwards, arm-over-arm, propelling himself higher. Once he was level with her, he called from his joist. 'Can you copy me?'

Wren shook her head. 'My arms are just so tired.'

'Okay.' Raw stretched across and grabbed her wing straps. He could just reach, but the Dome narrowed above them; they would get closer together. 'I'll pull you.'

'You can do that?' Wren swallowed and tried not to think about the amount of pain he had to be in.

In answer Raw used one arm and his legs to push himself higher up and dragged Wren after him. She resisted his pull at first, unable to relax her grasp. He grunted at her. She had to trust him.

'I've got you.'

'I know.' Slowly her fingers and thighs loosened. She didn't let go, but she relaxed enough that she slid a few inches up the pole when he dragged her.

She looked up. They had a couple of body lengths to go; this was going to take forever if she didn't help. With Raw holding her, Wren finally felt confident enough to reach above her with one hand.

This time when he pulled her, she pushed with her thighs and dragged herself with one arm and moved twice as far.

They kept moving. Wren tried not to look down. If she fell her wings would probably save her. Probably.

Her back grew hotter – the fire was still raging below. They had to vent the O_2.

The world shrank to the movement of her hands and legs. Sweat made her palms slick and her legs throbbed and trembled.

Raw drew nearer as their joists ran closer together. Then, suddenly, he wasn't pulling her any more. She looked at him with one arm stretched above her head, and blinked. Her fingers touched a platform. They had reached the apex.

'Go.' Raw boosted her up and she pulled her chest onto the metal grid. He followed, panting.

'We made it,' she said. She rolled onto her back and stared upwards. The sun was almost directly over-head. 'It's almost mid-day.' She groaned and rose awkwardly onto her knees.

'What do we do now?'

Raw crouched beside her and looked up. There was a mechanism on the side of each panel and a large central node with a dusty screen and keyboard.

'All right, these are pretty much the same as ours.' He touched the semi-rusted hinges on the panel nearest him. 'They were constructed so that when the Domes come down, the solar array can be repositioned at ground level. Right now, they stay at one optimal angle because the populations of the Domes and therefore their power needs remain consistent –'

'And if they moved, everyone inside the Dome would die.'

'Right.' Raw rubbed his chin. 'But when the atmosphere becomes breathable and the Domes come down, human populations will spread and more energy will be needed. So, the panels were actually designed to rotate – when they're needed to, they can track the sun and gather maximum possible energy.

'They go around.' Wren grasped his meaning immediately.

'Here's the axis.' Raw pointed. Each panel had a line running through the centre.

'So, we can push them open?' Wren tried. She shoved the nearest panel with her shoulder, but it didn't budge. Screaming sounded from below and she bit her lip. 'It didn't move.'

'It won't. The panels are programmed to remain closed because they're still on the Dome top. I'm going to have to re-programme the central panel.' He indicated the dusty screen. 'When I say so, you need to depress the 'unlock' button on the individual panel, then you'll have to push it open – it'll be hard to move.'

Wren nodded. 'I get it. How many should we open?'

'One should be enough.' Raw cracked his knuckles. 'Ready?'

Wren moved into position under the closest panel. 'Which button?'

'This one here.' Raw's hand hovered over hers, warm. He took her finger and guided it to a square red button. 'It takes two – I've got to key the button on the central node, while you do this one. It's a failsafe.

'Because of sabotage?'

'Of course. After Keirnan's Day the Originals put in as many fail-safes as they could, so don't press it till I say so, or you'll freeze up the process.'

He moved to the central node and rubbed the screen with his sleeve. '*Designers,* this is old.' He had to hammer at the keys to loosen them.

He thought for a moment, his green eyes narrow. Then he tapped the keyboard. He hesitated; then tapped again. Wren couldn't tell what he was inputting.

She closed her fists and her eyes, resisting the temptation to check the colony below. 'All right, I've reprogrammed its horizon. The computer thinks we're at ground level. I'm going to release the tilting mechanism in three … two … one –'

Wren jabbed the unlocking button. Then, as her panel gave a metallic whimper and didn't move, she set her shoulder to it. 'Come on.'

'I've got to stay leaning on this button, Wren, or it'll relock. You have to move it by yourself.'

Wren put her whole back against the panel and bent her knees; then she tried to straighten her legs. The whole panel groaned.

'You're doing it.' Raw shouted.

'It's not moving.'

'It will. Keep trying.'

She yelled and pressed her hands against the silicone at shoulder height. '*Move!*'

With a suddenness that shocked her, the panel suddenly tore free and swung outwards. The wind, which had been kept from the colony for so long, rushed underneath with a howl and swept Wren off her feet. Her wings fluttered and she grabbed the edge of the panel. O_2 hissed as it was sucked through the hole and past her into the atmosphere.

'*Wren!*' Raw yelled and leaped for her. He grabbed one of her feet and wrapped his other arm around the console.

Then there were flames. Blazing O_2 raged past Wren almost too fast to burn. Screaming, she closed her eyes and wished for her goggles. She could feel her eyebrows charring and her hair crisping on her head.

Her cheeks and bare fingers heated and her tunic smouldered.

Her wings were almost tearing from her back, fluttering so madly in the power of the escaping gas that she was sure they would soon be torn into the sky.

She screamed as Raw's grip on her leg loosened. She couldn't hold on much longer. She couldn't see, but she could imagine herself tossed into the atmosphere if he let go. If she was dragged out of the Dome, she could fly, but the mid-day gale was coming and who knew where she'd end up.

'Don't let go,' she screamed.

Her ears throbbed as an alarm higher pitched than any she had heard before started to wail: low O_2.

Suddenly the panel shook as something hard slammed into it. Then more hands grabbed her; lending their strength to Raw's they defied the wind, pulled her inside, and dragged her under the console.

Wren collapsed against Raw, chest heaving, and split open her eyelids. Escaping O_2 shrieked around them making their wings flutter into a blinding silver funnel.

Colm faced her, his dark eyes intent on her face. '*Skies*, Wren, we didn't think.' She had to read his lips to understand him.

'*Designers* …' Raw went to touch her face, but then stopped. 'How much does it hurt?'

'How did you get up here?' Wren yelled. She stared at Colm. Jay was crouched behind her. His hands knotted around her stomach, pinning her to both Raw and the joist and crushing the breath from her.

'On the O_2,' Colm shouted his reply and his jaw tightened. 'Like rockets. Are you all right?' The wail of escaping gas abruptly eased, almost as quickly as it had started. The wind once more pushed into the Dome.

Wren didn't dare feel her cheeks. Her skin was numb.

She nodded. Then rolled onto the edge of the platform and looked down. A few masked colonists were staggering, apparently shocked, others had collapsed. There was no sign of fire.

'Let's go.' Jay pointed to the open panel. 'It's the perfect take off point. We don't need the Runway.' His hair streamed in the wind.

'We can't.' Wren cocked her head at the sun. 'The mid-day gales are coming.'

'And we've got to shut the panel.' Raw gripped the central node. 'I can't do it from outside. I have to re-programme.'

'Screw the panel,' Jay snapped.

'O_2 is escaping as fast as it's being generated.' Wren frowned. 'They're already suffocating.' Below them sirens still wailed.

'I don't care.' Jay folded his arms.

Raw squared up. 'I'm not going to be responsible for wiping out a whole colony.'

'The world needs them.' Wren exhaled shakily. 'Jay, we've already lost Tir Na Nog, we can't lose the Vaikunthans too.'

'Wren's right,' Colm sighed. 'We'll have to take off from the Runner platform with the others.'

'Wren can't.' Jay reminded him. 'If the Runners see her alive, they'll take her wings and throw her off.'

Raw put his arm around Wren's shoulders. 'We'll wait until the others have all gone and then go. The Councillor said he'd free us if we opened the panel.'

Colm nodded. 'All right. What do we do?'

'I'm going to restore the programme; you'll need to pull the panel shut against the wind.'

Raw typed more slowly this time and one-handed. He was holding himself close to the keyboard with the other, resisting the pull of the wind.

Wren tried to go to the panel, but Colm held her back. 'Stay back, hold our legs.'

He and Jay set themselves in the centre of the panel and gripped the edges. Their wings flapped and snapped around them.

'The button,' Raw shouted.

Wren pushed the unlocking mechanism. Something clanked

deep inside the panel.

'Pull!' he yelled.

Colm and Jay hauled downwards. The wind blew ever harder, the gale rising and tugging at the square, desperate to keep it open.

'It's not moving.' Jay leaned his full weight and the whole section groaned.

Wren leaped across and grabbed his legs, lending her weight to his.

Colm gasped as a gust lifted him skywards. 'Colm!' Wren screamed. Jay released the panel and grabbed him. Then the wind, fickle as ever, changed direction for a mere heartbeat and the panel slammed downward.

Colm was shaken free and Jay gasped as his fingers were trapped in the seam.

Colm slammed into the metal grid and Wren pulled Jay's fingers free as the panel locked back into place. 'Let me see.'

Jay pushed her off and shoved his hands under his armpits. 'I'll be fine.' He looked at Raw. 'Happy now? We're trapped here.'

Raw squatted on the platform. 'Look.' He pointed at the stirring colonists. The O_2 alarm whispered into silence.

'They'll have to live on low O_2 for a while,' Wren murmured.

'But they'll live.' Raw gripped her hand. 'I didn't kill them all.'

Wren shook her head. 'Are we staying up here till the gale dies?'

Colm nodded. 'No-one else is getting up here, we couldn't be safer.'

They leaned against the central node, arms and legs around joists and watched the last of the colonists lurch into their homes. Around them the solar panels shook as the wind drove biting sand against the Dome.

Raw put one arm around Wren and she closed her eyes.

26

When Wren awoke, her brothers were muttering to one another. She stirred and Jay looked at her guiltily. 'Didn't mean to wake you.'

'It's okay.' Wren rubbed her eyes and winced. Her skin felt as if it had been sanded. 'What's happening?'

Raw pointed towards the Runner platform. Even from their perch, Wren could see that the airlock had cycled green.

The first Runner was already through it and racing along the platform. As soon as his feet left the red line, the second pelted out onto the boards and, like a silver ribbon, the row of Runners unfurled into the wind; escaping from Vaikuntha to Run over the delta.

Wren was used to seeing far reaching views; she lived at the top of Elysium Mons, yet the sight of the Runners from the top of the Dome was one she knew would stay with her for the rest of her life.

She turned slowly, taking in the whole delta. Around them, rocks, abraded to smoothness, formed organic looking ridges like veins across the desert. They glittered with seams of mica, quartz and obsidian, gold and other precious metals, bright colours that the height of Elysium made bland orange or brown. The recent gale had ironed out the dust, but even as she watched, arrows grew and moved, sand-writing drawn by the Creatures. If she squinted, she could almost read meanings in the senseless scrawl of their movement.

Clouds scudded across the violet sky and patches of green shimmered in the distance like mirages. Beyond them the rising grey line of the approaching mega-storm and then the Runners, seeking height and distance from captivity.

When the last of them had left the airlock, Colm stood. 'Time to go.'

Wren stretched and Raw helped her to stand. She shook her legs, trying to loosen them.

'Just glide to the platform,' Colm said. 'There isn't any wind, but we're heading downwards, so we should be all right. You just have to keep your wings locked till you get there. Don't forget to drop your legs at the platform.'

'She knows what to do.' Raw straightened. 'The question is, do *you*?'

Wren touched his forearm. 'Stop it, Raw.' She looked at Colm. 'I'll be fine.'

'All right then.' Colm frowned. 'Follow me.' He leaped from the platform and thrust out his arms. His wings locked and Wren held her breath as he started to glide downwards, too fast; there wasn't enough air, they had vented it all. Colm aimed for the platform and slammed into the staircase below it with an audible thud.

Wren clutched her wing straps until he waved. Then she relaxed. Colonists were hastening towards the platform; she thought she recognised Erb, the fat Councillor among them. She indicated their rush with a tilt of her head. 'We've got to go.'

'You next,' Jay said.

Wren shrugged. She rotated her shoulders and then set her face towards Colm's swiftly climbing figure.

Before she could jump, Raw caught her shoulder and spun her around. His lips touched hers. He released her almost before she realised what was happening. 'Good luck.'

Wren touched her lips and smiled. Then she turned and, in one smooth movement, leaped from the metal grid.

Joists flashed in front of her face, silver against the violet of the sky beyond the stippled Dome. She angled herself between two and felt the gentlest of air beneath her unlocked wings. Unable to prevent herself, she half closed her arms and rolled into a joyful spin, slanting downwards and whooping as she heard Jay's horrified shout. She evened out, flicked her arms straight and locked. Catching the updraft from the damaged O_2 tanks, she glided smoothly towards the Runner platform and her brother who had turned at Jay's cries.

She landed lightly just above him, closing her wings neatly into her sides as she touched down.

Colm was flushed red. 'What did you think you were doing? You could kill yourself flying like a … like a –'

Wren laughed. 'It was an easy glide, Colm.' She looked up. The Runner platform was only a level above them. A shout from below demanded that they stop. She peered over the railing: Erb. She waved at Raw and Jay. 'Come on!'

They leaped together from the top of the Dome, a pair of wings flashing in a ray of sunlight.

Like Colm, Raw was almost too heavy for the weakened air. Jay flew above him, his lighter frame giving him more lift. Raw came in first, almost too fast to see. He crashed into Colm with the force of an uprooted gingko. Colm grabbed him and they reeled backwards to crunch into the railing. The staircase juddered with the force of their impact. Jay followed, hammering into the pair of them, in a tangle of wings and limbs.

Colm groaned. The staircase creaked and Wren looked over the side. The Councillor was taking the steps two at a time. 'No time to lose.' She dragged Jay off Raw and the relief in his green eyes told her that his back had taking a beating. She pushed Jay towards the last set of stairs. 'Climb!'

She grabbed Raw's arm and helped him to his feet. Raw took his own weight, put an arm around her and drove her forward. She looked back to see Colm running to overtake them.

The four Runners raced to the platform, their wings flying behind them.

Jay gripped a railing and jumped over, saving himself half a staircase. Colm copied him and was soon in front. Raw pushed Wren ahead of him. Coughing and gasping for breath she looked back. They were leaving the fat Councillor several flights below them.

Then they were facing the Runner platform. Wren put her hands on her knees, choking for breath. There was a Runner station behind them and ahead, an airlock cycled red. The platform itself was built so that it went through the airlock and continued on the other side. The leaping lines were outside the Dome, above the desert. A ragged net hung beneath the platform. It would catch her only if she fell straight down.

'Who first?' She moved towards the airlock but Colm raised his eyebrows. 'We fly in order of seniority. I go first. Then Jay, then you and the *Grounder* is last.' He glared at Raw and then strode past Wren, towards the airlock.

He pressed a palm against the reader and it cycled green. Then he stepped backwards shook out his wings and bent into a starting position

For some reason the snick of an opening door caught Wren's attention when she should have been wholly focused on her brother. She glanced over her shoulder and her eyes widened. 'Genna!'

The Sphere-Mistress emerged from the Runner Station. She was almost unrecognisable; her face was so twisted with hatred. Her eyes blazed and her lips were pressed together, pale with rage.

At Wren's whisper, Colm stopped his preparations and turned. 'Sphere-Mistress Genna.' He nodded a greeting. 'You can come out of hiding. Your Council has agreed to let us go.'

Genna came closer, one hand was snarled in her skirt, the other fixed behind her back. Wren couldn't take her eyes from the hand she could not see. As Genna came nearer, some instinct made Wren retreat towards Raw.

'You're alive,' Genna rasped. 'We thought you were dead.'

Wren shook her head; she had no answer.

'We're going to deal with her in Elysium.' Colm said, keeping his tone low and calm. Why was he talking like that? Wren frowned.

'So, you're going to let her fly again.' Genna spat. 'Blasphemy on blasphemy.' Her voice rose.

Colm held his hands out, steady, and walked carefully forward. His voice remained low and clear. 'Patriarch Chayton will want to deal with her. I promise to make sure the wings get back safely. We'll send word once her punishment has been carried out.'

'Why wait?' Genna lurched forward. 'Why not throw her from *this* platform?' She reached with her free hand for Wren's wings and Raw yanked her out of Genna's reach.

Colm kept talking. 'I'm not Elysium's Patriarch.' He gave a deprecating smile. 'I can't make the decision. Once Chayton is back from Lake Lyot –'

'You don't need your Patriarch to pass judgement. You know exactly what Convocation would decide.' Her lip curled.

The platform shuddered again and Erb appeared at the top of the stairs. The fat Councillor was gasping for breath, his halfie half dangling from his nose, his chin wet with spit. Damp patches crept from his underarms towards his waist and his breath heaved in wet sucking rasps.

He saw Genna and froze.

Wren wriggled from Raw's grasp. 'Genna, I didn't cause the plague. Runner's spread it, that's true, but not me. I've never Run before this.'

Genna wailed, an insane sound, full of fury, hatred and frustration. 'The plague? What has that to do with this? You stole Runner wings, you filthy, irreverent, disgusting, blasphemous …' she sputtered, seeking further insults and Colm moved nearer. Now he stood beside Wren. He edged a hand between her and Raw and pushed her backwards, towards the platform.

'What are you doing?' Genna roared and her hidden hand came into view.

Wren saw what had stopped Erb. Genna wielded a long knife, one of the tools of a Sphere-Mistress that would have been kept inside the Runner station. 'Hand her over, Elysians,' she growled.

Wren's gut tightened.

Colm glanced at Erb, who held his hands up, still unmoving.

'We've been granted clemency.' Colm said again. 'The Councillors have said we're free to go.'

Then why is Erb here? Wren thought: trying to stop us from leaving.

'What has the Vaikunthan Council got to do with Runner

law?' Genna spat. 'I don't care about the rest of you, but that vile witch has to die.'

'We're not giving you our sister.' Jay's fists were clenched.

Wren backed towards the platform.

'No!' Genna wailed. 'You won't get away.' She lunged, twisting like water beneath Raw's arm and Colm's grasping hand. Wren could only stumble backwards, her hands raised defensively, as the Sphere-Mistress came at her screaming vengeance. There was no-one between them. Genna was already lifting the knife and jabbing at Wren's ribcage.

Colm leaped, his wings spreading to give him distance and lift. He landed right in front of Wren; his arms closed around her, and his eyes met hers. The force of his landing knocked the breath from them both and they fell together onto the platform. Wren struck her head on the airlock rim but, over the ringing in her ears, she heard the hiss as it opened and Jay's shriek, like nothing she had ever heard before.

There was a rush of silver above her and a tangle of limbs and skirt. Genna's furious cries shattered in her ears and Wren writhed.

'Colm, get off me, I can't breathe!'

She craned her neck and saw Raw bundle the Sphere-Mistress into the airlock.

Erb shouted at them to get away from the airlock, but she was pinned, couldn't move; could only watch as Raw ripped Genna's halfie from her face.

'Raw, no!'

Raw was beyond hearing. Genna fought and scratched, but he hurled her to the back of the airlock, leaped back into the Dome and slapped his hand on the palm reader.

Genna hammered on the airlock door for whole seconds. And then it cycled open over the desert. Her eyes widened, her hands went to her throat and she collapsed. Wren could no longer see her, but she could hear the drumming of her feet against metal. And then that too, stopped.

'What have you done?' She struggled to get out from under her brother. Why wasn't he moving? 'Colm, *get off*!'

Colm's eyes were still focused on hers. 'Wait a moment, Wren,' he whispered. Blood flecked his lips. Had he bitten his tongue when they fell?

He freed one arm from around her and touched her face. 'Do you remember flying kites with me?'

Wren nodded. 'We can talk later, there's no time now.'

Colm swallowed and more blood appeared on his face. It dripped onto Wren's neck. She couldn't wipe it away. For some reason Erb wasn't coming closer. Jay thudded to his knees at her side and there was something wrong with his face.

Raw remained standing.

She looked once more at Colm, a horrible suspicion growing. 'Colm ... are you all right?'

'Don't worry about me.' Colm's lips twitched. 'You'll have to lead the other two home, Wren ...' he coughed this time and Wren winced as gore spattered her cheeks.

'What do you –'

'You're the best Runner in the family.' Colm shook his head slightly and his eyes unfocused. 'I wouldn't have believed it, but –'

'Colm, *you're* leading us home.' Wren's chest tightened; she could hardly speak.

'Bear right from the ... Runway,' he whispered.

Colm shifted his gaze to Raw and Raw nodded. He reached down and caught Wren's shoulders. He eased her out from beneath her brother.

Wren struggled to her knees and held onto Raw for one precious heartbeat, stealing one moment when she could pretend everything was going to be fine. But she knew it wasn't. She pulled her face from Raw's chest and turned.

Erb stood like a loose-limbed statue, fat and sweating. She ignored him and looked, finally, at her brother. Now she could see only one thing: the graphene knife, sticking out from Colm's back and pinning his wings to him. Her eyes flashed to Jay. His met Wren's, so wide with horror that the whites were showing. He was silent, but Wren knew what he was saying – do something.

She turned to Raw, knowing it wasn't fair, knowing her eyes said the same thing as her brother's.

Raw swallowed as Colm's breath started to come in terrible rattles. 'I don't think we should pull out the knife.' Raw wrung his hands. 'It could kill him.'

Colm lay on his stomach, facing Wren. Now his blood pooled towards her knees. His wings fluttered around his body like escaping breath, and the knife twitched jerkily with each hitching inhalation. 'Take … it … out.'

'No!'

He half rolled and reached into his pocket. He pulled out a small packet and Wren's breath caught in her throat. Her mother's medicine, she had almost forgotten about it. He pressed it into her hand. 'Get this home.'

Wren shook her head, but she took the packet with trembling fingers and tucked it into her belt.

Colm looked at Raw. 'Do … it.'

Terror blocked Wren's throat, she choked on the bitter taste, but found Colm's hand. She interlocked her fingers with her brother's, crouched down as low as she could and forced him to look into her eyes. 'You're going to be fine.'

His hand was cold, as if dipped in the river they had swum through. He tried to nod, but agony shot across his face.

'Hold him still.' Wren's head shot up, but Raw was looking at Jay.

Jay pressed his forearms on Colm's back, one either side of the knife. 'Ready?' Raw shouted.

Jay nodded, his face drawn, his teeth showing outside his lips.

Raw didn't look at Wren but she saw him take a deep breath and close his hands around the handle.

Colm's hand convulsed in hers' and immediately she shifted her attention back to her brother.

She pressed her mouth to his ear. 'It's going to hurt, but it'll be okay.'

'On three?' Raw's voice trembled as he shouted. 'One … two …'

'Three.' Wren whispered it with him and kept her eyes locked on Colm's as Raw pulled the knife.

Colm bucked and his hand tightened so hard over hers' that she thought he might have broken her fingers.

She refused to look away as Jay pulled Colm's ripped wings from the wound. 'There's so much blood,' he choked.

A bundle of material was thrust into his hand and Wren looked up, surprised. Erb had removed his tunic. His bare chest heaved in the afternoon light. Rolls of fat hung over his trouser top and the folds of his skin were flushed and damp.

Jay's fingers cramped on the linen and he pressed it to the wound. Instantly it reddened.

Colm's eyes drifted closed and Wren shook him furiously. 'Don't you *dare* go to sleep. You think this is a good time for a nap?'

His eyes opened again and Wren risked a quick look up. Jay was sobbing hysterically as he tried to stem the blood flow. Raw's hands too, were working madly beneath her brother's wings.

Quickly, Wren looked back at Colm's face. His cheeks were white, but splashed with livid blood that was drying to brown on his lips.

'There's less blood,' she croaked. 'That's good, right?'

No answer came from her brother or Raw and suddenly she didn't dare look away from Colm's face. Somewhere deep inside she knew that if she let Colm close his eyes again, he wouldn't open them. 'We're going home, Colm,' she whispered into his ear. 'Mother's waiting for us.'

Colm sagged into stillness.

'No!' Wren snapped. 'Stay awake.'

Colm's lips twitched as if he was trying to smile. Tears blurred Wren's vision and when she could see again, the light had fled Colm's eyes.

'Colm!' She shook his hand, but he made no movement. She leaned right down, lying so that her ear was by his mouth. There was no rattle of breath. She shot onto her knees. 'Raw!' She hammered his shoulder.

He immediately turned to her, his face tragic. Jay was already still, his head hanging, his hands useless.

'What're you doing? Don't *stop!*'

Raw caught her hand. 'He's gone,' he said quietly.

'It's your fault,' Wren sobbed. 'We should have left the knife in.'

Raw jolted as if she'd punched him, but Jay reached over Colm's body and pinched her face, forcing her to look at him. 'What else could we have done?'

'But he's dead!' Wren's face contorted with the power of her agony. 'Colm's dead.' She collapsed over her brother's corpse, tears shaking her aching heart. A weight half crushed her, and only when she felt his warmth on her back, did she realise Jay had fallen himself, bawling in her ear as loudly as he had when he was seven years old and broken his ankle.

Strangely Jay's wailing forced an odd calm through her, just as it had when she was five and had to half carry him home.

She struggled out from beneath him and, still clutching Colm's hand, she spoke to Raw. 'I'm sorry.' She looked at Colm again, her hands shaking with the force of her grief. 'I – It wasn't your fault.'

Then, searching for somewhere less painful to rest, her gaze went to the Councillor who now stood with his head bowed.

'You're here for us,' she said.

Erb swallowed. 'You saved the colony.' He wiped sweat from his brow. 'Here.' He held out a twist of paper. 'The Runners have gone, spreading the plague.' He shook his head. 'So, we have to spread the cure. This is the formula for the medicine. If you can get it to Aaru they might be able to mass produce …'

Raw took the formula and tucked it into his shirt. 'And what about …?' He indicated Wren with a tilt of his head.

'Yes.' The Councillor licked thick lips. 'It's a shame about the girl.'

Jay's head shot up.

'A shame that the Sphere-Mistress killed her before your Convocaton could exact justice.' The Councillor gestured pushed past to lift Colm's body and began unstrapping his wings.

'What are you doing?' Wren leaped to her feet and Erb paused with Colm pressed to his chest, the bloody wings half off his back.

Colm looked peaceful. His eyes remained open and now, in the arms of the Vaikunthans, his face was half turned to the sky.

Raw reached down to close his eyes, but Wren caught his wrist. 'That's not our way. He's looking at the sky, that's right.'

Jay nodded miserably. 'I'll lie as I lived, under wings, under sky ...'

Wren could barely finish. 'Don't bury me deep in the dust when I die.' She leaned gratefully against Raw for just one moment. Then she followed Colm's final gaze upwards to the lavender sky.

'Say good-bye, Wren.' Raw whispered.

'What are you–?'

The Councillor spat to one side. 'Your Runners will want to see proof of your death.' Awkwardly he released Colm from his wings. 'Now I have something to show them.'

'But – what about Colm?'

Raw met Erb's lizard glare. Then he turned Wren to face him. 'We have to get rid of his body. Someone will see three Runners heading to Avalon. Colm has to be one of them.'

Wren's heart turned to stone. 'You can't mean –'

Raw nodded. Erb left the wings on the platform. He took Colm's shoulders and Raw his feet. As Wren and Jay stared, hopelessly, they carried him like a sack of seeds to the airlock and, silently Raw pressed his palm against the reader. It cycled open.

'Wait.' Wren took Jay's hand and led him to Raw's side. 'Not without us.'

They stepped through the airlock and over Genna's crumpled body. They stood inside, nothing to say, only the sound of their breathing tainting the air.

Then the door opened onto the desert and the wind whipped inside, welcoming them back.

They walked forward, staggering under Colm's weight. The wind tore at his hair, as if wondering why he didn't rise and fly.

Then Raw and Erb lifted Colm up and swung him over the edge of the platform. The Creature's trails showed them accelerating towards her falling brother before he even hit the ground.

27

Wren couldn't watch. She turned away, letting the wind whip her hair into her face, and the next time she risked a glance at the sand, he was gone.

Raw's face was drum-tight while Jay's sagged as if his skull had turned to mush beneath his skin.

Erb nodded, turned and strode back into the airlock. He sighed and started to drag Genna's body out.

'Should we …?' Jay murmured.

'Let him do it.' Wren shook her head and coughed. 'We're going home.'

She didn't bother stretching, or even taking a starting position. She pulled her goggles on and then jogged out over the net, she could barely bring herself to run. Heavy with grief, she did not leap, but rather fell from the end of the platform and allowed the wind to drag her wings out as it caught her.

Her wings locked and she was pulled from the platform. She circled to see Jay leaping and Raw following him, both hurling themselves into the wind as if they could hurt it.

The two sets of wings rose to meet her and Wren's stomach churned; neither were wearing goggles. She had to be their eyes and Colm had known it. Somehow, she had to get them safely home.

She looked outwards, seeking Elysium Mons. She could see nothing clearly. Then she remembered Colm's final advice: '*Bear right from the Runway*'.

She wheeled right.

There it was; a bump on the horizon. The dust from the impending mega-storm swirled, like a heat haze, but the bump rose higher still. It had to be the Mons.

'Look at the Runners,' Jay shouted and Wren redirected

her gaze. The Runners who had preceded them had scattered like seeds, each blown towards his own settlement. But as they dipped and whorled in the air currents, flashes of nimbus-like light glowed from their wings and created patterns of light as though they were still connected.

Wren released her breath and tears filled her eyes. 'Follow me,' she called. 'We're going home.'

Aiming for height, Wren tried to watch both Raw and Jay at the same time. Her eyes watered with the effort and her chest went into spasm as she fought the agonizing tingle of an impending coughing fit.

If only she could have a drink of water.

Water was suddenly all she could think about. Despite all that had happened all she could think about was the cup of water she could not have. She licked her cracked lips and moaned. Her wings matched the sound as the wind carried her ever further and the sun slid across the sky.

Wren's jacket clung to her, sticky with sweat. Suddenly a cloud hid the sun and her heart rose in anticipation of a reprieve from the post-Perihelion heat. However, she felt no cooler. If anything, it was as though she had been plunged into a over-hot bath. Sweat dripped down the inside of her goggles.

'Are you all right?'

With a start Wren realised that Raw had flown to her side. 'What?'

'You're wobbling. I've never seen you wobble before.'

Wren forced herself to answer in a voice loud enough to carry. 'I'm tired.'

Raw nodded. 'Can you make it?'

Wren looked down. Familiar arrows traced their shadows on the eddying sand. 'We can't stop.'

Raw nodded again and they flew on.

Wren's wings, once so light, weighed on her until her muscles quivered with effort. Now her throat not only burned for water, but her arms felt like dead branches. Only the wind pressing against them prevented her from trying to shake some life back into her shoulders. She tried to watch the desert skimming by, but her eyes watered and it was all she could do to focus on the Mons. She had to fly in the right direction; Raw and Jay were relying on her. And they were close now, so close that she could see strata of colour in the cliff and shards of white in the bone-yard.

Abruptly the wind growled and she rocked, dangerously off-balance.

She leaned right, fighting a pull to the left, but the wind buffeted her playfully and held its breath. Wren's wings fluttered and her stomach lurched; she had flown them into turbulence. Then warm air picked her up again. Struggling to remain parallel with the ground, Wren rolled to regain her balance. Slowly she levelled out and released a sobbing breath.

This time Jay flew to her, pitching and yawing jerkily.

Wren staved him off with a shake of her head, feeling as though blood was sloshing inside her skull. She dipped her shoulder to find a stronger current and Jay dropped behind her.

Wren began to cry. Her legs were shaking and her chest felt as though it was being slowly crushed. She struggled to breathe and phlegm clogged her tonsils. Helplessly she filled her goggles with tears as she coughed uncontrollably and waves of heat rippled through her.

'I want to be home,' she whispered, wretched.

'Come home, baby.' Her mother's face appeared in front of her. 'I'm waiting for you.' She began to dance – twirling around Wren in a purple dress the colour of the sky.

Cheerful music filled her ears and Wren blinked to find Colm, grinning around his tin whistle as he played to the beat of their mother's drumming heels. In the background Raw gave his slow twisted smile. Her heart did a flip as he mouthed her name.

'Wren?' Raw's voice was raised; he had clearly been calling her for some time.

In front of Wren, the sky whirled like a purple dress.

'Wren, can you hear me?' Raw was shouting at her, but she could not stop her head from drooping. 'Stay with me, Wren. Jay – help!'

It was strange; although Raw looked happy to see her, his voice was filled with alarm. She looked down at herself. Her dress hung wrong because she was holding her arms out at an odd stiff angle – she looked like a tree. She tried to drop her arms to her sides, but they wouldn't move. She frowned. There was some sort of resistance and for some reason her elbows were locked and aching. She forced her arms down.

Raw's shout turned into a scream.

As the wind fled her folding wings, Wren dropped silently and without protest.

Raw hurled himself after her, clutching at the space she'd occupied as if she had left part of herself behind that he could save. 'Jay!' The wind burned his streaming eyes and he could hardly see, but he heard Jay's answering cry. Rolling, Raw saw Wren's brother shooting downwards, his wings narrowed as he pointed himself after his plummeting sister.

Immediately Raw copied him, tipping his torso and streamlining his wings. The wind had already tipped Wren onto her back and her wings fluttered around her as if to cushion her from the coming blow. A tiny amount of lift was all they offered, but it was enough to slightly slow her descent.

The wind whistled mockingly in his ears as he dived. He wasn't sure what he could do when caught up to her, but there had to be something.

Jay's head turned. 'Her arm,' he screamed.

Raw assumed the gale had stolen his true meaning. 'What?' he shouted.

'She's lighter than any man. Catch her!'

Instantly Raw understood. He set his jaw. This could be suicide. But he didn't care and, apparently, neither did Wren's brother.

Raw saw only the blur of silver below him. He had no intention of losing Wren and had fixed his eyes on the glowing corona of her wings, which didn't seem to be getting any closer. Then he was on top of her and everything happened in an instant.

Recklessly he tilted, trying to grab her hand. His fingers brushed hers and the heat of her skin on his cold palm made him gasp. Then she slipped free and he lost her. On Wren's other side, he could sense Jay grappling with her other arm, but his peripheral vision was long gone and he could not see him properly.

Suddenly Wren tipped. Her wings flattened across her face and her gentle fall whipped into a frenzied plummet.

Jay must have caught her and now he was going down too.

Raw snatched desperately. He rolled and his own wings tried to unlock, but the end of Wren's wing smacked into his hand.

He remembered trying to catch her once before; her wings sliding out of his fingers as she ran from him. Now they slid again, slippery as blood, but he flicked his hand and wrapped the material around his wrist, grabbing a strut to ensure his grip.

For too long the three of them fell. Then Jay and Raw managed to straighten out. They hung almost suspended, neither falling nor rising, with Wren dangling awkwardly beneath them.

Jay had her arm and Raw her wing, so she hung facing her brother, one leg flopping over nothing, the other tangled inside the span of silver material.

With every outward breath Jay sobbed, frantically trying to catch his breath and failing. Raw's jaw was clenched so tight it was agony. He tasted blood. Desperately he looked for the cliffs of Elysium but he was disoriented and had no idea which direction he was facing.

Then Wren's weight started to pull them downwards. Slowly they dropped in an ungainly, but controlled glide.

Jay's bloodshot eyes were wide. 'If we land in the desert, we're dead.'

Raw nodded grimly. Neither of them let go. They spiralled inside the wind, their wings trapped by Wren's weight, unable even to guide their descent.

Raw gave up squinting into the biting blasts of air. He couldn't see where they were going; only vague splashes of colour that came and went as they turned.

On one rotation a snatch of turbulence stole his breath and turned Wren's face briefly towards him before it fell back down. She looked completely at peace.

He closed his eyes and focused on his grip. He would need all the strength that remained to him if he had to carry her up the Mons.

Jay was shouting at him. Raw opened his throbbing eyes. A green blur filled his vision then suddenly Wren's wing was yanked from his hands. He rolled forward, pitched sideways and his face smashed into solid ground. Jay spun past him, a tangle of arms and legs and a blur of cracking wings.

Ignoring the pain in his arm and the agony of his back, Raw forced himself to his feet. Blood ran into his eyes and he slashed it away with an impatient swipe of his wrist. His face throbbed and he was weather-blind.

'Wren,' he shouted. 'Jay?' There was no answer.

His arms were pinned from behind. Raw fought, but there was no reprieve. A man's wide chest pressed against his back and his arms were held to his waist. Frantically Raw blinked. Where were they? He had to see.

Gradually his vision cleared, and his eyes widened with shock. Avalon hunched on the edge of the cliff in front of him, defiant in its stand against the wind. Wren really had brought them home.

Then his ringing ears caught the full force of the fury of the man who held him. 'What *in the skies* is going on?'

Tortured by the exact words he had heard once before, when he had tried to save his own family from Caro's disease, Raw filled with terror. Able to do nothing else, his chest convulsed with bitter laughter. Chayton was back from Convocation. They were dead after all.

28

Wren first became aware of the voices. They sounded barely human, so full of anger. So, she had woken in hell, doomed by her sacrilege. Silently she laughed: the colonists had been right all along. The Designer really had been watching over them and cursing Wren's blasphemy.

Still she struggled to comprehend the hatred that singed the air around her.

'You thought I would believe this?'

'When Jay wakes up –'

'You think he'll back your story? It wasn't enough to let Caro's destroy your face, boy?'

'Any Runner there –'

'– will kill my daughter on sight, thanks to you.'

'Blasphemy …' Wren's lips formed a whisper and immediately the snarling stopped.

Then it started up again. 'I heard that. You said she would support your wild tale! You just never thought she'd wake.'

'Wren, can you hear me?' Hands closed around her own; not Runner's hands, but comforting all the same.

'Get away from my daughter, Grounder *filth*. To think I fought Convocation for you and yours.'

The words had meanings. Wren had to try harder to understand. The voices, angry as they were, soothed her. She strained to focus, trying to hear more. Then the hands were torn away.

'Let me go to her.' That voice made her lips tingle.

With a great effort Wren opened her aching eyes. 'Water?'

In moments a cup was held to her mouth and she gulped. Cool liquid spilled down her neck and dampened her collar. It was musty, not freshly pumped, but it soothed her burning throat.

She tried to lift her head and immediately someone lifted her to a sitting position. Her nose pressed into a tunic and the scent was wonderful. 'Father, did you die too?'

Chayton's arms tightened around her but she struggled to look past him; she had heard Raw, where was he? Confused, she realised that she recognised the room.

'This is Avalon,' she murmured. 'We made it home?'

Raw was slumped against the far wall. With a surge of relief, she sought her brother. Jay lay motionless on his cot, his breathing heavy as a snore.

Almost reluctantly her eyes searched Avalon's last corner. The curtains around Mia's bed were closed and the floor remained covered with untouched jugs and cups of old water.

'Mother?'

'Hush.' Chayton wiped ragged tails of hair from her face.

Wren fought free of his hold. 'I have a cure.' With fingers that felt like sticks, she fumbled in her belt for the packet Colm had handed her.

Raw surged to his feet. 'Wait!'

Chayton had already taken the medicine from his daughter and turned to the curtained cubicle. His fingers tightened around the prize. 'Wait?'

'Wren's sick too.'

Chayton stared at Raw, then at the packet in his hand. 'There's only a single dose? Enough for only one of them?'

Raw nodded.

'So, I have to choose: my wife, or my daughter.' Chayton's face tightened.

Instantly Raw clenched his fists. 'Why should *you* choose?'

'What did you say?' Chayton's reply was a whip of sound.

'Did *you* bring the cure back?' Raw strode forward. 'Did *you* save the Runners? What right have you got to choose?'

'What *right*?' Chayton's chest expanded. 'I'm the *Patriarch*. I am the only one *with* rights.'

Raw's eye flicked to the graphene knife hanging by the airlock. He jumped over the table and grabbed it in shaking hands. 'You won't take her from me.'

Chayton looked at Raw with a blazing gaze. 'You're both condemned to death for your blasphemy. Why should I lose my wife too?'

'Wren's your *daughter.*' Raw's knuckles were white on the knife handle. 'No Runner need even know she's still alive. The Vaikunthan Councillor will tell everyone she's already dead. Send her to the Women's Sector. Send her to *me.*' His eyes were watering. Wren gaped: Raw was crying. 'You already lost a son today. Don't lose a daughter too.'

'And Wren's mother?'

'I –'

'Wren.' The voice was whisper soft yet it silenced every sound in the room. Chayton dived towards the curtained alcove and swept back the material. Mia was not moving, even the rise and fall of her chest barely disturbed the air above her yet, somehow, she had managed her daughter's name.

'Mother!' Wren tried to lurch out of bed and Raw leaped to her side.

'Her mother would want Wren to take the cure,' he pleaded.

Chayton waved him to silence and dropped to his knees at his wife's side. 'I don't want to lose you.' His voice was a murmur.

Mia's hand trembled violently on the coverlet. 'Wren,' was all she said. Chayton's shoulder's shook.

'I didn't bring the cure back for myself,' Wren said wrenching her arm from Raw's.

Then she clutched her head as an alarm reverberated through the room, warning them before the airlock cycled open.

Wren stared at the figure silhouetted against the sky.

'Why have I had to come all the way up here?' the man snapped. 'Incoming Runner's were seen, yet no-one has informed the Council. You are neglecting your responsibilities, so maybe we should neglect our tithes, what do you think?'

Wren tried to focus through the glare as the setting sun glowed red behind the newcomer and set him on fire. She could not see who it was but her ears supplied the answer. 'Grandfather Win?' she whispered and the airlock closed behind him.

'Councillor.' Raw dropped the knife with a clatter but Wren's grandfather strode right by him, his pendants swinging.

'While I'm here, where is Mia?'

Wren saw his shoulders stiffen as he saw the figure on the bed. 'She really is dying?'

His eyes flicked to a swaying Wren. 'And the girl too. I should never have left them here with you. You brought Mia to her death, Runner, I hope you're happy.' Although the words were spat, Wren heard the tremor beneath the poison.

'We have a cure,' she rasped.

'Then why haven't you used it?' Her grandfather sneered. 'Too stupid I suppose. Give it to me.'

'No.' Raw stumbled forward and Chayton shoved the packet behind his back.

Win growled. 'What are you doing?'

'Give it to Wren,' Raw shouted.

Win glowered and the creases around his mouth and hooked nose deepened. 'What's going on here?'

'There's only enough cure for one.' As he spoke, Raw kept his eyes on Wren.

Win stared. Then he strode slowly across the room. He knelt by his daughter's side. 'Mia?'

For a long time, Mia did not move but then her eyes opened a crack. 'Father?'

Win held her hand in his, and Wren was shocked to see him tremble. 'Mia,' he said again, her name like a prayer. Mia closed her eyes and Win pressed his forehead to hers. 'I missed you. The pain was so great that I punished you for your choice. I should have forgiven you your decision. I'm so sorry.'

Mia tried to shake her head, but only managed to allow it to flop to one side. Win wiped the hair from her forehead. Her breath rasped slower and slower.

'You've not long left,' he muttered and Mia blinked her assent. She did not seem afraid.

Win fingered his black pendant as he stood. His hands were shaking. 'Give the cure to the girl.'

'No!' Chayton lurched towards Win and Raw blocked him. 'Why?' Chayton groaned, ignoring Raw. 'Do you hate her so much?'

Win's face tightened. 'Do you hate your own daughter?'

Chayton paled.

'You have *one dose*.' Win rubbed his face with trembling fingers. 'Mia is out of time. A single dose may not be enough to save her and then you'll have lost both of them. The girl … my grand-daughter … is sick, but she isn't yet dying. She can be saved.'

Wren collapsed, her canister suddenly feeling airless. 'You don't mean it. Give the cure to Mother.'

'Wren, you don't want to die from this plague,' Raw pleaded.

Win whirled. 'Plague? What do you mean, *plague*?'

Wren hung her head. 'Tir Na Nog is gone. Vaikuntha is dying.'

Win started to back towards the airlock. 'Are you telling me that you Runners have brought a plague on us?' His voice was ice.

'Don't be ridiculous,' Chayton snapped.

Raw swayed and closed his eyes. 'Yes, that's what we're saying.'

Chayton spun to face him, fury on his face, but Raw pointed at him with a finger like Death's. 'Only *you* could have infected Mia.'

Chayton sneered. 'Then why aren't I sick?'

Wren bit her lip. 'Erb said some could be carriers, not getting sick, just spreading the disease.'

Her father staggered, like a drunk at the end of a night. 'If I'm carrying this, half of the Runners at Convocation will be taking it home.'

He lurched past Win and ripped off his mask as he headed to the airlock like a man on fire looking for water. 'I must not be allowed to live.'

'Raw, stop him!' Wren coughed as agony ripped through her throat.

Raw leaped to the airlock, slapped his hand over the keypad next to the palm reader and entered a code that made it blink red. They were on lock-down.

Chayton folded as he turned back into the room. 'Give the cure to Wren then,' he muttered. 'Mia and I will be together soon enough.'

Wren's grandfather stood next to him. 'You disgust me,' he snapped. 'Be a man, even if you *are* a Runner.' He snatched the cure from Chayton's frozen fingers.

'Give the girl a three-quarter dose,' he said eventually. 'It'll have to be enough. Maybe our scientists will have time to synthesize more of this and we can save the colony when it hits.'

Raw shook his head. 'I've got the formula here. Can you use this instead?' He pulled the twist of paper Erb had given him from his shirt.

Win untwisted the paper and looked at it with a frown, then a nod.

Chayton clutched the door frame. 'We're the lungs of Mars, not the medics.'

'We still have a working synthesiser.' Win handed Raw the packet containing the cure. 'It isn't used often. Emergencies only. Save my grand-daughter. Once we have synthesized enough of the cure, Chayton can take samples out to Aaru and the other colonies. Maybe they have operational 'sizers left too.'

Chayton shook his head. 'I'm a carrier and there are no other able Runners here.'

Wren crouched over a cough; then straightened. 'Raw can do it.'

Chayton and Raw jerked in unison. 'No.' Raw shook his head. 'I'm not a Runner. I only followed you.'

Win looked at the unconscious Jay then tipped his chin at Raw. 'You're the closest thing to a Runner that we have right now. Chayton, you'll have to teach him what he doesn't know.'

Chayton opened his mouth and snapped it closed. 'Convocation would sentence me to death,' he muttered. Then he groaned. 'But ... I've broken with Convocation. The tithe they expect me to demand – it's insane. Grounders already mistrust Runners.' He hung his head. 'The decision Convocation have made will be the end of us all.'

Win's lip twitched as if he was trying to sneer, but could not. 'You have broken with Runner law?'

Chayton nodded grimly as Wren gasped.

Raw raised his head, hopeful. 'If that's true then Wren doesn't have to be punished.'

Wren's heart rose. 'Then Raw and I can Run for you.' She coughed again.

Wearily Chayton rubbed his face. 'Not you, Wren. If the Runners find out you're still alive, the High Patrions will come for you.'

He held out his hand and Wren placed her palm in his. Then he turned her arm so that her inner elbow faced the ceiling. 'Do it.'

'No!' Wren tried to jerk away, too late. Raw pressed the tab against her inner elbow and depressed the button. Air needled through her skin.

'What have you done?' she screamed.

Chayton lurched brokenly to his wife's side. Win strode to the window port and turned reddened eyes on his daughter.

Wren collapsed and her back sagged against the wall. Raw crouched next to her and she pushed him away. 'This is your fault. You should have let them give the cure to my mother. I hate you. I hate you all.'

Raw dropped his chin and pulled his hair down over his scarred face. He crouched at her side for a long time; finally, when she refused to look at him, he rose and sat at the table.

Chayton spoke without lifting his gaze from his wife. 'Wren can't be Sphere-Mistress any longer; she can't even stay here. When Runners come in, she'll be noticed.' His lips pursed as if he tasted something sour. He glanced at Raw. 'You want her?'

Raw nodded.

'I'm not a broken pot,' Wren cried. 'You can't just give me away. I'd rather join the damned baby exchange.'

Raw winced as if she had shot him and he pulled his hair

even lower. Her heart stuttered, but Wren ignored it. He had betrayed her.

Suddenly Mia's hand dropped from the bed and Wren froze. Chayton's head dropped to his wife's chest and Win held his own hand to his face. His breath came hard through vinegar-tight lips.

'She's gone?'

Chayton nodded.

Win turned to the airlock. 'Unlock this, I have work to do,' he snapped. Raw entered a code into the keypad.

Win looked once more at the unconscious Jay and then his eyes whisked around the otherwise empty room. He hesitated with his hand resting on the palm reader. 'I can see your eldest did not come home. I'm sorry for your losses.' Then he was gone.

The wail that ripped from Wren's throat was almost inhuman. Without thinking she groped for Raw's hand and pressed it to her heart as if only his touch could loosen the bands that had tightened around it.

One Month Later

Chayton watched as Raw swooped into a thermal above the platform. 'I didn't believe anyone but a Runner could Run.' He shook his head at Wren. 'There'll be some changes here before the other Patriarchs arrive.'

'The Patriarchs are coming?'

'Of course.' Chayton pushed his hair from his forehead. 'They'll want someone of their own to take over Avalon.'

'We won't let them.'

'Perhaps.' Chayton shrugged.

'What changes do you mean?' Wren frowned at him.

'We need to trust one another, Grounders and Runners. I'll offer lessons in Running to anyone that wants them. And, if a Runner wants to stay on land –' He glowered at Jay, who had refused to touch his wings since he had woken, 'I will allow it.' He raised his hand before Wren could speak. 'We won't have much time. When Convocation has finished repairing the damage caused by the early mega storm, they'll come.'

'What will they do?'

'Maybe they'll see a settlement that's working and leave us alone.' He stalked towards the platform where Raw was sweeping in for a landing. Wren looked at the scarred face as he touched down and her heart filled with hope.

Wren picked sullenly at a loose thread on the bedspread. Her grand-father had forced Tee to accept her into the Women's Sector and the days were slipping by. Soon someone would spot the Patriarchs Running in. She was going to have to leave Avalon.

Jay took her hand. 'It might not be as bad as you expect.'

'Remember the last time I went into Elysium, how they treated me?'

Jay sighed. 'You won't be in the Women's Sector long. It's the Choosing in a few days.'

'And then what? Where do I live?'

'Things between Runners and Grounders are improving. They'll have to accept you when you're married.'

'Raw betrayed me? I don't want to be with him.'

Jay's lips twitched. 'Are you sure about that?'

Wren looked away; her chest had tightened at the lie.

The airlock opened and Chayton stamped in. He had a pair of wings in his hands.

Wren held her breath and Jay's eyes immediately went to the window port. 'Have they …?'

'No. Not yet.'

Wren frowned a question at the wings. Did he have a repair job for her? They looked like her own and those had been fine when she had seen them last. Her father dropped the wings on the table.

'I'll take you down to the Women's Sector.' He shook the weather from his coat and stretched.

Wren swallowed. 'Now?'

He nodded. He said nothing about the wings. Maybe he figured they weren't anything to do with her now that she was never to be Avalon's Sphere-Mistress.

Wren stalled. 'How's the training going?'

Chayton grunted. 'He's doing well.' He avoided her eyes.

'He's better than Jay was, isn't he?' She smirked at her brother.

Reluctantly Chayton nodded. 'And two other lads have asked to be taught.'

'So that's why you need the extra wings.' Wren's eyes went to the silver material draped over the table.

Chayton marched to her side. 'He says –' he paused.

'What?' Panic clutched at her heart. Chayton continued to avoid her gaze and the air left the room.

'He says you were better than him. Better than Colm

even.'

Wren choked on the missing air. 'Raw said that?'

Chayton gestured at the wings. 'It would be a waste to send you away wingless.'

'I –' Wren stopped. She didn't dare believe that Chayton was actually giving her the wings. 'But I can't *Run*. If the Patriarchs find out I'm alive, I'll be killed. That's the whole point of sending me to the Women's Sector, to hide me, so they don't find out.'

'You can fly out that way.' He gestured behind them, 'where there are no colonies.'

Wren gaped.

'And you can help me teach the Grounders: Run demonstrations.'

Wren wrapped her hands around her chest, holding herself together against the shock. She felt as if she might fly apart. 'You'd let me Run?'

Chayton nodded and finally met her eyes with his own, older versions of Colm's. 'If it's true what Raw says, then you're a natural Runner. It would be cruel to take your wings.'

'But – blasphemy?'

Chayton sighed. 'Wren, I've broken laws myself now and your mother is dead. What do I have to fear from the High Patrions?'

Wren ran to the table. 'They're really mine?' Her arms went around the struts and her tears ran freely.

'Raw made it possible.' Chayton avoided her eyes. 'Perhaps before you go to the Women's Sector you would do one last thing for Avalon.'

Wren looked up. 'What?'

Chayton smiled. 'Fly with me, Wren.'

The air streamed over her wings and Wren looked over at her father. He grinned widely and tilted so that a gust of wind flicked into her face. Her eyes widened. This then was a lifetime of flying experience.

She unlocked her wings and closed them around her. As Chayton cried out his surprise, Wren spiralled downwards; then she forced her wings out again. The wind snapped them into place and she flew up to meet him.

His face smoothed out and suddenly he whooped and they were racing the sunset back to Avalon. Light played over silver graphene and the fluttering material sang alongside Wren's laughter.

As the platform came towards them her father grinned up at her, a challenge in his eyes. He started in for a landing, but before his feet touched down, he yawed forwards, tucked his legs into his chest and closed his wings. He turned a somersault and landed unmoving dead centre in the middle of the platform. Had he missed, he would have crashed into the net.

Wren gaped. Then she calculated. She had seen how he had done it. Raw had copied her all this time. It was her turn.

She tucked her legs beneath her.

The Women's Sector hunkered low to the ground. Lines of laundry were drying outside and an avenue of dresses led them to the door.

Before Chayton knocked, he dragged Wren out from behind him. 'For the sake of the *skies*,' he snapped. 'You stood up to the whole Vaikunthan colony.'

Wren snarled under her breath, but moved to his side and straightened her mother's skirts, which hung in an unfamiliar way and tangled around her ankles.

When he knocked, the door opened as though someone had been waiting on the other side. Wren blanched.

'My daughter is a woman grown.' Her father propelled her forward. 'And I should like her to enter the Sector.'

Wren shuffled her feet as Tee glowered down at her, the pendants swinging beneath her pendulous breasts. Then the councillor took her arm and Chayton stepped backwards, abandoning her in the doorway.

'Follow me –' Tee tugged Wren into the house. As soon as Chayton was out of view, she finished her sentence '- *Runner*.' Then she dropped Wren's arm with disdain.

She suppressed a sigh. It was going to be a long few days.

Wren was used to sharing a room with her family, but not with so many other girls. They twittered and giggled until long after lights out, and the nearer the time of the choosing came, the more twittery and giggly they became.

Not one of them had said a word to Wren since her arrival. She sat on her mattress in an island of silence, but because she was the only one quiet, she was the only one who heard the shutter rattle. Curious, she slipped out of bed.

Gravel continued to patter on the slats. Wren reached for the latch and a shriek stopped her.

'What are you doing?'

It was Cara, she of the shiny blonde hair and falsely pink cheeks.

'I'm opening the shutter,' Wren explained patiently.

'You can't!' Cara snatched at her hand.

'Is it a rule?' Wren groaned; she seemed to be coming up against a lot of those.

Cara stared at her in confusion. 'Of course not. We don't need a rule to tell us not to open the shutters.' She looked at the other girls who were all nodding and gaping at Wren as if she had two heads.

'I don't understand.' Wren shrugged and raised her hand again. 'If there's no rule –'

Cara's impressive bosom swelled. '*Nice* girls don't open the shutters at night. It's the *Designers* law, to protect us.'

Wren rubbed her short curls. She really wanted to know who was on the other side. Her skin tingled and her heart beat faster. Somehow, she knew who it was.

Ignoring Cara's whining, she unhooked the latch and pushed the shutter open. Fresh air rushed into the stale room.

'I thought you hadn't heard me.' Raw grinned.

Wren forced a scowl. 'I'm not speaking to you, remember?'

'Can you come out?' Raw held out his hand. Buoyed by the horrified gasps from the girls behind her, Wren climbed through the window.

Wren glanced back. 'I shouldn't be doing this.'

Female faces clustered around the window, obviously torn between slamming it shut and watching Wren committing yet more sacrilege.

'Then you certainly shouldn't be doing this.' Raw trapped her in his arms and claimed her mouth with his own.

This time there was no-one trying to take Wren's life, no raging fire and no illness to steal her breath, yet her pulse still raced and her stomach tied itself in knots.

Raw's mouth was hot and Wren held on tightly to stop herself from drifting away.

Raw pulled back and pressed his forehead to hers. 'I missed you.'

'I missed you too … I suppose.' Wren clutched his shirt between her fingers but then an image of the blonde Cara flashed through her head. Raw had once said to her that his disease had cost him his chance to Choose. Had he really wanted Cara, or someone like her? She had to know.

'Raw.' Her voice sounded foreign to her ears. 'You don't have to pick me.'

He shook her shoulders. 'You still hate me? Because it didn't feel like that a moment ago.'

'I know you feel that you owe me because I saved your life but … you don't have to go this far.'

Raw's eyes flashed and he stepped back from her. He twitched his hair back over his face as he retreated. 'Is that what you think? That I'm here tonight because I owe you one?'

Wren couldn't look at his flushed face. 'I don't know.'

'Was none of this real for you?' Raw snapped. 'Nothing that we went through?'

Wren gasped. 'Of course.'

'How could it be, if you think that about me?' He turned his back and Wren's gut lurched as he prepared to leave. 'You don't want me, that's the truth isn't it? I saw how you looked at Orel. I've seen how you look at my face.'

As his feet found the path, Wren leaped for his broad shoulders. 'Don't leave like this.' She grabbed frantically at him. 'I didn't want you to feel as if you had to choose me over one of the others. Any of them would have you.' She swallowed. 'You're beautiful.'

Raw stopped his headlong rush away. 'That's not true. You don't have to spend the rest of your life looking at me if you can't. Just say so.'

Wren forced his face round. 'You're beautiful, Raw.'

He caught her chin in one hand. His eyes had filled with tears. 'You *did* save my life, Wren, but I saved yours right back, remember? You got me home, but I caught you when you fell. We're even. We're not doing this because we owe one another anything, all right?'

She inhaled air that seemed too thin. 'You really don't feel like you owe me?'

Raw rubbed his scar as if it hurt him. 'Of course I owe you. Before I knew you, I was bitter and vengeful. You changed that. You're strong and brave; you're the beautiful one. I'm going to choose *you*, not because I owe you, not because I want to, but because …' His eyes glittered and Wren gulped. 'Because I *have* to. Without you I'm nothing. And if you went with someone else, I'd kill them with my bare hands.' He scrubbed his hands through his hair, nervously revealing his whole face to her. 'If you still hate me, you don't have to agree to the choosing. I betrayed your wishes and I know it.' His eyes flashed. 'But I wouldn't change anything, Wren. You're alive.'

Carefully Wren put her arms around him. 'We saved each other over and over again. I can't blame you for doing so one last time.'

Raw tilted her chin upwards. 'You're mine, always. I'll say so in front of the whole settlement in a few days.'

'All right.' Wren nodded, relief leaving her weightless. 'Except that I'm not yours.'

'But you just said.'

'I'm not yours, you idiot.' Wren punched his arm. 'You're mine.'

Raw smiled. 'That works too. I just wanted to make sure you were okay in there.' He nodded at the watching girls and Wren glanced back. She'd have to go around the front to get back in. There would be some awful punishment. She grinned.

Everything was going to be all right.

About the Author

Bryony Pearce is the multi-award winning author of seven novels for young adults: *Angel's Fury, The Weight of Souls, Phoenix Rising, Phoenix Burning, Wavefunction, Windrunner's Daughter* and *Savage Island.*

Her work has been translated into Russian, Polish and Turkish and is sold in the US as well as the UK and abroad.

She also writes short science fiction stories for adult anthologies and her work has been included in *Stories from the Edge, Now We Are Ten, Once Upon a Parsec* and *Soot and Steel.*

She has lived all around the country but is currently settled, with her husband and two children, in the Forest of Dean, Gloucestershire. She is working on her next novel.

Other Telos Titles
You Might Like

PAUL LEWIS
SMALL GHOSTS
Horror Novella

PAUL FINCH
CAPE WRATH AND THE HELLION
Horror Novella
TERROR TALES OF CORNWALL Ed. Paul Finch
TERROR TALES OF NORTHWEST ENGLAND Ed. Paul Finch

SIMON CLARK
HUMPTY'S BONES
THE FALL

FREDA WARRINGTON
NIGHTS OF BLOOD WINE
Vampire Horror Short Story Collection

STEPHEN LAWS
SPECTRE

RHYS HUGHES
CAPTAINS STUPENDOUS

DAVID J HOWE
TALESPINNING
Horror Collection of Stories, Screenplays and more

SOLOMON STRANGE
THE HAUNTING OF GOSPALL

DAWN G HARRIS
DIVINER

SAM STONE CONTINUED
CTHULHU AND OTHER MONSTERS
Lovecraftian Style Stories and More

LEGENDS OF CTHULHU & OTHER NIGHTMARES
Lovecraftian Style Stories and More

HELEN MCCABE
THE PIPER TRILOGY
1: PIPER
2: THE PIERCING
3: THE CODEX

TELOS PUBLISHING
www.telos.co.uk